WILL POWER

BOOKS BY A. J. HARTLEY

The Mask of Atreus
On the Fifth Day
What Time Devours
Act of Will
Will Power

WILL
POWER

A. J. HARTLEY

TOR®

A TOM DOHERTY ASSOCIATES BOOK
New York

WILL POWER

Edited by Liz Gorinsky

A Tor Book
Published by Tom Doherty Associates, LLC
175 Fifth Avenue
New York, NY 10010

www.tor-forge.com

Tor® is a registered trademark of Tom Doherty Associates, LLC.

Library of Congress Cataloging-in-Publication Data

Hartley, A. J. (Andrew James)
Will power / A. J. Hartley.—1st ed.
    p.   cm.
"A Tom Doherty Associates Book."
ISBN 978-0-7653-2125-1
1. Outlaws–Fiction.   2. Goblins–Fiction.   3. Space and time–Fiction.
4. Adventure and adventurers–Fiction.   I. Title.
PR6108.A787W56 2010
823'.92—dc22 2009040643

First Edition: September 2010

Printed in the United States of America

0   9   8   7   6   5   4   3   2   1

To my parents, who, unexpectedly, liked the first one

—AJH

ACKNOWLEDGMENTS

I'd like to thank my agent, Stacey Glick; my editor, Liz Gorinsky; and my wife (always my first reader), who helped make this book a reality.

Please visit my website, www.ajhartley.net, to pass along comments and see details of other projects, completed or in the works.

Thanks for reading.

A. J. Hartley

WILL
POWER

BY

WILLIAM HAWTHORNE

Translated from the Thrusian by

A. J. HARTLEY

TRANSLATOR'S PREFACE

It is with some trepidation that I present to the world this second installment of the Hawthorne saga. Like the first volume, *Act of Will*, it has been translated from the original Thrusian—as preserved in the now famous Fossington House papers—with the aid of notes left by the Elizabethan translator Sir Thomas Henby. As readers of the first manuscript will quickly see, the second volume is different in key respects from the first, and raises still more vexing questions of provenance, locale, and issues of how much of the narrative—if any—is derived from fact. My initial assumption—for reasons that will become apparent as the story unfolds—is that the work is pure fantasy, though other manuscripts from the Fossington House collection have since emerged that seem to root elements of the narrative in fact. The details of those materials will be published in a series of academic papers in forthcoming issues of *Philological Quarterly*, though I doubt they will hold much interest for the general reader.

Since the history of the manuscript collection is now well known, I will say only that I remain in the debt of Sir Thomas Henby, whose notes from the 1580s and '90s remain the core of my own translation. The tone, however, is the result of my own efforts to maintain some of the precocious energy of the Thrusian original, as I did with Volume One. Due to the rushed nature of the publishing schedule, I write this before beginning even preliminary work on the other pages seemingly penned in the same language, so I am not in a position to say whether there is more of the Hawthorne Saga to come or whether these two self contained narratives are the entirety of Mr. Hawthorne's labors. If more come to light, I will, of course, endeavor to make them available to the public in English so that they may become more than curiosities for ethnographers and linguists.

—*A. J. Hartley, 2010*

Unadulterated Hawthorne

Far be it from me to blow my own trumpet, but I was about to become a bit of a legend. We had been lying around Stavis mulling over our triumphs in Shale three weeks ago like a family of pythons that had recently gorged on a rather less fortunate family of gazelles, or whatever the hell pythons eat. Now we were going to see a little excitement. I had, I must say, been quite happy doing the python thing, but sleeping late and producing no more than bodily excretions for a whole month had started to wear a bit thin even for me. The others had, of course, tired of it rather earlier.

Garnet and Renthrette, our straight-from-the-shoulder brother and sister warriors, had been spoiling for a fight with anyone who made eye contact for a couple of weeks now. Even the generally placid, if surly, Mithos, the famed rebel and adventurer who had tormented the Empire for close to twenty years, had recently started pacing the Hide's underground library like the proverbial caged cat. Orgos, our overly noble weapon master, had begun polishing his swords again, barely concealing a mood as black as his skin. I saw little of Lisha, our girlish but revered leader, because she was usually busy poring over maps or gathering news on Empire patrols. Yours truly—Will Hawthorne, former dramatist, actor, and con man, current apprentice adventurer, and damn-near-professional gorged python—couldn't really see what all the fuss was about. We had solved the riddles of Shale and environs, or most of them, and had come away feeling virtuous, and, more importantly, rich.

With me so far? I hope so, because—as is now graven in theater lore—nothing kills a story like exposition. I once had to be in this play when nothing happened for twenty minutes because all this backstory had to be wheeled out for anything later to make sense. Not surprisingly, we got booed offstage a quarter of an hour in. So I'll be moving on. That's who we were and what we'd been doing. But by this point, even I had become conscious that—if I might milk the python meta-phor one last time—the flavor of warm gazelle meat was becoming a rather distant memory.

Thanks to my investigative brilliance, this was about to change, but before we got to the adventure bit there was food to be eaten. We were dining in the Waterman, one of Stavis's many traders' inns, in the northwestern part of the city. It was eight o'clock, and, perhaps for the first time this season, the landlady was lighting a fire in the main hall's grate to ward off the chill that came with early autumn. To our left was a party of wool merchants who ate nothing but baked pota-toes straight from the oven: no butter, no salt, no herbs. Yet they were munching with an enthusiasm which meant they either came from somewhere that had little or no food of any kind or that they were se-riously delusional. To our right was a family of ebony-skinned Trel-lenians swathed from head to foot in lustrous silk and eating a curry that would strip varnish. At the bar was an elderly man in dignified black, sipping Venarian claret. And on the table in front of us was a large game bird known locally as a rossel, roasted and carved to per-fection, surrounded by tiny links of smoked sausage and a moat of thick, hot sauce made from tart red berries, the whole sumptuous dis-play sitting among spinach leaves and wedges of lime, steaming invit-ingly. Even the wool traders' mouths were watering.

"Where was I?" I said as the serving boy left us. "Oh yes. So then Venario is on stage by himself, lying in wait for Carizo and Bianca. His sword is drawn and he's ready to attack Carizo and have his way with Bianca. He has a few smug words with the audience and takes his posi-tion behind one of the front pillars. Then, hearing a noise, he leaps out. But it's not Carizo. It's the ghost of Benario, rising out of a trapdoor and wailing: 'See here, O cursed wretch, the gaping wounds/Which thou didst carve into my living flesh . . . '"

"Who's Benario?" said Garnet.

"What? Oh," I began, "he's the bastard son of Duke Ferdinand, the one that Venario killed in the first act because he saw . . ."

"Who's Venario?" said Lisha.

"Who's Venario!" I exclaimed. "Haven't you been listening at all? All right. Venario was exiled from the court for having an incestuous relationship with his sister, who he later murdered with a poisoned pot of geraniums and . . ."

"I thought you had word of a job," murmured Mithos.

I gave him a long, pained look. "Don't you want to hear what happens next?" I said, injured.

"Sorry," he said, "but I thought we'd come here for a job."

"Fine," I replied, testily. "Fine. Right, forget the play. It's not important. After all, I only wrote it. . . ."

"All right. . . ." Mithos sighed.

"No," I inserted. "No. We are here for a job, so that's what I'll tell you about. Firstly . . ."

"Wait a moment," Orgos said, eyes glued to the rossel's golden brown breast.

"Do I get to finish a sentence tonight?" I asked.

"Not yet," said Orgos. "It would be criminal to discuss business over so excellent a feast."

Mithos sighed again and added, without any enthusiasm whatsoever, "So serve it."

He had a way of discussing the most exotic or delicate meals like they were day-old porridge. He ate them like that, too, mixing things together and spading it down his throat so that it barely touched his tongue. Garnet regarded the great bird with the blend of curiosity and distaste he usually reserved for me and took a forkful gingerly, as if it might come back to life and bite his hand off. Only Orgos seemed to accord the food anything like the respect it deserved.

This had been intended as a surprise feast to celebrate our next adventure, though I should have known that the adventure itself was the only sustenance they needed. I, still sulking about not being able to finish my story, chewed in sullen silence and resolved to make them wait for the day's big news: news which, with a tremendous effort, I had managed to keep to myself thus far.

Earlier that day I had been sampling a pint of milk stout in one of Stavis's less seemly hostelries, nostalgically reliving my Cresdon days as a cardsharp, actor, and storyteller, when I fell into conversation with a man of about fifty-five whose eyes held a strange and compelling light. He had some very interesting news.

In a matter of minutes this helpful chap, whose name was Mensahn, would join me and the rest of the party in the Waterman and give us vital information which would allow us to release Dantir, the famous rebel hero. Yes, *that* Dantir: the guy who had pinned down the Empire's fourth army during the conquest of Bowescroft with little more than rumor and a handful of well-trained archers. He was the Empire's prize captive, and they periodically threatened to execute him when things got unruly anywhere in Thrusia. The rebels (and that included most adventurers) wanted him back, partly because he was a bit of a legend and partly because he knew just enough about rebel operations to be dangerous.

And we could save him. Pretty heady stuff, eh? And it was all thanks to me. Our recent inactivity had allowed some of the suspicion with which the party had first greeted me to resurface, if only in muted forms, but this new triumph would remind them of my genius, and my usefulness. After one brief operation they would be feasting me, putting my name in songs, throwing gold at me, and—in Renthrette's case—maybe herself, too. As I said, I would soon be joining Dantir himself in the rebel's Hall of Heroes. I munched on the tender flesh of the rossel and my good humor returned.

"I've not been in here for weeks," said Orgos, glancing around the place. "Months, even. Not since that idiot Lightfoot took over the Empire's intelligence sector."

There was a flicker of amusement around the table and Orgos snorted to himself, as if remembering something funny.

"Who's Lightfoot?" I asked.

Garnet took up the story, an uncharacteristic grin splitting his pallid face. "He was a staff sergeant in the Oakhill garrison for years. Then—God knows how—he got himself posted here to intelligence, probably because nothing ever happens here for him to get in the way of. He must have been a terrible liability in Oakhill."

"I heard he once slaughtered and burned a flock of sheep that the garrison had impounded for their winter meat," inserted Renthrette, "because one of them reminded him of a local rebel. Something in the eyes, I suppose. The soldiers were famished for weeks."

"He's insane?" I ventured.

"Let's say 'eccentric,'" Orgos qualified. "He sees rebels everywhere and has devoted his life to lunatic schemes designed to flush them out. Almost every month he goes from tavern to tavern trying to lure adventurers or members of the resistance into an ambush with tales of Empire treasure convoys or defenseless generals. Then, at the appointed time, he shows up at the pub or wherever with a hundred soldiers and storms in. It is always deserted except for a few random traders. He interrogates them for a few hours and then lets them all go with an official pardon and a couple of silver pieces in compensation. It costs the Empire a fortune."

"Really?" I said, slightly uncomfortable.

"Lately," Garnet joined in cheerfully, "he's reverted to that ludicrous yarn about Dantir the great rebel hero. As if the rebels would do anything to get that old drunk back anyway. The only secrets he had concerned the whereabouts of the Empire's cache of Thrusian grain whiskey."

"Hasn't Dantir been dead for years?" asked Renthrette.

"At least two," answered Mithos, distantly.

"Really?" I managed again. Against all odds, I had lost my appetite. Beads of cool sweat had pricked out across my forehead. This was not good.

"How could even someone as harebrained as Lightfoot believe that anyone would fall for such an obvious ruse?" Renthrette wondered, sipping her wine. "I mean, how asinine can anyone be?"

"The story which is supposed to bring us all running into the arms of the Diamond Empire this time says that Dantir is being moved around," Garnet continued, now breaking into outright laughter, "with an escort of elderly ladies, or something. . . ."

"One Empire platoon, actually," I spluttered thoughtlessly. "It's not *that* preposterous!" My voice was rising defensively. "All right, it might not be likely, exactly . . . but it is, you know . . . *plausible*. Kind of. I don't see why you think it's so *obviously* ridiculous. If you lot didn't already know of this Lightfoot character you might have fallen for it. It is possible, you know, that your bloody perspicacity wouldn't be so dazzling if you didn't have all the facts in front of you. They *could* have been moving Dantir around. They could!"

There was a momentary silence as the smiles and good humor slipped away as if I'd mentioned that one of their elderly relatives had just kicked off.

"You didn't," growled Mithos across the table.

"Well . . ." I began, but, unable to shake off his eyes as they burned dark and hard into mine, I decided to leave it there.

"*That* was the big adventure you promised us?" stuttered Garnet as realization dawned like an unwary sun in a very cold place. "*That* was what you brought us here for? You stupid, simple-minded, moronic . . ."

"Lightfoot is going to arrive here any minute with a hundred troops?" said Lisha quickly, clarifying.

"Actually," I faltered, glancing at the clock over the bar, "he's slightly late."

There was a thundering of chair legs on the wooden floor as they leaped to their feet. Almost simultaneously, there came the distinctive creak and slam of the inn's door being flung out onto the chill evening air. I spun to see the white cloaks and silver scale of Empire troopers filing in, two abreast.

We weren't exactly armed to the teeth right now, and a pitched battle against a force this size would have led pretty quickly to our being carried out in casserole-sized joints. There were no obvious ways out of this situation. Our options were starting to look like hanging or beheading (at best) when Lisha prodded me firmly in the ribs. I turned, my face aghast and sickly, to find her staring up into my face, her black eyes even narrower than usual. She took hold of my wrist and gripped it firmly, as if I was about to run (she knew me pretty well by now). Through barely parted lips she hissed, "You got us into this, Will. Now get us out."

That was all she said, but the looks of menace I was getting from Garnet and Mithos underscored the point. Renthrette had closed her eyes, frustrated at herself for believing for a moment that I wasn't a walking death trap with the mental agility of a beer keg. Orgos glanced around the room as it flooded with soldiers, as if he was still calculating the odds of a last-ditch stand. His hand strayed to the hilt of that huge sword of his, the one with the yellowish stone in the pommel.

Turning swiftly toward the approaching footsteps I found myself looking into the slightly wild eyes of Lightfoot himself, now out of his rags and dressed in his best uniform. Uncertain what else to do, I smiled warmly and extended a hand. "Commander Lightfoot," I announced heartily, "how good to see you again."

There was a flicker of confusion in the officer's eyes. After a pause he shook my hand cautiously, saying, "I wasn't aware you knew my name."

"How could I not, sir?" I breezed. "Commander Lightfoot, the supreme intelligencer, the Empire's most acute and watchful eye."

"But when I spoke to you earlier," said Lightfoot, dimly, "I gave you no clue to my identity."

At his elbow, two officers exchanged knowing glances.

"I'm sorry," I said, "it seems we were talking at cross purposes. I was under the impression that you wanted me to try and locate Mithos and his gang for apprehension using the Dantir ruse to lure them to this place? No?"

"Well, yes," he muttered, "but I don't see . . ."

"I am a good citizen of the Empire, sir, and, knowing your methods, resolved to do all I could. Alas, as you can see, I was unsuccessful. I decided to dine with my friends here so I could pass on the news."

"Indeed . . ." said Lightfoot, uncertainly. One of his soldiers smirked and looked down.

Encouraged by this, I went on. "But I do have word, from a very reliable source, close to Mithos's party, that a raid is intended on the south garrison where they believe Dantir is being held."

At this, two things happened. Lightfoot's eyes lit up with anticipation, but the looks exchanged by his men changed. What had been a mixture of bored exasperation and embarrassment instantly became suspicion. It seemed that out of the entire population of Stavis (no small city), only Lightfoot and me were stupid enough to believe that Dantir was alive and worth rescuing. I thought I heard Orgos groan.

One of them, decked out in the white linen cuirass and silver helm of a young sergeant, stepped forward, hesitating awkwardly. Then, in a stage whisper, he addressed Lightfoot. "Excuse me, commander, sir, but these people do actually fit the descriptions we have of Mithos and his group."

"Nonsense," spat the commander, with barely a glance at where we stood around the table. "Mithos is on his way to D garrison. We should be on our way to intercept him."

"Sir . . . if you don't mind me saying so, sir, I doubt it."

"What is this insubordination?" muttered Lightfoot, turning on him.

"I don't think this man is to be trusted," responded the sergeant, with a glance for support at some of his comrades, "and I don't think we should act on what he tells us. In fact, we should take him and his 'friends' into custody immediately."

"Custody?" bellowed Lightfoot.

"Yes, sir. The party that arrived in Stavis three-and-a-half months ago was described as looking just like them," the sergeant continued, his voice rising, as he opted to disregard protocol. "I was on gate duty then and I remember. A pale man and a blond woman"—he said,

indicating Garnet and Renthrette—"a black man"—stabbing a finger
at Orgos—"and an olive-skinned man with dark hair and eyes, who
may be Mithos himself."

The sergeant stepped closer to make the identification clearer and
spoke the last words into Mithos's face. The soldiers who had been
lounging carelessly around the room were now alert and attentive,
their spears swinging toward us menacingly. There was a new urgency
to the situation, and the troopers felt it. Only the idiocy of their commander could save us now, and, given the grim surety of the young sergeant, even that might be insufficient.

"And what about her?" asked Lightfoot, gesturing to Lisha in an
offhand and slightly juvenile so-there gesture. The sergeant looked
over Lisha's almost childlike frame, her impassive face with its small
Eastern features and long, raven black hair, and he faltered.

"I don't know, sir," he spluttered. "I do not think she was with the
party when they entered the city, but . . ."

"Exactly," said Lightfoot, "and I will not have these good and
loyal citizens harassed further."

"May we go?" I inserted, a little too eagerly.

"Have you finished your supper?" asked Lightfoot. He looked
doubtful.

"Oh yes," I blustered. "You're welcome to what's left. It's quite
good, but I had rather a large lunch and . . ."

"Yes, yes," agreed the commander, hasty and anxious to be off.
"Go on your way, and thank you."

"With all due respect, sir . . ." began the sergeant, now with
undisguised anger.

"We'll discuss this later, young man," said Lightfoot, ominously.

"You're damn right about that," murmured the sergeant, turning
his back on his superior contemptuously.

We needed no further encouragement. Within seconds I was holding the door to the street open as Renthrette and Garnet filed out. Behind us, Lightfoot growled formal charges to his sergeant. Perversely, I
couldn't help feeling a little disdainful pity for both of them. Still, this
was not the time to show sympathy for the enemy. Taking up the rear,
I stepped into the open doorway, smiling to myself at a job well done,
some dignity saved, and so on. Then, the young sergeant, presumably
figuring he had nothing to lose, walked away from his commander,
dipped into The Book, and looked up the oldest trick.

"Oh, Mr. Hawthorne?" he called.

And, like the death trap/beer keg that I am, I turned. "Yes?" I began guilelessly.

At that, even Lightfoot's face fell. Then they started running.

For a second I was rooted to the spot as if I'd been blinded by a combination of my own stupidity and the glittering of all those steel spear tips aimed at me. Then Orgos shoved me out into the street, drew his sword, and closed his eyes.

For a split second there was amused disbelief on the part of the soldiers—*this guy's going to try and hold us off singlehandedly?* But then the stone in Orgos's sword seemed to swell with golden light, and there was a pulse of energy that radiated from it like ripples in a pond. I shut my eyes at the last second, but I still felt the firelight amber of the stone burst forth. When I opened them again, the soldiers looked dazed.

Knowing the moment wouldn't last, Orgos slammed the double doors shut.

"Wedge them closed," gasped Lisha. Garnet and Renthrette dropped to the ground, looking for suitable rocks or bits of wooden crate as Mithos joined Orgos, shoulders to the door. In seconds it jolted with the impact of the soldiers' first charge, but the pale siblings were already positioning a pair of heavy planks up against the door handles. They would buy us a few moments till the troopers levered the doors off their hinges with their shortswords.

I stood there, as I am wont to do in situations like this, looking vacant, uncomfortable and, more to the point, useless. As soon as the doors looked like they would hold, Garnet wheeled around and hoisted me up against a wall, plucking a knife from his belt. Déjà vu, eh? Still, at times like this, it's nice to know that some things can be counted on. Why worry about the Empire plowing the door down like crazed buffalo when Will Hawthorne is there to beat up on, eh, Garnet?

Fortunately, Garnet wasn't the only one in character. With a strong arm and a baleful glare, Orgos liberated me and began spitting insistent words like "prioritize," which I could sympathize with, and "time for this later," which I was rather less keen on.

Lisha interrupted him. "Garnet, run back to the Hide, load as much of our campaign equipment as you can onto the wagon, and meet us tomorrow morning at the Black Horse Inn. It's about twelve miles north of here on the road to Vetch. Go. Quickly."

Garnet paused only to shoot me the briefest but most murderous look imaginable, then was off and running. Lisha began walking swiftly, talking as she did so. "We have to move quickly, avoid the major roads. We need to get past city limits before news of this fiasco spreads. Run! Mithos, go with Will."

"You mean," I gasped, wheezing to keep up with her as she strode through the dark streets, eyes fixed ahead, "we're going to walk twelve miles? In darkness and on foot? You must be out of your . . ."

"Will," she said, coming to an abrupt halt and turning on me, an edge in her voice that I hadn't heard before, "I suggest you shut up and run, or, and I mean this quite sincerely, this is as far as you go with us."

I wasn't certain if that was a warning that they would abandon me, or the prelude to a possible stabbing, but I couldn't really chance it either way. And I didn't like the way that Mithos had slipped soundlessly behind me, as if waiting for the word to lop my head off. Back down the street, the doors to the Waterman roared and splintered. They'd be after us in seconds.

"Right," I said. That was the last word I uttered for some time. When I turned I saw Lisha running away to the west, Renthrette and Orgos having already ducked around a corner out of sight. Mithos laid a powerful hand on my shoulder and, almost lifting me with the force of it, pushed me into motion. We sprinted into an alley and were barely in its shadows when the door of the tavern burst asunder. Orders were barked, then came the sound of running feet, their armor jingling with each pounding step as they came after us. We ran.

SCENE II

Who Goes There?

I had no idea where we were, where we were going, or what we were doing. All I knew was that there were Empire soldiers behind me, and that Mithos was the only person I could count on to keep me alive. Given the fact that he was almost ready to kill me himself, this was kind of ironic, though not in the way that actually makes you laugh.

We were in a residential district, the houses built of bluish stone in large, regular slabs, each street narrow and numbingly similar. We took a right, then two lefts. I wouldn't have been at all surprised if the next turn had brought us back to where the Waterman still spewed forth soldiers through its ravaged doors. Not an appealing prospect. Still, Mithos seemed to know where he was going, and since it was taking all my energy to keep up with him, I stopped thinking about it. This is often the way I deal with alarming situations.

We came to a corner and Mithos peered around it. He froze. "Listen," he hissed.

Horses. Some of the guards had grabbed mounts from the stables and were gaining on us fast. Mithos reached into his tunic and drew out a sword wrapped in leather, its blade not much more than a foot long. He glanced at me. I, Will the idiot, Will the confirmed cretin who should have learned by now to always carry a weapon, could only shrug and smile sheepishly. He sighed and dashed around the corner. Then I heard the clatter of horse hooves and turned to see a mounted soldier, his armor glinting palely in the twilight. Enter Will the decoy.

The rider had been passing the end of the alley, but brought his horse to a stuttering, sliding halt when he saw me. The horse's hooves sparked on the cobbles as he turned the beast and spurred her at me, his shortsword drawn and raised to strike.

I sprinted thoughtlessly in the direction Mithos had gone, tripped and fell heavily on the stony ground, where I opted for one of my favorite combat strategies: blind hope along with the appearance of having unexpectedly died.

The soldier charged out of the alley toward me. Mithos, emerging suddenly from the shadows to the rider's right, flung himself at the horse's flank. The steed, no combat-trained mount, whinnied with surprise and reared on its hind legs, tipping the soldier back and out of the saddle. Mithos was on him before he could get to his feet. Since the trooper's weight had fallen on his sword arm, he could not block the blow across the face with the sword hilt and was knocked unconscious.

I winced at the idea of knocking out Empire soldiers. I had not seen any fighting for some time and its reappearance in my life sent my heart racing with exhilaration and panic.

Oh joy, I thought, more adventures.

Mithos, meanwhile, was tugging at the horse's bridle, bringing it back under control and then vaulting into the saddle. Once mounted, he turned and saw another Empire soldier advancing up the alley. After a fractional hesitation, which I rather resented, he offered me his hand.

Wordlessly I staggered to my feet. He caught my wrist, dragging me up behind him in one rough motion. I straddled the beast's broad haunches painfully and clung to Mithos, wheezing my terror and exhaustion into his shoulder. Then he set his boots to the horse's sides and we were away.

We surged down narrow, empty streets of locked doors and shuttered windows, passing the soft, warm light of taverns gasping whiffs of beer and song. We thundered through the night and each turn in the road was a looming disaster, a dead end, or an Empire patrol. We charged through the deepening shadows, scattering cats and rats in garbage, waking the good citizens of Stavis from blissful dreams of profit and safety. A drunk stepped out in front of us, bickering with himself and rolling like a war barge. Mithos spurred the horse on all the same. We missed him by a whisker, and the rush of wind through his hair made him pause in curious thought.

Then the houses fell away and the roads broadened. Mithos paused, looked doubtfully about him, and wheeled to the right, uncertainty in his eyes and sweat on his face. At the next junction he brought the horse to a complete halt. It snorted with fatigue in the sudden silence. Mithos was glancing wildly about, his desperation all too apparent. Not good. He turned and looked at me for assistance and then I knew we were really in trouble. My sense of direction is legendary, meaning that it is a minor miracle that I can make it to and from the toilet by myself. I shrugged, as bewildered by his asking me as I was about where we might be. He gazed quickly about him and made a snap decision. We went straight for another block and turned right. The street ended abruptly in the irregular brick of a tanner's yard.

Cursing under his breath, Mithos turned the horse and headed back the way we had come, but at the second junction, three infantry-men saw us and called out. They were directly ahead, blocking the street, their spears raised to shoulder height like javelins. I caught the sound of footsteps behind me and turned back to the junction we had just passed. Five more soldiers—their cloaks and armor spectrally pale in the gloom—were emerging and advancing on us like phantoms.

So this, as they say, was it: the end of my rather erratic career as an adventurer, and probably a lot of other things, including—the thought butted in like a friendly moose—my life. The Empire, in their idiocy, had elevated me to the same rank as Mithos and the rest of them, and while this had brought me a faintly invigorating sense of notoriety, it would now bring no more than a pretty horrible death. I had faced the possibility of being reduced to a sobering lesson for the people of Stavis rather a lot over the past few weeks, but I can't say the novelty had ever really worn off. The prospect of the rack, the curved and spiked knives they used for disemboweling, the gibbets, the flails, the thumbscrews, and the other knickknacks the Empire used to make passing into the next world just a bit less enticing filled me with the same cold dread it did the first time I found myself running from a pa-trol. The sight of the soldiers now in front of me had me clutching desperately at Mithos's back without a coherent thought in my head.

Mithos put his head down and I felt his muscles clench across his back and shoulders. Then, as if waking from a nightmare and finding that reality was just as bad, I felt the rolling leap of the horse as it powered forward like a tidal wave. We were charging them.

The three soldiers in front of us were almost as surprised as I was, but they recovered rather quicker. As I clung to Mithos's waist, barely daring to look around him to see what was happening, they formed a tight line across the street. Mithos raised his sword and dug his heels into the mare's flanks. She leaped on, but she was distracted and scared. I doubted she'd try to break through all that muscle and steel. Not that I could really blame her.

The impact, when it came, was more of a thud than a crash. The soldier in the middle panicked and dropped his spear as the horse's great breastbone barreled into him and sent him sprawling. The man on his right held his position but abandoned his lunge to defend himself from Mithos's fearsome sword strokes. The other stabbed at us from my left with his spear. Crying out in terrified desperation, I kicked wildly at him.

He dodged my boot, like someone avoiding a wasp, and stepped back. This was no retreat, however, but a way of better picking his striking spot. His spear was poised in his right hand, pulled back and ready to plunge into me with full force as I sat there with no weapon or armor to protect me.

With a cry of aggression, the product of a dubious marriage between horror and bravado, I flung myself on him, falling from the saddle and sending him sprawling backward. The spear clattered to the ground. Rather than trying to recover so unwieldy a weapon, he dragged his shortsword from its sheath. I was virtually straddling him, my right hand holding his left from my face, my left fumbling for his sword hand. I grabbed it, but his arm was strong. A dark smile spread across his face. He hissed through his teeth and his blue eyes lit with triumph. The weapon was almost completely under his control, and I felt its blade pressing below my rib cage. He pushed upward, and I struggled to hold it down. His strength was too much for me. His hands came on, one reaching for my eyes, the other pushing the shortsword into my thorax.

With a sudden shift of my lower body I put a knee to his stomach, and, as he gasped for air, rolled off and seized the fallen spear. By the time I had turned on him again, he was up and ready, the sword extended and his body hunched over and balanced, feet apart. He was a big man. I, by contrast, was not as athletic as an eighteen-year-old probably should be, wiry of limbs and a touch overfed about the middle. Still, I gripped the spear with both hands as Orgos had shown me, and, nervously, held my ground. At my back, the other troopers were hurrying toward us and the soldier who had fallen in front of our horse was getting to his feet.

My adversary cut at me, testingly, and I parried neatly, turning my left shoulder toward him and throwing my weight onto my right leg as I'd been taught. A flicker of a smile crossed his angular features, as if the fact that I was less incompetent than I had looked would actually make his inevitable victory more entertaining. He launched a feint attack, pulling back and actually chuckling as my block and lunge whistled through empty air. The footsteps behind us were getting closer. This was not the time to play for a draw.

I stabbed at him, extending my left leg, keeping my right planted and then, as he parried and cut, pulled back to my original position. Textbook. He grinned. I lunged short and, as I recovered, set my body weight squarely over my front foot, throwing my balance off in ways I could only hold for a couple of seconds. He had parried my attack easily and was looking smug, overconfident. I sprang forward, landing on my right foot and lunging as far as I could reach.

The speed and aggression of the flèche attack caught him off guard, and by the time he saw it, it was too late. The spear tip punched through the starched white linen of his cuirass just below the shoulder and a spot of crimson blossomed and spread. His eyes rolled back and he sank to the cobbled road, holding his wound.

"Will!" called Mithos, from the saddle. I turned and found the others were almost upon us. Though Mithos had dealt one of the original troopers a cut across the shoulder blade, which had been enough to take him out of the struggle, the other was now trading blows with him, clearly reluctant to get too close till his fellows from the other end of the street were on hand. This was our chance.

Once again, I took Mithos's powerful hand and was hoisted into the saddle. As I warded off the remaining soldier with the spear, our steed shuddered into motion. Behind us, the remaining soldiers, realizing they could not hope to catch us on foot, threw their spears in an erratic volley. One whistled over my head and clattered on the road ahead, another sparked against the stone wall to my right and fell to earth.

Three more turns, seven or eight blocks traveled, and no sign of the enemy. Our mount, however, was struggling. One of the flung spears had caught her hindquarters and the weapon's point had torn a hole in the tissue of one thigh. It was a minor wound, but it was bleeding heavily and giving the animal a lot of pain. She wouldn't run much further. Two more blocks and her canter became erratic as she tried to favor her other legs. Then, even this became too much for her and she stuttered to a halt.

Mithos glanced at the wound, slid to his feet without a word, and began to run. I followed, amazed we'd held off death this long, but still fully expecting to begin our Kingdom of the Damned tour within the next ten minutes or so. Unless they caught us and took us back for

Lengthy Torture and Languid Execution, in which case the tour might start later.

What we saw on rounding the next corner suggested that ten minutes had been optimistic. This road marked the northernmost reaches of the city and, while the town lacked the fortifications of Cresdon or Ironwall, there were sentries at every exit. Stavis, you'll recall, is an isolated bit of Empire territory connected to its lands in the West by little more than a road across the Hrof wastes. But except for that ribbon of paving across the desert, everything around the city was neutral territory. What that all added up to was that we were about twenty yards from never seeing another Empire soldier again, but from what I could see it may as well have been fifty miles.

There were soldiers everywhere. Lisha and the others may have been long gone, but we had lost several minutes in our earlier wanderings and news of the events at the Waterman had reached the city guards. A great throng of people had spilled out of the adjoining houses and inns to watch the inevitable capture of the notorious rebels as they attempted to leave. If this wasn't bad enough, the remainder of the guards who had pursued us would be here in moments, complete with even fuller descriptions of the escapees, their probable locations, and some colorful suggestions for what to do with them. Down the street was a stone tower, four stories high and topped with a white flag with a diamond motif: inside it would be soldiers. For once, Mithos's instinct matched my own. He found the first open tavern door—an inn called the Fisherman's Arms—and made for the bar.

The place was buzzing with anticipation and, since everyone was clustering around the door and windows, we had no trouble getting served.

"Two pints of bitter, please, mate," I said to a barman as he looked over my shoulder to see what was going on outside. "And close the door, will ya? It's spoiling the fire."

"What the hell are you doing?" Mithos growled with a disbelieving stare.

"I'm ordering a couple of . . . you know. I thought you wanted . . ."

"We came in here to get out of the street and to think, that's all."

"Well, since I've ordered them, we'll just drink up and be on our way, eh?" I ventured.

Mithos sighed and closed his eyes tightly, his brow creasing with intense concentration. I turned to see a face I recognized entering by the same door we had. He was a tall man in his late fifties, clad in a suit of black, his hair and beard an even silver, carefully trimmed. His eyes met mine blankly and he stepped on toward the bar.

"Mithos," I whispered, turning away and utterly failing to look casual.

"Quiet, Will," muttered Mithos, "I'm trying to think."

"Yes," I agreed hastily, "but a man has just come in who was in the Waterman."

"What?"

"He was at the bar when we were eating. I think he has seen us." I glanced around with a nonchalance I did not feel. "Yes. He's coming over."

And in seconds he was there, standing beside us and politely asking the barman for a drop of claret. Then, as the barman walked away, he spoke without turning to face us. His voice was smooth, refined even, and was touched with a smile I did not like. It spoke of dry, distanced amusement. Cold.

"Well, gentlemen," he said, "you've had quite an evening."

"I'm sorry?" said Mithos.

"No need to disguise it," he replied, "and certainly no point. You have led Lightfoot and his men in quite a merry dance, though it seems you are, shall I say, *tiring*."

That last word was spoken with an ominous emphasis that had floated behind the slightly amused tone of his other words.

"Who the hell are you?" I muttered, turning on him and caring nothing for Mithos's irritated sigh. He knew who we were well enough, so why pretend?

"My name is Dantir, rebel hero," he said, turning to face me. Then a joyless smile cracked his face and he added: "Just joking. Sorry. I am Linassi of . . ."

"Why the hell would I care . . ." I began, rankled by his composure and confidence.

"Excuse me," he replied with a calming gesture. "Perhaps I should have made myself clearer. I am *Ambassador* Linassi and I have a coach outside."

This was clearly supposed to mean something to me. It didn't, but that was a feeling I was used to. Mithos looked up and met Linassi's eyes for the first time. Apparently, something was going on here that I knew nothing about.

"And you have? . . ." began Mithos.

"Full diplomatic immunity, yes," answered the stranger, gazing emptily across the bar. "My driver is waiting in the yard. I suggest we move quickly."

"What?" I asked, looking from one to the other. "What's going on?"

"Don't be obtuse, Will," said Mithos, taking a hurried swill of beer and getting to his feet. "Just follow the ambassador."

"He could be anyone," I spluttered, ignoring the fact that the man was standing beside me.

"My papers," he said, plucking a wad of parchment from inside his jacket. "You can examine them as we go."

Out in the street, the sounds of the curious crowds dwindled significantly. A glance toward the open door told me why. The unit from the Waterman had regrouped and were mingling with the sentries.

"It looks like the decision has been made for you," said the ambassador, if that was what he was.

Mithos nodded solemnly, returned his papers, and indicated that he should lead the way. The older man inclined his head gravely and, without another word, led us in a series of long strides across the room.

I say "us," but, for most of those strides it would be truer to say "Mithos," because I stayed where I was, considering the odds of just losing myself in the crowds and finding a way out when things had died down. Then the crowd at the door parted and I caught a glimpse of white and silver. I didn't know if the guards were coming to search the place, or if they were just looking for refreshment, but I couldn't wait around to find out. So with eyes down and one hand rubbing my face in as obfuscating a manner as I could manage short of putting a bag on my head, I half-ran in pursuit of Mithos.

A door by the hearth gave way to a narrow passage smelling of damp and animals and leading to the stableyard, where, beside a wagon piled high with crates, sat a single coach. It was black as pitch, painted over with a highly polished lacquer, and trimmed with delicate ropes of gold. A crest hung on the side doors, featuring a dragon and a lamb on an azure shield.

"Pretty flash," I muttered to no one in particular, which was just as well since it was universally ignored.

A man in a dark and heavy overcoat who had been standing close to the coach knocked his pipe out against the wall and climbed up the stoop. Picking up his lash, he began cautiously walking the horses, all white geldings, until the coach was in the middle of the yard and ready to go. He leaned over the side and flipped a latch deftly with the butt of his whip. The carriage door swung open and Ambassador Linassi, with a small and wordless gesture, indicated that we should get aboard.

I glanced uneasily at Mithos, far from comfortable at the prospect of taking a spin in this glorified hearse with its questionable ambassador and his taciturn driver. Mithos's eyes said nothing and he climbed in, sitting himself comfortably on the red velvet seats inside. I followed, gingerly, and perched on the opposite seat, facing him and looking for assurance. The ambassador sat beside him, and his sharp, blue eyes met mine for a brief, blank instant, before he pulled the door shut behind him and rapped on the roof. As soon as we began to roll off, he stretched across toward me. I, with a start of panic, recoiled.

"Relax, Mr. Hawthorne," he said, his voice as smooth as before but touched with that same gentle amusement, "you are quite safe in here. For now."

Then he continued to lean across and, with a sudden tug on a cord, pulled down the window shade. He did the same on the other side and we were plunged into absolute darkness. Only several minutes later did my eyes seem to adjust, and even then I could make out little beyond shadows.

The coach rattled out of the inn yard and onto the road.

"She gives a very smooth ride, does she not?" said the ambassador suddenly, his voice unwinding in the darkness like an unseen cobra.

"Very good," I stammered, rather louder than I had intended, and was struck by the curious sense that I was alone in there, that I was talking to myself. Many moments passed before the ambassador added, "Steel sprung suspension. Nothing finer."

I felt obliged to say something but could not think of the words. I found myself nodding agreement to the darkness and then, as the silence extended itself, I abandoned speech altogether, focusing instead on my own anxieties, all of which seemed to be amplified by being in this curtained box, this cave, this pit of darkness on wheels. Still, it was likely to be a short journey, even if it was into the arms of the Empire's leading torturer. How bad could things get?

"Papers," said an imperious voice outside, perhaps only a foot and a half from my head. With sudden insight I realized that things could get pretty bad.

Something touched my knee and I jumped, striking my head on the roof. Then it came again, more insistent this time. Putting out my hand, I found myself holding the ambassador's documents. Barely daring to breathe, I pushed them through the crack in the window blind, leaning back in my seat to avoid being seen. As I did so, I caught a glimpse of steel helms plumed with white. Then the papers were snatched from my grasp by the invisible sentry and I flinched again.

"You have got to be joking," growled the unseen soldier, inches from my right ear. I sat very still, muscles tight and bowels clenched.

There was one of those half-decade pauses that actually lasts about three seconds. Then we heard the sibilant hiss of exasperation that can only come from an Empire sentry foiled by red tape. The papers were stuffed back through the window in a fist that didn't care if it caught one of the passengers on the jaw. Then it was gone, and a voice commanded the driver to "Move on" in a tone that left us in no doubt as to what the speaker thought about diplomatic immunity.

In a spasm of relieved joy I contemplated leaning out of the window and shouting something witty as the carriage rolled off. Something told me, however, that the one thing the guards would thank me for now would be the word or gesture that would lead to one of those unfortunate incidents which leaves huddles of troops standing over civilian corpses and muttering to their knowing superiors about how one of them had seemed to be brandishing some lethal, garrison-leveling weapon that had turned out to be a salt shaker. . . .

I considered Mithos, who was sitting silent as the grave in the darkness opposite me, and wondered if the guards would have had the chance to finish me off. He probably had his sword point poised for a discreet lunge at my liver in case of precisely such an eventuality. I figured I'd stay where I was and keep my mouth shut for once. We rolled off, smooth as ever, and I swallowed hard. Behind us the voices faded and we headed north.

"There now," said the ambassador, as if he did this every weekend, "that wasn't so bad, was it?"

If it was a real question, no one treated it as such. There was another long silence and then the ambassador added, in the absent tone of one remarking on the chance of rain, "You gentlemen seem to find danger wherever you turn."

"Thus far our luck seems to have held out," said Mithos. It was one of his usual faintly grim but otherwise toneless remarks, but the impenetrable darkness of the carriage lent it a certain low hostility.

"Indeed," replied the elderly man, and his voice matched the other in its steely but otherwise unreadable quality. "Thus far."

It could have been just the oppressive and disorientating blackness of the carriage, but, for whatever reason, I realized that my body had not relaxed one iota since we left the Empire guards and territories behind us.

The Only Way to Travel

We sat like that, silent and edgy, for about two miles. The darkness in the carriage was thick and liquid, giving the slightest rustle of clothing or creak of its steel spring suspension an immediate and unnerving resonance. I almost leaped out of my seat several times at the sound of someone shifting fractionally in theirs. Eventually, I mustered the courage to squint through the window blind, only to find that the land beyond it was almost as dark as the inside of the coffin on wheels we were riding in.

I could just make out a line of tall and narrow trees running along-side the road and pointing up into the heavens like spear tips. Cedars, perhaps. A quarter moon had just begun to rise, casting no useful light, so even the trees had a slightly sinister aspect that made absolutely no sense whatsoever. I noticed—from outside myself, as it were—that I was clinging to the edge of my seat with one claw of a right hand while the fingers of my left drummed silently, obsessively, on the seat cloth.

Mithos, his sheer grimness rivaled for once by Ambassador Death's, reached across to hold the shade open. What little light there was fell on his dour features as he gazed out into the passing trees. "This is the Vetch road?" he said.

"Yes," said the ambassador. "There is an inn where we can rest before we reach the village."

"The Black Horse?" Mithos asked, turning from the window. "Good. We have companions to meet there."

"That is most convenient," said the ambassador. "Our roads lie together."

Convenient indeed, I thought to myself uncomfortably. Everything about this little jaunt was extremely convenient, as if it had been arranged weeks ago. The idea that it was all coincidence seemed no more plausible to me than the tale of Dantir, renowned rebel-drunk and gypsy wanderer. I was wary of getting caught out twice.

"Perhaps your friends can join me on my road north," ventured the ambassador.

Perhaps not. The sooner I got out of this mobile graveyard, the better.

"What is your destination?" asked Mithos, casually enough, though I guessed he was probing.

"North," he said simply.

"Specific!" I muttered, my discomfort switching suddenly into irritation.

"No," agreed the voice of the ambassador, calm and unoffended. "But accurate."

"Just not very helpful," I persisted.

"The ambassador has a right to keep his own business to himself," Mithos remarked coolly.

"I can't say it fills me with confidence, that's all," I said sulkily into the blackness. The hint of skeptical hostility this remark contained had not really been intended, but I was wound as tight as a Dranetian merchant's purse and in such situations tended to be the tool of my words, rather than the other way round.

The ambassador chuckled invisibly, a rich and throaty gurgle of a laugh that raised the hair on the back of my neck.

"Ever the realist, eh, Mr. Hawthorne?" he said when his amusement had passed. "Will Hawthorne the pragmatist. William the cynic, Bill the perceptive. A man who knows the world and sees through its various shell games as if they're made of glass. A man too shrewd for principles, too practical to be distracted from the truth. . . ."

This was an alarming speech, particularly for someone who had never set eyes on me before. He had pigeonholed me a little too accurately. It was like he had somehow seen into the way my head worked and seen the way I—in my less humble and bewildered moments—tended to see myself. I shifted in my seat.

Suddenly there was a flash of light and the inside of the carriage flickered into the shifting radiance of a greenish flame. It sprouted and guttered from the tip of the ambassador's right forefinger. As my jaw fell open, he spoke again, looking me squarely in the face with an odd smile. "But what *is* real, Mr. Hawthorne? What is true?"

His bright eyes fastened on mine and held them for a moment, then his face loomed large, as if it had swelled to a great size, and filled the carriage, dwarfing me beneath it. I cried out and looked to Mithos, who sat in the strange light, his head lolling with sleep. The vast face of the ambassador hanging over me split into a broad grin and he began to laugh.

With a start I awoke to find myself sitting in the darkened carriage as before. There was no sound or movement from my companions. As my heart slowed to normal again, I laid my head on the rest behind it and watched the trees pass until I slipped into more restful slumber. It took some time.

❧

It was still dark when we reached the Black Horse, tired and cramped from sitting. The motion of the carriage had caused a dull nausea to settle in my gut like some spawning shellfish. I found an outhouse and splashed some water on my face, though the predawn air was cold and damp. Then the stench of the toilet overwhelmed me quite suddenly and I vomited into the foul pit below, my stomach wrenching in great, painful waves till my eyes watered and I swore I'd never eat, drink, or travel again.

I groped my way across the courtyard to where a boy, bleary-eyed and yawning, helped our silent coachman to unyoke the horses by the light of a lantern. He gave me a sullen glower as I passed. Given the fact that we were responsible for dragging him from his bed at this ungodly hour, I could hardly blame him, especially since it was often touch and go whether I'd be up in time for lunch. Still, empathy didn't improve my temper. I returned his scowl with interest.

The inn staff were already up, or some of them, at least, and they were busying themselves with the preparation of breakfast. I requested a mug of water and swilled it down hurriedly, as if we'd just emerged from the Hrof wastes, rather than the elegant sophistication of Stavis-by-the-Sea. A fire was burning in the hearth of the main bar room. Sitting in front of it, silently warming their hands, were Orgos and Renthrette. I joined them hesitantly, expecting the usual torrent of abuse, but Renthrette was too tired to bother. I quickly realized they were also anxious. Lisha and Garnet had not yet arrived.

"Bacon and eggs, sir?" inquired a far-too-perky maid as she skipped toward the kitchen.

"God, no," I managed.

"Rough trip?" inquired Orgos, observing this rare instance of non-gluttony.

"Grim," I said, and left it at that. The three of us returned our eyes to the fire, lost in our own thoughts.

Mithos joined us and announced that he had got us a pair of rooms. "You can rest for a while if you like," he said.

"I'll stay down here," said Renthrette, "in case the Empire comes looking. . . ."

"They won't," said Mithos. "They lost interest in us the moment we left their territory."

"Still," said Renthrette, ignoring him. "I'll wait here."

Mithos nodded minutely, understanding, and walked away. It was unlike her brother not to be here first, raring to go with his axe at the ready, and I had just assumed that we would find Lisha silently studying maps at the breakfast table. Their absence was worrying.

I followed Mithos, chose a bed, lay down, waited for the room to stop spinning, and, as dawn was breaking with an irritating flurry of birdsong, fell asleep.

⁂

I awoke to find some kind of meeting going on around me. Actually, "shouting match" might be more accurate, and that despite the fact that I had been snoring away pleasantly.

"We can't just leave them behind!" Renthrette was shouting, her face as strained as her voice. "We have to go back."

"If we go back," answered Orgos, "we endanger them far more than we help them, as well as putting ourselves at risk."

"Is that the issue?" Renthrette snapped. "Are we just going to abandon them to protect our own skins? If Garnet and Lisha had got out and we hadn't, I think the situation would be a little different."

"Are you listening to me, Renthrette?" Orgos said, biting off the words. "By themselves they might lie low and then slip out of the city unnoticed. If we go back we will only make them fifty times more visible, more recognizable. Lisha, of all people, would understand that. And your brother would be the last person to endanger the whole party unnecessarily."

"Then why don't we just stay here and wait?" she retorted. "You said yourselves that the Empire won't stray out of its own lands to look for us."

Mithos, who had been sitting silently in thought thus far, turned and said, "They might if they know we're still here. There are travelers passing through this place on to Stavis all the time. The Empire won't pursue us if we're moving away, but if they know we're sitting less than a day's ride away . . . who knows?"

Renthrette dropped angrily into a chair and sighed. Seeing what looked like a convenient break in the conflict I sat up and said, "I could murder that bacon now."

"I could murder you, Hawthorne," snarled Renthrette, "very easily. This is all your fault. As usual."

I thought that a little uncalled for, but I knew better than to get in the way of the tigress protecting her cub. Well, sibling, actually, but you take my point. Her pale cheek was flushed and hollow, her eyes cold and hard, her slim lips tight, and there was a strand or two of golden hair straying unheeded into her face: appealing, in a homicidal kind of way.

"Do I smell sausage?" I muttered, attempting to slink out of the room with a semblance of preoccupation.

"Whether you do or not, you aren't getting any," Orgos remarked, his eyes still on Renthrette. "You're getting fat again. And we're moving out in ten minutes."

"What?" I exclaimed, almost as outraged as Renthrette. "I'm starving!"

"If you ever had been," the black man responded, "you wouldn't toss that expression around so casually."

"I have!" I shouted. "Almost."

"Do you ever think with anything other than your gut?" Renthrette spat.

I started to giggle uncontrollably.

She just shook her head with the kind of disgust that took me right back to when we first met. As she stormed out and down the steps to the bar, I couldn't help wondering how I had managed to dispel that mood for those few weeks in Shale when we had almost been friends. Ah, well. What goes around comes up short, and a stitch in time is worth two in the bush. But life goes on, and on, and on . . .

Mithos and Orgos merely looked at each other and then set to packing their things.

"So where are we going?" I grumbled.

"North," said Mithos.

"Not with Mr. Cheery and his traveling clownschool?" I bawled.

"What?"

"What's-his-name: Diplomat to the Damned."

"Ambassador Linassi?" said Mithos expressionlessly. "Yes. He has asked us to serve as an armed escort for him on the road, and has purchased a horse to the purpose."

"He will buy us some basic weapons in Vetch," added Orgos, "for those of us who came unprepared," he added with a glance in my direction.

"And in the meantime," I muttered, "I'll just bite the arms off any bandits who attack us. After all, I'd risk everything for a total stranger."

"Who saved your neck when it was on the block," Orgos concluded.

"I'll sacrifice my firstborn child in his honor," I responded, bitterly

"How about doing the world a real favor and just not having any children at all," said Orgos.

*

The ambassador oversaw our final preparations in silence. I'd say he was dour, but there was always that touch of sparkle in his eyes that suggested a disarming private amusement, so I did my best to stay out of his way. Since I was also keeping clear of the more definitively dour Mithos, and Renthrette had reverted to treating me like a mangy and probably rabid dog, that left Orgos. As ever.

I found him sitting on the carriage's driver's plate, testing the edge of his sword with his thumb.

"I hate fighting with only one sword," he remarked. "The balance is all wrong. Perhaps I am getting too set in my ways."

"Change isn't always good," I said, thinking ruefully of our trip into "the North," whatever that meant.

"I'm not sure," he answered, looking up into the morning sun. "I was beginning to feel hemmed in in Stavis. A spell on the road will be pleasant. Invigorating."

In Orgos's mouth, that last word had an ominous feel. It was like "excitement." For years "excitement" had conjured serving maids divesting themselves of unwieldy apparel, but when Orgos said it I shivered at the blood-smeared images charging through his head, lances poised to skewer the unrighteous. A spell on the road may indeed be pleasant, but if things got invigorating, according to Orgos's definition, I might find myself looking for a way back to Stavis. Or somewhere else.

Somewhere quiet and peaceful, where adventure means a new kind of beer and excitement follows you upstairs by candlelight. . . .

"Are you driving?" I asked, changing the subject. The black man nodded.

"The other driver was hired here two nights ago," he said.

"What was the ambassador doing in Stavis for so short a time?" I asked.

Orgos shrugged. "Why so suspicious?" he said.

I shaded my eyes from the sun to see if this was a serious question. Apparently, it was.

"He just seems to have been exactly what we needed exactly when we needed it. Plus," I added, as a slightly embarrassed afterthought, "he bothers me."

"Bothers?"

"You know," I hissed, glancing around as if he might be behind me, listening with that oddly watchful mirth of his. "He seems so . . . I don't know, calculating. Deceptive? No, that's too strong. He looks at me like someone looking at a kind of ape, you know? Something that is intriguing and kind of funny because it is almost—but not quite—human?"

"Renthrette looks at you like that, too," he grinned.

"She's better looking," I returned. "But it's different. She's obviously revolted by what she sees. He's just *fascinated*. It's like he's joining in a child's game, you know? He's involved, and yet he isn't."

"I think you're overanalyzing." Orgos laughed.

"It wouldn't be the first time," I admitted. "I just have to come up with a reason for why he makes me feel so strange."

"What is this, intuition? A hunch?"

"I suppose."

"A bit metaphysical for you, isn't it?" Orgos smiled.

"That's why I'm trying to rationalize it," I agreed. He took my hand and pulled me up beside him, and I found myself smiling. If we had to ride off into the unknown, I would at least have a companion who would exchange the time of day with me.

Renthrette appeared. She was mounted on a dapple-gray filly and still looked sullen. "Let's go, if we're going," she said. She had tied her hair back with string and wore a long mantle of creamish wool. A sword hung beside her, but she had no other weapons or armor, and I couldn't help thinking that we were ill-prepared to be anyone's escort in unfamiliar territory. Her face, almost white with sleeplessness and anxiety save for lips tightened to pinkish lines and eyes rimmed with shadow, was hard, stoic, under my gaze. Then, without waiting for a response, she turned the horse and began walking it out of the inn yard. Orgos watched her quietly, his face showing that curious emotional elasticity it had. He could slip from violent rage to easy and expansive laughter in the blink of an eye without ever seeming remotely insincere. Now his brow was clouded with concern and fears he dare not speak.

"Garnet and Lisha are on their way," I breezed. "Be sure of it."

Orgos looked down for a second and then grinned at me, knowing I was trying to encourage him, and grateful for it.

"Where's your crossbow?" said Mithos to me as he strode out of the inn with a basket of bread and cheese.

"I didn't have it with me, exactly," I faltered. "I . . ."

"If you are unarmed," he said, cutting me off briskly, "you're no use up there. Get in the back with the ambassador. I'll ride with Orgos."

So that was it. I climbed down and loitered for a while, but it was clear that we were ready to go. I kicked at the gravel of the yard and then looked up to find the carriage door swinging open. The ambassador met my gaze from inside and he smiled slightly, knowingly. Even in daylight with the windows open, the interior seemed somehow dark and uninviting. It was like he exhaled shadow, or the sunbeams which came shafting through the windows like golden smiles took one look at him and thought better of it. I glanced round as if he might have been waiting for someone else but then, when no one came to my rescue, climbed in.

"It's nice to have fellow travelers for company," said the ambassador evenly.

"Yes," I said, barely disguising the extent of the lie.

"And such a nice day."

"Yes," I said.

"Well, perhaps we ought to be getting on."

"Yes," I said.

He rapped on the roof with his knuckles once, and we set off. I tried not to look him in the face, though this was difficult to avoid since we were sitting directly opposite each other. As we turned out of the inn,

I stared out of the window as if there was something extremely interesting about the countryside outside.

In fact, there wasn't. We were only a dozen miles north of Stavis and about the same distance east of the river Yarseth, so although the ground was sandy and hard, the area was irrigated well and the near continual sun made the land fruitful for miles. How far it went, I really couldn't say. I supposed there were isolated villages and little market towns, but if there were settlements on the scale of Stavis or Cresdon, or, for that matter, of Adsine or Ironwall, I had never heard of them. So we were heading aimlessly into the back of beyond, and I got to make the journey with the world's funniest undertaker. Another smart career choice by all-knowing Will, clear-sighted clairvoyant extraordinaire.

After a few minutes studying the fields of green stuff we were passing as if my life depended on it, I sneaked a peek at the ambassador in the hope that he might have nodded off. He was sitting with his head tipped forward and his fingertips pressed together. His eyes, rolled slightly upward, were fixed unwaveringly on me.

"Oh, er . . . Lovely countryside," I blurted out. "So, you know . . . green."

"Yes," he said, throwing my taciturnity back at me.

I flushed, awkward and embarrassed. He, predictably, smiled to himself as at a secret joke. I returned to the window, though I could feel his eyes on me continually as the miles passed.

❧

We stopped for lunch three hours later and I was out of that coach before you could say Mobile Tomb. After a morning two feet from the prince of darkness, even Renthrette's steely gaze seemed welcoming. Another misreading. She met my smile with a look that could turn milk to cheese at fifty paces and returned her attention to her horse, who she probably deemed a more worthy companion.

I had wandered cheerlessly off into the underbrush to relieve myself and was returning to the road up a shallow embankment when, glancing up, I saw that the sky, which had been bright and clear only moments before, was now darkening with huge purple storm clouds. They were moving at great speed, steadily obliterating the blue beyond, though I could feel no wind to speak of. There was a rumble of thunder and, almost immediately, there came a pattering of rain.

I scrambled up the slope to the road just as a distant lightning flash set Renthrette's filly snorting and stamping. She dismounted hurriedly and whispered to it. As she did so, I glanced at the coach horses which, by contrast, were curiously still and unaffected, even as the thunder bellowed loud overhead. Orgos and Mithos slid down from the driver's plate, hunching over to keep the rain from their faces, and, for a moment, the four of us were together in the road, caught quite off guard by the sudden storm. We exchanged bewildered and irritable glances and then I heard, from inside the carriage, the faintest laughter.

The ambassador, who was watching us through the coach window, clearly found the idea of great adventurers caught out by a cloudburst extremely amusing. His eyes fell on mine. "The pragmatist gets drenched!" he exclaimed with strange rapture. "How easily the unlikely takes you off guard, Mr. Hawthorne!"

There was something oddly knowing about his manner and, recalling my dream, I felt a shiver course through my spine. He continued to laugh, staring at me, and then, with a great sigh as if he'd finally got what he wanted, he turned his face up to the sky. "See, William," he said. "Reality dawns."

I followed his gaze and found that the clouds were now a charcoal gray marbled with wisps of violet and pea-soup green, thick and impenetrable. Light had fallen to a fraction of what it had been moments before, and the clouds seemed to be swirling like some heavenly maelstrom. Then, with a deafening roar and a crack like the splitting of a great tree, there was a flash of lightning that burned the world away, searing everything white and throwing me onto the ground.

I don't know how long I lay there. It could have been seconds, but it felt like more. I thought I might have been blinded by the flash, but when I opened my eyes I found that they, and the rest of me, were quite unharmed. I was face down in the dirt and everything was still.

The dirt was dry.

Dirt?

I rolled over quickly and found Orgos already on his knees beside me. Mithos was a few feet away, and Renthrette, who was still holding her horse's bridle, was standing a little to his right. They were all gazing about them in silence. There was no rain, no coach, no ambassador, no road.

"Where the hell are we?" I gasped.

Mithos gazed around the grassy vale in which we stood, his eyes lingering on the steep snowcapped mountains which hemmed us in on all sides.

"I have no idea," he said.

Bird Watching

What do you mean, you have no idea?" I spluttered. "We are a few miles north of Stavis, right? Where we were a few minutes ago. I mean, we have to be."

"No," whispered Mithos, still gazing about him as if he were in a trance, "we're not. I've never seen these mountains before."

"I've never even heard of mountains close to Stavis," added Orgos in the same awed tone. "Outside Thrusia, the nearest range is Aeloria in the northwest."

"Home of the Diamond Empire," said Mithos. "And if we're there, we'll know soon enough. There'll be fortifications, patrols. . . ."

"But Aeloria is three or four hundred miles from Stavis," added Renthrette, breaking silence for the first time. Her surliness had melted in the face of this new and thoroughly astounding development.

"More," said Orgos.

"So where in the name of all that's rational are we?" I demanded irritably. They were the adventurers after all. They were supposed to know these things.

"Like I said," Mithos replied, turning to me at last. "I have no idea."

"Well could you think a little harder, please?" I shouted. "I mean, we were only doing, what, six or seven miles an hour? And we had been on the Vetch road for about four hours. The Black Horse is twelve miles from Stavis, so that puts us . . . What? What the hell's the matter with you lot, eh? What are you staring at?"

Mithos took a deep breath and sighed. Then he took a step toward me and said, "I don't know the land north of Stavis as well as I might, but there are no mountains in that region."

"Yes there bloody are!" I yelled back at him. "Look around you! Use your bloody eyes, for God's sake! Mountains! Everywhere. Of course there are bloody mountains north of Stavis. You think they grew overnight like some kind of apocalyptic mushroom? You think maybe no one spotted them before?"

"Have you ever seen mountains on maps of this area?" he responded, cool and hard.

"So they got left off. They aren't especially interesting mountains. The mapmakers must have just figured they'd stick to the key stuff like towns and rivers. Maybe they had to write 'Vetch' in big curly letters and there was no room for the bloody mountains. Maybe—"

"We aren't on the Vetch road anymore, Will," he said with a touch of irritation. "Use *your* eyes. There is no road. Something happened to us and we are somewhere else. That's all."

And suddenly my brain gave up and it just wasn't worth arguing. He was right. There had to be an explanation, but he was right. We weren't where we were supposed to be.

"This has something to do with the ambassador," I muttered.

"Quite possibly," said Mithos, himself again.

"If I ever see that bloke again . . ." I began, but couldn't think of anything that seemed suitable. "I'll bet he drugged us and then drove us somewhere, dumped us and waited for us to come round. . . ."

"Hundreds, maybe thousands of miles?" said Renthrette skeptically, but too confused herself to give the remark the withering disdain she would have mustered in other circumstances.

"If I've been unconscious," said Orgos, "it hasn't been for long. My beard hasn't grown."

"Maybe he shaved you," I tried, lamely. Everyone ignored me and turned their eyes back to the mountains. A cold wind rippled the meadow in which we stood and, for the first time, I felt the chill of winter. Something was very badly wrong. It had been early autumn when we set out.

"So where to now?" Renthrette mused aloud.

"Shelter," said Mithos, "and any signs of people we can track to civilization."

"Which way?" said Orgos.

No one replied for a second, and then, with a half-shrug and no word of explanation, Mithos began walking across the valley. We followed, eventually, Renthrette remounting her horse, Orgos catching up with Mithos and striding silently along with him. I brought up the rear, in a stunned silence.

If the sun was going down, then we must be heading north. Presuming, of course, that the sun still set in the west. For all I knew, round here the sun might rise in the south, hang around for a bit and then go back the way it came. Maybe it didn't go down at all, and would turn into the moon, or a side of beef. . . .

This was getting me nowhere, except perhaps on a fast horse to mental collapse. With that in mind, I chose to focus on what *was*, rather than what *might be*. In truth, I still suspected that what *was* was more a matter of what *seemed to be*, but there was clearly little point in dwelling on the distinction. My brain hinted that we'd get past the first mountain and find Vetch nestling at its foot as expected, and there would be the ambassador looking lost and hurt and saying, "Where on earth did you get to? I just turned my back for a moment and . . ."

Yes, not very plausible. Less plausible, in fact, than the aggressively real brush of the long grass about my ankles or the wind that burned my ears with each frosty gust. I pulled my totally inadequate jerkin tight about me and tried to pick up the pace a little before bits of me started falling off.

After almost an hour we had made our way to one side of the valley. There we came upon a stream, frozen at the edges, but fast and clear. Crossing it brought us to an embankment of some sort, like the wall of a dam formed by the scree and rubble which fell from the mountain. After a moment's deliberation, we scrambled up it awkwardly, sending little avalanches in our wake. Renthrette and Orgos had to virtually drag the skittish horse up the treacherous slope. I slid halfway down and took the skin off the palms of my hands trying to stop myself. The others waited silently at the top for me, showing the kind of patience that you might bestow on an imbecile child as he failed repeatedly to spell the word "moron." By the time I got up, sweating in spite of the bitter wind, even the horse looked bored.

A few steps, however, swept this mood away. For atop the embankment was a cinder trail that wound its way through the mountains. It promised more than shelter, it promised civilization. Given that I was freezing, irritated, totally confused, and bleeding slightly from wounds too minor to get any real sympathy, that promise was as good as a hot bath, a joint of venison, and a flagon of strong ale. Well, not quite, but you take my point.

But the idea of the bath cooled rapidly as we strode along the blackened track for an hour or more with no sign of intelligent life. The road, if that was what it was, felt like it was going somewhere, but it dragged through the mountains, curling aimlessly here, doubling back around an outcrop of rock there, so that its progress was random to say the least. After a while I felt like I was riding some huge, lazy, and very confused—or possibly blind—earthworm. After a second hour, I gave up on the beer and venison, too.

The one thing we did have on the path was protection from the icy wind and, though the air was still crisp and clear, the sun brushed our upturned faces and warmed them gently. Around us the mountains loomed: great angular crags of pale russet and violet-gray, towering as hard and impassive as a gold merchant's wife and fading into distant peaks white with snow. Of Vetch there was little hope and no sign.

After another hour, the company grew restless again. The sun had clearly begun its descent (in the west?) and we couldn't go on walking till dark with no plan for what happened if we didn't stroll into a cleverly concealed city around the next corner. Mithos grew even more surly than usual, and as he muttered earnestly to Orgos, they began walking a little faster. Renthrette, still mounted, trotted up to them and exchanged a few insights on our condition. Apprentice Will, man of dubious talents, tired legs and all-round miserable bastard, trudged behind and counted off all the places I would rather have been.

Suddenly there was a bird call, high and caustically harsh, from in front of us. It was a starling, feathers ruffled, wings aggressively half-spread, and it sat in the bare branches of a small and withered yew tree just left of the path. We hadn't seen many trees in the mountains, and even one as blasted as this was something of an event. Moreover, the bird's position in it, coupled perhaps with the way it fixed us with its hard bird eyes, gave it the aura of a guard or sentinel. I couldn't help but smile as the bird, small though it was, continued to screech its anger at us, flicking its wings and bobbing its head up and down as it called.

Mithos and Orgos stopped in their tracks before reaching the little tree, giving me time to catch up.

"Odd that it doesn't seem afraid of us," Mithos remarked.

"Probably used to people 'round here," I answered, snide. The bird cried again and flashed its wing feathers, dark and glossy as polished steel. Then it took to the air, circled us once, and flew away over a great purple boulder, calling all the time.

That was the highlight of the afternoon. We walked on for another mile or two before Mithos came to an abrupt halt.

"We have only two or three hours of good light left, and there is no sign of a town or an inn," he said, as if we might have missed that fact. "We are going to have to spend the night outdoors."

I opened my mouth to protest, but the others seemed quite unmoved by the patent idiocy of this suggestion so, for the moment, I held my peace.

Turning to Renthrette, Mithos asked what we had with us.

The saddlebags on the horse were the only luggage that had completed the "journey" from the Black Horse. Most of the rest had been inside the carriage, and we had been traveling light even then. Now, as Renthrette's quick inventory of the leather satchels across her mount made clear, we were virtually weightless.

"Two blankets, flint and tinder, an oil lamp, one small hatchet, some bread and cheese, and a length of rope. About thirty feet," she said, not exactly exuberantly.

"No tent?" I ventured.

"Did I mention one?" she snarled, her eyes still on Mithos and Orgos.

"Then you'll have to build a bivouac," I said. Actually, I was far from clear what bivouacs were, though they were reputed to save the lives of outdoor types from time to time.

"Do you see large numbers of trees around here?" Renthrette spat, lips curled with that special talking-to-Hawthorne contempt.

"What?"

"Branches," she said. "Leafy boughs? Clods of soft earth and turf? Yards of twine or vines to hold the thing together?"

Her scorn suggested that these things were somehow connected, even integral, to bivouacs, and that construction of one in our present conditions seemed unlikely.

"You, no doubt," I began, "would rather construct a three-story villa with a pool and one of those tiled porches with a little fountain and . . ."

"Shut up, Will," said Orgos, thoughtfully.

"I was only trying to be helpful," I said.

"We need to find a cave," said Mithos with a shrug. "And we'll need to build a fire, so gather what wood you see as we go. There won't be much, and we'll need all we can get. Renthrette, you can walk from here. Use the rope to bundle up the firewood and tie it to the saddle."

She nodded once and slipped easily from the horse's back, managing to hide her inevitable disappointment at no longer being the mounted escort poised to charge any dangerous but misguided beast that should come lumbering down the mountain into range.

Above us came a screeching call, so sharp and loud that we all turned our eyes upward.

"A kite," said Orgos.

"No," I corrected him, "it's a bird."

"A kite is a bird, idiot," he said without malice. "A kind of hawk."

The bird was circling perhaps a hundred feet overhead, its tail black and forked like a swallow's and its head down, watching. Its head and body were a brilliant white, even against the pale sky, and set off the black of the tail and wings strikingly. I was about to turn away from this before Orgos started one of his lectures on the wonders of nature, when a curious thing happened. A smaller bird flew up to the kite, chirping shrilly, then veered off and swooped low at us with only a yard or two of clearance.

"A starling," said Orgos. There was a note of confusion in his voice as his eyes followed the smaller bird to where it rejoined the kite, calling as before. The raptor, continuing to glide in tight circles, wings out straight, pinions splayed, returned a series of sharp whistles.

"It's not a starling," said Mithos, eyes upturned. "I mean, it's not *a* starling, it's *the* starling. The one we saw before."

"Based on what?" I asked. "You've seen one starling, you've seen 'em all."

"Based on nothing," said Mithos, dropping his eyes to mine. "A hunch. A sense of being watched."

This was, of course, quite absurd, but "absurd" is not a word which leaps to the lips when confronted with Mithos giving you one of those looks. Orgos? Maybe. Renthrette? Certainly, though you should expect to pay for it. But *Mithos*? Absurd? No. Mithos kept himself to himself, showing little emotion and letting the world go on around him till he told it to stop. When he gave orders, people followed them without question because he seemed so sure of his own mind and so dangerous to challenge. Not that he was violent or overtly threatening, you understand. He was just grim and powerful. Yes, that's the word: *powerful*, in every sense.

Now, though my brain said that the idea that these birds were keeping an eye on our progress and discussing it over a sandwich and a couple of pints was preposterous, the fact that it was Mithos who had said so gave it a kind of weird credibility. Renthrette watched him for a moment as if expecting further explanation, but he did not give any, and when she turned away, her face was blank, expressionless. Orgos nodded thoughtfully to himself and advanced along the cinder track, eyes skinned for an opening in the rock that would get us out of the freezing night winds.

I watched as they set off again and wondered, as I have often wondered in their company, what the hell I was doing with these people.

The cave which Mithos's keen eyes picked out of the mountainside was almost obscured by a great slab of granite. Behind it a fissure in the rock admitted us into a short corridor which we passed through two abreast, and thence into an L-shaped chamber, a long entrance stretching back into the cliff and then curving left through a narrow fissure. Its walls were irregular, in parts jutting out sharply, and it was, if anything, colder than it had been outside.

I crossed the uneven floor with a sour look on my face: There was a musty, almost rancid scent to the place and the air was moist as well as cold. Droplets of water pearled on my face. I brushed them off, wandering to the back of the cavern and the hollow, which cut to the left. This was dry, though much of the larger cavern (the two parts of the L were virtually separate "rooms"), was mossy, and a thin slime covered the floor by the entrance, where a trickle of water ran down the wall. No hand had carved the cave: only the wind, the rain, and the awesome splitting power of freezing winter and spring thaw, if spring ever came to this frigid wind-trap.

"Excellent," said Orgos in a voice apparently without sarcasm.

"Just like home," I added.

"We'll soon warm it up once we've got a fire going," said Mithos. "Renthrette, see if you can hang the blankets across the doorway. Keep the wind out."

The horse was led inside, much to my distaste, and offered what little greenery Renthrette had found.

"Must we sleep with the animal?" I whined.

Renthrette gave me an angry stare and said, "We've had to ever since you joined us."

"Funny," I observed. "I mean that great stinking manure factory."

Renthrette glanced at the horse to make sure it hadn't been offended.

"Can't leave it outside," said Mithos. "There may be wolves about."

"Oh, great," I said. "Knowing our luck we've probably holed up in their den. The horse would be safer as far from here as possible."

"No animals have lived here lately," said Orgos, our resident naturalist. "There's no dung, bones, or anything."

"Pity," I said. "There might have been something edible. Do we have anything for dinner at all?"

"One loaf of bread and a block of goat cheese," said Orgos, fishing through a saddlebag.

"I suppose we could always eat the horse," I mused. "Better than sleeping with it."

"I'd rather sleep with the horse than with you," Renthrette snapped.

"I'll bet," I said. "I'd suggest you invite it over for dinner first, but since we've sod-all to eat . . ."

"Give it a rest, Will," she muttered, balefully. Orgos grinned at me briefly and then joined Mithos in the center of the chamber.

They squatted down and began striking the steel and flint into the few dry leaves we had managed to find. When a flame appeared they cupped hands around it, whispering nurturing words as they fed it twigs and blew softly at its base. Renthrette joined them and the three of them crouched together, urging the fire to life as if tending a newborn calf, willing it to breathe or to take its first step. I watched from the back of the chamber, oddly distant from their seemingly familiar ritual. When the flames were strong enough to set their teeth to some of the larger branches we had gathered, the group shared a collective smile of comradeship and achievement. I shivered, as much at the exclusion as at the cold.

The cave did warm up, and within an hour or so, after a meager supper and the smallest gulp from Orgos's water flask, I was as comfortable and ready to sleep as I was likely to get. The four of us were seated quietly around the fire, watching it as we had done months before, only days after I met them. Bearing that in mind, I was half expecting the request for a tale of some sort when it came. It was, after all, pretty much all I could do. What I wasn't expecting was that it should come from Renthrette.

"Got a suitable tale, Will?" she asked.

I gave her a searching glance, but her eyes were lost in the fire. Briefly they flicked up to me, expressionless, then returned to the hearth without comment.

I considered for a moment, then spoke. "Once upon a time, in a land far away, there lived a girl with hair like spun gold and eyes of blue clear as a spring sky. She was fourteen and lived with her brother and her parents in a town that sat in a range of tall, imposing mountains. The parents doted on the girl and gave her everything she could wish for and, since they lived in a fine, spacious house with a maid and a butler and a nurse for the children, she did as she pleased and was as happy as a girl has ever been in life or story.

"But one day, her father came home from the market and his face was anxious. He was distant, preoccupied, and barely looked at the girl when she asked him what he had brought for her today. She was upset and sought out her brother. Together they watched as her father's worry spread to their mother and among the servants, but they did not know why until there was a loud rapping at the door.

"A man was outside, dressed in armor and a white cloak. His face was stern, and twenty other soldiers stood in ranks behind him, all with spears and shortswords. The children watched as the soldiers marched into the house and began helping themselves to food, drink, and whatever valuables they came upon. Plates were smashed; ancient crystal, passed on through the family, was brushed aside to shatter in pieces on the floor; and priceless furniture was overturned and chopped up for firewood. The servants, beaten by the soldiers, fled. The mother wept loudly over the ruins of her possessions and the father sought out the soldiers' commander, pleading with him to spare the rest of their belongings.

"But the soldiers just laughed and went on stealing and destroying everything in the house. Then one of them caught sight of the girl, and, catching her by the hair, he thrust her against the wall. As others gathered around them, the father burst in upon them with a hatchet and felled one of the men with a single blow. The others turned on him with their swords. The mother ran to tear them from her husband, but it was too late, and she too received her death wound. The children saw all this, but were too afraid to weep. Instead they fled, from the house, from the town, from the mountains.

"They fled for several years, living from hand to mouth, hiding in the streets, lurking in shadows, learning the ways of the downtrodden and the poor. Learning to hate the soldiers in their armor and white cloaks. . . ."

"Is this your idea of humor, Will?"

I looked up from the fire to find Renthrette staring at me. Her face was drawn tight and her already pale skin had a strange bleached quality. Her eyes were cold but full of rage.

"I'm sorry?" I said.

She gave me a long, hard look, and the anger in her eyes froze hard. Then, quite suddenly, and with a studied casualness which did not register in her face, she rose to her feet. "Forget it," she said, then added, "I'm going to get some sleep." She walked toward the back of the cave, gathering up one of the blankets in a single, irritable gesture.

"Don't you want to hear the end of the story?" I asked. She turned and her glance chilled me to the bone. I was used to her distaste and loathing, but this was different. This was close to hatred.

Her voice, when she spoke, however, was casual, almost jocular. "The part where she and her brother meet up with a group of rebels and become adventurers, but they get separated by the stupidity of this idiot actor they found in the street? I don't think so, thanks."

She turned and walked away, leaving the three of us in silence by the fire. I shrugged.

"That was way out of line, Will," said Orgos, his voice cold, his eyes boring into mine. "You're lucky she didn't put a dagger through your lungs."

There was another long and awkward pause as he refused to let me out of his gaze.

"I would have," said Mithos. His eyes never rose from the fire and his tone was soft, almost thoughtful. But he meant it. Hit with a wave of fear—fear of Renthrette, of Mithos's words and, even more, fear of the hint of agreement in Orgos's dark eyes—I struggled to my feet and blundered out into the night air.

It had been a stupid and mean-spirited thing to do and I was far from clear what I had been trying to achieve: trying to make her look slightly stupid for ridiculing me, I suppose. And I was trying to make myself look shrewd at having put together the half-clues I had been given over the past few months. Maybe I had hoped she would take it all with a half smile and a wink, impressed, even touched that I might give her background so much consideration. Or maybe I was just trying to claim a little insight because this place made me feel so stupid and lost. I had no idea how close to the mark I had been, but the fact that they all knew what I had been shooting at suggested I hadn't been far off. Suddenly the cleverness of my story fell away and I glimpsed something of its awful truth. If she had been through something like the picture I painted, Mithos was right: it was a wonder she hadn't killed me on the spot. To bring it all up to score a cheap point at her expense . . . Standing out in the cold, windy darkness and the silence of the mountain, my motives looked pretty shoddy.

I had convinced myself that I was no longer really interested in Renthrette. Even when I had been, it had been pure, unmitigated lust, as she had been quick to point out. Hadn't it? There were times I had begun to wonder, but they had passed quickly enough. I had felt quite sure that given the choice between a lifetime of friendship and one night with her under the sheets followed by no relationship of any sort, I would have taken the latter without hesitation. The patent spitefulness of what I had done made me wonder, with something of a start, what my feelings for her actually were. It was an unnerving thought.

Me and Renthrette? You must be joking. There might be—in fact, I know there are—some men who jump at the chance to be spurned by a woman, their feelings trampled and their poetry mocked, but not me. Not Will Anything-for-a-quiet-life Hawthorne. The Bill Hawthorne who had patronized the Eagle in Cresdon and who lived for beer and cards, the dashing apprentice actor and minor playwright, had a formula for love which ran as follows: flirtation, seduction, consummation, satisfaction, evasion. Afterward, when one is gathered with one's mates over a few pints of Old Seymore's chestnut ale, the cycle is concluded with a little recollection and narration. All that hearts and flowers stuff was merely part of steps one or two, and anyone who thought otherwise was doomed to a life of quite unnecessary pain. That was strictly for the birds.

And as if on cue, one appeared. It perched on the slab of rock across the cave mouth only ten feet or so from where I stood and looked at me in silence. A moment passed and I realized that it was doing none of that shifting, twitching, head tilting stuff that birds do. It was quite still, its eyes fixed on me.

The moon was riding high and three quarters full, casting a pale glow on the rocky landscape, which flared softly and then faded as clouds passed overhead. Suddenly, the sky cleared and the night shapes grew harder edges as the moon brushed the track and the crags around it with a watery silver light. The bird's distinctive blackish green plumage sparkled metallically and I recognized it: It was a starling.

While this thought was registering in my head, I caught movement elsewhere, out among the strewn boulders and rocky outcrops beyond the road. I turned to face them, and, as my eyes adjusted a little, I saw a flicker of shapes—no more than shadows—moving quickly. Then one by one I saw pairs of clear green eyes pricking out of the darkness like fireflies.

I turned awkwardly, scraping against the stone in my haste, and dipped into the little corridor with its curtain of gray wool. "Wolves!" I shouted. "There's a pack of wolves outside. Or something."

"What does 'or something' mean?" said Orgos, casually and without getting up.

"I didn't get real close!" I shouted back in panic and anger. "They looked like wolves. All right?"

"Renthrette is trying to sleep," said Mithos, his eyes on a piece of wood he was whittling with his knife.

"Are you people deaf or just stupid?" I yelled again. "I said there are . . ."

"Wolves," said Orgos. "Yes."

"Well?"

"Well, what?" said Orgos.

"Well, what are you going to do?" I demanded, body and voice beginning to tremble with exasperation.

"Nothing," said Mithos. "Stay here. They'll be gone by dawn."

"Are you out of your tiny minds?" I retorted. "There's a pack of ravenous, bloodthirsty beasts out there. Wolves, for God's sake! Listen!"

They had started to howl, great falling bays that rolled through the night air and trailed into plaintive whines like the music that drifts from a madhouse. A paralyzing chill seeped into my bloodstream and spread throughout my body. I went pale, fumbled for a weapon I didn't have, and then turned to find Orgos gazing off as in a trance. His black face, glowing softly in the firelight, was transfigured with a strange contentment, an almost spiritual delight in the wolf voices.

"Is there something wrong with you?" I bawled at him. "Do you find the idea of wolf muzzles poking into your ribcage for the juicy bits somehow amusing? Or is this more of that harmony-with-nature bollocks? They'll tear your throat out as soon as look at you."

"No they won't," said Orgos, with a sigh which suggested we'd had this conversation a hundred times. "They almost never attack people unless the winter is unusually hard and nothing else has survived. Not the case here, evidently. Nor would they seek us out in a cave like this, especially when there's a fire. No wolf that wasn't desperate for food would consider coming through that curtain. Just relax and enjoy the music."

And, as if on cue, a black muzzle sprouting with pale grayish bristle pushed through the woolen hanging at the cave's mouth. Slowly, guarded and low to the ground, its teeth bared and a low growl emanating from its throat, a great wolf entered.

SCENE V

❧

Sorrail

It's a funny thing, but sometimes—not often, you understand, but from time to time—it's nicer to be wrong than right. This was one of those times. The fact that Mithos froze, reversing the grip on his knife carefully, and Orgos scrambled awkwardly to his feet, eyes flashing to the sword that lay a dozen feet away, really didn't help at all. We were in a very small space with a wolf whose teeth, at this none-too-comfortable distance, looked like kitchen knives. Moreover, as the shifting of the curtain testified, there were more behind it, and they were coming in.

The horse went berserk. It had been standing over in the corner, as far from the fire as it could get in relative comfort, but the scent of the wolf induced sudden and total terror and it began to rear and paw the air. It ran to the back of the cavern and then paced to and fro, neighing and shaking its mane, its dark eyes bulging.

The wolf came on, right into the cave, undaunted by the fire, and there were at least three following it. I glanced around wildly, but there was nothing even resembling a weapon to hand and none of us had bows. We would have to fight at close quarters, with those great jaws snapping at us from all sides. In true Hawthorne fashion, I backed off slowly, my eyes fixed on the foremost wolf.

It was a huge dark-gray beast with a shaggy collar of longer fur stretching back like a mane from its slim face to its shoulders, while in its eyes was a cold light that suddenly and curiously reminded me of the starling. The association made little sense so I discarded it, returning to the more important matter of putting some yardage between me and those lupine chops. Backing off into the hollow at the back of the cave, I stumbled into Renthrette as she was getting to her feet and finding her sword.

I turned to her, but she looked through me as if we had never met, and then glanced from the advancing wolves to the leather-bound grip of her broadsword. It was a long, keen-bladed weapon, almost like a rapier but heavier, and she held it outstretched before her to hold the animals at bay. Instinctively, I stepped behind her.

There were five wolves in the cavern now, all snarling, hackles rising and falling like wind-blown aspens as the muscles beneath flexed and tightened. They had arced around the fire and now held their ground, their eyes amber with the leaping flames which were doing nothing to discourage them. The horse, now quite mad with terror, bucked one last time before its heart stopped and it fell heavily to the ground.

"Wait!" said Mithos, as the four of us huddled together, blades outstretched. "They may yet withdraw."

This seemed unlikely to me and I didn't like the idea of those jaws coming at me, cowering as I was back there with no weapon to hand. Moreover, there was something about the wolves which I didn't like; something beyond the obvious, I mean. They didn't move right. They exchanged glances and made noises unlike any beasts I had ever seen. And their eyes: in their eyes there was, what? Something I didn't want to name. . . .

The back of the cave was littered with stones of various sizes as if part of the cave wall had collapsed decades ago. As I watched the wolves no more than four or five yards away, I had been weighing a rock in my hand thoughtfully. Now I flung it, hard as I could, at the nearest and largest of the wolves.

He saw it coming and tried to duck, but it struck the mound of his shoulder and knocked him to the floor with a yelp. He was barely down for a moment, however, before he was on his feet again and coming for us. And the others came with him.

The cavern exploded with the noise of their rage as they set upon us. For a second the room seemed full of their gaping throats and gleaming fangs. Renthrette's sword, orange in the firelight, cut and lunged, and a wolf howl died on its dark lips. Mithos felled another, but there seemed to be more coming in. Orgos slashed one across the side and it collapsed, whining, but another was on his back and snapping at the nape of his neck. I saw Mithos call out and step toward Orgos, sword smoking with fresh blood.

Then I felt hot breath on my arm and a shock of pain. A wolf, paler than the others, almost white, had got past Renthrette, launched itself at me, and clamped its jaws around my left wrist and was worrying at it. I screamed, trying to shake it free, and blood, my blood, spattered on the cavern wall. The wolf let go, only to throw its forepaws onto my shoulders and send me crashing hard onto my back. Then it was on my chest and its muzzle was dipping for my throat as I flailed uselessly at it.

I didn't see Renthrette's sword pierce the beast until it had stiffened and slumped lifeless on top of me. Her eyes turned back to the fight. I just lay there feeling the wild thumping of my heart.

When I rolled out from under the warm and bloody fur of the animal, my left wrist stripped raw and streaming blood, I found I was too weak to stand, and my arm felt as if it had been thrust into the heart of the fire. I was gripped by an agony as tight as the wolf's jaws. Gathering myself into a sitting position with my back to the rock wall, I tried to stay the bleeding with a piece of my shirt. In truth, I also had to cover it up because I thought—wrongly, as it turned out—that I could see bone. Briefly my eyes misted over.

When I looked again, the wolves which remained, four or five of them, had withdrawn a little and now hung back around the cave mouth. They watched us still, but more warily now, and the sounds they made to each other were different. One of them, a silver-gray beast with a white blaze on the fur of its throat, met my gaze and returned it with eyes like yellow moons floating in black oil. Orgos still stood beside Renthrette, but he was bleeding from his neck and leg. Drops of crimson trickled down Renthrette's sword arm, and Mithos had backed up to the wall and leaned against it. His sword hung wearily from his hand, his face was pale, and there was a great wound in his side. His right hand was clasped across it, but blood seeped through his fingers and fell like rain to the cave floor.

"I do not think we can hold off another assault," said Renthrette.

"But we will show them what human muscle and fine steel can do before we perish," Orgos replied, darkly.

There was a commotion at the cave mouth. The wolves parted on either side of it, as if by agreement, and their growls grew low and ominous. Something was coming in.

The curtain was torn down and a great bear shambled into the cave. It was immense and brownish and it filled the corridor completely, squeezing into the cave with difficulty. Its head and paws were vast, the latter equipped with claws perhaps seven inches long. I'd seen bears back in the Cresdon baiting pits, but this was bigger than any of them. And then there was the way it looked to the wolves and growled strangely, and the light in its eyes.

Renthrette blanched and Orgos's dark skin seemed to cloud over. Mithos's jaw dropped slightly and there was dread in his eyes. For once, I knew what he knew. The bear's reach would tear out our hearts and crush our skulls before we could get close enough to stab at it.

It took a step to the right of the fire and the wolves followed in its wake, grinning malevolently. We backed off still further, though there was clearly no escape. If we had bows or spears, we might have had a chance, but as it was, this was not going to be so much a battle as a kind of grotesque buffet.

The bear roared, a vast and deafening bellow that made the walls tremble, and presented a gape that could have taken me head first and closed about my waist. Then it lowered its muzzle and advanced, its bulk blocking out the firelight as it loomed over us.

Suddenly there was a flicker of light, a bluish flash that rippled around the cave's uneven surfaces. With something like panic, the bear began a great, lumbering revolution, but before it could complete the turn, it shrieked with what could only be pain. The wolves whined and fled, the bear shook its great head from side to side, and blood fell from its terrible maw. Once more it began to turn toward the entrance, and once more it cried out in sudden pain.

Then its nemesis appeared.

In the cave mouth was a man clad in a hooded robe the color of new cream and armed with a long, two-handed spear whose tip flared with a dazzling light. It seemed like a flame, though it did not consume the spear and its light was hard and white and hurt my eyes when I looked directly at it. The bear, now facing him, bellowed and stooped to lunge, but the spear slid past its wild claws and found its chest. The beast lurched, but the spearman held on to the shaft with uncommon strength and determination. The pale light flared in the bear's face and, with one last cry of pain and—so it seemed to me—horror or hatred, it tipped forward. The man wrested the spear from its breast and stepped sideways as the beast fell dead before him.

A stillness fell and, for a moment, we looked in wonder at our timely savior. He, quite calm and still, looked back. His age was hard to guess. I might have said something over forty, though his movements had the ease and vigor of a younger man. He drew the hood back from his head and his hair, which was fair, spilled out over his shoulders. His skin was also fair, but weathered and tanned by the sun. His eyes were an ice blue, startling and intelligent. His countenance, though severe as Mithos's, flickered into a smile and he bowed politely.

"It seems my finding you was fortuitous," he said in a clear and faintly musical voice. "There are dark creatures abroad these days."

There was a pause, then Orgos spoke. "I am Orgos, from Thrusia, and I offer our thanks for your help. As you can see, however, we have all suffered some hurt and Mithos, our leader, needs particular attention."

"Forgive me," said the stranger. "I am Sorrail of Phasdreille, a watcher of the paths. I first observed you an hour before sundown. I would have come to you earlier, but I was unsure of your allegiances. Your appearances are, shall we say, misleading."

"Allegiance to who?" asked Orgos. "We are travelers in this land and know little of its business."

"Indeed," said Sorrail, "you must have come from far afield not to know what stirs in the mountains here. But come, bind your wounds and rest. I must chase these creatures of foulness to earth. I will return at first light to guide you."

So saying, he took from inside his habit a leather satchel full of bandages and ointments. These he gave to Orgos and, without further comment, turned on his heel and left us, taking his strange spear with him.

"Helpful chap," I remarked. This was a laughable attempt to make light of our brush with being steak (heavily marbled in my case). No one, myself included, was taken in for a moment.

There was another long silence and Orgos got to work on Mithos. Renthrette, whose injury was not so bad that she could not use her hands, took another roll of bandage and squatted beside me.

"Let me see your wound," she said.

I removed the sodden rag of fabric about my wrist and her face darkened.

"I can bind it for now, but this needs more expert attention."

I winced as she began to wind the fabric about my arm, but said nothing. The dressing was cool and slightly moist and gave off a sweet scent like honey and rose petals. Renthrette kept her eyes on her work but, as if considering the question even as she spoke, said, "Why did you throw that rock? This could have been avoided."

"You have got to be joking," I said. "They came in here after us."

"They were beasts hunting. They might not have attacked," she answered.

"True," said Orgos from where he was examining Mithos, "but they did, and I don't know why. There was something strange about these creatures, and never have I heard of bears and wolves hunting together so deliberately. These were no ordinary animals. Perhaps, as our new friend said, there are dark creatures abroad."

Renthrette fell silent, thoughtful. I spoke up. "So what the hell were they? They sure looked like animals to me. Wolves and a bear. No question, no mystery."

Orgos looked at me, and he could see that I was looking for agreement that would silence my own doubts. "Have you ever seen bears or wolves of that size?" he asked.

"Clearly they get a lot to eat," I remarked, considering how close we had come to being just another meal on the run.

"Their voices," gasped Mithos. We all turned to look at him. He was pale and still bleeding heavily. His words came with a struggle that clearly filled Orgos with alarm, and the feeling spread to Renthrette. "I have not heard . . ." Mithos managed. "I have never heard animal voices so . . . so coherent. . . . So much . . . like . . . *speech*."

"Quiet," said Orgos gently. "Lie still."

But Mithos was right. It made no sense, but I had had the same feeling about the noises the beasts had made to each other. It was something similar to that deliberation with which they moved and the glimmer in their eyes. It wasn't just watchful, and it wasn't just hungry. Indeed, it wasn't animal at all. There was a keenness there that had made me catch my breath. It was like you could see a *mind* through those eyes, a mind that was working, processing. It was an alarming sensation, and though I wanted to put it down to never having been this close to a wolf before, I knew that that wasn't it. I have seen the eyes of beasts in cages before, and I have looked into the faces of dogs and cats and cattle and pigs, and what I have always seen is a blankness that tells of instinct, a gateway not into mind but into body, the creature's impulses for food and self-protection. This was different. In the eyes of those wolves there had been *thought*.

Except, of course, that there couldn't have been.

Gradually, and with some effort, the questions slipped from our minds and we grew quiet, finding our own ways into rest, even into sleep. When I woke there was a soft light in the cave and, for a moment, before the pain of my wound spiked through my wrist like a pickaxe, there was a sense of calm and contentment. The morning was fair and cold and I woke slowly, the corpses of great wolves gradually painting the night's events as if they had been experienced by someone else.

We were sharing out the last of our sparse rations when Sorrail returned. He had been walking most of the night but still seemed a good deal fresher than I felt. Smiling, he drew a pair of rabbits from his satchel and laid them on the ground by the fire.

"Breakfast," he said. "Not much, I'm afraid, but you need to restore your strength."

He inspected our wounds and, though he paused long over my wrist and longer over Mithos's side, he seemed satisfied. "We will need to carry him to the rest house," he said, "but it is not far and the day is mild as yet. You sir, can you walk?"

"Yes," I said.

"Good. It is unfortunate that your horse perished, but we can make a sling of the blankets and fasten them to my spear. It is a sturdy weapon and will bear his weight, I think."

"And it's magic," I said. "Orgos has one of those."

Sorrail gave me a swift glance, and there was something hard and unreadable in his eyes.

"Is it a secret?" I said. "I won't say anything."

He blinked, then said, "Orgos, you and I must carry Mithos between us. Perhaps the lady could roast us that brace of conies before we set out?"

So that was that. Sorrail told us what to do and we did it. He was a politely straightforward fellow, but he was companionable enough so long as you didn't ask about his spear. I would never have dared presume to tell Renthrette to do anything as obviously "feminine" as cook, though she did it often enough. In this case, however, she set about skinning and preparing the meat without the slightest suggestion of having taken offense. In just over an hour we had dined and were ready to set out.

Sorrail said little as we made our way along the cinder path. His eyes were always scouring the crags and embankments and he barely responded to my questions, and then only obliquely. Like Mithos, he seemed to ration his words, as if there may not be enough to last him till the end of the week. He said that these were the Violet Mountains and that we were "many leagues" from the northernmost reaches of Thrusia. I wasn't certain what a league was, exactly, but it didn't sound promising, and despite his words I wondered if he had ever even heard of Stavis or Thrusia, since he clearly knew nothing about either. Given the fact that he styled himself a wanderer, this was not a good sign. I pressed him for names for this land, but he only repeated absently that these were the Violet Mountains and that beyond them lay the White City. Just when I was getting used to the idea that names had been shelved in favor of colors round here, he added that the White City was properly called Phasdreille.

He spoke like someone in a play: an old play, full of larger-than-life heroes. It was odd. I'd spoken lines like that, had even written a few. But the closest I had come to hearing them delivered as actual speech in real life was listening to Mithos and Orgos encouraging me to do my duty or some other damned thing, and neither of them came close to this character. I wanted to ask him if he was for real, or if he was rehearsing a part or something, but he also had Mithos and Orgos's demeanor, which didn't encourage questions, much less mockery. I risked a sort of smirk at him after he had made some remark about Phasdreille being "fairest of the cities of light" to suggest he was overdoing it a bit, but he just stared at me.

"What about the creatures we fought last night?" I asked, figuring that I may as well play along. "What were they?"

"It is better not to speak of such things," said Sorrail, his eyes meeting mine for the first time. "The enemy is abroad and his shapes are many. This land is full of his spies. We will talk of this in more secure surroundings, not before."

Right you are, squire, I thought. You stay in your heroic tale and I'll ignore it as best I can. Now that I thought about it, if no one mentioned our little encounter with those . . . whatever they were till we were back in Stavis, I'd be positively ecstatic.

So Sorrail strode on, Mithos slung between him and Orgos, his eyes seeking out every stump of tree or boulder that could be hiding the servants of this nebulous "enemy." Renthrette brought up the rear, a good twenty yards back, her sword drawn. On the pretext of getting a stone from my shoe, I dropped back. Though she loitered as long as she could, she eventually caught up.

"Listen," I said, dropping my eyes, "about last night . . ."

"Forget it," she said, picking up the pace a little.

"No, I mean," I began, though I wasn't sure what I *did* mean. She kept walking and I, after a pause to gather resolution, scampered after her like a puppy and blurted, "I mean, I'm sorry."

She stopped and turned to me. "I said, forget it," she said.

"I was well out of line," I persisted, "and I'm sorry."

It was a relief to say it, and I took a deep breath. She looked at me in that careful, scrutinizing way of hers, like someone picking over meat that was suspiciously under-priced, then said, "It was an honest mistake, I suppose."

This was curious.

"Was it?" I said, uncertainly.

"I suppose. It wasn't very clever tactically. . . ."

"What are we talking about?" I interrupted.

"I thought we were talking about you throwing the stone that nearly got us all killed," she said. "Aren't we?"

"No," I gasped. "I'm saying sorry for the story by the fire last night. I thought I was being clever, you know, stringing together a few bits of information and filling in the blanks with guesswork. But I didn't mean, you know . . ."

There was the briefest pause, a momentary hesitation on her part that was completely unreadable. "Forget it," she said. The words were the same, but her face had frozen over like the surface of a pond, hiding whatever lay in its depths. A wall had gone up around her and, like a face seen through thick, imperfect glass, she was momentarily distorted by it: barely recognizable. Then she brushed her hair from her face and walked away.

~❦~

After about an hour, the path began to descend, winding in a slow, erratic spiral down the side of a great russet peak whose stone gleamed with flecks of metal ores. Sorrail said its name was Naishiim, but it was commonly called The Armored One. I suppressed a derisive snort of laughter and stared at it to hide my grins. Absurdly melodramatic though it was, the title did seem appropriate, since the mountain had steep shoulders and a rise in the center which, at certain angles, looked like a head. It stood as a giant sentinel on the edge of the clustered range, glowering down on the path, which traced its way into a series of lower rises, sheer-sided, but mere swelling hills in comparison.

"It is good that we have passed the mountain," said Sorrail as we paused to rest. His eyes moved from the path ahead back to the foreboding mountain. "From here on, the journey will be easier and we will be in less danger of assault. Dread creatures dwell on the upper slopes of The Armored One, and it is just as well that our journey has kept us largely at its feet. Few have passed a night on its top unscathed, and recently the place has become a haunt for still fouler beasts than those you saw last night. A company of goblins passed through here some months ago, and it is thought that they have made their home in one of its foul crevices."

"Excuse me, what?" I stuttered, not bothering to mask my incredulity. "I think I misheard. What passed through here?"

"Goblins," said Sorrail, his face straighter than an Empire road. "About two hundred of them, large and well equipped. The road has been barely used since."

"No doubt," I said, brushing aside his traffic concerns. "And what exactly do you mean by goblins? I mean, where I come from, goblins are nasty fairies or something that you tell children about to make them eat their porridge."

"Indeed?" said Sorrail, serious as before. "I fail to see the connection."

"I mean," I said with a sigh at having to spell it out, "they aren't real and never have been. They are just a barely remembered ingredient from old folktales that relied on nasty beasties running around so the good guys would have something to kill without feeling bad about it. You know what I mean? I guess, for some reason, you use the same word for something more mundane. Some large and unpleasant squirrels, perhaps, or some bad tempered beavers, or . . ."

He cut me off with a word and a stern glance that was almost offended. "These are not squirrels," he said.

"Well, no," I persisted, "probably not. I'm just saying that they are probably something that we call by another name. . . ."

"These are the spawn of the enemy and they are not to be made light of," he said coldly. "They are creatures of darkness and hatred, corrupt to the core. They are like men but twisted by the evil which dwells in each of them and shows forth in their speech and their deeds, even in their very countenance. You would look upon them, Mr. Hawthorne, and despair. They are dreadful, and since they have become organized and armed, they lead the enemy against all which is true and fair in the world. You would do well to speak of them less frivolously."

Well, that, not for the first time, was me told. I shut up and we marched on. The others did not speak and avoided my eyes when I rolled them in their direction. Goblins? What was he on? I shut up, feeling irritated, righteous, and a bit confused, and started to lag a little behind—separate enough to show my discontent, close enough to have support should I get assaulted by some shrieking hoard of mythical monsters. Mixed feelings, in other words. My brain said that this was lunacy, but I had to admit to having seen beasts that moved with human deliberation, birds that conversed, and the flash of unearthly light from a long spear.

Not long ago you didn't believe in magic swords, either, I reminded myself.

And then there was the mystery of how we had got to this place. We had no idea where we were, after all. We could be a thousand miles away from Stavis, on a different continent entirely. Maybe the bears did talk here. Maybe there were whole cities of cats and monkeys ruled by a big blue pig.

No. It was all bollocks. Some wolves had decided that following a bear got them the scraps the bear didn't eat. Simple as that. I could believe in flashes of power from swords and spears—just. But goblins? Come on. I'd accept lions playing poker before that. At least lions existed.

If the others questioned the fact that all semblance of reality as we knew it had been abandoned the moment we set foot in this place, they gave no indication of it. I shot Orgos an inquiring glance and pulled a comically skeptical face, mouthing "Goblins?" soundlessly. He did not respond except to give me a hard look, as loaded with dour concern as it was long. I drew closer to the rest of the company and kept my eyes open.

A couple of hundred yards farther on, a yew tree grew beside the path. It was windblown and stunted so that its limbs were twisted up as if with long anguish. Sorrail set his foot onto one of the lowest branches, and, in seconds he was fifteen or twenty feet up, scanning the land about us. The mountain was behind us and ahead, just visible through a fine morning mist, I could make out a valley that spread wide below us. I caught my breath with surprise. So much had my attention been fixed on the slopes at our sides and rear that I had barely noticed the territory in front.

"Good," said Sorrail. "The worst is past. After this last descent, our way becomes easier."

He slipped easily down the tree and turned smilingly upon us. Then his head tipped slightly to one side and he became very still. I began to ask what the matter was, but he cut me off with a quick gesture of his hand. He was listening intently, his eyes squeezed shut.

So we listened, too, and, for a while, heard nothing. Then, distantly, as if carried on the breeze, we heard a low booming which I might have ignored were it not so steadily, deliberately repeated. Drums, I thought, and getting louder.

Sorrail turned on his heel and stared back the way we had come, eyes flashing hard and alert across the steep sides of the mountain. Then, after the briefest double take, his gaze rested on a point midway up one of the slopes. His face, which had been pale but full of energy, faded somehow. I turned.

Barely visible in the gray haze which slept on the armored head of Naishiim, shapes were moving. They were moving down the mountain toward us and they were moving fast. The drums were clearly audible now and, if I wasn't mistaken, there were voices among them which chanted darkly, though I did not know the words.

"This is a most evil fortune," gasped Sorrail, his eyes wide. "We must fly! Down the path into the valley. Fast as you can go! Run!"

I looked from him back to the mountain and saw, though I couldn't—wouldn't—believe it, bears: dozens of them. And on their backs were forms like armored men with lances. But they were not men. Aghast, I looked back to the others, stunned into inaction.

"Don't you understand?" shouted Sorrail. "We cannot fight such a force. Even on foot they are dreadful: cruel and strong. Mounted they are terrible. We must flee! Now!"

He waited for no further comment, just pulled at Mithos's stretcher, dragging Orgos after him. Renthrette looked back once and then bounded off on the heels of the others down the path which dropped into the valley.

Ironically, I was the last to run, though that had more to do with disbelief and stupidity than with valor, in case that still needs pointing out. I watched them run and felt the possibility of armed goblins mounted on giant bears offering itself for debate. Then, just as my brain was settling into a comfortable chair with a drop of whiskey and a satisfied, slightly ironic smile, all ready to leisurely prove the nonexistence of goblins, talking bears, magic moonbeams, and pots of gold under rainbows, there came a cry. It was a blend of an animal roar and a human, or near-human, scream of hatred and aggression. Others joined in until the mountains resounded with a single dreadful voice. It came from a force which bristled with teeth and sprouted lance heads like a forest. I began to run, faster than I would have thought I was capable of, all sense of irony gone. And, as if the gates of Hell had burst apart, the goblins came after.

SCENE VI

~※~

Flight and Refuge

Renthrette quickly took the lead, sprinting ahead with leaping gazelle strides as the cinder path plummeted down the incline and turned into scree. Sorrail and Orgos, struggling with the wounded Mithos, slowed painfully till even I passed them, though I was too scared to take much notice. Behind us the noise of pursuit was growing ever louder and I fancied I could feel the earth itself shake. I tripped and slid on the loose stones of the downward slope, barely keeping myself upright as my momentum carried me on and out of control.

Then Renthrette, who had hit the level and tussocky ground of the valley floor at breakneck speed, pulled up short and scuttered to a halt. Turning, she looked past me and her mouth fell open in a soundless cry. I had no choice but to keep running, not daring to risk looking back and losing my footing completely. It took me no more than a second to reach her, but in that time she had drawn her sword and was climbing back up the treacherous slope.

"What the hell? . . ." I gasped, wheezing heavily as I came to an awkward standstill. She ignored me. Looking up the way we had come I saw the bears charging forward at a speed that a fast horse would struggle to match, their heads low, their shoulders high and angular, and their vast paws eating up the ground in great bounds. Astride each was a dark rider with helmet and armor, a keen lance, and a round shield. The immense bulk of the bears roared forward toward, less than a hundred yards in front of them, the body of Mithos. He was lying on the ground with Orgos standing over him, sword outstretched and body braced futilely against the inevitable impact.

Sorrail, a little further down, shouted wildly up at Orgos. "Fly! You cannot help him! Save yourself!"

"Go!" Orgos replied. "I will stand by my friend."

Without another word Sorrail turned back toward where I stood, his eyes wild, then began once more to run. Then he saw Renthrette advancing, and managed to slow himself before colliding with her. He seized her sword arm briefly. "You must leave him! You cannot hope to repel such an enemy."

He gave a desperate gesture back up the slope. Five or six of the bears with their goblin riders were only paces from Orgos, and two more were coming down each side toward us, one with a pair of huge drums slung across the beast's back. How many more were behind them I could not say: a dozen at the very least.

Doubt flickered through Renthrette's eyes as Sorrail pulled at her. She hesitated a moment and then ran with him, down into the valley, at the same moment that one of the bears reached Orgos's position, reared, and struck him a heavy swash of its forepaw across his left shoulder. He did not have time to land even a single stroke from his sword. He was knocked back and sideways with the incredible force of the blow and fell against a boulder where he lay quite still. With precise brutality they set upon him, fallen though he was, and upon his friend of so many years, who lay defenseless close by. The onslaught hemmed them in until I could see their bodies no more.

"Orgos!" I screamed, but the foul beasts and their fouler riders were everywhere now, and still pouring toward us. I turned and began to run once more.

❧

And I kept running. There was nothing else for it, and no one in their right mind would say otherwise. Sorrail had had to virtually drag Renthrette away, and she wept bitter tears as he pulled her, but I was watching my own path. Since where I was going mattered less than what I was getting away from, I paid little heed to the direction or to my companions. I dashed between the bushes and hollows of the vale which, as it turned out, was marshy and pocked with still, leaden pools. The grass was waist deep, so I was running blind, with no sense of where I might hit a rock or a pothole. I got the latter.

My foot sank calf-deep into a boggy hole and I pitched forward. I fought to get up, but my boot slid in the mud. Then it occurred to me that I might have more chance of survival lying low in the long grass and swamp than trying to outrun the enemy. So I hugged the ground and desperately tried to shrug off the pictures that rose, uncalled for, to my mind: claws and lance tips tearing flesh, great ursine jaws closing on limbs. Perhaps if I had not seen it happen, the images would have been less terrible, less savagely real. Then again, perhaps not.

I tried gingerly inching up enough to look through the grass for Sorrail and Renthrcttc, but they were nowhere to be seen. I lay on the edge of a pit, cold water seeping into my clothes, face down in the hard grass and rushes that grew around it, and wondered how I could have been so stupid as to lose them. I felt a sudden terrifying and unexpected grief for Orgos and Mithos welling up inside me, so I focused on the fear that I was nursing like a hole in the belly. This seemed to help. Perhaps it's just me, but other people's fates seem less pressing when you're waiting to have your throat torn out by a creature you didn't believe in a few hours ago.

⁂

I lay in the marshy hollow for about fifteen minutes, though I had no way of knowing exactly how long it was. The air was still and rank with the smell of stagnant water and decaying plant life. "Rank" is a bit of an understatement. A few years ago my housekeeper, Mrs. Pugh, cooked a pot of potatoes and then—God knows how—forgot about them for ten days of sweltering Cresdon summer. I wouldn't have believed I would ever smell anything worse than that harmless-looking pot of olfactory horror. Right now, I would have bathed in it to rinse the foulness of the pool off me, a foulness you could almost see rising off the thick water.

The cries of the enemy had ceased and, after only a few minutes, the sound of their breakneck pursuit had faded to nothing. But I figured that if I stuck my head up I was still liable to have it lopped neatly off, so I stayed where I was, kept my head down, and felt sorry for myself. Little stirred except the wind in the reeds. A warbler burbled happily to itself before taking flight, and a small brownish toad caught sight of me and hopped into invisibility. I speculated darkly that they might be reporting back to creatures considerably larger and nastier than they, but there wasn't much I could do about it if they were.

Then something moved only a few feet away from the lip of the pool, something large and careful. I held my breath and waited, catching the slightly bitter scent of an animal, then a muted grunt. I kept my head down, but felt—or thought I felt—a fractional chill as of a shadow passing over me. The reeds on the rim of the hollow shifted and snapped, and something huge inhaled, a series of powerful sniffs trying

to gather an aroma, a trace, perhaps, of me. If I saw that bloody warbler again I'd give it something to sing about.

With infinite care I tipped my head slightly and looked up. Ten
yards away, just on the lip of the pit and surrounded by eight-foot reeds
and elephant grass with plumed white ears, was a goblin lancer mounted
on a great steel-gray bear. The animal had its left flank toward me and
was sniffing, its muzzle to the ground.

The goblin was squat, heavily muscled, and about my height. It was
armored with black and rusted mail and heavy leather pads. Its head
was unhelmeted and quite bald, its skin cracked and yellow-brown, like
old mustard. Then it shifted, turning toward the center of the wet hollow, and I saw its face. It was thin and tight, each bone of the skull
showing through the strained skin. It looked like a man, but hairless
and with malice smoldering in its small, hollow eyes. The goblin
seemed to look at me, but its eyes were focused elsewhere and the reeds
screened me for the moment. It spoke, a stream of guttural noises and
hard syllables spiked as sharp as the barbs on the lance it brandished in
its sinewy right hand, and another goblin answered from close by. I put
my head back down and hoped that the rancid stench of the pit itself
would confuse the bear or whatever the hell it was.

Back in Cresdon or Stavis, people would pay good money to see
a bear that would let you ride on it without demanding bits of your
thorax in return. If I ever got out of here, maybe I could take one back
with me and corner the market. Such thoughts were, however, prema-
ture. As the most experienced merchants will tell you, long-term eco-
nomic plans must bow to surviving the next thirty seconds. Moving less
than an inch at a time I began to slide backward into the cold, thick water of the pit. The movement was painfully slow. The thick, freezing water welled round my thighs, then around my waist, and then my chest,
and still the bear and its rider did not stir. I slid back still further, my
legs sliding in the slime under the water until they encountered something long and heavy lying on the floor of the pond: a log. I pushed until it shifted and my feet squeezed under it. I felt the water's icy hand
close about my throat.

The bear snorted, shifted, and uttered a sound that might have been
a word in the goblin's own filthy tongue, at which the rider turned to
peer into the pool. I breathed in deeply and, eyes tight shut, pushed my
head completely under the water. I clutched at a clump of weeds with
one fist and pushed the other into the muddy ooze up to the wrist, to

keep myself from floating to the surface. My feet squirmed under the fallen log, helping to anchor me in place. Though this all took less than five seconds, I felt that I was running out of air. Wildly I remembered how heroes in stories hid from pursuers by using reeds to breathe through as they floated downstream. Well, it was too damn late for that. Another five seconds passed and my wind pipe contracted and buckled as if I was going to vomit, but I swallowed it down and held on for another few seconds.

Then the log resting on my ankles shifted and—to my horror— swam slowly away. The gorge rose in my throat again and I could hold it no longer. I broke the surface as gently as possible and gasped at the air. The bear had not moved. Terror of the goblin and its mount warred in my breast with the gut-wrenching nausea inspired by whatever the creature in the pond was. Before any decision had been made, I was scrambling out in blind terror of brushing against the chill skin of whatever was under the water. I snaked almost completely out and into the reeds, moving too quickly and thrashing slightly with involuntary revulsion. The goblin heard me.

It turned like a sprung trap and its muscles tautened, eyes and ears concentrated on the pool. It was motionless. I froze and held my breath as if I was still under the reeking water, but I could not look away. Its thin lips were parted slightly and I saw teeth in its immobile jaws. Its small, deep-set eyes flicked around the surface of the pond, and suddenly, as if caused by the hard stare of those eyes, the water broke with a small splash. Ripples coursed away and the body of some great eel or serpent, an oily olive green streaked with gray slime, arced back down to the bed from whence I had roused it. It sent a stream of heavy bubbles to the surface and, as it did so, the goblin's face and body sagged. He grunted some word to his mount and turned away disinterested. The bear made another semi-articulate sound. There was a momentary pause, and then they moved off with remarkable stealth. I, pulling my feet from the water completely and huddling into a childlike crouch, breathed again.

I waited in the same position till the sun had begun its descent, sure that any movement would bring the monstrous riders back. All that time my eyes moved from the grass around the rim where the goblins might reappear and back to the dark water with its nameless inhabitant. But the shadows were lengthening fast, and this was not my idea of a fun place to spend the evening. If I wasn't going to spend the night wandering around this desolate hole in total darkness, stumbling into bogs or the jaws of whatever nightmares lived in them, I was going to have to move quickly, goblins or no bloody goblins.

I crawled out and up, conscious that the mud clotting on my skin was beginning to stink even more as it warmed to my body heat. Nice. Peering out and across the valley floor, I scoured the land for signs of the enemy, but could see little through the long, coarse grass. Bugger all, in fact. Nothing of friends or town, road or track. And as if on cue, it began to rain, a cold, misty drizzle which didn't rinse any of the mud off, but did manage to make me just that bit more miserable.

I clambered awkwardly to my feet and began, for want of a better idea, to move in the vague direction the path had been pointing before it petered out in this swampy wasteland. My mouth and nose were full of the pond's stinking ooze and grit, and no matter how much I spat, there seemed to be more under my tongue or between my teeth making my drool brownish. I skulked forward, all hunched over, glancing furtively about and dropping to a hurried crouch in the long grass every few seconds like a crippled rabbit with a lot of enemies.

This went on for about two hours. The light began to lessen perceptibly, though I have no idea how far I traveled or if I was still heading in the same direction. With dull alarm I began moving faster and less cautiously, knowing full well that with the grass this long I could slam into the side of a bear without seeing it until it was ready for a second helping. I kept going, pressed on by the swelling darkness, the growing chill, and the absolute certainty that if I had to spend the night out here *something* would get me.

The ground began to dry out under my feet and the reeds thinned until I was crossing great fields of long tufted grass. Turning around, I thought I could make out the dim silhouette of the crags behind me in the far distance. Large insects, beetles, and some evil-looking form of cricket leaped and blundered out of my path as I sped away from the mountains and the creatures which lived there. I was filthy, miserable, and exhausted, but I picked up the pace, hoping against hope to find something more in my milieu, if you know what I mean. A pub with a friendly barmaid would be nice, but I'd settle for a house. And a beer. I could murder a beer.

I rested on a fallen tree which had been lying in the grass donkeys' years and was overgrown with moss and strange leathery fungi. Sitting on it, I wheezed heavily, sucking the air into my lungs like a man at a desert oasis gulping water. I had a stitch in my side from running, and I found myself wishing, ironically, that Orgos had made me exercise more in Stavis. But that was not the way to think now, for lots of reasons. I thought of one of the heroes I had played in those old Thrusian history plays and figured that if I could make two-and-a-half-thousand bitter Cresdonites believe that Will Hawthorne, scrawny and fat at the same time, was Lothar the Wanderer, scourge of the unchivalrous and iambic-pentametered all-round good egg, once a month for two years, I could do anything. I got to my feet and began to run again with new and grim determination.

Ten minutes later, clutching my aching side and gasping with weariness, Lothar the Wanderer was flagging. I squatted in the grass and parted one great tuft (if "tuft" isn't the wrong word for a clump of leaves twelve feet high), looking desperately around. There, directly ahead of me, I saw smoke: not the smoke of carnage and destruction, amazingly enough, but chimney smoke, hanging like a smudge of steely blue in the dark sky. Rising till I was almost vertical, I began, once more, to run, but this time I could see the audience admiring me. Lothar was doing the epilogue; I could smell it in the woodsmoke.

At times the gray billow disappeared behind the matted stalks of grass, but soon the land cleared and I could make it out plainly. I was in a meadow or pasture of some kind and only a few hundred yards ahead I could see the outline of trees, black against the sky. I stumbled on, ignoring the way my legs buckled with pathetic exhaustion, crossing the field to a crudely fashioned wooden fence. I paused and inhaled through my nose, and the smoke was bitter and woody over the damp greenery. Gasping for air though I was, I sucked it into my lungs like life itself. The audience's applause swelled in my ears, and suddenly I saw it, appearing through a thicket of hawthorn hedge: a gabled roof, a gray stone chimney, and a sign hanging on a bracket above the door: The Last Refuge Inn.

"Thank you, ladies and gentlemen!" I said aloud, bowing to the field. "Thank you! Thank you!"

But the door of The Last Refuge Inn was locked. This rather un-pub-like development dashed my spirits a little, but I beat heartily on the door and called in a commanding fashion such as the long dead and probably fictional Lothar would have been proud of.

> "The Wand'ring Knight has come to taste your cheer,
> Since he has 'scaped his journey's fearful doom,

And longs for hearth and dinner and a beer,
And welcome given to your daughter's room."

Hardly great verse, but not bad for the spur of the moment. There was no answer, but a curtain in a bay window moved, so I waited.

Nothing happened.

I tried again, knocking loudly and grinning as I called out, "Come throw the latch and summon Lothar in, since he is weary and he seeks for rest."

Still nothing.

"Open the bloody door!" I yelled, losing patience and good humor at a stroke. "What the hell kind of pub is this? Should I have made an appointment? Do I need references? Come on, open the damn door."

And, with a heavy clang, the lock turned and the door creaked open. With it came the point of a fine silver rapier which came to rest about two inches from my windpipe. It was held by a tall, fair man. Others were behind him, weapons in hand and eyes fixed on me with undisguised hostility.

"Hello?" I tried, leaning slightly away from the sword point.

The others did not speak, but their eyes hardened and the sword moved steadily under my chin. Gasping wordlessly, I wondered if I had perhaps violated some sort of dress code.

Farcical though such an instinct undoubtedly was, it wasn't altogether wide of the mark. There was fear behind the menace in their eyes, and recognizing this, I guessed that the principal reason for this rather unwelcoming behavior lay in my appearance, since I was still caked from head to foot in a dark brown slime and the light in the inn was low. The truth struck me with sudden and comic force: They thought I was some sort of goblin. Imagining how I must appear to these quiet, law-abiding folk already spooked by tales of bear-riding demon assaults to have me banging on their door like a ravaging swamp troll, I laughed with relief. This was apparently the wrong thing to do and seemed, momentarily, to convince them of my hellish origins.

"Strike!" hissed a young man peering round the doorjamb. He was addressing the rapier wielder and had one eye on me, the other on an axe he was raising.

"Wait!" I spluttered, specks of mud exploding from my cracked lips unhelpfully. "I am Will Hawthorne, a traveler and friend of . . . of, what the hell is his name . . . ? You know!"

"Strike quickly," advised the young man spitefully. "Heed not the words of the enemy, for his tongue is foul."

Truer than you know, mate, I thought, spitting out more pond filth.

"It called itself Lothar. It is surely some devil from the waters beneath the mountains."

"No," I assured him. "That was just a bit of a joke. A sort of poem, you know. I was happy to see the tavern and . . ." This no longer seemed plausible even to me, so I reverted to my previous tactic. "I'm a friend of that blond-haired chap. You know . . . tall guy, pale, blond." Since this brilliant description fit all four men I had glimpsed behind the door I added, "He's got a spear with a kind of torch thing . . . a light. And he killed a bear with it. You know. Whatsisname. Mr? . . . Sorbet? Sor . . . did? No. Sorrail. SORRAIL!"

There was a hesitant moment as the men exchanged glances. Clearly they recognized the name. That would keep my blood flowing internally for the moment. I grinned to myself, exultant, and then, unsure of what such a grin looked like through my new skin, scrapped it.

They watched me warily, then the young man leaned round the door. His glance was both cautious and menacing. "We'll see about that, goblin," he said, a remark which, if it hadn't been accompanied with that just-give-me-an-excuse-to-kill-you kind of hatred, would have struck me as riotously funny. He drew a long knife from his belt, put the flat of the blade against my throat (causing a little pattering of dried clay at my feet) and said, "Get Sorrail."

Someone inside moved away from the door. Then he caught hold of my arm and dragged me inside, never taking the pressure off the knife blade.

"He's here?" I exclaimed with relief as I stumbled into the barroom.

"Silence, demon-vermin," shouted the young man, pressing the knife a little harder. "You speak when you are spoken to and not before. Is that clear?"

I emitted a little trickle of bubbling filth from the corner of my mouth, along with a sound designed to show just how clear it was.

There were footsteps from the corridor outside, booted feet entering the room hastily. I tried to turn, but my captor demonstrated his dislike of this with the brilliant rhetorical strategy of pushing the blade against my windpipe till I coughed in nervous exasperation. The resulting spatter of brownish phlegm which caught him in the face might have ended my life right there and then if not for a familiar voice from my right.

"Yes, it's him," said Renthrette, bored and thoroughly disinterested. "A little dirtier than usual, but otherwise the same, I'm sure."

"Renthrette! Thank God!" I exclaimed, pausing to rub my throat as the blade was withdrawn and pointedly wiped clean. I grinned widely and extended my hands to her, and to Sorrail, who was loitering at the door. His chiseled features were grave.

"Spare me," she muttered, turning on her heel and striding back out. "And if you can tell where the slime finishes and you begin, get a bath."

Sorrail eyed me cautiously for a moment and then followed her out. The rest returned to their seats by the fire and watched me suspiciously, in complete silence. A rank steam had begun to rise from my skin and clothes, touched with the scent of stagnant water, decayed plant life, and whatever other unspeakable slurry had collected in that pit. Though I had seriously doubted I would ever want to be immersed in fluid again, the bath was beginning to sound like a very good idea.

∼✤∽

In fact, I didn't have a bath. I had five. The first time I stepped into the copper tub the water instantly turned an opaque and foul-smelling brown almost identical to the pond I had been lying in. I didn't even get to sit down. Tipping the sluggish water out of the window I saw that it was raining hard now. I clutched an old washcloth to my mud-caked loins and went downstairs. There I asked a startled maid to refill the tub and went to stand in the courtyard, letting the chill downpour beat the mud from my body. Some of it, at least.

A minute or two after the initial cold had worn off, it started to creep back over me and I decided to retreat to my hot bath. I removed a few strings of mossy pond weed, adjusted my makeshift loincloth for maximum coverage, and headed back inside, via the tavern's sitting room. The same collection of faces turned from the fire to look me over.

Grimy and bedraggled as I was, I had expected laughter at best or more hostility at worst. Instead, I got a stunned silence and then a series of pattering apologies as they each got to their feet.

"I'm sorry, sir," murmured the young man who had been so keen to examine my neck from the inside half an hour before. "You never can tell what might come in through that door, sir, we being so close to the mountains, and all. I seem to have made a terrible mistake. I'm so sorry. . . ."

"Forget it," I answered, echoing Renthrette from before while I tried to figure out what new strangeness this was.

"It was a terrible misjudgment of you, sir. . . ." he went on.

"Not at all. Really," I interrupted, trying to sound sincere and nonchalant at the same time—not easy when one is clad in nothing but a damp, strategically positioned washcloth. "Don't give it another thought."

He began again, his friends glum as whipped puppies in the background. Unable to bear any more of this bizarre exchange, I shook his hand and bolted for my bath, presenting my bare behind to them as I did so—though the realization of that last bit came after it was too late to do anything about it, so I just clambered back into my foaming kettle and considered drowning myself. Still, I thought, after a life like mine, why bother trying to salvage any personal dignity now? In this somewhat defeatist mood, I glanced hurriedly over all that had happened since that dinner in Stavis, thought better of it, and did my best to forget everything. Being warm and comfortable, if exhausted, for the first time in several days, I succeeded.

An hour or so later I woke, rolled out of the frigid water, dried myself absently, and tumbled into bed, where I remained till morning. I dreamed of Orgos and Mithos and then lay awake for at least an hour till sleep, mercifully, took me again.

❧

It was still raining when I woke, and the chamber was positively icy. I blew a long breath, watched it billow across the room, and decided to stay where I was. I removed the dressing on my wrist and was amazed to find the wound almost completely closed. Sorrail and his people might be annoying, but they seemed to know something about medicine. An hour later, just when I was dropping off again, the door burst open and Renthrette, unannounced, strode in. The air temperature seemed to drop. I moved the covers on one side of the bed, smiled suggestively, and gave the mattress an inviting pat.

"Get up," she said, "and spare me your suggestive remarks and all the usual garbage you spout. It should have become clear, even to one as insensitive, degenerate, and dull-witted as you that I will never—"

"I am not dull-witted."

"—*that I will never*," she continued pointedly, "be found in the same bed as you. I can barely stand being in the same room. The only way you would get me into bed with you is if I had been bound hand and foot. . . ."

"Renthrette," I said playfully, "I'd no idea . . ."

"No, scratch that," she said, "the only way is if I was already dead."

"There I draw the line," I said with mock indignation. "I have been accused of various fascinations in the past, but there is a limit. Rob the cradle, I might, but the grave? Never. And before you get indignant, *robbing the cradle* is a figure of speech. I have no interest in or sympathy for . . ."

"Do you ever tire of hearing yourself talk?"

"Not often. I am both a good listener and a lively raconteur. For someone as self-centered as me, the combination is quite magical."

"Just get up and save your witty banter for someone who doesn't get nauseated by the sound of your voice," she spat.

"Now you're getting it," I encouraged. "But next time . . ."

I stopped suddenly. Something was odd. She had been spirited since she came in—confrontational, admittedly, but spirited nonetheless. Moreover, at that last little jibe there had been a flicker of a smile. I had various ways of dealing with sadness and loss, ways which rarely allowed me to experience either for long. She did not.

"They're alive, aren't they," I said.

"Who?" she said, not bothering to conceal the twitch of her thin, pale lips.

"Mithos and Orgos. They're alive, damn them! After all the effort I've put into not grieving . . . Where are they?"

"Come downstairs," she said, turning for the door.

"They're here?!" I exclaimed, leaping out of bed, depressingly safe in the knowledge that she wouldn't turn to catch me naked.

"Of course not," she said. "But they are alive."

I grabbed my breeches and stepped hurriedly into them.

"How do you know?" I said, trying to keep my balance as I tottered about the room pulling up my pants.

"A spy was taken late last night from a company of goblins which has moved out of the mountains to raid the surrounding villages. If the creature is to be believed, Mithos and Orgos are alive, and being held in their mountain stronghold."

"So what are you so bloody happy about?" I said, fastening my belt and turning her to face me.

"Sorrail knows a way in," she said, unsuppressable excitement breaking through her veneer of calm dignity.

"What?"

"We can rescue them!"

"Did you see how many of them there were? Or the bears, or the . . ."

"It won't be a battle, idiot," she laughed. "It will be a small party breaking in unseen and getting them out."

"Wishful thinking, if you ask me," I snorted.

"Fortunately, I'm *not* asking you," she riposted. "A two-man party will do just fine. One man and one woman, that is."

"You and your friend Sorrail are going to get yourselves killed. And that," I said, "is a promise. A guarantee. If I had a farm, I'd bet it. This is the most harebrained exercise in self-annihilation I ever . . ."

"It's not Sorrail," she said. "He has to go on to the White City to report on the goblin movements, and the other men will be defending their own homes. It's you, Hawthorne. You're coming with me, so you'd better hope the odds improve. Good thing you don't have that farm, huh?"

I just stared at her with my mouth open. For once I could think of nothing to say.

SCENE VII

Hawthorne to the Rescue

Given that my general dislike for wild animals had recently taken an alarming new turn, and that creatures which had always seemed dodgy even in folktales had turned out to be real and meaner than reports had suggested; and given that the word of a goblin spy who assured us that our friends were alive was about as reliable as mine; and given that the mountains bristled with sinister troops and our mission was therefore destined for death (ours) and destruction (ditto); and given (finally, I promise) that Renthrette was a maniac only content when poised for slaughter, and that she valued my skin a good deal less than that of her horse, the fact that I had agreed to go with her on this sortie into the Abyss made absolutely no sense whatsoever.

Still, what the hell.

I am not, alas, without feeling, nor (and this was the real spear in the buttock) without principle. Not utterly. I had fallen victim to a rising sense of guilt which I had been beating into silence every step of the way from Stavis. Now, with Renthrette's careful prompting, it leaped to its feet and started roaring about talking to Empire guards, throwing stones at wolves, and generally laying the fate of our trusty comrades squarely at my door like an unwanted child. In short, she had me where she wanted me. As we trekked back into the reedy grasslands which I had fled through the day before, I couldn't help considering how wildly different this was from where I wanted her.

This playing on my sense of responsibility had been accompanied by that hint of a threat which her family relied so heavily on with varying degrees of subtlety. While his sister talked wistfully of how sad it would be if something unpleasant befell me, Garnet preferred the grab-him-by-the-throat-and-shout-about-cutting-his-liver-out approach. This difference in form belied the basic similarity between them, an endearing little detail of sibling character which made me glad I had never met their parents.

Of course, all threats aside, it was the thought of my friends that made me agree to this little excursion. We weren't exactly popular at the Refuge (I suggested they consider renaming the inn to something more suitable: the Hostile, perhaps, or the Surprisingly Unwelcoming) and Sorrail looked at me like he was wondering if I might be part goblin after all. I felt more comfortable with Renthrette, however distant she was currently being. But it was the thought of other friends—Orgos in particular—that made me steel myself for another encounter in the mountains.

And it wasn't like we were going to knock on the front door and then fight our way in. This was a stealth mission, one which—if it went right—wouldn't involve any fighting at all. I wasn't thrilled by the prospect of Heroic Deeds, but if they came disguised as sneaking about and going home quickly if anyone spotted us, I'd consider it. Factor in my sense of responsibility and genuine desire to be back with people I actually liked, and I was in.

So as the inn emptied of its clientele, all beetling off home to bar their doors and windows against rampaging goblins, and Sorrail galloped off to the White City carrying his lance and Renthrette's all-too-sincere good wishes, I got what little money I had together and tried to drum up a few basic weapons. The innkeeper wasn't thrilled with the idea of parting with anything that might help him against the demonic attackers which would soon come howling out of the night, but Sorrail had had a word with him, and a few extras had been found and set on the bar. Renthrette had got herself a hunting bow, a quiver of arrows, and a small shield to supplement her sword, but she was making do with a leather hood and corselet. What little metal armor there was in the area was being held onto, and our few silver pieces couldn't loosen the owners' grasps. I got a large round shield, about a yard across. It was oak, covered with reddish hide, and rimmed with copper. It was also heavy and old. With it came a one-handed axe: not a weapon I was used to, but my skill with a sword was so meager it made little difference. The one real find was, inevitably, a crossbow: a two-handed thing bigger than the Cherrati toy I had wielded in Stavis, though nothing like the massive Scorpions we had mounted on the wagon back in Shale. It was slow and difficult to load, but had a hefty punch which might save my neck if I could aim the thing straight. It would, more importantly, keep the enemy at a distance. Briefly.

I had, in a crazed moment, thought that a regular bow might be better, it being lighter and faster than the crossbow, but after an embarrassing experiment with Renthrette's bow in which I came close to blinding several of the innkeeper's family members, I decided to stick to what I knew. All these tales of marksmanship with a bow, splitting arrows at five hundred yards and such, are a lot of old horse manure. Renthrette could hang a plate on a barn and hit it at a hundred yards if she was composed and there was no wind. On a good day, I could hit the barn. The beauty of a crossbow is that, unlike with a regular bow, the stretching of the string, the aiming, and the firing are all quite separate actions. You bend over, brace the thing against the ground, and use your body weight to pull back and latch the cord. After that, casually and whenever the mood takes you, you slip an arrow in. Then, when you're well rested and at one with the universe, you point it at something, put a little pressure on the trigger with one finger, and there you are: the hero of the hour. With the kind of bow Renthrette used, all those actions were pretty much simultaneous. I could do each one by itself, but put them all together and I turn into some kind of random death machine. That anyone can hold one of those things steady when it's bent tight, let alone aim it, is a mystery to me. But I digress.

The inn also boasted a two-handed sword with a hilt almost a yard across. It hung on a wall over the fireplace. I lifted it down and hefted it thoughtfully. It was a weighty piece, and the blade was as long as a spear and broad as my hand. I couldn't see myself using anything so unwieldy, since I figured you'd need arms like tree trunks to brandish it effectively, but it had a kind of powerful menace and I wondered if a warrior who could carry such a terrifying weapon ever had to actually use it.

"How much for this?" I inquired of the landlord, idly.

"Not for sale or rent," he said, in a tone of finality. "That's an heirloom, that is. My great-grandfather bore it when Phasdreille was besieged by a vast goblin horde which crossed the river to sack the White City. He rode with a cavalry force raised here in the borderlands, and they met the goblin ranks as they lay outside the great city."

"Oh," I said, trying to head him off. "That's fine. . . ." But he had a glint in his eye, and he was going to finish the story whether I wanted to hear it or not.

"The horsemen caught the goblins unawares and routed them,"

said the landlord, "though many tall and fair soldiers fell in the battle. My great-grandfather survived, but he was killed shortly afterward. That was the last time he wielded this, his mighty sword. With it he struck down many dozens of goblins, cleaving a path through their ranks until he came upon their chieftain: a huge brute dressed in red and black, great ugly spikes on his helm and a weapon like a vast cleaver in his massive claws. My ancestor faced the beast and, after many blows were struck on both sides, felled him, cleaving his skull in twain. But the goblin was wearing an iron collar and the great sword was notched, as you can see. A diamond was taken from the dead goblin and set in the pommel, see? Like I said, it's not for sale."

Well, thanks for that, I thought. I wondered if he would go into as much detail about dishes that weren't on his menu. Ah yes, sir, tonight we don't have steak with grilled mushrooms and garlic sauce, which would be followed by sticky toffee pudding, if we had any, but we don't. . . .

I took what weapons we had, and there we were, wading through the elephantine grasses of the pockmarked valley that led through the marshes to the escarpment, the cinder path, and the mountains. It didn't seem to make a lot of sense to me, but Renthrette was in charge and claimed to know what she was doing.

"Rather than following the path up and through the mountains," she whispered, "we will cross the valley floor and then veer off to the right, heading east for half a mile. Then we climb toward an outcrop of rock which is overgrown with lichen so that it looks pale green from a distance. From its top, a few hundred yards to the east, we should be able to see a stone lion. This marks an old guardhouse and a forgotten corridor into the depths of the goblin fort."

All this was said in a hushed voice with a good deal of glancing about, as if we might be overheard by the enemy. Having seen something of the wildlife in this doubtful region, that was probably wise. I found it hard to be so collected. "And the goblins have never noticed this huge stone lion behind their house, I take it?"

"They have not been in the fort long, by all accounts, and do not know all its secrets. It is an ancient structure locally called the Falcon's Nest, built long ago to protect the pass from invaders, and the goblins have only expanded this way in the last few months."

"Oh, I see," I muttered. "I know when I move into a new place it always takes me the best part of a year to find the back door."

"Sorrail says the goblins have only been inhabiting the parts of the fortress that open onto the pass itself. They are a lazy and short-sighted race who can't see past an immediate profit or easy conquest."

"How convenient."

"Yes," she said, missing the irony.

"So if they are so lazy and shortsighted, how did they take the fortress from Sorrail's pals in the first place?"

"Treachery."

"Of course."

"Sorrail says that it's everything in their nature that makes them so terrible—their delight in causing pain and incapacity of thinking beyond their own swinish desires—that also makes them vulnerable. Where we are explorers and nurturers, dedicated to life and learning, they are destroyers, filled with hatred against even their own kind."

"Who is this 'we'?" I wondered aloud.

"You doubt our friendship with the fair folk?"

"The what?"

"That's how they are termed locally, the 'fair folk,' because they are tall and pale and golden-haired," she said, still forging ahead and refusing to meet my gaze.

"Termed by who? The goblins? I doubt it. By themselves, per-haps."

"Well, Sorrail says . . ."

"Can we drop Sorrail for a while?" I said. Her admiration for the blond lancer was becoming pointedly and irritatingly apparent. I marched on through the wet grass, avoiding the sucking, water-filled pits with a shudder of remembrance. My shield and axe were in my left hand and my right supported the crossbow, which was slung about my shoulders on a leather thong.

"It's a good thing Sorrail is so familiar with this country," said Renthrette suddenly. "He knows this mountain fort like the back of his hand."

"I had a feeling he might," I remarked, bitterly. "Too bad I didn't have chance to cut it off. We could have used a map."

It took us several hours to cross the reedy vale, then we veered east and began to skirt the foot of the mountain range. Before, the whole range had been visible and the Armored One had been scowling down at this, our foolhardy approach. Now, flush to the steep slopes them-selves, we could see nothing but the granite wall in front of us. The ground was rocky enough to prevent much vegetation, and a species of path had thus developed, tracing its way round the almost vertical sides of the peaks, which rose sharply out of the wetlands.

A cold wind had picked up since we left the inn and it tousled Renthrette's hair and made her eyes water. She proceeded without a word. I battled on behind her, trying not to think about what we were doing, where we were, how we were going to get back, the bloody miserable weather, and so forth. From time to time we would round a crag and a gust of wind would hit us hard and knock the breath from our bodies like some specter barreling down the mountains to ward us off. There were no birds, nor even any bird calls, but I couldn't decide if that was good or not. There was only the wind, which, just occasionally, seemed to whine up there in the ramparts of the mountain and through its hidden crevices, so that I wheeled and looked up and about me with momentary panic. Renthrette scowled at me and sighed to herself, as if wondering if it had been such a great idea to invite old Liability Hawthorne along for the ride. Ignoring this unhelpful attitude, I kept my eyes skinned for whatever hostile brute was likely to pop up and rip my legs off.

But the journey passed without event. Renthrette gestured suddenly and stood still, smiling. Above was a great rock face like a cliff, smooth as a sea-washed pebble and green as the shoots of spring saplings. The stone glowed with the emerald light that shafts through a wooded glade, and jutted out like it was the knee or elbow of the crouching mountain. Below that it came down, sheer and unblemished as a frozen waterfall on a winter morning. Getting up it was going to be an absolute bugger.

Renthrette, inspired, no doubt, by the memory of Sorrail, all-purpose warrior and romantic hero, was undaunted. While I slumped into the grass and pawed through my haversack for something edible, she paced the ground, gazing up at the lichen-covered rock face, stepping up onto boulders and testing hand and footholds. Then there would be a little shower of stones and she would jump down, muttering irritably.

"Are you just going to sit there, or what?" she said. "I don't know why I brought you."

"I did wonder," I answered, dragging myself to my feet and starting to pace around as she had been doing, as if this was going to help somehow.

"I looked there," she said, irritably. I moved east along the rock face and tried to look busy.

"Not that far, idiot," she said. "Try over there."

I did. "Over there" was a point directly beneath the great green outcrop. It was, so far as I could see, completely featureless. Still, far from wishing to upset the tyrant queen still further, I snuffled about like a lost dog and listened to her whispering to herself as she searched. And then, while my attention was almost completely on her, a remarkable thing happened. I took a step to the left, a spot I had passed over a dozen times, and the rock face changed. I repositioned myself very carefully and it happened again. When I was in just the right position, motionless, and the light was falling on the rock at a certain angle, stairs appeared recessed into the stone three feet from my face. For a second I stood dumbfounded, then I called to Renthrette, not daring to turn away in case I never found the place again.

They were camouflaged so well that it took her a couple of minutes to see them, and she muttered doubtfully the whole time. I suppose she thought I was pulling her chain. When she finally saw them she grew very still, an expression of mute wonder on her face. Because it was more than camouflage. It was an extraordinary piece of engineering and artistry. The stairs were cut to be invisible anywhere but in the precise spot I had been standing, and the rock about them seemed to just blur them away. Perhaps when the sun was higher or casting longer shadows, the edges of the recess would be more sharply defined, but the rock around it sheltered them so perfectly that the face seemed unbroken. I was still admiring this remarkable craftsmanship when a voice came from halfway up the face.

"Come on," Renthrette was hissing, with more enthusiasm than impatience. "What are you waiting for?"

My flicker of delight was doused, as ever, by her yearning for blood and glory, and I was left with that trembling, dreadful anticipation that came in its wake. In this case, the "wake" I had in mind had less to do with passing ships and more with farewell drinks round a coffin. Of course, were I to perish in this mountain stronghold, it seemed pretty unlikely that the goblins and their hungry mounts would host a wake where my corpse could be mourned by my loved ones. Not that I had any loved ones.

With such encouraging thoughts, I ascended the stairs, wondering all the while if the recess concealed me as effectively as it concealed the flight of steps. I had, till fairly recently, lived a pretty quiet life, much of it with my head down, an eye on the door, and an ear open for the approach of the authorities. But even in my days as an actor the notion of invisibility had always had its appeal, no more so than now. Imagine being able to take this ingenious little recess with me, to melt into the walls or trees around me whenever I felt like it! To just turn into scenery as soon as the audience got volatile! To be able to just slide away until the world forgot my existence: Wouldn't that be a kind of bliss?

At the head of the stairs we emerged onto a narrow granite shelf that ran onto the greenish outcrop, onto which we crossed. I stared fixedly ahead, trying to avoid considering the drop to our right, which was about fifty feet and quite sheer. Up close the greenness of the smooth swelling was patchy and pale, covered with a carpet of tiny pale lichen, and moss rich and vibrant. I squatted and ran my hand over their surfaces, the one rough and brittle, the other soft as deep velvet.

Renthrette put one booted foot on a rock splashed with a mustard-yellow lichen and looked about her. "There," she said simply, shielding her eyes from the sun.

And sure enough, only twenty-five yards from where we stood, the head of a stone lion peered out over a boulder as dark as charred timber. Its sightless eyes looked past us and across the wetlands stretched out beyond.

"The world's most useless sentinel," I said to myself, "I hope."

Renthrette was already stroking the beast's mane absently and peering into what I soon found to be a corridor, the mouth of which was overhung with the dead or dying branches of some twisted shrub. The tunnel cut into the cliff wall in a perfectly straight line, its floor level and paved, its ceiling vaulted, buttresses intricately carved out of the mountain's living rock. Impressive though this all was, the thing that really struck me was that ten feet inside, a shadow fell across the corridor and from that point on you couldn't see a damn thing. A chill, moist air condensed on my skin like sweat and I swallowed hard.

"You aren't thinking of going in there?" I breathed.

Renthrette just gave me one of her blank looks, drew her sword, and edged into the blackness, disappearing almost immediately. Invisibility no longer seemed like such an obvious plus.

"You will get used to the darkness," she said under her breath. "Just wait a little while before you go farther in."

"Good idea," I replied. "I'll give it a shot when I'm fifty."

"Quiet, Will," she answered, drifting off into her adventurer's world and advancing, sword poised to champion justice, defend virtue, and win honor, all by hacking bloody great holes in whatever came out of the blackness ahead: a scary way to live but, at least for Renthrette, one uncluttered by dilemma.

I fixed my attention on the shifting of her dark, blurred form and followed, swinging the crossbow round and wondering how the hell I was supposed to shoot enemies I couldn't see. This was a bad idea. I turned to the rectangle of blinding light through which we had come and considered just walking back that way, but then a hand grabbed me by the scruff of the neck and dragged me on.

It was Renthrette, which—in the circumstances—was probably for the best. Sensing the flagging of my barely existent resolve, she had pulled me around the corner where the light vanished. Relief that it was only her who had her claws in my shirt quickly turned into something unpleasantly like terror.

The darkness was complete, opaque. Every sound echoed like rolling thunder or empty wine casks. I stood stock still and lifted the heavy shield in front of me, figuring that it was only a matter of time before something that could see better than I could launched itself at me. I waited, braced for the impact. There was sweat running down my neck and my knuckles were white. Probably. In this light (joke!) I was as likely to see the rooftops of Stavis as I was the color of my knuckles.

"Will you stop that," hissed Renthrette, making me jump two feet in the air.

"What?"

"That gasping, breathy thing you're doing."

"Sorry," I said indignantly. "I don't like it here. And I do have to breathe, you know."

"Debatable," she muttered, walking away. Of course she started developing her withering banter when I was too petrified to think. I inched blindly after her, my right hand (no longer cradling the useless crossbow) stretched out in front of me.

Renthrette struck a shower of sparks from her flint and steel onto a tiny square of alcohol-soaked cotton: a standard and annoyingly useful part of her campaign equipment. With this she lit a tiny terracotta oil lamp that sat like a perching sparrow in her right hand. The walls around us flared up amber, every detail of their surface flickering tiny shadows as the lamp flame fluttered. Suddenly the tunnel was something quite different and, awful though it still was, it had a dark beauty. This was no natural cavern but a carved passage with a vaulted roof and rows of columns against the walls, rising like perfectly symmetrical stalagmites. So many months, maybe years, of work, now left to the darkness and damp and goblins! What a waste of bloody time.

And did I believe in goblins now? Tough not to, really. I'd seen them, and now I was poking around in their yard, as it were. Still: *goblins*, for crying out loud? Talk about difficult to swallow, especially for one as brutally realistic as me. And I suppose there, right there in the dark with the threat of these irrational monsters around the next corner, it finally dawned on me that we, or at least I, had been deliberately brought here. I remembered the ambassador's references to my sense of what was real and I knew that he was involved up to his neck, though where this got me I couldn't say. All I knew was that I was now living in terror of things which I hadn't believed in three days ago: no, things that *didn't exist* three days before, not in the world I knew, anyway.

I was exploring this seemingly important distinction when Renthrette hissed at me. I turned to find her standing on a great pile of rubble. Part of the ceiling had fallen in (not a terribly encouraging sign in itself), and the corridor was blocked right to the roof. It seemed we could go no farther. Ah, well.

"So," I said, "back to the pub?"

Renthrette, of course, had other ideas, and had already started clearing the rocks out of the way. She set her lamp down and gave me a wordless look. I helped, but slowly, far from sure I wanted to see what was on the other side.

Predictably enough, the blockage was minor and, after only a few minutes' work, we were able to clamber over the rubble. Renthrette went first, lamp and sword in hand. As soon as I heard her low, pleased whistle, I knew we were in trouble. On the other side of the rubble was a door, wooden with iron fittings. Judging by the webs across its hinges, it had been undisturbed for some time. Well, it was going to get disturbed now, I thought ruefully as Renthrette put her hand carefully on the latch and set her shoulder to the wood.

"Cover me," she whispered and, before I had chance to respond, she twisted the handle. With an agonizingly loud creaking and scraping, the door shuddered open and we found ourselves looking into a wall of barrels and crates, all dusty and apparently discarded. The timbers were broken and rotted, the metal bands rusted into nothing. Renthrette pushed a couple of the larger ones aside and we found ourselves in a corridor just like the one we had been in, apparently abandoned to low-priority storage. We paused, listening, then Renthrette stepped carefully past the barrels to where the passage ended in another door. This one was unlocked, and she dragged it open with little effort and almost no noise. For a moment she was absolutely still and silent, holding the lamp back within the doorway. Then she was gone and I was left darkling.

Fear and anger blended, leaving me in a blundering panic. I sprang through the door after her, collided with the hard stone edge of the jamb, and went sprawling on the floor of the corridor beyond. The noise seemed to have been deafening, but when I looked up, there was still only Renthrette, lamp held up so that its warm light made her faintly bored exasperation all too apparent. She motioned at me to get up, turned her back, and trotted silently off down the corridor on her toes. I limped after. God alone knew why she'd asked me to come here; I was obviously more than capable of maiming myself even if no goblins were around to do it for me. Moreover, taking me on a stealth assault was a bit like strapping a marching band to your ankle. We may as well have sent them formal notice of our visit a week ago. At least then they might have laid out a few drinks.

The corridor ended in another door, this one so small that even I had to stoop a little to get through it. It was dusty, but not disused, and it swung open easily and without a sound. This struck me as good, since not alerting the demonic hordes to our presence seemed crucial to our momentary survival, but Renthrette looked less happy. She touched the hinge and her finger came away oily. That meant that the enemy was at hand. I tried to ready myself mentally for meeting them. Fat chance.

The door admitted us to a triangular chamber, carved as before but lit by torches bracketed to each wall. Each wall also had a door like ours, so there were two others to pick from. Renthrette looked at me with something that might have been encouragement, blew out her lamp, and chose, either randomly or on some tip from Sorrail which she chose not to share with me, the door on the left.

Again, it opened quite easily, admitting us to another long, torch-lit corridor. It was narrower than before and the ceiling was lower, the effect being oppressively confining. The torches smoked and filled the air with the scent of burnt fat. I began to wonder what animal grease the goblins used, and then thought better of it. We were halfway along the corridor when we heard heavy footsteps approaching from round the next corner.

There was nowhere to hide, so I froze to the spot and did nothing. Renthrette flung herself against the wall farther up and waited. A second or two later a dark figure appeared, walking swiftly, a dull jingle that might have been armor accompanying each labored step. The goblin's silhouette filled the corridor, large and square, its head set on broad shoulders, its arms long and ape-like, its legs short and stocky, splayed to balance the weight of its barrel chest. As it stepped into the torchlight and its huge shadow flickered around the tunnel walls, I saw first its great shield, then the cleaver-like weapon in its immense fist, then its face. It was heavy-jawed, with teeth that seemed to protrude beyond its lips. Its nose and cheeks were broad and flat, and, glittering blackly in deep pits were small, malicious eyes which fell upon me and narrowed slightly.

The goblin, if such a name could apply to this hulking and savage creature, stopped and lowered its head. It began to say something in its own tongue, but the sound dried up quickly and a change came over its face and body. It became tense, and the blade of its cleaver, long and angular, moved forward and glinted in the torchlight. Then it grinned, or its face made something like a grin as it swung the vast shield in front of its chest. It advanced, its eyes on mine.

I suppose this had been the plan, for it gave Renthrette a fractional advantage as she launched herself at it, lunging with her sword as best she could in the confined space. Her adversary bellowed, forgot my existence, and slumped against the wall, blood rushing from its ribs. But however big and clumsy it looked, there was an astonishing agility in the way it wheeled its shield arm toward her second attack, fending off the sword point. In almost the same instant that Renthrette withdrew her blade, the goblin drew itself up and hacked at her. Its reach was astonishing—grotesque, even—and it was with a small cry of surprise that she responded, reaching up and catching the massive cleaver with her shield. The force of the blow seemed to drive her into the stone floor and her shield splintered, split quite in two. She crumpled to her knees and the creature loomed over her.

Enter Will the comrade-in-arms. I didn't know what else I could do, so I raised my axe and roared as maniacally as I could, running full tilt at the monster and hoping against hope that something would stop me from reaching it while it was still alive. The goblin eyes turned to meet mine again, and as its body twisted to face me, it raised its heavy blade to strike. I lifted my shield and slowed to a halt. Fear overpowered me and I felt the axe slipping from my grasp under the goblin gaze. It grunted and I thought drool dropped from its lips. It took a step toward me and its jaw fell open slightly, teeth showing tusk-like. I sagged still further.

Then, quite suddenly, Renthrette rolled from beneath her shattered shield and stabbed once, precise and hard. Once more, a change came over the goblin's face, its eyes losing their focus, its jaws becoming slack as blood trickled out. Its legs gave out and it fell forward with an echoing boom. I squatted and began to breathe quickly.

"Thanks, Will," said Renthrette.

"What?" I said, presuming sarcasm.

"I owe you one," she said, smiling sincerely. "I wouldn't have thought you . . . Well, thanks."

I nodded dumbly, trying to figure out why she couldn't smell the fear that was oozing out of every pore on my body. The axe had slid to the floor and was merely resting against the open palm of my hand, so I grasped it quickly, before she saw just how utterly useless I would have been if she had acted a moment later. And with that little dissemblance came words: "No problem," I said in a voice so calm and confidant that I felt like a ventroliquist's dummy. "You can count on me."

She touched my arm and said, "Come on. We shouldn't have far to go to get to the cells."

Her apparent confidence in me struck home and I followed her with something ludicrously akin to eagerness. I knew I was a coward, but she had thought I was a hero, and that somehow made me into one. I have said this before and I will say it again: Nothing astonishes so completely or so regularly as man's capacity for self-delusion. Mine, at any rate.

So the valiant adventurers proceeded. They found themselves, having rounded the corner, at a broad arch with caryatid gargoyles shaped like giant trolls, each supporting the roof on stone necks and hands, elbows turned outward and heads bowed under the weight. The chamber beyond was brightly lit with many torches, and from within came the sound of voices in some foreign tongue. My courage fluttered like a trapped butterfly.

"I thought there would be no guards?" I hissed.

"Sorrail said there wouldn't be," said Renthrette, peering cautiously around one of the columns. "But there are only two, and they're a lot smaller than the last one. The cell doors are right there."

She unslung her bow and nocked an arrow.

"This is pretty much always your solution to difficulties, isn't it?" I hissed again.

"What?"

"If in doubt, kill something."

"Do you have a better idea?"

"I'm just saying your approach isn't very, you know, *inventive*."

"You take the one standing," she answered. "I'll take the one sitting at the table."

"Take" was one of those little euphemistic expressions that she and her brother favored. It usually meant, as it did now, "kill." Feeling that things were moving far too quickly for my liking, I swung my crossbow round and fiddled frantically with the cocking mechanism.

When she stepped out into the room, she did so with quiet ease and confidence, her bow already raised and the string drawn back. I scuttered after her and dropped to one knee. The standing goblin was in my sights before it knew we were there. It turned at the swish of Renthrette's bow, but her arrow plunged into its comrade's chest as it struggled to its feet. It barely had time to cry out before I fired and the bolt silenced it forever. Renthrette was already grabbing the keys and running to the cell doors calling Mithos's name.

"Renthrette?" called a voice in answer. "Renthrette, listen, this is important!"

I was running over to join her, barely able to contain my delighted laughter, when there was a metallic sound behind me and I turned to find doors on either side of the arch we had come through, doors we hadn't even seen, opening virtually simultaneously. A great goblin clad in dark, waxed leather and brandishing a huge scimitar was coming in through one door. There were others behind him. A pair of smaller goblins, their skin ochre and their limbs thin, had already come through the other, and there were darker, bigger forms following.

Renthrette drew and fired again, and one of the smaller creatures fell, holding its stomach. I took the keys and fumbled desperately at the lock, but the first key I could fit in would not turn at all. I turned to find the large goblin already bearing down on Renthrette, who had dropped her bow and drawn her sword. I thrust my crossbow head to the ground, braced it against my stomach, and leaned all my weight on it until the slide clicked into position. By the time I had fitted a bolt and swung the weapon around, Renthrette was almost surrounded, and several blows had been struck. I picked the nearest goblin, fired hurriedly, and, as it fell, drew my axe. One of them was closing on me and there was no way I was going to be able to get Mithos and Orgos, who were shouting our names wildly, out to help. The doors behind the archway continued to breed goblin forms. Renthrette parried a goblin slash and looked wildly round. For a moment our eyes met, and for once the feeling was mutual: This was not going well. In fact, it didn't look like it would be going much further.

One of the goblins strayed close to me, leering through its narrow eyes. I cut at its legs with a savage sweep of my axe. The blow went wide and threw me off balance, and when I looked up, the goblin had edged cautiously closer, a slim spear aimed at my vitals. Renthrette was backing off, leaving her riven shield on the ground. One of the large black goblins had collapsed at her feet, bleeding, but another was advancing steadily, wielding a two-handed weapon that looked like an axe/sword hybrid, but bright and keen edged. She held her ground as the monster brought down its hacking strike. Her sword flashed up and parried, but as it did so, its blade shattered and fell in glittering shards.

"Run!" I shouted. "This way."

There was nothing else for it. There was one way out of the chamber, since the enemy had blocked the way we had come, and that was out toward the other side, to the pass where we had been attacked the previous day. Barely waiting for her, I fled down a corridor of doors and tunnels, not knowing where I was going but running as if every devil in Hell was on my tail. For all I knew, that was exactly what was happening.

A black-flighted arrow whistled over my head and clattered against the wall, and I heard Renthrette's bow gasp back its defiance. There was a cry of pain, harsh and loud as the bellow of a bull, but it was a token retaliation on our part. We knew we could not stand and fight. One of the doors ahead of me opened, and a goblin stepped out, curious about the commotion. I ran right into it and hacked at its neck once, barely breaking stride as it slipped to the ground, foaming blood.

Renthrette was immediately behind me now, but the pursuit had slowed. They were organizing themselves. If we were going to get out of here, we had to do something before they were on our heels again. I tried a door. It revealed a chamber full of shelves laden with pots, so I slammed it shut and moved on, trying the next: another storeroom. Then a third, and the sound of the door reverberated hollowly. It was dark inside, but I could hear the slosh and trickle of water: a great deal of water.

Renthrette grabbed a torch from the corridor, pushed me inside and pulled the door shut behind us. We stood on a rock platform in a huge square and high-ceilinged chamber cut out of the rock. The platform was only a few yards long. The rest of the room was filled with water.

"A cistern," said Renthrette, looking quickly about her. "There must be a spring or something that brings in the water. Maybe we could use it to get out."

"It's probably under the surface," I said. "Or it just seeps in through channels in the rock. Most of it is probably melted ice from the mountaintops."

"Then why doesn't it flood the whole fort?" Renthrette demanded.

"Good question. There must be some kind of overflow drain to stop the level from getting too high. Look around the edge."

She paced the platform with her torch outstretched, peering into the water to see how deep it was. I did the same but could see nothing under the surface.

"Quick!" I said. "They're coming!"

"There!" she said. "Over on the far wall."

There, barely visible in the torchlight, was a small rectangle of darkness: a channel cut into the stone right at the water's brim. My heart sank.

Renthrette jumped in without another thought. For a moment I thought she was standing on the bottom, but then she started to bob up and down as she treaded water, somehow managing to keep the head of the torch above the surface.

"Come on!" she hissed.

"I can't swim!" I whined, awash with self-contempt and horror.

"Yes you can!"

"No . . ." I began.

"You have to! Now get in! I'll help you get across. It's not far. Come on! They're coming!"

I sat on the shelf and lowered my feet and legs into the still, freezing water. "I can't!"

She reached over and tugged at my boots, pulling me in. I sank into the cold and silence, bobbing up a moment later, terrified and gasping for air. I began to go under again and she caught me, dragging me along as she began to swim.

"Hold the torch and kick!"

I tried, but my legs were too stricken with cold or the paralysis of fear to respond. All I could think about was the depth of water beneath me. Then the door into the cistern clicked and opened.

I pulled the torch underwater and it hissed briefly. Then all was dark and quiet, save at the door, where a pair of goblins stood framed in the flickering light of the corridor.

Renthrette's hand slipped over my mouth and her legs began to kick silently. I let the torch go and began to move my arms and legs to her rhythm, my heart thumping. The goblins came in and looked around, but the chamber was pitch black and even their night eyes would have difficulty seeing us if we kept still.

If. I flapped my arms like a wounded duck and prayed not to break the surface with my hands or otherwise make some telltale ripple that would leave us floating here shot full of black arrows.

It was only a few seconds, of course, but it seemed like an hour before the goblins stepped out into the corridor and closed the door. Renthrette uncovered my mouth and began to swim for where the hole had been. I got a mouthful of water, spat it out as if it was acid, and began flailing my way after her like some hyperactive puppy.

Fortunately her sense of direction was better than mine. She swam to the wall, pulling me after her, then began testing the stone with one hand till she found the space which marked the mouth of the drainage channel. It was a rectangular hole cut into the stone about five feet high, its floor no more than an inch below the waterline of the cistern. She swung herself up and in, then offered me her hand. Once in, I lay on its wet stone floor and breathed.

"There's no time to lose," said Renthrette. "They'll notice the missing torch and be back soon enough."

And so we set off, stooping, hands in front of our faces and still trying to run, though we were utterly sightless. I hit my head, painfully skinning my right temple, and the roof got steadily lower. After only a few yards we could go no farther upright.

"We'll have to crawl," Renthrette breathed.

We did so, and the passage descended gradually, just enough to keep the chill water around our hands and knees flowing. But soon the walls narrowed and the roof dropped still lower and I began having to squeeze myself through the tunnel. The water level had risen proportionally, and over half my body was now beneath its surface. I was freezing, but I desperately wanted to slip out of my jerkin and cloak, which were now taking up valuable inches of space. I tried to shrug myself out of my cloak, but there wasn't enough room. A horrible, fearful sense of paralysis came over me. I flexed my back against the dripping rock overhead as if I could somehow push through it, expanding the way. When I couldn't, and the passage seemed almost to contract against me, I felt the urge to scream building in my throat. My eyes closed tight and my fists clenched and, for a second, I thought I would go mad. Then the sound of Renthrette splashing and scrambling in front of me came to an abrupt halt and I got hold of myself, bracing for some new development.

"What?" I stuttered, desperately. "What's the matter?" My words boomed in the tight, dank passage.

"It gets narrower," she said. "I don't know if we can get through."

"If it's worse than this, I don't see how we can. But I can't turn round here. I don't think I can get back this way. I can't move."

Neither of us said anything for a long time. We stayed where we were, still in the darkness, and the icy water flowed around us.

"We'll have to go on," she said eventually.

And then she was gone. I crawled a little ahead and found that the ceiling of the tunnel stepped down abruptly. I knelt at this new gateway with growing fear. There was only an inch or two of space between the stone and the top of the water. And farther inside even that might be filled.

Renthrette had gone. She might have been drowning only a few feet away from me, but there was nothing I could do about it. I could try to inch my way back, but I was unsure that I could get all the way to the cistern without getting stuck. And even if I did, then what? What mercy could I expect at the hands of the goblins after our little assault? They would have found the way we got in and it would be guarded even if I could get that far unseen.

Loneliness, if that is not too tame a word for the crippling sense of isolation that struck me, won out. I could not stand to be left there by myself or to attempt to escape without Renthrette. I lay down in the water. Then, with infinite care, I rolled over onto my back. For a terrifying second I was completely immersed in the black water, then I thrust my neck and shoulders up on my elbows and lifted my face out into the ribbon of air between the water and the rock. I breathed, then inched backward, walking crab-like on my elbows, into the smaller tunnel. My face was pressed up against the stone and the water lapped around my cheeks and ran into my ears. I put my lips right against the granite, inhaled, then held my breath and continued my backward crawl.

I had been making my painstaking and nightmarish passage like this for several minutes when the water closed over my face altogether. I spluttered and pulled back, jerking involuntarily toward a sitting position and cracking my forehead hard against the rock. I retraced a few feet of my slithering steps, surfaced, and breathed, calming myself. Then I filled my lungs to capacity, rolled onto my face and clawed my way along the bottom of the channel. In so little water buoyancy was hardly a problem, and I was able to wriggle against the walls of the now tube-like tunnel, but the rock was closing in. The water above and around me was running faster, and, as I pulled myself along, nearing the end of my air, I hit my shoulder hard against a stony outcrop.

I gasped, swallowing water and losing what little air remained. My stomach contracted and my knees snapped hard against the rock beneath me, then the outcrop ground into my waist and I stuck fast. The gorge in my throat rose and I fought against it, stretching out as much as I could, flattening myself to the floor of what had turned into a pipe less than two feet in diameter and full of rushing water.

I remained lodged there and panic overcame me. I began to thrash as much as I could, but the sides of the pipe were quite smooth and I could get no purchase to drag myself through. I lunged forward with the little strength I had left and a strong, slender hand took mine, tightened and pulled. Sinews in my shoulder cracked and a flash of pain went through my arm, but then I was sliding forward and out. The water and darkness fell away and I found myself retching into the weedy pools of a waterfall on the western side of the mountain.

Renthrette watched me with her usual detached curiosity, as if she was looking at something in a museum case, while I continued to vomit water onto the grass: not a technique renowned for impressing women, but that was, for once, far from my mind. She didn't speak, but she looked stern. Our survival, harrowing though it had been, had not taken away from her awareness that our mission had not been a raging success. I sat up, coughing. The swollen stream into which the waterfall flowed wound through the wetlands we had crossed that morning, and squinting in the noon light I thought I could just make out the smoke from the Last Refuge Inn. I suppose I was grateful to be alive, but I had been so close to *not* being that all I felt was my customary petulant anger.

"There are only a couple of them, she says," I wheezed bitterly. "Sorrail knows this place like the back of his hand, she says. Has he ever looked at the back of his hand? It's probably crawling with goblins."

"Shut up, Will," said Renthrette. "Well, at least we know Mithos and Orgos are alive."

"If our little visit doesn't change that," I replied grimly.

All peril and near-death experiences aside, I was puzzled. I still didn't understand how we had got in, why the side door wasn't better protected. Maybe the goblins had only been there a little while, but . . .

"Mithos was trying to tell us something," Renthrette added, pensively. "I wonder what it was."

"We may never know," I answered. "I hope it wasn't important."

❦

Eventor

Renthrette prowled the inn, brooding, muttering curses and shooting me black looks. We had to go back, she said. We hadn't tried hard enough. We could still get them out. I let her rant and pace for a while and then told her she was talking nonsense, that we were lucky to be alive, and that going back was like taking a swan dive off the Cliffs of Doom or whatever they called that damned mountain that was full of teeth, scimitars, and other nasty, spiky things I wasn't about to get stuck through my throat. Amazingly enough, she actually listened, and eventually nodded in silence.

That evening, over a melancholy dinner of meat and potatoes utterly devoid of flavor, we came to the obvious conclusion. We couldn't get Mithos and Orgos out alone, presuming they hadn't already been killed in reprisal for our botched "rescue," and the locals were too concerned with protecting their own property to consider helping. We needed to go somewhere where we could mount a less suicidal rescue attempt with real soldiers instead of relying on incompetents like yours truly. The idea that the locals were "concerned" with protecting their farms and houses was an understatement. There was a frenetic mood approaching paranoia in the tavern's sitting room that night, the men sitting armed and talking about how best to defend their houses and barns against the "hand of evil" which was expected to extend from the mountains. They feared, they said, for their wives and children, it having been confidently reported that the goblins had a taste for human flesh, raw or broiled. Moreover, the goblins, foul and twisted though they were themselves, prized human females as their concubines, and their brutal lust was legendary.

"My Alsary would die before she submitted to their loathsome hands," said one, a large man, pale and blond as the rest but with a weathered look about him. This met with general agreement. "And if she could not, she would find a way later. She would not foster their brood or bring forth any creatures of tainted blood."

"Tainted blood?" I repeated. Even given the subject matter, I thought the phrase a bit rich.

"I mean that she would stifle at birth any monstrous bastard fathered by such as they," said the man, his blue eyes hard on mine. "A child with goblin blood, however little, is a goblin through and through and must be destroyed as such."

I frowned and he responded instantly, leaning forward with an odd, disarming light in his eyes. "Do you not yet know what they are? Can't you see it when you look upon their horrid blasphemy of the human form? They are born with a malice and cruelty so intense that it shows through in their very features, their twisted faces and foul hides. That is their nature as a species! They breathe the stench of death and corruption. They yearn to cause misery, to practice acts of obscenity and torture, to ruin the living and defile the dead. Nothing pleases them like the tearing down of all that is fair and beautiful, the ravaging of virtue, the perverting or violating of all which is true and bright. They bring terror, and in their path they leave destruction of a savagery you cannot conceive."

There wasn't much you could say to that. A grim silence had descended on the room during this dreadful litany and all I could do was nod respectfully as their pale faces clouded over and they each turned to their own thoughts. It was some time before anyone spoke again, and in the end it was me who tried to break the awkward silence. I wanted to ask about interesting local cuisine, their attitudes to plays and music, but I couldn't think of a segue.

"So the goblins have always been on your borders like this?" I began.

"Far from it," said an elderly man with a growth of silver-gold beard. "They used to cross the river rarely, and they have been in the mountain fastnesses only a few months."

"But they have always been in this land with you?" I asked.

"God, no!" said another. "They first appeared only four or five generations ago. A wandering, vagabond race of cutthroats, they are. They steal and murder for their living, moving from place to place, sacking what they find and settling only when all is laid waste. Then they move on. Five or six score years they have been here, loitering away yonder on the far side of the river, inching into the mountains when we could not defend them adequately, mainly in the winter. But lately their numbers have grown, and they have massed an army bent on conquering our lands and cities."

"The forests fell to them first," said the older man, to whom the others seemed to defer. "A hundred years ago it is said they were fair and golden, full of deer and birdsong. Back then the forest west of the river was called Lucendale, the bright place, and the portion on the east bank, twenty miles south of here, was Eventor. Since then, the goblins have taken the forest west of the river and it has changed. They call it Sarak-Nul; it is a darksome place of blasted trees and stinking swamp into which few, save the enemy, will travel. On this side, Eventor remains ours, but goblins have been seen in its glades and clearings and the mark of their corruption is feared to be spreading, souring the air and rotting the earth. Their grasp on the mountain passes grows steadily stronger, and our Warders can no longer keep them at bay. The Falcon's Nest, the ancient bastion and lookout, whose strength and beauty you can affirm, fell but recently as our warriors gathered in the White City. We have been sleeping and it has cost us dear. You have looked upon the wonders of the Falcon's Nest, but many of us have not. Our ancestors carved its magnificence out of the very mountain, sweating and bleeding over their hammers and chisels. We will no longer lie silently while goblin filth soils the labor, the memory, nay, the very lives of our forefathers with their presence. Dark times are ahead and the struggle which you have seen begin will be long and bloody. It has been long in the making and will not end until they have destroyed us completely, or till we have vanquished them."

Well, so much for music and theater. There didn't seem to be much to say about their local cuisine either, since these people seemed to have no concept of the word "gourmet." Never before had I tasted beef so cunningly disguised as tree bark. I know: tough to imagine, but the chef at the Refuge clearly had special gifts. Renthrette swore it was wholesome and nutritious, but since she rarely ate anything other than raw vegetables and rice, her opinion did little to sway me. I poked at the gray meat and wondered what day they had begun boiling it. The fact that no one remarked on this study in the culinarily bland and stodgy did not bode well.

The beer wasn't much better, either. It looked like a kind of lager, but paler, with almost no alcohol content and absolutely no flavor.

When I first sipped the fizzy, yellowish stuff, I presumed there was something wrong with the barrel and took it back to the bar. The landlord helpfully gave me another glass of the same gutless liquid and followed it up with a blank look when I asked to sample something else. The Refuge served only one kind of "beer" and this watered-down donkey urine was it.

Taking into account what we'd probably be eating and drinking if we stayed at the Refuge made it easier to consent to Renthrette's desire to leave. We couldn't save Mithos and Orgos alone, and there was nothing to do here, so she wanted to go on to the White City in pursuit of her beloved Sorrail. I hadn't actually ascertained that he *was* her beloved Sorrail, but it aided my put-upon mood to think so, and I wasn't about to bring the subject up with the ice queen herself. What did not initially occur to me was that the journey to said city took us through, or at least close to, the forests which had been so ominously depicted for us earlier in the evening. Renthrette pointed out that we wouldn't be crossing the river and would thus be close to "the good bit." This snippet of arrestingly vivid description referred to Eventor, the woodland which was, by all accounts, a little less rancid than its counterpart on the western bank. This was supposed, in so far as she gave a damn one way or the other, to make me feel better.

❧

The first day of the journey passed without event. Our meager supply of silver had managed to wring us a pair of horses for the trip and some oh-so-inspiring bowls of something resembling gruel. (I hoped we were received favorably in the White City, because we didn't have another penny to our names.) The horses, old and listless beasts with heavy feet and long, thick manes the color of new wool, had probably been used for pulling plows, and they seemed as likely to canter as they were to fly. The villagers wanted them back and the fee we had paid was a deposit we could ill afford to lose.

A series of rills and streams—including, I expect, the overflow from the Falcon's Nest cistern—came down from the mountain and congregated randomly over the two miles north of the Refuge Inn. Thereafter our route followed the eastern bank of a slow river. This was the Snowborne, a southbound frigid curl of clear, shallow water only twenty or thirty feet across for much of its length but swelling, we were told, to several times that as it passed the White City. It was reedy and its surface was broken by rocks and stones, but there was never any chance of us losing it altogether, and it was as good a guide as we could have wished for.

That was presuming, of course, that we wanted to go at all. I was pretty ambivalent about the whole thing, but I sure as hell wasn't going to sit around in the village of the damned while Renthrette rode off looking for her knight in shining armor and his heroic pals. I wanted to get some distance between me and that nightmare fort, at least until I could do something constructive to get my friends out of it. I did still feel responsible for them, to be honest, but I couldn't wish myself into being something I wasn't. If I could I would have been Will the Heroic and Invincible long ago. Well, probably.

Incidentally, I had not given up on finding some other road, one that got us away from these lands of legend and myth and back to more predictable problems and petty miseries, but when I had asked the residents in the Refuge about Stavis and Cresdon, the mountains of Thrusia and the Diamond Empire, I just got blank stares. One of the barmaids pointed out that someone had once had a cow called Cresdel. That was very helpful.

So what was I supposed to do? Take off by myself and go wandering through this land of goblins and talking bears? Good scheme. So I sat astride my ponderous mount and kept my eyes on the riverbank just in case something grotesque came striding over to tear my head off. It was, after all, only a matter of time.

Renthrette, by contrast, was quite jaunty. For her. She seemed to have gotten over our catastrophe in the mountains and the imminence of the denizens of Hell now that we were "taking the right course." She rode on, talking idly about reforging her sword blade and how much she missed riding Tarsha. To these observations I made wary agreement, which seemed all that was required of me. We didn't speak of the others—any of them, the ones we lost in Stavis or those we had left under goblin guard—as if even breathing their names would be bad luck.

Then we saw the forest. It appeared along the western bank of the Snowborne and it was all the villagers had said it was and more, a dank and sinister-looking wall of trees. Sarak-Nul, they had called it. An ugly name for an ugly place, though "ugly" doesn't begin to describe it. The trees along the riverbank—those that were still standing, that is—were pale and gray, stripped of their leaves by more than winter. Their branches clawed the sky, and, at their feet, piles of dead lumber blackened and sprouted flesh-like fungus in great tubes and swellings clearly visible even from this side of the black water. The wood was swampy, silent, and vast, its dead, waterlogged foulness stretching farther than the eye could see. The horses snorted and tossed their heads uncomfortably, and a chill ran down my back, making me look sharply away. Renthrette stared at it fixedly, as if getting to know the enemy or staging her defiance. I just thanked God that we were forty feet of water away from it and did my best to ignore it.

I was less than completely successful at this because the woodland had a way of making you feel like you were being watched. I realize that sounds clichéd, but that's how it felt. There is, after all, usually a degree of truth at the bottom of every cliché, only the familiarity of the words making the thought sound insincere. So, trust me, I'm being sincere. The trees had, I was convinced, eyes. If they didn't, there were things among them that did, and the eyes were trained on us like a thousand crossbows. Could a place be evil? I had never thought so, but this soul-sapping forest was doing a pretty good impression.

An hour after the forest first appeared, we came upon a collection of buildings too small to call a village. None of them advertised itself as an inn or tavern, so we didn't even dismount. We slowed, however, to discuss whether it was worth checking our route with one of the locals. As we did so, we became aware of doors and window shutters stirring fractionally. More eyes. Then the doors were closed carefully and bolts were thrown into place. Shadows passed across upper windows and vanished. The hamlet became quite still and we, it was apparent, were not welcome.

"Such warm people," I remarked to Renthrette loudly. "Hard to believe the place isn't awash with tourists! I mean, considering their openness and their exotic cuisine, amiable wildlife, and picturesque scenery"—this last bellowed with a broad gesture toward the fetid forest over the river—"it just takes my breath away that we aren't fighting for road space. Well," I concluded, in a bitter roar at the shuttered windows, "I'll spread the word, have no fear! I'll say, 'If ever you're passing a cramped and run-down shanty on the edge of a dead forest, a lousy collection of ruinous hovels populated by a bunch of inbred, misanthropic gits,' I'll say, 'do yourself a favor and keep passing.'"

"Quiet, Will," sighed Renthrette predictably. "Let's go."

"Oh, I'm not sure I can tear myself away from this. . . ."

"Shut up, Will."

❧

That was the last haven of civilization (if you could call it that) that we saw for ten days. Thereafter it was just us, the river, and the forest, and a right hoot that was.

We slept alternately during the deepest hours of the night, taking a couple of hours each to watch by the fire. It was cold, but there was no wind, and we had brought extra blankets from the inn. Strange birds called from the river at night, great booming rolls that didn't sound like birds at all; Renthrette said they were bitterns and that I should go back to sleep and stop being so pathetically infantile. There were other noises that she said were birds, too, lunatic cries that came out of the darkness when you least expected it, chuckling and whooping insanely to themselves, then stopping abruptly. The sooner we got to this White City place, the better I'd feel.

Then the forest crossed the river. I don't mean that the trees of Sarak-Nul uprooted themselves and splashed their way across, though I was beginning to think anything was possible in this land of goblins and their conversational pets. I mean that the forest spread onto our side as we had been told it would. This was Eventor, the wood which was supposedly still largely untainted by the black hand from the western bank. Still, it was a forest and, given recent associations, I was more than happy to give it a wide berth, and said so.

"No," said Renthrette in that apprentice-party-leader way she sometimes had. "We have to stick to the riverbank, and the forest is big. To go round it would take us twenty, thirty miles out of our way."

"To go through it could cost us a good deal more than time," I pointed out.

"Eventor is not Sarak-Nul. We've been told . . ."

"We were told the goblins wouldn't be living in the southern chambers of the Falcon's Nest," I reminded her.

"This is different," she said, coming close to me and speaking straight into my face. "The sooner we reach the White City, the sooner we can come back with a force to help us get Mithos and Orgos out. We can't take the chance of another two or three days on the road."

"And if we don't get through?"

"We don't get through," she said, shrugging. "But at least we tried."

And there it was, Renthrette's good old lust for glory and honor, that never-say-die spirit that led her to endure, no, *to seek out*, against-all-odds situations where she could put her neck on the line for a righteous cause. Unfortunately, there always seemed to be other necks involved, the owners of which (take me, for example) were less convinced of the value of principled martyrdom. Not that this ever mattered to her.

"Then let's start moving," I said, knowing better than to keep backing a three-legged horse. Her eyes held mine and a flicker of doubt rippled across them. Then she smiled, pleased—impressed, even. And then she walked away, a little spring in her step as I, knowing that my resignation had somehow been misread as resolve akin to her own, felt unaccountably guilty for not clarifying matters. But she didn't smile at me that often these days, and when she did, it usually meant she was thinking about something else and I had just happened to be there, so I let it go.

Four days after passing through the Hostile Hamlet, we stepped into the forest of Eventor. I wished Orgos was with us, for his smile and his singing voice as much as for his sword. But Eventor wasn't all bad. The night had been colder than before and the wind had picked up so that even I was glad of the shelter the trees gave us. The grass in the open had been frosty this morning, but the forest was dry and felt warm by comparison. While many of the trees were hardwoods and therefore bare, there were enough conifers of various shapes and sizes to keep the forest green and touched with life in defiance of the winter. The horses snorted and steamed softly with what I took to be pleasure or a sense of relief. Overhead in the canopied air, songbirds fluttered about, twittering to themselves. No maniacal starlings, hawks, or lunatic cries—just birds, small and pretty and generally barely worth noticing. I, with my new appreciation for wildlife that didn't approach with vast, slavering jaws, noticed.

That evening we rested in a glade where copper beeches stood, still clinging to their oddly metallic leaves. The horses had browsed happily, and we had made a fire (or Renthrette had), cooked (likewise), and eaten (I helped). We were now sitting quietly as the last light dwindled and the stars, just visible glinting through the sparser branches above, came out cold and clear.

I told a story. She didn't ask for one, and the last time I had told one she had come as close as ever before to slitting my throat, but we had been getting on better of late, so I gave it a shot. I chose something that would appeal to her, all knights and monsters, chivalry, and tests of loyalty and truth. She sat silently and watched the fire as I spoke—listening, I think, though she may have been thinking of other things. When I finished, she didn't move for a while, then she wished me good night and got ready for bed. I hadn't leaped to the front of her list of personal heroes, but seemed at least back in favor. For reasons I was not exactly sure of, this pleased me.

Renthrette had wrapped herself tight in a blanket and curled up like a kitten by the fire. Her hair fell across her sleeping face and, touched as it was by the flame-light, flickered like molten brass and copper running together in the finest streams imaginable. A little overly lyrical, perhaps, but not an altogether inappropriate image, since she had a good deal of fire about her even when just walking around in broad daylight. She could stand in a drenching rain and still light a fire with her glance. I felt it constantly, and while it could be appealing in a hopelessly unattainable way, the version I got was usually the red-hot-plowshare-on-the-bum kind of heat.

I was ruminating on this, and considering the heat that might break out of her if I could somehow convince her that I was her long lost handsome prince and not the septic rat-tail she had taken me for, when I heard the distinctive sound of whistling. It was a musical whistle, a snatch of an old Thrusian melody delivered with expert and easy confidence. I wheeled, pulled up my crossbow, and stared into the darkness of the wood, locating the sound at the same moment that I saw the man stepping unhurriedly toward me. I raised my weapon and he came on unabashed. Then the firelight picked him out.

"Orgos!" I exclaimed. "What the? . . ."

"Sorry to surprise you, Will," said the black man, smiling broadly so that his teeth shone. And there he was, large as life, tall and strong as ever, clad in his black armor with russet tunic and trousers beneath, his two long cutting swords strapped across his back so that their hilts stood proud on his shoulders like horns. He was the original sight for sore eyes.

"How the hell did you get out?" I began, approaching him quickly and slapping my hand into his. "God, it's good to see you!"

"You, too, old friend," he replied, laughing.

"How's Mithos?" I spluttered, swallowing back something almost like the proverbial lump in the throat. Probably a remnant of dinner.

"Almost completely recovered," he beamed, slipping a casual arm about my shoulders with that familiar ease of his. Relief and the courage which had always emanated from him blended and coursed through me.

"I can't believe it!" I exclaimed, hugging him again. "I thought . . ."

"What?"

I laughed and shrugged it off.

"So what are you doing here and how did you escape?" I demanded again, smiling wide.

"Sorrail sent a cavalry unit to get us out and I immediately came looking for you. Fortunately you aren't too tough to track, and I knew where you entered the forest and when. It was just a matter of time before I found you."

"What's the hurry?" I said, observing the concern in his face.

"We have to get out of here. Not just the wood, the whole country, the region itself. We have to get back on the road and head south for as long as it takes, and we must leave this place to its own troubles."

"But the goblins . . ."

"There are dark forces at work here, Will: things we cannot comprehend and are too feeble to influence. Our first encounter with the goblins should have told us that much. There is *power* here, the kind of power we might call magic, and those who live here wield it. We don't. We are just people, and our blades are insufficient. We must leave while we still can."

I sat down by the fire to think, glancing over to where Renthrette lay motionless.

"Let her sleep," said Orgos, as if reading my thoughts. "She needs the rest. We have a long journey home ahead of us."

He was quite right, of course, and I was, I confess, relieved to hear him say it. The idea of leaving had been in the back of my mind since we arrived, but it didn't appear to have occurred to anyone else. I kept it quiet because from me such a remark would mean cowardly flight, while from the others it was tactical withdrawal.

And I, who have spent my life fleeing, was suddenly unsure. Orgos wanted us to run for our lives because we were less powerful than our enemies? Since when? I thought for a moment, and something struck me.

"When we left Stavis," I said, my eyes fixed on the dying fire, "you were virtually unarmed. Your equipment was back in the Hide. You had one of your swords. Now you have both of them again."

I looked at him quickly and his expression was blank. "I *don't* have them," he said, apparently confused. "This is all I have, the blade I had when you saw me last."

And sure enough, there was no sign of the second sword he had been wearing at his back.

"You did have them," I said, getting to my feet, my body feeling like it had been plunged into icy water. "I saw them. Only a moment ago you had them."

"No," he said, his expression as before, "you are mistaken. I have only this."

"Where did you get it?" I spluttered, nodding at the sword.

"What?"

"Where did you get it? Tell me about the first man you killed with it."

"I don't remember."

He was quite calm, but his face had changed. A grayness had come into his eyes and his features had grown hard and implacable.

"I do," I shouted. "I remember but you don't? Does that strike you as terribly likely, swordsman?"

I turned hurriedly and kicked at Renthrette. There was a pause, and then his voice—or a voice like his but quite changed now—came low and cold as a mountain ice storm.

"You cannot wake her," it said.

I spun and found that Orgos had risen silently and now loomed over me, all semblance of my friend running from him like melting wax. The grayness I had seen in the eyes was spreading cloud-like throughout his features, and with it came an odor, increasingly foul and pungent, but dry as old bones. It was decay.

"You are not Orgos," I announced, somewhat redundantly in the circumstances, hoping that this would dispel whatever it was that was materializing.

"I am what is left of him," the creature rasped. The cloud dissipated and the blasted corpse was revealed, desiccated and crumbling. The lip-less jaws parted, but the sound that came out was more an emanation of the whole body than it was a voice:

"Fly, William, or perish utterly. Fly, or cower in despair. Fly, or have your body rent by pain, your mind by terror, and your heart by misery. Fly, or learn to wish for death and grieve unceasing that it never comes."

The specter's sightless eyes held me fast and, as its lower jaw fell away completely, its fleshless arms rose and bony fingers closed hard about my shoulders, pinning me to the spot. A new coldness, like the moist chill of grave earth, seeped into my body. I screamed, a long wail of horror, right into the skeletal face which closed on mine like some deathly suitor. One of its fingers splintered. Then another. Part of the face collapsed into the hollow skull, and the forearms snapped abruptly. The ribcage caved in, and in less than a few seconds, the entire corpse had crumpled in a shower of dust. It fell in a pile at my feet, dwindling still, fragmenting, disintegrating, reducing to powder.

And still I screamed.

SCENE IX

The White City

An hour had passed, an hour in which I talked a skeptical Renthrette through the details of my ghastly encounter bit by bit, over and over, as I worked to convince her that this wasn't some bizarre prank. As the incident faded I expected to rediscover my sanity and find some ingenious way to dismiss it, but I didn't. The visitation had happened and it had been a conscious force, not the product of some hallucinatory mushroom accidentally included in dinner: a dubious claim which was impossible to substantiate, of course, but one I was sure of nonetheless.

Renthrette was equally certain that this was a none-too-clever ruse on my part to justify fleeing for Stavis as the apparition had instructed. I told her that even if I did want to leave this bloody place—which, obviously, I did—we still had no idea how we would actually do that, so conjuring this spectral advisor just to change her mind made no sense. Go back to Stavis? Fine. How exactly? Which direction was it in? Did I have to summon a storm and a black carriage like the one which had brought us here in the first place, and, if so, how precisely was I supposed to do that? She grudgingly backed off, which was just as well, because I was on the verge of telling her that the thing which had come walking up to me in the forest had claimed to be what was left of Orgos, which would mean that he was already dead. If that was true . . . Well, there seemed little point in confronting that possibility right now.

And there was one bit of evidence on my side. The bones hadn't all collapsed into dust, and those fragments that remained—including part of the skull—looked to me more goblin than human.

"So what does it mean?" I asked, staring into the fire. I couldn't quite shake the feeling of a deep cold in my bones.

"Mean?" said Renthrette distractedly. "It doesn't mean anything. Not everything *means* something, you know."

"Yes, it does," I insisted. This was the one thing I had learned from my years in the Thrusian theater. Everything *means* something, even if you can't control what that meaning is. If you ever doubt that little unimportant-seeming things mean something, try farting on stage during a tragic death scene. Trust me on this. "This means something."

"Then, what?"

"I'm not sure, but I'll make a guess," I said, fiddling with a stick which had caught fire at one end. "Some goblin force, a spirit or something, crossed over from the other forest, from Sarak-Nul, I mean, and came looking for us. It was very specific in its choice of identity and there has to be a reason for that. It animated a goblin corpse, perhaps, and used my thoughts to *clothe* it, as it were, as a person I knew. I had been thinking of Orgos earlier—missing him, I guess—and it somehow seined my mental picture of him and fashioned its form accordingly. Something like that. It chose a person I respect, a person whose company I missed, and presented him as he exists in my head, which is why it got the swords wrong. When that mistake was revealed, the spell (or whatever it was) fell apart for some reason, as if the controlling force couldn't sustain the illusion once I became suspicious. The question is, why go to all that trouble?"

"Maybe it was just some wandering ghost—" began Renthrette.

I cut her off, swallowing back the now ludicrous urge to say that I did not believe in ghosts. "No," I said. "It had a purpose. It was trying to get rid of us by saying that we were in danger, out of our element, guaranteed to fail. . . ."

"Whatever it was, it read you like a book," Renthrette remarked, a sly little smile crinkling the edge of her mouth.

"Thanks," I said. "But my point is that it was willfully *misreading* the Orgos in my head. He never would have said all that stuff about running away. That suggests real purpose. It wanted us gone enough to violate the disguise in a very risky fashion. There is more to this than meets the eye. If we are so impotent, why did it want us out of the way? If we are so obviously doomed, why go to the trouble of trying to get rid of us? Maybe we actually aren't completely out of our element. Maybe we can do something aside from getting ourselves killed. . . . Tough to believe, but there it is."

⁂

We continued our trek across the forest for the rest of the day. Renthrette led, sedate and watchful. I followed, glancing behind me from time to time in case that rustle of wind in the trees was actually the corpse of an old mate coming to share some thoughts on what we should do next.

The air was moist and cool, and wisps of mist still trailed along the forest floor and over the still, dark surface of the river. Then a rocky escarpment rose up on the bank and we had to turn from the water and into the forest to get round it. It was about thirty feet high, irregular, and creviced in ridges and craggy, tuber-like growths. A few withered bushes and weeds struggled out of the thin soil in its cracks, and boulders dropped from God knew where were scattered among the undergrowth. And in one horseshoe hollow was a cave. Its mouth was tight, only a few feet across, and inside was a dark tunnel that burrowed back toward the river.

Renthrette brought her horse to a standstill and I looked from her to the cave and back. "You must be joking," I muttered.

"Quiet, Will."

"Can we just get on and leave this adventurer stuff for the people with nothing better to do? Remember the last cave we spent the night in? Or our little jaunt through the cistern at the Falcon's Nest? Two words: *talking bears*. And goblins. No, four words: *talking bears and goblins*. Riding them. OK, six words. . . ."

She had already dismounted and was approaching the cave mouth cautiously, bent over to peer in. I stayed in my saddle.

"Don't expect me to come," I began. "Don't expect me to help pull you out when a great set of grinding incisors grips you round the waist and . . ."

But I had already dismounted, had even begun to follow, so this show of defiance had become futile even by my standards. She paused at the dark entrance, adjusted her grip on the axe I had given her, stooped further, and was gone. I hesitated, looked down at the crossbow in my hands, cocked it, and fitted a bolt into the slide. Then I bent over and stepped inside.

The cave was shallow and only the very back was completely dark. There was ash and charred sticks on the ground and, as I turned them over with the toe of my boot, I saw what looked like chicken bones.

"Here," said Renthrette, from my left. She was holding a satchel made of coarse, olive-colored fabric. She upended it and a series of small packages spilled out onto the floor. I was stooping to pick one up when I caught a sharp aroma, momentarily unpleasant, then wonderfully familiar.

"Cheese!" I exclaimed. "Thank God. Look at this, Renthrette. Cheese. Good cheese at that. Real cheese that tastes of cheese, not that petrified rubber they gave us in the pub the other night. There's a strong, crumbly white; a smoked; and, what's this? Oh God . . . a blue. Oh yes. Taste this, it's superb!"

She gave me a superior look and I scrambled to my feet.

"Nothing else?" she said.

"Nothing else?! Taste this!"

"Is that all there is?" she demanded with slow patience.

"Eh . . . no. There are a couple of small knives, a metal pot, a spoon, a cloth of dried herbs, and half a bulb of garlic. Oh, and a small onion. Great!" I enthused.

"Great," she echoed halfheartedly, striding back out into the forest. I followed, nibbling contentedly on a sliver of the smoked. "Probably a hunter's camp," she remarked uninterested.

"I left the pot," I said, guiltily. "I only took the cheese and the garlic. Come on, don't be so damned moral. My need is greater than whoever can get hold of this stuff."

"Whatever, Will," she remarked with a slightly sour expression. "But keep that stuff downwind of me and don't come breathing on me after you've eaten it."

Fat chance, I thought. If it was only a matter of giving up garlic and onions, I'd have been living on celery for months now. Well, probably.

I was just pondering the wholly academic question of which of my appetites would have won out if I had been given the option when Renthrette's horse turned sideways abruptly and pattered to a halt.

"What? . . ." I began, but she waved me into silence with a sudden gesture.

She turned and hissed, "Get off the path!"

She led the way, pushing her mount into the trees off to the right. I followed, looking wildly around but seeing nothing. Then, as I slid from the back of my horse, landing awkwardly on my left ankle, I heard voices coming from up ahead. I couldn't hear words, and the sound fluctuated as it carried on the breeze, but the language raised the hair on my neck. It was caustic and abrasive, dark and spiked like the head of a mace: goblins.

My horse flinched and I patted it desperately, pushing it farther into a thicket of tangled leaves and branches. Renthrette had already tethered hers and was on her way back, axe in hand in a way reminiscent of her brother Garnet, her eyes cautious and resolute like an animal's. She slipped furtively past me and crouched behind the gnarled and heavy trunk of an oak. I bit my lip hard till the blood ran in my mouth, and pressed my horse further into cover.

There were four of them, dark and squat, armed with knives and long spears. Two of them wore half-helms, the others had hoods of leather. They were talking among themselves and laughing: nasal, rasping laughs which creased their eyes to nothing and set their heavy jaws lolling. Their skin was a grayish-yellow and thick, almost scaly, snake-like. Their limbs were short and powerful. I swallowed the blood in my mouth and froze, squatted in the dirt beside Renthrette, one hand on my crossbow, the other braced against the tree trunk. Renthrette looked at me and her face, though blank, seemed somehow to ask what I thought we should do. They would pass within fifteen feet of us in less than ten seconds. I held my breath.

Then one of the horses snorted. The goblins reacted immediately, their conversation evaporating in an instant as they went stock still, eyes and ears scanning the woodland. One of them paused and then began to inch along the path toward us, head down and spear horizontal. Renthrette tensed like a cat poised to spring. I glanced down at my weapon and stretched my index finger to the trigger. The first goblin's yellow-green eyes met mine and his mouth fell open in a cry of warning.

I tried to aim, but Renthrette leaped in front of me.

She bounded out onto the path from the other side of the tree, the axe held behind her, ready to strike. He barely saw her before her blow connected. He screamed and fell forward. I jumped to my feet and leveled the crossbow at the next, whose eyes were on Renthrette. He wheeled his spear toward me too late and the bolt hit him between shoulder and neck.

Two more. Renthrette cut at one with her axe and it bit into the goblin's spear, breaking it cleanly. He gripped the top half of the shaft with its metal tip like a shortsword and swung it at her. Simultaneously, the last closed on her and she took a step back. The crossbow was too slow to load and I dropped it, pulling a knife from my belt. It felt small and inadequate, but I had to do something.

Those creatures, I thought, must not touch her.

One of them was glancing warily around for other attackers.

I nodded pointedly, my eyes staring across the path and into the trees. The goblin closest to me, a thin, gray-skinned creature brandishing a scimitar, caught the glance but did nothing. I felt my bluff had been called. I glanced from the goblin back into the forest behind him and shouted—quite convincingly given how unoriginal the idea was— "Now!"

The goblin spun in the direction I was staring, raising his blade, and I launched myself at him, knife extended.

The leap was poor and I fell short, managing only to gash his leg as I fell. He shrieked with surprise nonetheless and collided awkwardly with the other one who, thinking he was under attack, stabbed blindly with the remains of his spear. The point caught his fellow just above the waist, bringing him to his knees as Renthrette flung herself at the other. They fell together, each clawing for the handle of the axe which had been torn free in the fall. The gray one, sensing I was upon him, turned and looked up. The blade of my knife was already sweeping toward him and his eyes met mine as it stabbed home through his vest. Almost simultaneously, Renthrette seized the axe, raised it and brought it down hard. There was a sickening splitting sound like a bursting melon, then silence.

I sat on the ground breathing hard.

"That was a terrible idea," said Renthrette after she got her breath back, "that let's-pretend-there-are-more-of-us thing. I couldn't believe you actually tried that."

"It worked, didn't it?" I reposted.

"Barely," she answered. "It's a good thing the goblins weren't exactly crack troops."

I gave her a sardonic look. I still hadn't got to her level of casualness when it came to carnage, and the idea that someone had, however briefly, really wanted to kill me, always left me a little disoriented.

"Never mind. With a bit of luck we'll get ambushed by some real pros later in the day," I remarked.

"They must have been a patrol, but they were pretty damn casual given the fact that they were in enemy territory," she mused, ignoring me. She picked up one of the dead goblin's spears and looked it over critically. "Odd," she said.

"What?"

"See this little crosspiece just below the head? That's to stop it going in too deep. It's a hunting spear. Which means they're either just using whatever weapons they can steal regardless of their purpose—always possible for the likes of them, I suppose. . . ."

"Or?"

"Or they weren't a military patrol at all."

"Hold it," I said, getting to my feet. "You're saying they were here hunting for food?"

"There probably isn't much that lives on their side of the river. Here there are probably deer, wild boar maybe. It's probably their cheese that you have in your pockets."

"So you don't think they were looking for us?"

"I wouldn't have thought so, no."

"Well, that's good," I said. "I suppose. Still, we had to attack. After all, goblins are goblins, right?"

"Of course," Renthrette answered, but she didn't look at me, and seemed strangely preoccupied.

We both fell silent and got on with readying our horses. We didn't make eye contact at all for a while, though I can't say what was going on in Renthrette's mind. I'm not really sure what I was thinking, but there was something, a feeling of anticlimax or uncertainty. I think we both sensed it in each other but chose to keep quiet, holding the feeling at arm's length as if we were warding off an unpredictable dog.

❧

The forest ended quite suddenly two days later, and Phasdreille—the White City—was visible as soon as we stepped out of the trees. It was still a few miles off but it lay on lower ground and was spread out before us, gleaming pale and beautiful in the afternoon sun. We halted and looked at it, silent and hardly breathing. From here it looked sculpted out of alabaster, walled and towered like the citadel in a fairy tale. I had seen walled cities before but they always seemed so purposeful and strong. This place looked effortlessly unassailable, as imposing as Cresdon or Ironwall, but with a grace, an unearthly dignity that sparkled on its white stone and flashed off the glass in its windows like sunlight on a waterfall. It looked like a city such as might exist above the clouds, ruled by a benign monarch whose daughters sent their suitors on quests for dragons and treasure . . . an impossible place.

"Now if we can't get a decent piece of beef and some strong ale there," I remarked, "there's a problem."

But my flippancy was strained and felt curiously inappropriate. Renthrette just stared off toward the white towers as if lost in a dream, or perhaps in a memory of childhood, when such places seemed plausible.

"It's breathtaking," she whispered. "Perfect."

And, as my cynicism failed to kick in, I nodded.

❧

We were there before sundown and the light had yellowed, turning the city to gold, which warmed and deepened as we reached a long, ornamented bridge. This spanned a wide moat filled by the Snowborne and it was broad and fair, supported on smooth arches with carved capitals and lined with marble balustrades. At its head was a gatehouse, with a pair of turrets filled with tall warriors with long, pale hair that rippled with their cloaks in the breeze.

"Who comes from Eventor?" called one of them.

"Renthrette and William from Stavis," called my companion, who always rose to occasions like this, "friends to the fair folk and to Sorrail. We seek aid and bring news from the mountains."

A door opened and three or four of them emerged.

"You have been looked for," said one. "Sorrail has been here many days and is expecting you. Welcome to Phasdreille, the White City. Enter, before it grows dark, and seek him out in the house of the king. We will send word."

The gates were framed with iron, burnished to a high shine, and paneled with a pale wood inlaid with brass, though whether this was decorative or defensive, I could not say. They opened easily, despite their great weight, and we walked our horses into the barbican and onto the twilit bridge without another word. Ahead of us, a rider cantered off across the bridge toward the gatehouse of the city, and we followed, gazing down to the river and up to the great, pale walls in an awed silence. At the far side we passed through another pair of imposing doors and entered the town.

Even with the onset of evening, the streets seemed bright and mythically fair, the city holding an air of serenity, as unlike the squalid bustle

I had been used to in Cresdon as could be imagined. There was no one else about, but the city felt cleansed rather than deserted. All was quiet and peaceful, as if the very walls were watching paternally over residents who were sleeping or gathered around their hearths with their families, watching as they had for centuries.

Sorrail met us at the entrance to the king's palace. He was handsome and smiling, pleased to see us, but he stood atop the little flight of marble steps with formal reserve. With him was an entourage of some sort, men and women dressed in vivid silks and adorned with bracelets and necklaces in which shone precious stones. They hovered at his back, their eyes upon us.

"You are most welcome to Phasdreille, home of the fair folk," said Sorrail in a rolling, modulated voice that was addressed to those at his back as well as to those in front of him. "And to the court of King Halmir, son of Velmir, you are welcome, too. Enter and feast with us. Let us find you new raiment fitting to this place, and then you can tell us your news. For as the diamond should be cut, polished, and set in gold to show off its quality, so should the doers of virtue be clad in wealth and beauty so that their worth shines forth."

At this slightly odd remark, there was a smattering of applause from those clustered around him. Their smiles flexed and deepened.

"Er . . . thanks," I said. "I could use a change and a bite to eat."

There was a momentary pause, a series of fractional glances between them, and then more simpering smiles. If I didn't know they were glad to see us, I'd say we were being condescended to. Sorrail bowed carefully at the waist, nonchalantly adding a little flourish of the hand that invited us in: very polished. He was barely recognizable as the ranger who had met us on the road.

Just as we were ascending the stairs, a distant trumpet call echoed through the air. Everyone paused and it was answered by another, closer this time.

"It seems," said Sorrail, "that our horsemen have returned, and in triumph."

His tone was low, amused rather than exuberant, as if he'd just heard that a friend had won a few coins at dice. The ripple through the entourage matched his own contented swagger. I shot Renthrette a bewildered glance. Her eyes were narrowed, confused, even surprised, but further speculation was abandoned as the drumming of horse hooves swelled to a deafening pitch. The courtyard before the palace filled with fifty or sixty blond riders, caped with white, fluttering cloaks and armed with silver-tipped lances. As another smattering of polite applause broke out from the assembly of the steps, I saw one of the riders who was not uniformed as the others. His helm was full and great horns grew menacingly from each side. He bore a heavy axe, a round, crimson shield, and sat astride a great white charger. His face was pale, almost white, and his hair, when he removed the great and terrifying helm, was short and brownish. He glanced toward us and his eyes shone green as emeralds.

"Garnet!" I exclaimed. Renthrette was already running toward her brother, who swung himself to earth easily, smiling. There they embraced as the unit's captain ascended the stairs and bowed to Sorrail. I left them to their reports and hurried after Renthrette.

"Hell's teeth," I exclaimed, laughing aloud. "I never thought I'd be this pleased to see you!"

"Likewise," he grinned over his sister's shoulder. He extended his strong, thin hand and I clasped it briefly.

"I had heard you were around," he said, "but we've had no news since you set out to rescue Orgos and Mithos."

"How long have you been here?" asked Renthrette.

"Almost as long as you have, I think. I laid low in the Hide for a couple of days and then took a horse and whatever I could carry and came after you. When I got to the Black Horse I found you had already gone on ahead, but some ambassador chap said he could lead me to you if I served as his escort for a few miles. I'm not sure what happened next. I think I fell asleep in the saddle or something, I don't know. It doesn't really make any sense, but when I woke I was in sight of this place and there was no sign of the ambassador. I've been here ever since and, after Sorrail brought news of the rest of the party, I've been riding with the armies of Phasdreille against goblin encampments this side of the river."

"Any sign of Lisha?" Renthrette asked.

"None," said Garnet. "I don't really know where we are, let alone where she might be. Until Sorrail arrived, I thought I was by myself. Still," he added with a smile at the horsemen around him, "there are worse places to be. I mean, I missed you all and everything, but this place . . . It's just so, I don't know, *right*. It's like I should have been born here, or something. God, Renthrette, you are going to love it here. You'll never want to leave."

⁓✻⁓

This last remark troubled me. Don't get me wrong: You couldn't fault the city. It gleamed with nobility and courage and light and truth and, well, *fairness* in every sense. In other words, it made concrete all that Garnet and Renthrette lived for. Here they were no longer the principled few struggling against a dark, self-interested, and vicious world. Here they were part of the majority and could be vicious on its behalf. Nor, I had to admit, could I really fault Sorrail. He was everything he had first seemed to be, and if Renthrette looked at him as the best thing since cold steel, I could hardly blame her. I had been a little confused by his odd, courtly greeting to us earlier and by the perfectly decked out little band that had been hanging on his exquisitely tailored coattails, but I suppose that was just the way things worked here. No, nothing had really shaken my faith in the place or its people but Garnet's rapturous enthusiasm for them.

You see, Garnet is about the worst judge of pretty much anything that I have ever come across. He couldn't tell a pint of stout from a cream sherry, and if he ever swore that someone was a great fellow, said fellow would probably slip something lethal in your pint (or sherry) before the night was out. This isn't just sour grapes on my part. Garnet and I have not always seen eye to eye, I confess, but he can be very useful to have around. If you need someone hacked to pieces, he's your man. Tell him that the friendly stranger across the room made a lewd remark about his sister, hand him an axe, then sit back and watch the fun. But analyze something and come to a shrewd conclusion? When camels write poetry.

Garnet is a terrible reader. I don't mean he couldn't pick up a menu and spot the salad; in fact, like his sister, he could wade through the most complex legal documents and figure out their details with alarming rigor and clearheadedness. What he couldn't do was read *between* the lines. Just like Renthrette, who had told me that the apparition in the forest hadn't *meant* anything, Garnet took things at face value. Neither of them looked too closely or asked too many questions, since that took valuable time away from getting their weapons bloody. They would leave this place and its rosy hue uncriticized because it offered such a neat solution to all their ethical problems. Here goodness was built in the stone of the city and the flesh of its people; across the river was evil. Their mission was clear.

Too clear for a charlatan, actor, dramatist, cheat, and liar like me to swallow without at least looking more closely at the label.

But what really burned me up was that they seemed to be right.

⁓❦⁓

The royal palace came alive before dawn. Unfortunately, since we were due to meet the king today, that meant that the banging on the door at half past five in the bloody morning was supposed to be taken seriously. The journey had taken its toll and I had slept like a particularly exhausted log right until Garnet started bludgeoning my door down.

I crawled over, threw the bolt, and admitted him with a sour grunt. He was dressed in burnished armor that, even in this miserably low light, sparkled like a box of mirrors. He wore a tunic of immaculate white linen and a matching cloak. He was cradling his great horned helm in his arm and beaming like he'd just found a bag of gold in an alley. Or at least, that's what would make me beam like an idiot. I couldn't imagine, especially with my brain still fogged with sleep, what could make him so happy short of meeting the goblin king (if there was one) in single combat.

"Ready?" he chirped.

"Hardly," I muttered, rubbing the sleep from my eyes and clambering irritably into a pair of trousers. "Do we have to meet him so bloody early? Couldn't we, like, have lunch together or something?"

"No."

"Dinner, then?"

"No," said Garnet, still cheery and indulgent with that schoolboy exuberance that occasionally takes the place of his homicidal nobility. "That's not the way of things here. But you'll see. This is going to be one of the most fantastic days in your life, Will. Just wait till you see the court: the clothes, the sophistication. I could listen to them talk for hours."

"Who?"

"The courtiers," he laughed, like he was assuring a four-year-old about how good a piece of chocolate was going to taste. "You'll be in your element."

"Right," I agreed hollowly, suspecting the chocolate was really spinach.

"Come on, Will. Are you going to put a shirt on?"

"Oh!" I exclaimed, parodying his childlike excitement. "That would be a wheeze."

I dressed, irritably.

"You're wearing *that*?" said Garnet, with a sour look.

"Evidently," I said, checking to be sure. "Why?"

"Don't you have anything . . . you know, *classier*?"

"I thought we were adventurers," I said. "These are adventurers' clothes. Shirt and britches. Leather belt. Some bits of ring mail here and there to denote manly purpose. I thought you'd approve."

"Weren't you wearing them yesterday?"

"I was indeed," I agreed. "We adventurers are hardy folk. But the britches are fairly clean and the shirt is not actually unpleasant. Yet. Maybe when the day heats up a little . . ."

"Can't you wash them?" said Garnet, like someone's grandmother.

"Not now, and I didn't have time last night. If I'd known you cared so much I wouldn't have bothered sleeping at all, then I could have spent the night running something up in pink satin and lace."

"Well, at least wash yourself. Here."

He tossed me a piece of soap shaped like a seashell. I sniffed at it suspiciously. It smelled of rose petals, only stronger and powerfully sweet.

"It's wonderful," Garnet said. "All produced locally, I hear. There's quite a lot of soap around. They are a very clean people. They bathe daily. It's a sign of spiritual purity. But it's not just about being clean; it's also about elegance. Look how intricately that has been molded," he said, nodding at the shell-shaped soap, "and smell the fragrance!"

"Yes," I scowled. "Very nice. And the next time I want to go round stinking like an expensive whore I'll put it straight to use."

"Just get a move on," he snapped. "And brush your hair."

And so we left, him in front, striding off and making pleasant little bows every time someone passed, me straggling after him, doing up buttons and cursing quietly to myself.

We entered a large room, flagged with black and white marble like a chessboard and arranged with padded chairs and benches. There were torches and lanterns everywhere and it was like daylight inside, except for the wreath of smoke that hung about the ceiling. It was packed with men and women in silks and satins and jewels, many seated or reclining elegantly on pieces of furniture that looked like chairs with pretensions

to couch-hood. Others were poised artistically against columns or leaning with studied nonchalance on mantelpieces. And all were engaged in
hushed conversation. Occasionally there would be a ripple of laughter
or a soft pattering of polite applause from restrained, gloved hands.
Somewhere a wistfully plucked harp was accompanying a woman
singing in a high, lilting tone about a lovelorn shepherdess.

"What the hell is this?" I breathed to Garnet.

"It's a waiting room."

"What are all these people doing?"

"Waiting," he said, as if this was self-evident.

"For?"

"A summons from his lordship the king."

"And us?" I pressed, losing patience.

"We wait, too."

"Hold it," I whispered, venomously. "Are you telling me that you
dragged me out of bed before cockcrow so that I could stand around
with this bunch of overdressed cretins for an hour?"

"More," he said.

"What?"

"More than an hour. Probably several. But being here is half the
fun."

I gave him an oblique look. Was this a perverse brand of humor I
had never glimpsed in my generally surly companion?

"I mean it," he said, guilelessly. "Just watch and listen."

Too exasperated to do anything else, I did.

Seated on one of the extended chairs close by were two ladies
lounging elegantly in cream-colored lace and taffeta. They dripped with
pearls and other forms of conspicuous opulence. One wore a necklace
of the largest diamonds I had ever seen. Another pair of ladies sat beside them on velvet cushioned chairs. All four were turned to a pair of
gentlemen who held court in their midst. Both were tall, lithe, and
blond, one in a doublet of sea-green velvet trimmed with golden cord
and matching hose, the other, an older gentleman, in royal-blue and
silver silk. Both were immaculately groomed and wore trim beards that
tapered to waxed points.

"My lord Gaspar," said the one in green with a wry smile, "affects,
I fear, a disposition toward my lady Johanna that he feels not. For as
flames give off smoke, so love breathes forth the sighs of passion for
all to see. It seems that though my worthy friend bewails his love for

fashion's sake, there is no passion like to mine for my lady Beatrice. I fear his mistress's disdain has finally quenched his fire and smothered his smoke."

The ladies smiled among themselves and waited for the elder to reply. He did, with the smallest step forward and the most casual positioning of one hand upon his hip. "My Lord Castileo," Gaspar intoned, smiling, "embers and smoldering leaves produce a smoke most bitter and unwholesome to the senses, yet the heat from whence it rises is but a poor and mean thing at which one might not even warm one's hands. The heart of a furnace burns pure and hot, consuming all and leaving little there to smoke withal. So my love for Johanna, like the core of the forge, blazes with white, undying passion, while yours for Beatrice, I fear, so cool and, doused with overlong laments, smokes merely."

"And yet," retorted Castileo, "are my words from the heart, not crafted in forges or furnaces where men beat out their labors with the sweat of their brows. My words, like my love, are natural and proceed thoughtless from my consumed heart."

This met with another burst of applause. I turned, befuddled, to Garnet only to have my confusion increase. He was spellbound, hanging on every word with an awestruck expression on his face.

"What the bloody hell was all that about?" I breathed. Garnet didn't respond, so I tried another tack. "This is what they do all day?"

"Yes. Isn't it wonderful? Hush now," he whispered, his eyes not straying from the peacocks in front of us. "Gaspar is going to respond."

"The anticipation is crushing me," I muttered, walking away in search of something more closely resembling entertainment.

There wasn't any. I circled the room twice and, save for a little dice rolling here and there, that witty little study in who loves who more seemed the rule rather than the exception. A shepherdess in silk and rubies worth about a thousand acres of grazing land bewailed her lost love ("Alack the day, my Corin's gone away"), and a curious species of high jump contest flared up for a while. But spoken words were the order of the day: elegant, polished, and memorized. They pretended they were making them up as they went, but I know a rehearsed performance when I see one, and I was looking at about twenty. But, there being bugger-all else to do, we sat there for about four hours and listened to what the fair folk did when they weren't slaying goblins.

Renthrette had arrived midway through this study in futility, and her appearance took my breath away. This was not simply because she was beautiful, in a flame-colored satin gown and an extravagant diamond necklace, gold in her hair and crystal studs set into her bodice—though I suppose she was—but because I barely recognized her. She looked like one of them, blending in so well that it depressed me a little.

"Sorrail sent it," she said simply, glancing with a kind of delighted uncertainty at her dress. "To help me fit in."

"Quite," I said, fitting in less and less by the minute. "Look," I said, opting for something direct and virile to offset all this court culture, "shouldn't we be doing something useful, like organizing a rescue of Orgos and Mithos or something?"

"Patience, Will," said Garnet, a remark so out of character that I was still gaping at him when the liveried lackey who had just arrived started whispering to him.

"They're ready," said Garnet, eyes wide with delight. "The king will see us now."

"Already?" I said. "I mean, I could listen to this I-love-you-more-than-he-does stuff all day."

"Be quiet, Will," said Garnet. And suddenly his eyes flashed with that dangerous impatience that I knew so well. It was, strangely enough, sort of a relief to see it. At least some things don't change.

SCENE X

The King

The lackey, a small, obsequious man in a carefully tailored suit with brass buttons and little epaulettes, led us through a series of corridors and double doors, several of which opened onto smaller versions of the room we had just left. In each, diamond-encrusted courtiers sat around swapping witty banter, reciting lousy sonnets, and singing to each other about their disdainful mistresses. Fortunately, we were moving quickly, so I only caught the odd word, but I'd already heard enough of this verbal poncing about to last me a lifetime, and each half-heard quip, each shrewdly worded jest, each ripple of polite amusement stuck me like the blade of a stiletto.

"Don't these people have anything better to do?" I murmured after one particularly sophisticated remark about how kissing a beautiful lady was a rung on the ladder to the divine.

"The question," said the lackey who led us, tossing the remark over his shoulder in a manner one of his masters would have been proud of, "is whether anyone could do it better than them."

This was obviously supposed to close the matter. I thought otherwise.

"But if what they're doing is worthless, who cares whether they are any good at it or not? It's like being the national champion of balancing a spoon on the end of your nose. I mean, so what?"

Our little procession stuttered to a halt and the lackey turned on me with an offended look that flushed his cheeks.

"These are the elite," he said stiffly, "and their accomplishments do not merely accompany their station, they demonstrate it and show why *they* are courtiers and others aren't. A tradesman can buy clothes and friends, but these people are different, superior. No tradesman could enter here without being shamed. These people just know how to behave, how to dress, and how to converse in *civilized* society. It is in their blood, and that is why they have the ear of the king and the tradesman does not."

With a curl of the lip which neatly coincided with the word "tradesman," the lackey turned on his heel and marched off. Garnet and Renthrette shot me the obligatory looks of hostility, amazed I could have missed something this obvious, and stalked after him. Someone in the corner began to sing about how beauty and virtue were really the same thing. I, the tradesman who didn't belong, hurried after the others.

We had to be announced before being admitted to the king's chambers. This, for reasons unknown, took a good ten minutes. During that time we stood at the door and tried to look reverential, something which seemed to be an effort only for me. The somber siblings, despite having spent their adult lives fighting the hand of authority, were clearly very impressed with all this ritual and glamorized hierarchy. I suspect that if the Diamond Emperor himself condescended to invite them and their rebel brethren to tea, all organized resistance would collapse overnight while they basked in the glow of his magnificence and that paradoxical "human" quality which apparently justified any semblance of tyranny. *"Such and such a lord butchered my father to get his land, but he personally sent a basket of fruit to the funeral. What a decent chap—you know, always has a smile for the locals. Sure, he lives in a castle and eats gold, but if you meet him he's so genuine, so ordinary. What's it to us if he wants to turn our village into one big sheep farm and send us into whoredom and beggary? I mean, I'm sure he knows best. After all, he is a lord."*

Anyway, the announcements started echoing down the halls and through the palace's sumptuous chambers. "Garnet and the Thrusian wanderers," they called us.

"We sound like a pub act," I remarked, with bitter amusement. And all at once I could see the three of us playing for a crowd in Cresdon's Eagle Tavern: Renthrette with a lute, Garnet with a bloody big drum, and me with a pair of bent spoons, dodging insults and rotten fruit. But before I could share this little vignette with my companions, we were hustled down yet another corridor, through three more antechambers and, with a silvery fanfare, into the presence of King Halmir, son of Velmir, lord of Phasdreille.

He was seated in an alabaster throne padded with purple velvet at the end of a long chamber with high windows along the walls. A narrow carpet of the same rich purple led up to it, and on each side stood guards and courtiers, their eyes turned toward us. The king himself was pale and blond, perhaps forty, his hair breaking around his shoulders in luxuriant ringlets, but these were details I noticed later. My first impression of him was one of spectacle. He was dressed from head to foot in cloth-of-gold, and the early afternoon sun splashing down in great diagonal shafts through the windowpanes picked him out and made him shimmer astonishingly, like a man seated amidst flames. We faltered, our eyes on him, and Garnet gasped audibly.

"Approach his majesty the king," said the lackey, a smug smile sprawling across his plump face as he took in our response.

There was a fluttering of fans from the female courtiers as the king inclined his head fractionally: a tiny nod which sent the light in the room dancing, as if a thousand burnished mirrors had been flashed toward the sun.

We began to edge forward, onto the carpet and down it, Garnet leading, then Renthrette, then me, all half-blinded by his brilliance. He did not move, but a ripple passed through the crowd as we approached and a number of men gathered at the foot of the throne: councilors and private secretaries, no doubt. Some were clad as the rest in bright, expensive fabrics and jewels, others wore the somber black of the archetypal civil servant. I noted that Gaspar, the middle-aged courtier I had seen earlier trading metaphors as proof of his love, was in the latter group. He was changed out of his finery now and looked positively funereal. Sorrail was among the courtiers. His eyes fell on Renthrette in her borrowed finery, and he smiled, pleased.

I had tried to wash my clothing for the event, but still looked like something dragged in by the proverbial cat: dragged, I might add, through hedges and waterlogged ditches, and then partly eaten. This had not gone unnoticed. While Renthrette got glances of quiet, polite admiration from the men and equally quiet, polite malice from the women, and Garnet got an inverted version of the same thing, the whole assembly found common ground once they'd looked me over: I was a scumbag. My shirt was yellowed with age and sweat, my breeches were stained disturbingly, worn at the seat, torn at the knee, and shredded altogether at the hem. It had been a tough journey, all right? If my comrades hadn't been so lovingly supplied with fresh and dazzling attire, they would look no better. Well, not much. The point is that I was an adventurer (I had just decided), not a fop. And anyway, I wasn't the

least bit interested in people who would evaluate me according to
what I looked like. Who did they think they were?

The problem was that all this elegance and spectacle was getting to
me, and the truth was that, yes, I did feel a bit awkward and out of my
element. I once witnessed a frog race in Cresdon years ago. (Bear with
me, and the relevance of this will become clear). Some idiot had marked
out a little course and people were expected to place bets on which of
the five uninterested frogs would finish first. People did, too. When the
"race" started, the frogs either sat where they were, went in the wrong
direction, hopped out of the course altogether, or tried to make friends
with the other frogs. The idiot organizer was press-ganged into paying
the gamblers as if everyone had won, and finished the afternoon badly
out of pocket and looking like a complete prat. Anyway, being before
the king reminded me of that, though I couldn't decide if I, surrounded
by courtly leers and polite smiles, felt more like him or one of his stupid frogs. (See? I told you it was relevant. Sort of.)

While I was musing on my frog-like status, we had reached the
dais where King Halmir, son of Velmir, sat like a human sunbeam. He
looked us over, opened his mouth pensively, and said nothing. Not a
sausage. So we stood there looking deferential, and lowered our eyes
as his gaze strayed over our clothes, lingering significantly on mine. I
felt my beard growing. Nothing happened and there was, for a moment, total silence. I felt . . . *something*, like I was being held under a
lens like a bug, an odd sensation that was more than being simply
looked at. I was being studied, evaluated, but since no one said anything I had no idea whether or not I had passed whatever test I seemed
to be taking. Then Gaspar, who was standing beside the king's throne,
no expression on his austere privy-councilor face, coughed politely.
We looked up and he bowed fractionally.

"Thank you," he breathed. "That will be all."

My jaw dropped. I looked from him back to the king, whose attention had turned to his finger ends in a manner which said that our
presence in his was no longer required. Garnet and Renthrette bowed
and turned. With a rushed and halting movement, I followed suit,
glancing back at the king, too bewildered to speak. He was conversing
in hushed tones, his mouth barely moving, to Lord Gaspar, who was
nodding thoughtfully. We got about a third of the way down the carpet before the crowd began to buzz with chatter as their ordered ranks
collapsed. Suddenly there was a throng of people about us, milling

here and there and taking no notice of us whatsoever. The king, I discovered, had left the room through a door at the far end. We were pro-
pelled out by the lackey, whose manner was now casual to the point of
brusqueness, and dismissed. The frog race had been abandoned.

"Excuse me?" I gasped, as we were virtually ejected from the inner chambers and directed toward the street entrance. "Could someone tell me please what the bloody hell just happened?"

❦

"What confuses me," said Garnet, pushing ornate little pastries around
his bowl sullenly, "is why we were presented to His Lordship in the first
place."

"Especially since he was just going to look us up and down like we
were maggots in the dregs of his salad," I added, taking one of the elegant little pies and sampling it.

"What do you mean *we*?" asked Renthrette, spitefully.

"Oh, it was *my* fault," I exclaimed, incredulous, spitting crumbs.
"I should have known."

"Couldn't you at least have changed your clothes?" she spat like
an alley cat disputing ownership of a fish head.

"Into what?" I shouted back. "This is it, my entire wardrobe, right
here on my back. I'm sorry, but all my golden suits are being polished
and I haven't found some horny courtier to buy me another, all right?"

At this last she wilted a little and turned irritably away.

"Have you any idea how much that little get up must have cost?" I
went on, pushing the point home and flicking my finger accusingly up
and down her dress and jewelry. "More money than I've seen in a long
time, that's for sure. Don't start with me because *I* don't look like what
happens when you tie a tailor to a goldsmith and ply them with cash.
And what the hell is in these pies?" I said, studying Garnet's ornamental
lunch. "They taste of nothing at all. Why can't we go somewhere where
people know how to cook? . . ."

"Shut up, Will," said Garnet, flaring. "I should have known you'd
humiliate us just by being here."

"Listen . . ." I began.

"I said, *shut up*!" he roared, his hand straying for his axe with that
just-try-me gleam in his eye. It was a familiar gesture, but it was one
of those that never got stale, somehow. It was sort of like watching a
favorite play: I always got a little something new out of it, something

I'd not seen before. This time it was a hot flush that rushed through me like a bison with its tail on fire and almost made me stain my britches. All right, stain them *some more*. Happy?

⁂

That night I sat in my room for a while and sulked. Our meeting with the king had turned into another of those "adventurer" games which I always seem to lose, at least partly because I'm the only one who doesn't know the rules. More to the point, I was no nearer to figuring out the real burning question: What the hell was I doing here? This was followed by a question which didn't so much burn as rage like some apocalyptic furnace: How could I get back home?

Home. An odd word, that, always brimming over with unsaid promise of comfort and a sense of ease, a removal of fear and pressure, a restoration of the familiar and the reassuring. Yet, for all these associations to kick in effectively, it helped to know where exactly home was. For me, home had been Cresdon, though it had never been especially comforting or reassuring under the guardianship of Mrs. Pugh— particularly when the Empire found my name on their "top ten seditious actors and playwrights" list and, more dramatically, tried to put arrows through my gizzard. So home had become a concealed fortification in Stavis where the company of my new friends had taken the place of the homely hearth and steak and kidney pie with the family that I'd never really had. But now I was hundreds, maybe thousands, of miles away, with the two "friends" most likely to slit my throat for belching at table, and a growing suspicion that all my other friends were dead. To top things off, there was a race of sinister goblins and specters who thought I was darkly important, and a race of handsome, sophisticated hero-types who thought I wasn't.

This last raised another question. If we were so clearly worthless, if we were the kind of human refuse you could glance over in a second and completely get the measure of, if we were such slime that we could be dismissed without a word in our defense, why the bloody hell had they wanted to see us in the first place? Garnet was probably making a name for himself as Goblin Slayer Extraordinaire, and Renthrette was, shall we say, *connected* by way of Sorrail, but so what? In a city full of would-be ladies- and gentlemen-in-waiting, why had we been so quickly pushed to the head of the list for an audience with his royal goldness? And impressive as the city was, why were Garnet and

Renthrette sitting around instead of moving heaven and earth to rescue their friends? I mean, I was in no hurry to go crawling about goblin-infested caves, but for Orgos and Mithos I would at least consider it. Shouldn't Renthrette, champion of the oppressed whatever the odds, be promising to charge back for her friends—by herself if no one would come with her—rather than sitting around the court playing fancy dress? The answer to all these questions was the same, and it came in a pint glass with a foaming head. I went out.

We were still residing in the palace, for reasons unknown, and our little suite of rooms had a tall and slender guard not unlike Garnet in physique but blond and quiet in that removed, dignified manner all the people around here seemed to have when they weren't improvising love poems to their mistress's eyebrows. I hadn't seen much in the way of passionate outbursts since I'd been here, now that I thought of it. Yes, the waiting rooms had been awash with wry chuckles and other forms of polite amusement, but there had been no real laughter, per se. I mean no side-splitting, eye-watering, thigh-slapping laughter, the kind people make when they think something is *really funny*, as opposed to, you know, amusing. Everyone was so controlled, so restrained. It was beginning to get me down.

So I had a word in our guard's shell and asked for directions to the nearest tavern. Nothing fancy, I assured him, in case he hadn't got a good look at my britches lately, just somewhere I could get a good beer. He gave me a blank look, one of many I had been getting lately.

"You mean, an inn?" he said uncertainly.

"Spot on, mate. Good shot," I encouraged him.

"The closest is some distance from this part of the city. Perhaps half an hour on foot."

No problem. I had begun to feel like a trapped rat in the palace and figured the walk would do me good. I jotted down some directions on a little rectangle of parchment which the guard had for just such an eventuality. No wonder Renthrette and Garnet were so fond of this place. In Cresdon the local militia's idea of giving directions is to turn you to face the appropriate compass point and then give you a hearty kick in the ass.

So off I went, ambling casually, in no great hurry, and content to soak up the quiet evening. It was always pretty quiet around the palace: hardly what you'd call *urban*. The streets felt like the neglected cloister of some vast monastery or temple: all pale stone, clean, faintly ascetic angles, and a slightly unearthly silence. I tried whistling to myself but it felt disrespectful so I gave it up. The few people who passed me, mounted or on foot, barely made eye contact with me as they went about their business or pleasure (you couldn't tell the difference) in a demure, even stately fashion. It didn't bode well for the tavern, I suppose, but I had to try.

The point turned out to be, as they say, moot. I had just consulted my parchment and taken a left into the closest thing to an alley I had seen thus far, when I heard soft, careful footsteps behind me. I came instinctively to a halt. A second later, so did they. I turned and looked up to the main street I had left, but saw nothing. I started to walk again, a little quicker this time. At first there was only the echo of my own feet in the tunnel like alley, but then I heard them again, slightly out of sync with mine, following me. I began to run.

The footfalls were joined by voices, urgent, hissing whispers that bounced off the walls. I ran on and the alley descended slightly, snaking through a series of arches to the left. In front of me was a narrow flight of steps, climbing about ten feet back up to a passage that joined a main street. With panic driving me on, I was almost on the staircase before I saw the squat, heavy figure that stood in the shadows at the top. It stepped forward as I scuttered to a halt, and the evening light picked out an evil-looking figure, cowled all in black. Clasped in his hands in front of him was a huge, bladed weapon, heavy and brutal-looking.

It was a goblin, and it wasn't alone. Another appeared out of the shadows to my left and a third came running up from behind. They were all lithe, dark, and strong.

I backed up without thinking, but they were too close. A swarthy hand took me by the arm and thrust my face against the alley wall. My hands were caught and pinned behind my back. A trickle of cold water ran into my shirt collar and I shuddered.

"I have no faith in prophecy, Mr. Hawthorne," the big goblin on the stairs hissed into my ear in a strangely accented voice, a voice cold and hard as steel, which filled me with the sense of certain death. "Nor will you, by the time your blood has been poured from your throat."

"Listen," I spluttered desperately, "if it's money you want . . ."

One of those holding me laughed softly, a throaty chuckle, rich and chilling. I closed my mouth quickly as if paralyzed. Neither money nor words seemed likely to help me now.

A gloved hand passed over my mouth, pulling my head back so that my throat was exposed to the air. I heard the knife drawn by the third goblin and braced myself for the pain, the momentary warmth of blood running down my chest, the drowning, frothing gateway to darkness that would follow.

Yet, through the terror, a voice in my head, faint and indistinct, was repeating a single word: *prophecy*? It grew louder and, as I saw the blade raised, a flash of bluish light on its razor edge, I spoke. "You do not need to believe in the prophecy to be part of it."

The knife hovered in the air. I could smell my assailant's hesitation, and pressed my advantage, fighting for calm and evenness in my voice. "Remember the words of the prophecy," I said, improvising desperately. "And remember what happens to those who forget they are subject to destiny. Strike me down and take the inevitable consequences."

It was a little heavy-handed, but the fact that I was still alive to say the words suggested they were having some effect. Words have a life of their own, as I'm fond of saying, and it's best to run with that fact rather than insist on them meaning only one thing. This time I was really running with it. Sprinting away at full pelt, no less. My would-be assassin apparently thought my words meant something, though what that something could be, I had no idea. The knife paused in the air, frozen in time. Then it lowered uncertainly.

There was an angry sputtering of sharp, unfamiliar words and a hand spun me round. A dark, leathery face with narrow and malicious goblin eyes was inches from mine. This was the one who had laughed and, absurd though it seemed to be choosing between them, I liked this one least.

"You do not scare me, Outsider," he said. "What magic will strike me down when I cut out your heart and throw it to the swine?"

"My spirit will pursue you in the form of a great, gray hound with eyes like lanterns and teeth like scimitars," I managed, coolly.

"Really?" said the goblin. There had been a fractional pause, but the word was touched with bitter sarcasm. "We shall see," it resolved. It held out its hand for the knife, and the other goblin—after a fractional pause—gave it.

Then the big one on the stairs spoke uncertainly in his own tongue. The knife-wielder replied angrily and perhaps threateningly, and the big goblin responded with guttural hostility. They were arguing. The one with the knife turned to him, spat, and answered in crisp, bitter sounds, thrusting me away as it did so as if to give itself more room to fight. The big goblin glared and took a step down the stairs, brandishing its great cleaver and shrugging aside its heavy black cloak. The one with the knife turned disdainfully and peered at me through its tiny, squinting eyes. The knife, gleaming along its edge slightly, hung in the air.

And then, quite suddenly, the goblin stiffened and sank into a heap. I turned, wildly looking around me, since neither of the other two had stirred. At the far end of the alley was a shadowy figure, one hand outstretched as if pointing to the fallen goblin.

There was a confused struggle behind me and the smaller of the two remaining goblins, with a bestial snarl, took a great bound down the dark passageway toward the figure. "*Pale Claw,*" it said, and I thought it sounded scared.

In one hand, a razor which had been concealed in its foul tunic sparkled. The other was stretched out, fingers splayed to grapple with the newcomer. I stepped back cautiously, glancing to the steps where the large, cleaver-wielding goblin was descending awkwardly. There was a startled cry from the alley and I turned just as the razor clattered to the street, the goblin slumping down after it. A slim spike of metal stuck out of its chest, small and delicate as a needle. The big goblin on the stairs had slowed uncertainly. Another moment, I thought, and it would try to flee.

"Hell's teeth, but you cut that fine!" I exclaimed, too delighted for there to be any real criticism there.

The figure did not move, and his reply was calm, detached, and suave. "Now William," he said, almost casually, but slow, as if savoring every word, "let us not count our chickens."

The voice was all wrong: too dry and quietly amused, too knowing. And suddenly, in a wave of chill sweat, I knew he was no savior. He meant to kill me as coolly, precisely, and methodically as he had killed the goblins. In fact, I was pretty sure the goblins had been an inconvenience, a distraction for him. And while being a tad more famous than the other people on stage had once been appealing, I suddenly thought it a very bad thing that though he had dispatched the goblins with ruthless efficiency, it was my name he knew. He had barely moved so far, but now I saw his head tilt microscopically and felt his eyes upon me from within his hood.

"Hold still now," he breathed almost seductively, as if he was taking a speck of dust from my eye. "The pain will be surprisingly brief."

For a moment I stood quite motionless, trying to shake off the dread that the ease and elegant restraint of his words sent through me. Stepping back, I looked to the staircase, where the large goblin was now inching out into the alley, cleaver raised, and flung myself backward into the shadows. The stone wall where I had been standing sparked briefly and the tinkling sound of steel rang out, small and musical. I stood up quickly, thought for a desperate second, and ran behind the goblin whose eyes were on the hooded stranger, toward the stairs.

The goblin heard me, made a stumbling turn toward me, bellowing and hewing the air with its cleaver, and caught the needle-dart meant for me in its shoulder. It cried out, sagging fast, and I ran, throwing myself against the stone and climbing the stairs in three-at-a-time leaps.

"Now, William," said the smooth, quiet, but perfectly audible voice of the hooded figure, "don't be tiresome."

I think the goblin took a second dart, but I was up the steps before it fell, and running from the purposeful strides I could hear coming after me. I found myself in another short passage which rejoined the main street. I ran hard, but my pursuer had made it up the stairs by the time I got to the corner.

The goblins had fallen quickly: too quickly. The killer's darts had to have been tipped with something particularly nasty. Bearing this in mind, I ran still faster, weaving erratically down the street. One deserted block, then another. Then a third. From some ways back came the voice again, raised fractionally, but still barely concerned:

"Till next time, then, William. Soon."

I ran one more block and then looked back. There was no sign of anyone following, but I only paused for a second to take a long, sucking breath. Then I ran again, waiting for the momentary sting of one of those poisoned needles sliding suddenly into my spine.

Words, Words, Words

It was three o'clock in the morning. It had taken me over an hour to work my way as circuitously as possible back to the palace, hiding at every corner, moving from shadow to shadow: You know the drill. It was, I knew, a complete waste of time. Should I have finished up within a block of my former pursuer, no stealth, speed, or hasty camouflaging would have kept those needle-like daggers out of my body. Before, I had been one of four targets, and the other three had been potentially dangerous to the killer, with their gorilla arms and their cleavers. Now I was by myself and about as dangerous to an assassin like that as a newborn lamb: a very irritated and hostile lamb, no doubt, but a lamb nonetheless. In the quick eyes and lethal hands of my would-be assassin, I could hear the crackle of flames around the roasting spit and smell the mint sauce. So I dashed back to the palace and hoped to God my enemy had opted for an early night.

At the palace, I had alerted the guards and sent them to wake Sorrail and scour the city for my multiple assailants. I woke Garnet and Renthrette myself and bombarded them with a version of my story: a version, perhaps, with a little more stoic composure and a little less bowel-shifting terror than I had felt at the time. But I'm not *that* good an actor, so they spotted enough of my fear-stricken panic to trust that I had actually been in danger.

The search of the city (surprise, surprise) turned up nothing. The assassin, unlike the goblins who had caught me first, had come and gone with all the noise and fuss of a ground fog, the kind you don't see forming till you can't find the floor anymore. I hadn't expected him to leave any grist for the investigator's mill: no carelessly dropped letters with names and addresses, no passing witness who felt sure he'd seen him somewhere before, no distinctive jewelry left at the scene. He had vanished from the White City's immaculate streets like the flame of a quenched candle, and if there hadn't been a little stack of dead goblins a few blocks from the palace, I doubt Sorrail would have given my tale much credence.

But there was, and he did. He came back to our rooms dressed in his military tunic and his face was grave and pensive.

"Tell me what happened," he said, running his hand thoughtfully through his hair.

"I already did," I said.

"Once more, please," he said. His voice was tired, but his eyes were still keen and alert. I began the story again, casually, bored with it already. Gaspar, apparently one of the king's closest advisers despite his part-time appearance as a dandified courtly love poet, took notes and looked as gray as his suit. Renthrette sharpened her knife carefully. Garnet yawned.

"And that's all you remember?" said Sorrail, as I concluded.

"No," I said. "I forgot to tell you that he said his name was Albert and he came from a village just north of . . ."

"Will," said Renthrette, barely looking up.

"Sorry," I said. "A joke. Yes, that's all I remember."

"What about his voice?" Sorrail continued, ignoring that last piece of stupidity.

"Urbane," I said. "No accent to speak of. Smooth, you know? Almost oily but not in a bad way. Precise, like the sound of a very finely made crossbow slide. Probably not the voice of a very young man, but I couldn't say for sure. Not a voice I knew, I'd say. So that ought to really narrow down the possibilities."

"Would you recognize the man again if you saw him?" said Sorrail.

"No," I said. "I told you: I didn't see his face and we really never got that close. Barely on speaking terms really. A nodding acquaintance, you know. Not a *mate*, exactly. . . ."

"Will," Renthrette warned.

"Sorry. I'm just getting tired of this. I really need to sleep and I never did get my beer."

Sorrail called a guard and muttered to him. The guard paused fractionally longer than he should have and Sorrail raised an eyebrow in that do-you-have-a-problem-private? way that commanding officers have. Five minutes later the guard came back with a tankard of what looked remarkably like beer. For me.

And at this unexpected delight, something struck me. "Hold it," I said, rising thoughtfully. "One of the goblins said something."

"I thought they spoke in their own language when they weren't speaking to you," said Sorrail.

"They did," I agreed. "But when the first goblin fell, one of the others said something that sounded like it wasn't one of their words. It sounded different. Like regular Thrusian or whatever you call it here. And I think it was connected to the appearance of the hooded assassin. Something 'claw.' An adjective, then claw." I thought frantically. I had begun to pace the room, hands to my temples. "Claw," I repeated. "Something-claw. Pale!" I said suddenly, snapping my fingers. "That was it, I think. Pale claw. I'm almost sure."

"Sounds like a name to me," said Garnet, regaining interest.

"Yes," said Sorrail, hesitating thoughtfully. "But I do not know how we begin to find who it belongs to. Moreover, if Pale Claw is the killer's name, then the goblins recognized him. He must have been one of their agents, and I do not know how we would find such a man."

"But he killed the goblins," I said. "No. He was a man. Tallish, slim. Not at all squat or heavy like most of the goblins I've seen."

"A human accomplice, then," said Sorrail. "A traitor. The goblins apparently came into the city in the back of a tradesman's wagon. We found the wagon and its driver this morning. The goblins could not hope to hide long in the city after their mission was complete, but if the other attacker was a man, he could be anywhere and be quite undetected. I do not see what we could do to identify him."

"Shouldn't you be organizing the raiding party that goes back for Orgos and Mithos?" I said, tiring of this circular conversation.

Garnet turned and gave me a curious look, eyes narrowed and head cocked like he was straining to hear something a long way off. He opened his mouth vaguely as if he was going to say something but couldn't find the words.

"Hell's teeth!" I spat. "You call this beer?"

⁓⚘⁓

Dawn showed up like an old lover I'd never wanted to see again. With it came a letter. It lay on my breakfast tray alongside a tray of cunningly fashioned and utterly flavorless confectionary and some bland liquid which, I was assured, was "very nourishing." I suspected it was made from some particularly nasty species of turnip. The letter came in a rich, creamy envelope bound with red ribbon and sealed with wax. My name was etched in copperplate, barely discernible beneath all the flourishes. It smelt odd. Perfumed.

"It would seem you have an admirer," said Renthrette, idly. "How nice. You've always wanted one."

I practiced my steely look on her but it bounced off as usual and broke against the wall. She smiled like a cat over a bowl of cream. Or, I suppose, a mouse.

The letter was written in a long, fine, curly print as if the world's most aesthetically inclined spider had fallen in an ink well and become slightly drunk. I was about to peruse it when Renthrette, unable to sustain her pretense at superior disinterest, snatched it from me and began to read aloud. " 'My dear and most excellent Mr. Hawthorne—' Whoever it is doesn't know you very well," Renthrette inserted, without pausing for breath.

"Just read the bloody thing," I muttered. "I think we can manage without your editorials."

She went on, her voice raised in mock passion. " 'I fear your aim be truer than my heart hath strength to fly, for I fall stricken at your conquering feet with my breast heaving. Take me up in your most valiant arms and save me, beloved William. Kiss my breathless lips back to life and I will live to serve and pleasure you. Love me as I love you and I will set the heavens with myriad stars to shed full daylight on your fair countenance though it were deepest night. Like Sytone in the play of old, I'll burn with joy—' "

"Hold it!" I said. "The play of old? There are plays here, and no one told me? I was beginning to think Thrusia had the only theaters on the globe. Where can I find these plays?"

"Don't you even want to know who it's from?" said Renthrette, warming to the intrigue of the thing.

"Depends," I said. "Does she give any more precise indication of how she intends to demonstrate this uncontrollable desire of hers? I mean, is it going to be all courtly verse, or do we get to, you know, mix our metaphors a bit?"

"Typical," said Renthrette. "No. And it's just signed 'an admirer,' anyway, so it looks like you're stuck with the words."

Nothing new there. But at least I had the words, and they could lead me to more interesting things. I leaned out into the corridor and flagged down the nearest guard. "You have a theater in this city?" I asked.

"A what?" said the guard.

"A place for plays. You know? Drama. A kind of entertainment where people act out stories."

He put his head slightly on one side like a chicken that has been asked to lay a side of beef for a change, and then shook his head slowly.

"What about a public library of some sort?" I tried.

"Oh yes, sir," he said, smiling proudly. "An extraordinary collection of our most ancient and modern manuscripts, I believe."

Renthrette sighed pointedly. "Books are for people who can't survive in reality," she said. "And stories are just empty wastes of time."

"Right, Renthrette," I agreed absently. "Real men can't read, I know. Go and kill something, will you? Cheer yourself up."

The library was over by the city's western wall, opposite the judicial courthouse. The two buildings gazed upon each other across a flagged square. They were, of course, elegant buildings fronted with white plastered columns whose capitals were discreetly brushed with gold and shone in the morning light. The square was empty and the series of turrets that surmounted the courthouse threw slightly austere, regular shadows across it. It was cold in the shadow and I was glad to pause for a moment on the sunlit side and admire the forum's colonnade and the library's great domed roof. It was still chilly, but the sky was clear and there was a brisk, invigorating quality to the air. I almost bounded up the marble steps and tried one of the doors, great oak things, almost black with age.

The latch clicked easily, but the door barely moved, though I put my whole weight upon it. I tried again and it scraped a few more inches and then juddered to a halt with a whine of protest. It wasn't going any farther. I tried the other, but it was bolted down into the floor and was impervious to my efforts. I knocked loudly, but nothing happened. For a public library, it would have made a pretty good fortress.

I stood at the head of the stairs and looked out across the forum into the sun.

"So much for that," I said aloud. Then I slowly descended the steps and began to cross the square. On a whim I swung across to the northern colonnade and began strolling along its stately length, vaguely pleased by the shelter from the breeze. Then I saw, straight ahead, just visible behind a series of stone benches that faced out into the square, a small door into the base of the law courts. Since these buildings had obviously been built to balance each other, probably at the same time, it struck me as at least possible that there might be a similar door into the library. I turned quickly and ran back, shaded by the roofed colonnade. At the far end, set in a little alcove so that it was virtually invisible from the forum, was a door about a third the size of the main entrance. I tried it.

It didn't open. Irritably, I twisted the handle, and a reddish dust collected on my fist like dried blood. I did it again, more vigorously this time, and the rust flaked all the more. Something shifted in the mechanism and the handle gave a little more. With a glance over my shoulder and one last wrench, something inside snapped, there was a little cascade of orange which had once been metal, and the door shifted against my shoulder. Leaning my back against it and setting my feet to the jamb for leverage, I forced it open and it was the hinges' turn to shower the stone floor with rust.

It was dark and cold inside and I had to push the door wider just to see where I was going. It was dry, but smelled unused, stale even. The corridor was narrow and, after only a few yards, turned sharply to the left. The light from the doorway was no use here and I stumbled and grazed my calves on the edge of a stone step. I felt with my hands: there were more steps ahead. Arms spread like a nervous chick poised to jump out of the nest for the first time, I ascended the stairs.

Different people have different passions, and you only have to find the right one to make them behave irrationally. My passions were few and fairly straightforward: food, drink (especially beer), money (not that I ever had any), women (likewise), books in all forms, and plays in particular. My days as an adventurer had brought me most of these, though when adventuring gave you anything you could be fairly sure that it would turn out to have a heavily muscled swordsman attached. I didn't like creeping around in dark corridors, but if there was reading matter as well as light at the end of the tunnel, I'd give it a go. If the seven-foot-tall, sword-wielding custodian was out to lunch, so much the better.

At the top of the stairs my fingertips found vertical wooden boards, a cold metal ring, and a keyhole through which nothing could be seen. I fumbled with the ring and, actually trying to be quiet for the first time since I had broken in, turned it till the door clicked. *Un-locked*, I thought, pleased with myself, and pushed. It shuddered and gave slightly, but there was clearly something solid against it on the other side. I tried again. No joy.

The trouble with passion is that it can make you singleminded to the point of stupidity. Perhaps that is why I found myself sprinting up the stairs and throwing myself in a shoulder-cracking thud against the door. The door burst open, the table on the other side turned over and crashed to the floor, and I followed suit, landing on my side in a heap of parchment. As things quieted and I began squeezing my collarbone tentatively, an inkwell which had been catapulted off the table rolled quietly away, leaving a thin black trail on the parquet floor.

After a moment of silence, I rolled over onto my back and found myself bathed in a chill, gray light. It came from the dome directly above, which was translucent, and glowed with a soft radiance, pale and easy on the eyes. It was stone, I think, and was supported with darker buttresses that arched up into the center like ribs, but it lit the entire building like a vast lantern with a paper shade. And all around me, on great lurching shelves, at the ends of sliding ladders, stacked into the very dome itself, were books. It was like stumbling onto a lake of cool, crystal water after three weeks in the desert. It broke over me like a crash of triumphal music.

I had never seen anything like it.

Half-delirious, I rolled over and onto my feet, sprang to the nearest wall of spines, and plucked one out.

"*A Rhetorical Method for Schoolmasters*," I read aloud, delightedly. The one next to it was *Tharnast's Rules of Logic*, and beside that, *A Discourse on the Structures of Grammar for the Edification of the Scholar*, with a revised appendix on *Practical Syntax in Rustic Dialect*. Things of beauty, all. I returned them to the stacks, barely able to contain a giggle of excitement, and began to pace the dim corridors of shelves, scouring their contents with my head tipped on one side and grinning like a child accidentally locked in a pantry full of cake, trifle, and cookies.

It wasn't that I had been starved of reading matter, but books showed up only rarely in the life of an adventurer, and even the library in the Hide back in Stavis tended toward the practical. If you were into siege tactics, herbal remedies, and how to turn a hairpin into a lock pick, that was the place for you. Lisha, Mithos, and Co. were, but while I will read such stuff in the absence of an alternative, I want books to pull me out of reality, not to plunge me into it, hairpin and broadsword at the ready. In Stavis, and indeed throughout Thrusia, the Empire had made books few and far between. Literacy is dangerous, and they had taken pains to discourage it. When they closed the theaters as similarly dangerous, they also impounded and destroyed whatever playbooks could be found. Then poetry, being considered frivolous, obscure, and, in some cases, lewd, was added to the list. Bonfires on street corners became a regular sight, enthusiastic young corporals standing over them full of the spirit of victory and righteousness. It had been some time since I had curled up with a good book; so long, in fact, that the "good book" category was now easily broad enough to include *A Rhetorical Method for Schoolmasters*.

It didn't need to be. After only a minute or two, I came upon a table piled high with huge tomes bound with cloth and stiffened with sheets of a board so heavy it took two hands to open them. A catalog. There, in minute, handwritten but perfectly legible print were the titles, authors, genres, and other details about the library's twenty-five thousand plus volumes. Each record was lettered and numbered to correspond with an area, stack, and shelf. In moments I had oriented myself and was gazing raptly at a ten-foot-high wall of irregular books and manuscripts, some bound with leather and etched with gold leaf, others mere jumbles of papers stitched together or folded into parchment covers, all qualified by a plate halfway up the wall which read, simply, DRAMA.

I shut my eyes and chose one, found a stained, ancient desk with a leather-covered chair in a dark recess between the stacks, and sat quite still and silent for two hours. The sun rose high over the dome and the soft effervescence grew, though I barely noticed it, so totally immersed was I in the world whose pages I turned—less hungrily now, but with a sense of peaceful joy spreading through me like the light in the dome. And though, like the starving man who rejoices over a stale crust, I would have been happy with anything, it was good stuff. Very good, in fact. It was romance: not in the sense of a love story—though that was an element of it—but a romance of the epic variety, dark forces propelling the play toward tragedy and the hand of some providential power pulling everything back from the brink of chaos and destruction, into comic resolution, victory, marriage, and the reuniting of sundered families and friends. Romance is the most painful kind of drama because it announces so clearly that only through art can such horrors be averted, such discord turned to harmony. The end is always joyful, but touched with a galling pathos that reminds the audience that in the world *we* inhabit, the treacherous survive; the grandfather never recovers his sanity; the fleeing virgin, instead of encountering her long lost brother in the forest, falls prey to bandits, rapists, and murderers. Painful, romance is, and hard to pull off. A badly written romance is, at best, predictably tedious, at worst, laughable and embarrassing. This was neither. The characters were carefully drawn with distinct voices and personalities. The plot was deftly woven, turning artfully in on itself like a serpent, balancing thematic unity and clever surprises. The whole had a lyric ease, a grace of diction, a flowing, intricate, spellbinding beauty that pulled me in so that the rest of the world was forgotten.

It was all the more striking, then, when I found myself pricking up my ears and glancing hurriedly about. I had heard something, could hear it still. It was distant and small, but regular, now slowing, not far from the door I had entered. As it stuttered into stillness, I realized what it was: the inkwell I had upset and left on the floor. Someone had kicked it.

I remained motionless for a second, then rose, quiet as I could, lifting my chair so it would not scrape on the floor. Then I listened. Nothing. Whoever, or whatever, had been over there, was intending to be silent. This bothered me. I drew my belt knife and took a long, incredibly slow, step toward the closest stacks, easing my foot down and rolling my weight from heel to toe soundlessly. Then another step, and I was against a bank of shelves about ten feet high. I moved sideways toward the central area where the great indexes were, eyes flashing from the north to the south ends of the narrow book-lined alley. Then I waited, still several yards from the edge of the stacks, and listened. Nothing.

Out of the corner of my eye, something moved, or seemed to. I turned hurriedly to my right, but the south end of the tight corridor was quite empty. I paused and had just managed to convince myself that it had been a trick of the light when the books directly in front of me exploded out of their shelf and, from behind them, I glimpsed first a pair of eyes which ducked away like an animal's, then the business end of a large crossbow pointed squarely at my thorax.

"Don't move," said a voice, before the possibility had even occurred to me, "and drop the knife."

It was a collected voice, as voices from behind crossbows tend to be, unruffled and in control. It was also a woman's. I did as she said and smiled sheepishly. There was a tiny rustle of movement, and when I looked up, the space in the shelves was quite empty. I turned and found her coming from the north end, the crossbow leveled at me but held in that casual way that comes from familiarity. Her eyes were on me and there was neither casualness nor familiarity there. They were blue-gray, large, and beautiful like a snowscape is beautiful: entrancing but cold, and best enjoyed through the window of a room with a fireplace.

"Who are you and what are you doing here?" she said evenly.

"Will Hawthorne," I said. "I came to read a book. I was under the impression that this was a library."

"It's a museum library," she said carefully, "and it's closed. What have you been doing?"

"Reading," I said. "What else would one do in—"

"*What* have you been reading?" she demanded with careful, impatient emphasis.

"*A Seasonal Storm*," I said. She did not respond. "A play by, well, I don't think it says. It's on the table there."

She stepped past me, the crossbow still trained on my breastbone a trifle melodramatically. At the desk she picked up the text, flashed her eyes over it, and dropped it carelessly back where I'd left it.

She was about about my age, maybe a year or two more, tall, and blond like everyone else here, but she was not dressed as a courtier. She wore a long dark smock with a white shirt beneath, open enticingly at her throat. Her arms were long and slender, her wrists and fingers similarly slim and pale as new ivory. Her hair was gathered tight to the back of her head with a silver clasp. Her mouth was small, her lips full in a permanent half-pout, her forehead and cheekbones high, her jaw sculpted. She looked like an alabaster statue which had come to life. To put it another way, she was hot.

"You must go now," she said. "And if you wish to see the library, you need express permission from the King's Counsel."

"How might I get that?"

"I really don't know," she said, "but I'm sure—"

"I mean, it seems such a shame to lock away all these wonderful books," I said. "People should be able to read them without 'express permission,' surely?"

"This is a museum. The stock here is too precious to—"

"I'd be very careful," I tried.

"Parts of the building have not been structurally sound since last year's earthquake," she said, not really bothering to conceal the fact that she found these explanations tiresome.

"Earthquake?"

"You're not from round here, are you?" she said, as if thinking the implications of this through for the first time.

"No," I began, "I'm a guest of Sorrail, as I said, and . . ."

"Of course," she said, and a light went on somewhere in her memory. "Well, yes, there was an earthquake. A large section of the outer wall has not yet been repaired, though it fortunately faces away from the goblin presence in the forest, so—"

"Perhaps you could show me around? You know, *supervise* me?" I said, pushing my luck a little.

"What?" she asked, caught off guard. For the first time it seemed like she wasn't following a script.

"I mean, perhaps you could show me the library."

"I'm very busy. I really don't have time to . . ."

"I'd love to just come and read a little. I wouldn't get in anyone's way. . . ." I began.

"Perhaps I could have one of my assistants take some books to your lodgings."

"Perhaps you could bring them yourself," I said with a smile. There was a pause and her gaze flicked away, as if uncertain of what to say next. I filled the silence for her. "Couldn't you just show me around the library?"

"I really am very busy," she answered, less adamantly than before. "And if you do get permission to visit the library, you will also get a tour escort from the library staff."

"Would that be you?" I smiled winsomely.

"It might be," she said and, for a fraction of a moment, her eyes thawed slightly.

"Then I'll make an appointment immediately," I said, relaxing. "Might I request your company by name?"

The crossbow moved fractionally, paused, and then dropped completely.

"Aliana," said the woman. "You'd better go."

"Yes," I said. "Er . . ."

"I'll let you out the front way," she said, and this time the smile, which had begun in her eyes, made its way to her lips. I was, momentarily, transfixed by the result. She saw me notice, recognized my interest, and turned away as her smile widened.

"This way," she said, turning back to me, but not meeting my eyes.

She moved quickly, leading me into a dark, cold vestibule where the great oak doors that I had tried to force stood. She stooped and pulled at the floor bolt, but it was stuck.

"Allow me," I said, bending with her till my cheek was inches from hers. She smiled, showing that little girlish flash of coyness again. As she straightened, I was struck with how different a response I would have gotten from Renthrette. The bolt moved easily in my hand and the great door shuddered as it came free. She held it open.

"Well, good-bye then," I said, lingering in the doorway.

"Good-bye, Mr. Hawthorne," she answered.

"Right," I said, stupidly, before backing awkwardly away, my eyes still on her. "I'll be back."

"I'll look forward to it," she said, smiling broadly now.

And with that, she closed the door and was gone. I turned, scuttled down the steps, and skipped across the forum.

❧

"Did you find your admirer?" asked Renthrette, without looking up from the feathers she was trimming for arrow flights.

"Not exactly," I replied, thinking wistfully of Aliana. "Why? Jealous?"

She snorted slightly and her thin lips creased into a dry smile. She lifted a goose quill to the light and examined it carefully.

"I mean," I continued, "you should let me know, if that's how you feel."

There was a long silence.

"What?" she said slowly, her eyes and attention still wholly on the feather, which she had now laid on the table, her knife poised above it. She adjusted the angle of the blade fractionally and cut delicately, meticulously, like a surgeon.

"I said," I explained, "that if you find yourself struggling to vanquish the resentment and envy you feel toward this unknown lady, then perhaps you should lay your heart bare. . . ."

"What are you talking about?" she said, looking at me for the first time since I had walked in.

"That special bond between us," I said, grinning. "Give in to that unspoken, secret desire which keeps you awake, yearning for my presence beside you. . . ."

"Oh, that," she said, returning her gaze to her work. "Well, what would be the use?"

This was new for Renthrette. My audacity usually irritated and flustered her in ways that made her prone to violence. I'd never seen her play along with such composure. For a moment I dried up. When words came to me, they did so slightly defiantly, though I grinned all the while. "Perhaps I would take you after all," I said, wondering how far I'd have to push her before she took a swing at me. "Perhaps I'd take you in my arms and kiss you hard on the mouth and run my hands through your hair and . . ."

She stood up abruptly. I smiled in quiet triumph as she took a step toward me, but her face was set, unamused.

"Would you really, Will?" she said. "Would you?" Her voice was soft, pensive. Even sad.

I stood where I was, my mouth open, dumb with surprise.

What the hell?

Her eyes searched my face and then fell slowly, sorrowfully. My mouth moved, but initially, nothing came out. Then I whispered, "I didn't think . . ."

"Don't you think . . ." She paused, catching her hand up to her mouth as her hair hung across her face, a picture of desolation. "Don't you think it could work? *Us*, I mean?" she whispered.

I hesitated, trying to catch up. "I think it could," I said, trying to restrain my enthusiasm. "Sure. Why not? I just didn't know that you were, you know, so . . . *keen*."

"Oh, I'm keen," she said, looking up with a little smile that could have been suggestive. "Keen as your wit. Maybe keener."

Then she laughed like I had never seen her laugh before. What had been a smile snapped wide and opened up. She threw her head back and roared hysterically. "You . . ." she screamed. "You *believed* me!"

I faltered and said nothing while she went on, laughing harder than a tree full of monkeys, tears streaming down her cheeks. Doubling up and holding her stomach, she sobbed, "Oh, Will. Admit it. I got you."

"Oh. Right. Yes. Very clever."

Then she was back to cackling and complaining about how her sides and belly ached.

I stood there and watched.

"And I thought *you* were the actor!" she said, curtseying to an imaginary crowd. "Thank you, ladies and gentlemen!"

"You malicious bitch," I managed. This was answered with another shriek of mirth.

"Oh, darling," she blurted out, "how could you say such a thing about *us*?"

This new gem of wit brought her to her knees with delight. She remained for some time, laughing uncontrollably. When Garnet came crashing through the door five minutes later, she was still giggling to herself.

"What is going on?" he demanded.

"Renthrette's just being oh-so-amusing this evening," I remarked.

"Oh Garnet," she said, "you have to hear this. Will came in and said—"

"Not now," snapped Garnet. "The city is under attack. A huge goblin army has come out of the woods and is assaulting the main gate. Everyone is needed on the walls! Everyone."

With that last word aimed pointedly at me, he grabbed his helm and armor and was out the door. Renthrette, former chief hyena and one-woman show, was now Renthrette the brave, a warrior stalwart, and grave. Garnet was barely out of the room and she was already half-buckled into her ring mail.

"Come on, Will," she said, throwing a quiver of arrows over her shoulder and grabbing her longbow from the corner of the room. "Come and kill something. You'll feel better."

She paused and gave me a grim smile, then thrust my scale corselet into my arms so forcefully that I nearly fell backward.

"Touché," I said, but she was already hurrying out the door. I stood there for a moment as if hoping to wake up, and then, with an uneasy apprehension tinged with nausea, I began to put on my armor. It took me longer than usual because my fingers fumbled with the buckles and straps as if I'd never seen them before. Pausing and raising my hands in front of my face, I could see that I was trembling palpably.

"Smug cow," I said aloud. This confession of anger at Renthrette seemed to help, and the straps slid into place as they should.

I grabbed my spear and crossbow and strode out into the palace corridor where guards were running with the quiet intensity of the genuinely alarmed, relying on trained discipline rather than thought. I pushed Renthrette's joke from my mind and decided to focus on the hordes of mythical beasts that had come to kill me.

SCENE XII

❧

Holding the Walls

Renthrette was out of sight by the time I was ready, but it wasn't too difficult to guess which way she had gone. I followed the running troops down the corridors and through a series of doors and courtyards that brought me out into the evening air, across a broad and chaotic street, and up a flight of fifty or sixty steps to the walls of the White City. The ramparts were wide enough for the town's defenders to stand three or four deep, and they were protected by huge crenelations with sloping tops. In fact, these walkways where we now stood were not the tops of the walls at all, but a series of galleries like theater balconies, a row of long boxes cut two-thirds of the way up the fortified city perimeter. They ran about a hundred yards from tower to tower and above them were other walls, cut with arrow slits, and other galleries.

A hundred men stood against the back wall of the gallery. They were clad in knee-length mail corselets, leather trews, and slightly conical plated helmets with nose guards and mantles of metal scale which hung to their shoulders at the sides and nape of their necks. I grasped the stone of the battlements and peered out over the walls.

My heart quickened.

Below and to my left, the bridge over which we had first entered the city arched its way across the river and ended in a turreted barbican. On the tops of the white towers and leaning over the bridge's stone balustrade were the shining helms and mail coats of the Phasdreille sentries. But all around them and across the entire far bank of the river was a dark, boiling mass bristling with spears and pikes and shrieking in wild and murderous joy: goblins. There were hundreds of them, seething like some foul volcanic geyser, spitting filth and heat at the walls which glowed with eerie beauty in the fading light.

The order was given, and the archers around me stepped up to the parapets in unison and released a long volley of arrows from their huge, tightly curved bows. For a split second, the sky darkened as their feathered shafts took flight in a long gasp, then the arrows flashed and burst into unnatural flame, greenish but so bright that I shaded my eyes.

I turned hurriedly back to the archers. On each end of their ranks were men clad in long white robes belted with silver rope. Their eyes were closed and their fingers moved rapidly in front of them, as if weaving invisible silk.

Magic.

The word jolted into my head like a kicking horse, but I brushed it aside and followed the arrows' trajectory. The river was a good fifty yards across and the bows fired from the walls barely cleared it before falling like strange, burning hail. The goblins, apparently unmoved by this unearthly fire, backed off slightly, jeering, as if they had been poked with a stick.

"They're a disorderly rabble," said Garnet, appearing at my shoulder and speaking with distaste, "aren't they? No tactics, just blood lust. No intelligence to speak of, just the desire to ravage and mutilate. But you should hear them scream when our blades find their loathsome flesh."

"And that fire," I began, "is it, you know, *magic*?" I said the word, but I could not keep the embarrassed snicker out of my voice.

"Magic," he answered, without looking at me, "holy. Call it what you will."

A cry of warning went up from the walls and I looked to see that several goblins had somehow bypassed the gatehouse and were now clawing their way up the bridge's elegant stone. One of them swung itself over the stone rail and stood dripping on the bridge, its head lowered furtively. Then it unstrapped a broad axe from its thigh and ran at one of the unsuspecting guards who was leaning out over the river with his bow drawn. The goblin felled him with a brutal shout of cruel delight, but one of the other guards, wheeling promptly, leveled and fired his bow hard into the creature's midsection before it could butcher anyone else. With the alarm raised, the couple dozen guards remaining returned to the barbican, bows trained on the bridge sides where the goblins were scrambling up and hanging back, like hyenas looking for the youngest or weakest buffalo in the herd. The sentries couldn't see from down there, but there must have been close to a hundred goblins poised to clamber up and join the fray.

"The bridge guard are massively outnumbered," said Renthrette, appearing from the bank of archers. "They'll be slaughtered! We have to open the main door and relieve them."

"Open the door?" I said. "The door of the city? You're insane. That's what they want us to do. What if we can't hold them there? They'll walk right in and that's your war lost."

"We'll hold them," said Garnet grimly. "We have to."

"They're not even animals," spat Renthrette. "Animals are less malicious and destructive. I despise them."

This she punctuated with a shot from her longbow fired with such effort that she gasped, almost losing her balance as the arrow left. It kindled in the air and fell smoking sulfurously into the mass of enemies. I gasped and looked at her.

"Did you do that?"

She shook her head and looked to where the strange priestly figures continued to work their fingers, eyes lightly, serenely closed.

"Who's in command here?" shouted Garnet. "We need horsemen and a tight group of heavily armed and well-trained infantry to hold the gate after us."

"Will," said Renthrette earnestly. "Run around the walls and find the senior commanders. Tell them what we're doing and have them support us if need be. Tell them we'll stay on the bridge. We will not venture farther."

And then they were gone. As the pair of them clattered off down the stairs with some corporal who was to lead them to the cavalry, I looked about me and tried to decide if this was a good development. No fighting for me, exactly, but a kind of importance: a kind unlikely to get me killed. An arrow with ragged black flights scudded over the parapet and fell against the back wall. I ducked my head and looked for the safest way out of there.

To my left was a tower with a door in it. I tried it and it opened, revealing a pair of fair-haired men who were loading and aiming a bolt-throwing catapult through a cross-shaped slit in the stone. They barely acknowledged me, so I ran behind them, out the other side of the tower, and onto the next section of wall. There, another group of archers were firing in ordered rows under the command of a stark, flushed sargeant.

"They're going to send horsemen onto the bridge. Give them some covering fire," I yelled at him.

"What? Who are you?" he shouted back, the veins on his neck bulging ominously.

"It doesn't matter. . . ."

"It does if you're going to give me orders," replied the officer.

"I'm a tactical advisor to Sorrail," I lied hurriedly. "Now slow your fire until those horsemen come out underneath us. Cover the balustrades and pick off any goblins that get behind the cavalry."

The sargeant hesitated for a second and then nodded and said, "Yes, sir."

I ran on, tried the next door, and kept going, repeating the order to the next group of archers. I did it again and again until the archers were too far from the bridge to be of use, so I told them to shoot at the goblins as they climbed the sides. The next group were barely close enough even for that and could only pick off those goblins that moved too far upstream. The next set of guards were standing around waiting for instructions, so I sent them down to help hold the gate behind the cavalry. After that, the sections of walls between the towers were patrolled only by isolated men who regarded me with alarm and expectation as I came barreling through the towers, panting heavily.

I was getting bloody tired, and I was too far round the walls now to even see what was going on on the bridge. The cavalry could have charged out with total success, or, for all I knew, they could have been cut to pieces, Renthrette and Garnet with them. I slowed a little and considered running back the way I had come. I had to be at least halfway round the central fortress by now, however, and to go back made little sense. I took a long, wheezing breath, straightened up and began to run again. Three towers later I realized why I should have gone back.

The wall ended abruptly in scaffolding and piles of masonry. To my right was the back of the library where I had spent the morning, and in front of me was a huge hole in the wall, left over, I now remembered, from last year's earthquake. The ramparts in front of me had buckled like parchment left in the sun and about twenty feet of impenetrable fortification had torn and slid into a dusty pile beneath. A timber structure had been erected over the top, presumably to aid in the reconstruction, but its highest point was a good ten yards lower than the level I was on. I leaned against a stack of immense stone blocks a yard on each side, lashed together and ready for the repairs to come, and peered down into the gorge beneath. It was quite a hole. It was a hell of a good thing that the walls sat at the river's widest point.

All of a sudden I caught sight of a figure running from the library and bounding up the steps on the far side of the breach with a large crossbow in his hands. Correction: *her* hands. It was Aliana, robed in a long, cream habit belted at the waist. I waved. She kept running and, on reaching the head of the stairs, crouched behind a shattered parapet and took aim at something down below.

The earnestness of her effort to be significantly involved in a battle taking place on the other side of the city amused me slightly and, chuckling, I leaned casually over the wall. My indulgent laughter perished.

On the bank below, three great war barges were beached. Each carried about thirty goblins, which were now spilling out and skulking cautiously, weapons poised and ready for the trap that wasn't there, inching toward the gaping, inviting space that had once been the wall. Taking in the other barges which were gliding silently across behind them, I came to the inevitable conclusion: The battle was lost.

The stillness was broken by the snap-twang of Aliana's crossbow. A large goblin fell to its knees clutching its shoulder and the others scattered instinctively, wheeling large, hide-covered shields up over their heads and scuttling for the cover of the boats and the walls. But no more bolts rained down on them from above and their high, caustic cries of alarm were quickly replaced by confused hissings. Their faces, invisible to me from the walls, turned to each other and they whispered fiercely. Then, with a cry of resolution, they began to emerge from their cover and, some shifting apprehensively, some running with long, rangy strides, they began moving toward the breach once more.

I, who had been clutching my parapet out of sight, allowed myself to breathe and looked hurriedly around. The guards, thanks to my tactical genius, had all gone to defend the gate, leaving the walls quite deserted. Then movement on the other side of the breech reminded me of Aliana. She fired again and, as before, the cry of pain from below was accompanied by a scramble for cover. But she was separated from me by twenty feet of air where the walls had been, and there was no one else to defend the place.

She looked across and recognized me in the dim light, but her eyes were hard. "Go for help, Mr. Hawthorne," she shouted, but I was still exhausted from running over here in the first place, and I'd have to cir-cumscribe three quarters of the city before I found anyone.

"Your side is closer to the front," I shouted, moving toward the twenty-foot pile of roped stone blocks which rose like some mono-lithic tower out of the breach's strewn boulders. "You go."

She looked from the enemy to me and back, then she nodded, rocked onto her haunches and up into a sprinting run toward the near-est tower. In seconds she was gone. I swallowed hard and glanced over the wall.

The goblins, who had emerged rather faster than last time, were now straightening up and moving toward us, their eyes flashing from the undefended walls to the heaped rubble and wooden scaffold where the repairs were. It was a narrow pass and would necessitate them climbing over the masonry-strewn foundation and timber frame, but it wouldn't take them more than a few minutes to get through. Perhaps I could pick them off one by one as they swung themselves over the scaf-folding. . . .

Right. Even if I can aim this thing better than I've ever done be-fore, I'll still be lucky to get three of them before they break through and come up the stairs after me.

This was crazy. I wondered if by moving around and firing from different spots I could trick them into thinking the walls were stuffed with guards lying in wait. No. I couldn't fire anything like fast enough to make that work.

So, as is often my response to finding myself in a tight corner, I started to talk. Aloud. To myself.

"Are they close enough?"

"Not yet."

"Just a few more feet."

"Are they ready on the other side?"

"Yes. They won't know what hit them."

"Get that catapult ready. Pass me those bolts."

"Ready, sir. . . ."

I was never that good at voices, really, but I figured I'd just created at least six different people with accents from various parts of Thrusia, Shale, and the Empire. One of them sounded drunk and another was mentally subnormal, but then, so was I for trying something this laugh-ably destined to fail.

The fact remained, however, that Aliana's shots had come from the other side of the breach and this exercise in auditory puppetry, however inept, had the goblins slowing and gazing up at the other side of the fractured wall with sudden apprehension. There was a pause as words were exchanged between them. For a moment, nothing seemed to move, then several of the goblins turned back to the shore and my hopes were shattered as surely as the wall itself had been.

Another barge had landed. Its prow was a great door that fell heavily on the shingle with a dull splash. The goblins close by limped hurriedly away and turned to watch with their eyes cowed, their bodies low and nervous like jackals abandoning a carcass to a lion. I stared fixedly at the barge and, from the darkness within, something huge began to emerge. I saw its eyes like glowing coals and the vast curl of goat-like horns that spread out and back, each wider than the span of a man's arms. I saw each forepaw's talons click on the gangplank like the claws of a great reptile and the waves of muscle that flexed and rippled beneath its thick and scaly hide. It gathered in a kind of crouch, and its form was something like a man's, but gargantuan and with bestially deformed features like the devils in ancient prayer books. As it emerged, its tail rose behind it, lashing the air as it lowered its immense, bullish snout and snorted.

A low gasp slid out of the goblins and they spread still wider, now in total silence. The beast gathered itself, shrugging off the cramp of the barge, and raised its thick, cabled neck and shoulders. The fiery eyes rose twenty feet into the air until they seemed to be looking into mine. When it reached its full height it stood only six or seven yards below me, its muzzle clearly moist, and its horns coiled and spread like giant shells, stretched and twisted by the hands of some terrible creator. For a moment, everything else was darkness and there was only me and that thing of night and malice, peering into my soul. Again it snorted—a deep, rolling thunder that seemed to shake the very walls—then it lowered its head. It took a step and the walls shook. A cascade of loose stone trickled down the splintered sides of the breach and the timber scaffold groaned. It seemed I could feel its thick breath on my face. Struck with a cold terror, I looked away and started to run for the tower door.

It clawed at me from below, a great sweeping reach with immense, ape-like arms covered with short, bristling hair and hands—*hands*— with fingers the length of my legs and nails like blackened sabers.

I dived low behind the parapet and the monster tore part of the wall away. Blocks of granite exploded in a haze of lethal fragments and landed in a shower of stones, one of which fell hard across my shoulders and left me breathless. I rolled painfully onto my back and saw the immense clawed hand reaching over the shattered parapet and grasping like some blind, nightmarish spider at the space where I had been.

Then it slid away into the air outside and there was complete silence, ominous and short-lived. I heard the rushing air as the hand came smashing in again. I scrambled up and, as the hideous paw tore through the wall by the tower door, found I had nowhere to run but to the breach itself. As the fingers crawled their way toward me, I scuttled to the end of the wall where the giant slabs of masonry were piled, lashed into place with guy ropes thick as my arms.

The hand swept toward me, wrenching the crenelations from the walls as it did so, so that I had no choice but to go down before it reached me. I clambered over the wooden rail and felt desperately with my feet for the rungs of a ladder. The giant hand clutched at empty space a yard in front of me and I heard the scythe-swing of its talons. One of them found the ropes that held the enormous stack of blocks for the wall repairs and slashed through them so that the tower of stone shifted ominously. Reaching lower, desperately feeling with one foot, I found the ladder and slithered down to the planked structure below, which straddled the rubble like a bridge to the other side of the breach. An arrow soared past me and another slammed into the pine rail in front of me. I ducked into a precarious crouch and looked out to the shore.

The goblins were preparing to enter the breach four or five abreast, and they were going to march, not climb. Whatever was in their way— foundation, fallen rocks, scaffolding; even me, if I stayed there—was going to be plowed aside by that creature, that thing, that blasphemy of all that was natural. And there was nowhere for me to go, nothing for me to do. In a pair of strides the size of a coach and horses, the beast was on the shore again. Then it turned toward the breach and lowered its immense horns to charge. There was a sigh of satisfaction from the goblins, then the sound of its footfalls, pounding and reverberating like thunder in a canyon.

There was no ladder on the other side and the narrow plank bridge had no way down to the ground. Unthinkingly, I dashed back the way I had come and flung myself back up the ladder as the animal, if animal it was, smashed into the breach like a dozen elephants. Stone and lumber exploded and the entire bulwark seemed to roll backward, hang in the air, and crash to earth. It took several hacking seconds for the dust to settle. Where the breach had been dammed with its own fallen weight, the rock and mortar had been thrown backward into the city. There was still a pile of rubble, but it was half what it had been and I found myself hanging over a fifteen-foot drop. Of the timber bridge and frame which had run over to the other side, there was no sign. Knowing that it could reach up and tear me away from the wall if it wanted to, I grabbed the rung above me and dragged myself up as the ground shook again and the monster came on.

This time I was looking up when it tore into what was left of the wall. The tower of granite slabs at the top of the ladder shuddered and a rope snapped free, whipping back on itself like the monster's tail. I didn't look down at the great horns which were surely below me; I just scrambled up as fast as I could, grabbed the shortsword from my belt and hacked at the first rope I saw.

The goblins were closing in on the breach now, but the clearance wasn't complete. The ground trembled again and with a noise like a bursting drum, the beast rammed its way through. One rope gave and lashed my face as it did so, though I was too busy hewing madly at the next to feel the blood run down my cheek. The stone blocks squealed and groaned and I looked up, sure I would be pinned beneath the tower. Below me, the beast was worrying the remains of the shattered wall, grunting as it stooped its huge, bullish shoulders and plowed at what remained with its horns. It clambered into the breach, its great clawed hands pushing through like a swimmer parting the waves before him. A cheer went up from the victorious goblins. It stopped and looked up and, in the sudden silence, it heard the song of the last straining rope, tight as a harp string, before my blade bit through it. I rolled out of the way and waited.

Nothing happened. The tower of stone rocked slightly, but it did not fall. I sat up and peered down into the dust that rose from the breach. The creature looked up very slowly and saw me. I rolled backward, leaped to my feet, and charged the pile of blocks with all my weight, slamming my shoulder into it. Again, nothing happened; I merely sagged, clutching my shoulder. I heard it coming before I saw it. When I looked down, it was climbing.

It scaled the rubble pile in the breach in under a second with an astonishing, gorilla-like reach and agility. It lunged at me and its claws cut the air inches from my abdomen. I stepped back, but the beast had, for whatever reason, stopped. I peered cautiously over the edge and it looked back at me with eyes that smoldered with hatred and anger. It was clinging to the shattered wall like a great bat, its claws biting deep into the very stone. Apart from a sudden flare of its vast nostrils, it was quite still.

"You obscenity," I said. "You filthy, twisted aberration! You unholy and unnatural—"

I doubt it understood me, but it leaped at me with a bellow of rage, clawing at me with its hands and splintering the stone where I stood with its horns. I jumped back as the monster reared up, and the great stack of masonry finally began to sway out over the breach. The beast roared again, but now the tower of stones was falling and the monster could not get out of the way. The pile fell as a single unit, a great slab of granite that only broke into its component parts on the creature's back and shoulders. The earth shook. The beast crumpled, broken by the weight of the stone, and almost filling the breach. Its breath escaped in a last roar that turned into a whine and trailed off into nothing. Then there was silence again.

A chill wind broke over the city wall and, still squatting on the shattered rampart, I shivered, suddenly conscious of the sweat which had broken out all over my body. A coarse, gray dust stuck to me like sand and, when I brushed my arm distractedly, it scraped the skin away. I stood and looked down into the half-filled hole where the dark, almost unbroken skin of the beast was growing pale and indistinct as the same dust settled all over it. Then a wail went up from the goblin force on the beach, a keening cry of confusion, fear, and even—it occurred to me—grief.

Some of them were already scurrying back into their boats; others stood motionless, staring at the giant carcass and considering the odds against their continuing the assault unaided. Then there was a new sound: a blanket of drumming hooves, so many hooves that their individual staccato was lost in a long, unbroken roar. I turned to see a column of horsemen rounding the far corner of the forum and galloping toward me. They wore plate armor and heraldic shields. At their head was Sorrail.

The goblins heard them, too, and their indecision vanished. In seconds they were scrabbling up the slick prows of their war barges,

pushing, struggling, and climbing over each other to get in and away.
A pair of the larger ones waited, glancing uneasily at the city walls,
while the rest boarded. Then they put their shoulders to the slick timbers
and shoved the vessels back into the river, all the while shouting over
the confused din of the others. As their oars folded out in an erratic
wave and began to stab desperately into the water, I turned and raised
both arms to greet the cavalry. Relief, gladness, and triumph blended,
and I bellowed over the retreating goblins.

SCENE XIII

※

Stranger Still

So the battle was won, and many more goblins fell to our horsemen as they fled into the woods. I say "our," but I felt like a part
of the victory only inasmuch as I was not on the losing side. You
might expect that I would be hailed as a hero for playing so instrumental a part in the triumph, showered with honors and wealth, given
the keys to the city's extravagant larder (I couldn't believe the king
and his cohorts ate the tasteless muck we'd been fed so far), and surrounded by beautiful court ladies all anxious to touch my greatness.
As you will have realized by now, I am not one to let minor scruples
stand in the way of serious reward, and I was more than ready to sit
back and wait for my golden goblet to be filled without pausing to explain that my actions were more self-preservatory than heroic, more
accident than valor. I didn't get the option.

The soldiers who relieved me at the walls were delighted to see the
monster fall, but an odd hush came over them when they saw me clinging to the shattered parapets. Sorrail gave me a long silent look and then
led the charge on the goblins, his face troubled.

The news of my actions spread round the troops quickly for a while
and then, though I wasn't sure when the change took place, there was a
conspicuous lack of interest in my doings. By the afternoon the news
was dead and I wandered alone through the marketplace where many
soldiers were marching back to their garrisons amidst cheers and applause from the townsfolk. I was ignored. I caught some soldiers talking
to each other about how Sorrail had led a unit of crack guardsmen from
the king's palace to pull the stone ramparts down on the invading monster, as if it had been planned that way from the outset. I thought this a
bit much, and said so.

"That's not the way I heard it," I cut in. "I was under the impression that Sorrail was on the other side of the city and that the monster
hadn't even been seen until one of the Outsiders . . ."

"You mean, one like you?" said one of the privates with something akin to contempt.

"Very like me, actually," I replied, curtly. "Yes."

"Oh, yes," said the other, a tall young man with mocking eyes. "I heard that, too. You met the black fiend and wrestled it to death by yourself."

"Of course not," I began. "But . . ."

"Of course not," said the young man coldly, "that's what I thought."

They turned on their heels and walked away, smiling grimly to each other.

As I was considering this, Garnet and Renthrette appeared.

"Can you believe I'm not even getting credit for this?" I demanded.

"For what?" said Garnet.

"My brave defense of the city!" I said. "Who do you think dumped ten tons of quarried stone on that goblin wall-crusher? Who do you think stalled the enemy as they boiled around the walls and leveled their hellish champion moments before victory was assuredly theirs?"

"Sorrail," said Renthrette, with a shrug that suggested she thought I was joking around and found it only mildly amusing at best.

"No, I'm serious. It was me. Sorrail was with you lot at the front."

"Only for a short time," said Garnet. "Then he led his men to encounter the horned beast at the breach."

"But it was dead by then!" I protested. "I killed it."

"No, Will," said Renthrette. "You didn't. You know you didn't."

She said it almost kindly. I stared at her.

"I'm sure you tried to help. . . ." she began.

"Oh, right," I said. "I tried to help but failed because I am—you know—incompetent and degenerate. And then Sorrail—who is a hero, virtuous and mighty—showed up to save the day. All hail Sorrail!"

Garnet scowled and looked at the floor.

"Must you always try to belittle whatever you are too unworthy to look upon, Will?"

That little mouthful of acid came from Renthrette's slim lips. Her eyes held mine and I stood there speechless. She went on. "Sorrail is a man of virtue and valor. I think the very least you could do is give him credit for his victories instead of trying to poach them like some petty thief. But maybe that's all you are. A petty thief. I thought you were past all that. In the future, if you're going to lie, at least try to choose something remotely plausible."

I was too amazed to speak and stood there spellbound as they turned and stalked away as if poles had been jammed up their rears. This made no sense. Not that bit about poles up their rears. That made all the sense in the world. But this erasing me from the story of the battle wasn't just irritating, it was odd. Bloody odd, in fact, and I was going to get to the bottom of it.

I would begin with Aliana in the library. She had seen everything and would vouch for me, so I would salvage a little dignity yet, if only from Renthrette and Garnet. I must admit that this Sorrail character was really beginning to wind me up as well. If I could take him down a peg or two, so much the better. And if I could prove my account of things, that would help: the virtuous and heroic Sorrail taking credit for winning a battle at which he wasn't present? Oh, yes, that would make him fall in the estimation of a certain streak of blond misery; fall like a ton of rocks had been dropped on his head.

But not yet. I didn't want to think about the battle right now because it just made me mad, and I figured I needed a level head to prove Sorrail the duplicitous fiction-monger he clearly was. I decided to take a walk and take in the sights of the city properly.

I wandered in the direction of the library, aiming to leave the bustle of the marketplace behind me. On the way out, I spotted a weapon-smith's. The place reminded me of Orgos, so I went inside, wondering if Sorrail or Garnet had put that raiding party together yet. It would have been delayed by the attack on the city, no doubt, and I found myself impatient and baffled by how long it was taking to mount the rescue attempt. I wondered if something was being done in secret, that I was being kept in the dark about it on purpose. I wouldn't put it past Sorrail—maybe even past Garnet and Renthrette—to assume I wasn't sufficiently trustworthy to be let in on their plans. Well, that was fine, so long as they actually did something and so long as it actually worked and quickly. If I didn't have to be involved in the actual crawling about in goblin caves, so much the better.

The weaponsmith's was full of the usual bits and pieces, but it quickly became apparent that its wares could be divided into two groups: the old stuff, which was elegant but unadorned, beautifully simple, and looked like it would be around for centuries; and the new stuff, which was often tricked out with gold and jewels but looked flimsy and poorly made by comparison. Orgos would have been very unimpressed. The new stuff, the shopkeeper assured me, was all the rage in the city. I didn't doubt it.

I was about to leave when I caught sight of one of those huge two-handed swords such as I had seen over the fireplace at the Refuge Inn. I remarked on this and the shopkeeper, a tall man in late middle age, replied, "Similar, perhaps, sir, but this is a special piece."

"Really?" I said. "How so?"

"It has been in our family many generations," replied the shop-keeper. "My great-grandfather bore it when Phasdreille was besieged by a vast goblin horde which crossed the river to sack the White City."

I had hardly been listening, but something made me stop and turn to him. He carried on his tale. "He rode with a cavalry force raised in the borderlands, and they met the goblin ranks as they lay outside the great city. The horsemen caught the goblins unawares and routed them, though many tall and fair soldiers fell in the battle. My great-grandfather survived, but he was killed shortly afterward, and that was the last time he wielded this mighty sword. With it he struck down many dozens of goblins, cleaving a path through their ranks until he came upon their chieftain: a huge brute dressed in red and black, great ugly spikes on his helm and a weapon like a vast cleaver in his massive claws. My ancestor faced the beast and, after many blows were struck on both sides, felled him, cleaving his skull in twain. But the goblin was wearing an iron collar and the great sword was notched, as you can see."

And sure enough, the blade was damaged, a v-shaped piece of the steel edge knocked out. I looked from it to the shopkeeper and back, confused.

"A diamond was taken from the dead goblin," said the shopkeeper, "and it was set into the pommel here."

I stared at it, then at him. Could this be the same sword I had seen at the inn? Could it be a popular local tale that everyone claimed, or was it just a ruse designed to drive up the price of the merchandise? Probably, but since I felt abused, I left and walked away from the marketplace, feeling slightly disoriented for reasons I couldn't pinpoint.

Quickly, the streets became quiet. The city was so clean, so carefully laid out, so beautifully carved, so crisp of corner, so graceful of curve, that if I hadn't just seen thousands of people cheering their conquering heroes (sic) I would begin to wonder if anyone actually lived here at all. It felt like a model made by some huge entity as a home for storybook heroes, incredibly detailed but ultimately lifeless. I paced its impeccable marble streets and saw no more than a handful of citizens, all quietly going about their business, ignoring me as was—apparently—the law of the land.

Then I saw the gate. It was curiously ornate and gilded. I stepped through, and found a very different world on the other side. The streets here were, if anything, brighter and cleaner than the rest, but there the similarity ended. Where the walls of plain, elegant houses had been before, vast windows of polished glass now stretched, each pane opening onto a different display of gowns, jewelry, fabric, sweetmeats, trinkets, silverware, glass, feathered hats, candles, mirrors, carpets, handkerchiefs, cosmetics, perfumes—in short, everything I could have imagined (and many things I couldn't). It was all for sale. The street rolled seemingly for miles and it was lined with sparkling, dazzling, painstakingly laid out, mouth-wateringly luxuriant *shops*. In front of each window was a group of people peering in, their eyes flashing with desire, from whom rose a hum of chatter, like the emanation of a bee swarm at a rhododendron bush, each insect buzzing happily to itself as it moved from blossom to blossom sipping the heady nectar. Each was dressed in elaborately ornate finery such as the courtiers had been wearing. So startling was the array of colors, so bright and vivid their hues, that for a moment I had to shade my eyes. It was glorious!

And bizarre. It was, after all, only hours since the city had been under attack from a massive goblin army. Now the great and the good were out shopping as if nothing had happened. And what shopping!

I moved among them, a thrill passing through me as I brushed between their stiffened silk skirts, their padded shoulders with golden epaulettes, their lace shirtfronts, ruffs, and cuffs, their sheer stockings and jeweled slippers. It was breathtakingly excessive, like rolling in money. It was as if the entire population of the town had spent the evening planning how to wear all their worldly assets. They had succeeded, too. If the purpose was to announce your value, I couldn't see how it could be done better, short of taking your annual income in silver, melting it down and making it into a hat. It looked like some of them had done that, too.

At one corner a line had formed, and at its head a small crowd of sophisticates were watching with interest, making delighted observations to their partners as people they knew appeared in the line.

I squeezed through the wall of satin and cambric to get a better view, and saw two small tables of wrought iron set outside the store front. At each sat a young couple, dressed as lavishly as everyone else and studiously ignoring the crowd which eyed them appreciatively from behind a single rope barrier some fifteen feet away. They seemed to be drinking from tall glasses of clear fluid, possibly water. I was bewildered. Then a man emerged from the shop and a hush you might call expectant fell on the spectators. He bowed to one of the couples and produced a velvet purse with a drawstring. He emptied this into the glass carafe on the table and the liquid glittered suddenly. The crowd sighed with pleasure and the couple, smiling at each other and continuing to act as if they were quite alone, poured and sipped. The crowd applauded politely.

"What did he put in the drink?" I asked of an elderly gentleman in a powdered wig. He peered at me through spectacles perched on the end of his nose with amused scorn.

"Gold," he said. "Obviously."

My mouth fell open. "Now that's what I call stylish," I said. Judging by the discreetly worded sign over the door, they brought their own gold to be ground on the premises.

"Would you care to sample some?"

"I'm afraid I'll have to pass," I said. He apparently thought this predictable. Another disdainfully minuscule smile twitched his thin lips.

"Quite," he remarked, turning away.

In other circumstances, this might have irritated me, but the place was so awash with color and splendor and, well, money, that I couldn't muster the appropriate indignation. On my right someone was selling ruby-studded hat pins and was making a fortune despite the fact that no one seemed to wear hats. Next to him was a jeweler selling delicate little cloisonné coats of arms filled with garnets, sapphires, and emeralds. It seemed that the buyers ordered them in advance according to the emblem of their house and then wore them on their collars. Another sold decorative badges shaped like flowers, made out of gold and silver wire and set with pearls like spots of dew. On the other side of the street, courtly lords and ladies gathered to watch portraits being painted of their acquaintances, who were dressed regally in fur and heavy gold chains. The jeweler next door was making a mint selling to those who would then have their pictures painted. I had never seen so many diamonds in my life: trays and trays of them in every size, cut, and carat you could imagine.

"Mined in the mountains not ten miles from here," said the jeweler, handing me a little magnifying lens and a velvet-lined box full of stones the size of buttons. "Cut expressly to the most discerning taste of our most demanding customer. Name the tincture, carat, purity and my staff can deliver what you want to the smallest detail."

"What I can pay for, more like," I said, giving him what was supposed to be a matey we're-all-men-of-the-world kind of grin.

"Indeed," he said, his obsequiousness curdling a little about the edges.

I wondered vaguely about buying something for Renthrette, but I couldn't afford even the diamonds you needed the magnifier just to see. I walked away, thinking derisively about Sorrail, who seemed to have bunches of the things lying around and could thus throw necklaces and pendants at her when she stepped into the palace. I remembered getting her a silver chain back in Graycoast and wondered if she still had it. Probably not.

Parked close by was a pair of wagons painted cream, ornamented with a purple trim, and hung with brass and gold fittings. Beside the wagons stood a stall where two men, one dressed in a full, velvet cloak, the other in a buff leather jerkin, sold scented soaps.

"The finest way to cleanse the softest skin," announced the man in the cloak in a high, nasal drawl. "Release the delicate fragrance of rose petals and jasmine as you bathe. Suffuse yourself with the aroma of luxury as you rinse the cares of the day from your hands. The highest quality natural ingredients made by the best perfumiers. . . ."

A cluster of women in taffeta conferred and began opening their purses. Soon they were sniffing admiringly and discussing how these were all the latest colors and featured a new range of shapes. A glance down the street, however, showed me that these two were only a small part of a convoy of such wagons all offering slightly different variations on the same theme, each proprietor attesting to their delicate perfumes, soft bubbles, and a dozen other qualities which left my head spinning. For someone whose approach to soap had been a reluctant encounter with a block of carbolic once a month, this was all pretty strange. But, as Garnet had told me, people here were pretty keen on soap.

Straight in front of me was a trim little stall where a trim little lady was selling trim little chocolate birds with what looked like real feathers in the tail. At first I was merely intrigued, but the elegant crowd who had already purchased her wares and now stood with rhapsodic looks on their faces and little poems of praise on their lips could not be ignored.

"How much?" I drooled.

"One silver piece," said the girl, with a doubtful look at my attire.

I paused, temporarily stunned. "A piece of silver?" I asked. "For a chocolate pigeon the size of a wren?"

"Vermilion hedge sparrows," she remarked with dry condescension. "Very rare. There are cheaper ones available from other vendors, but they are of inferior quality."

"They are indeed," agreed a lady to my left, who was daintily nibbling on a tiny area of wing tip. She was swathed in courtly, ultramarine satin fringed with lace and studded all over with pearls. Over her heart was a gilt-edged miniature of the king, which she wore as a broach. "Therahlia's were quite the thing last month, but these are *so* much finer," she said, then added amiably, "There is simply no one at her stall these days. It is thought that she will have to leave the market within the week! Ah, well, supply and demand, you know. Look at the detailing around the little creature's eyes! Superlative."

"Madame has exquisite taste," remarked the vendor. "These are specially handcrafted for the more discerning palate. Of course, if yours . . ." she began, turning to me.

"I'll take two," I said, fishing in my pocket.

"How very extravagant," said the courtly lady, catching me off guard with an admiring look that was almost erotic.

"I like the finer things in life," I managed.

"Indeed you do, sir," said the vendor, all trace of contempt evaporating like spit in a hot pan.

"Aren't you one of those Outsiders?" the lady asked, now sidling close to me provocatively and giving me a disarmingly direct look. She was a radiant creature with a sultry gaze that belied her pale skin. Large diamonds hung from her earlobes and her hair was gathered up to expose them.

"Well," I began, nonchalantly biting the head off one of my delicacies. I chewed for no more than a second and then it hit me. "Oh my God!" I spluttered, spitting feathers and chocolate onto the pavement. "What the hell is this?"

"Sparrows dipped in chocolate," she answered. "I thought you were familiar . . ."

"*Real* sparrows?"

"Naturally," inserted the vendor indignantly. "Did you expect some kind of substitute?"

"Oh, God," I repeated, spitting again, and trying to suck up the bits of dried bone and tissue already halfway to my gut.

"Really!" said the courtly lady, backing away from me rapidly, "your behavior is really *quite* inappropriate."

"Inappropriate?!" I spluttered between coughs that left dribblings of brown phlegm down my tunic. "Inappropriate? You give me chocolate-covered real dead birds and you think that vomiting them back at you is inappropriate? That is the single nastiest thing that has ever been passed off as food! God, I think I have a teeny piece of beak stuck in my tooth. What the hell are you people thinking?"

"My first instinct," said the vendor to the lady, "was that he lacked the refinement to appreciate sweetmeats of this quality. . . ."

"Mine, too," agreed the other, whose eyes had frozen over as if caught in a blizzard. "I don't know why they allow these people in."

And with that, she stalked pointedly away, though I was too busy hacking up bits of dirt-colored sparrow to take notice of her or the others who were looking me up and down with their noses wrinkled in distaste.

It's funny how one's enthusiasm for shopping can be dampened by a mouthful of chocolate-covered bird. The stores, whose excesses had formerly seemed so fresh and sparklingly inviting, a sumptuous feast for the eyes, a glorious display of wealth and good taste, were now merely excesses: grotesque and ridiculous. I traded my second sparrow for a thumbnail-sized tart with what looked like wafer-thin slicings of strawberry on the top. It was a beautiful little thing assembled with the skill of a goldsmith and the eye of a painter, and it tasted of absolutely nothing. I would have thrown it away but it had gone down in one swallow. Odd, really. The way everyone else was nibbling on them and extolling the "simply darling" subtleties of flavor, I began to wonder if I'd gotten a bad one. Maybe I hadn't paid enough.

"If you could take a piece of the sky," I remarked to the girl who had sold it to me, "and turn it into something edible, this is what it would taste like."

"They *are* wonderfully light, aren't they, sir," she agreed warmly. "Like a piece of the sky: a charming conceit! You have a most ready wit and a shrewd palate, sir."

"No," I said, "you misunderstand me. I don't mean it as a compliment."

She gave me a blank look.

"I mean," I persisted with overly slow clarity, "they have no flavor or texture. They have nothing that would make any sane person want to eat them, let alone spend a vast amount of money on them. I cannot say they taste like soap or excrement or chocolates stuffed with bits of bird, because they do not taste at all. They are a culinary vacuum and I have already wasted more words on them than they could ever deserve. You ought to sell something with a bit of bite. Try this, for example."

I produced a small piece of the blue cheese I had found in the woodland cave, wrapped in a thin leather cloth. "This is perhaps a bit bold for this place, but give it a try. This is a cheese with real character, a cheese to sample between sips of a dusty red wine, a cheese of boldness, sharp, but still warm, tangy but . . ."

I trailed off. As I pushed the cheese under her nose, her face had blanched first with distaste, then swelled to revulsion, and wound up in something oddly like fear. Her eyes flashed from the morsel of cheese to my face. I cannot imagine what she saw there, but it seemed to fill her with dread. She backed away, staring at me with her hand over her mouth, then began to run, sobbing as she fled.

Passersby eyed me with hostile curiosity. What had I done? I tried to shrug and smile reassuringly at the faces turned toward me, but this—not surprisingly—didn't help. Maybe I still had chocolate sparrow bits on my shirt.

I made for the library. At least there I wouldn't feel like some absurd fish flopping about on the floor. There I could lose myself in a good book or six. Even a bad one would be better than trying to blend in with these people. It had been an odd day. But as I have learned to remind myself, things can always get worse.

SCENE XIV

The Plot Thickens

I didn't bother trying the main door to the library, but went straight to the side entrance. The door opened as easily as it had before, though a key had been pushed into the lock from the inside, as if someone had tried to lock it without realizing that the mechanism was rusted away. The writing table had been pushed back up against the second door, but it yielded as it had done before and I was in before you could say "minimum security."

"Aliana?" I whispered, with the hushed reverence I reserve for libraries. There was no answer. I walked around a great case of medical books and peered at the main entrance, but there was no sign of her or anyone else, so I wandered through the aisles of piled and shelved volumes, wending my way back to the drama stacks. I settled here and randomly plucked a book from the shelf behind me.

"*The Tragical History of Shatrel, Lord of Dambreland, and the Horrid Revenge of Benath Kazrak,*" I read aloud. "Sounds good to me."

And so I settled and read under the pale, glowing dome for an hour. But when I reached the fourth act, with Shatrel's demonic machinations in full swing, the thing ended abruptly. There were thirty pages missing, cut out at the spine with a knife or scissors. I cursed quietly to myself and replaced it in the shelves. The next one I selected got a careful examination before I started reading, and this produced a curious discovery: The play's final pages were intact, but much of the second act was missing, cut out like the conclusion of the other play. I took down a pile of books and flicked through them. Over half of them had some pages missing: a couple missing only three or four pages, some lacking a good deal more, one being reduced to no more than a dozen leaves.

I put them back and sat pensively. This was not the result of decay, neglect, or the passage of time. These books were not accidentally burned, nor had their pages fallen out of rotted bindings or been casually torn out by owners who needed a piece of scrap paper. These had been rigorously and systematically mutilated. To someone like me who had seen similar work done by the Diamond Empire in Thrusia, this could mean only one thing: censorship. But of what and by whom?

I often find that I think better on my feet, so I rose and began to pace the library floor. It was a large building and I had seen only a fraction of it. Since there didn't seem to be anyone about, this seemed as good a time as any to see what else was there while I mulled over recent developments.

I saw it like this: Long ago, Phasdreille was the center of a glorious civilization and it produced much that was fair and wonderful to behold. The city architecture by itself would have been ample evidence of this, but so was the literature I had been reading and the paintings I had seen in the king's palace. In more recent years, however, something of the fire that had inspired the "fair folk" had gone out. What I saw now was a society devoid of passion and intensity except in their understandable hatred for the goblins: a society ruled by fashion and ostentation, by the shallowest performance and superficiality. In such a culture, even the great literary products of its past could be considered scurrilous and disreputable. So the good people of present day Phasdreille had opted to rid themselves of what they now considered degenerate.

It sounded right to me, but the real test would be to turn up some local history books and see what had happened to create this shift in attitude. Perhaps it was the appearance of the goblins themselves? With this in mind, I began to climb the stone-balustraded spiral staircase that coiled up to a great gallery which skirted the dome. It was lined with books and doors into other, darker rooms. Since I wasn't finding the books I had been looking for I began trying the doors. A few were open but led to tiny storage rooms with empty crates and boxes. The rest were locked.

I suppose some part of me had always known this, but my few months adventuring had driven the point home: The best doors are always locked, and how much you want to get into a room is directly proportional to how difficult it is to do so. Tell a child he can go in any room but the one at the end of the dark corridor and, as all good storytellers know, that's where he'll want to go as soon as he's left alone in the house. The same is true of romantic conquest, I suppose: forbidden fruit, and all that. This I offer as explanation for using my handy fruit knife (which hadn't seen much fruit lately) to throw the tumblers in the lock of one particularly interesting-looking door.

It was bigger than the others, heavy and studded with square-headed iron nails that were now quite black. The handle was a great iron ring that hung stiff and heavy, and the lock was old, purposeful but far from intricate. After no more than a couple of minutes probing and twisting in the massive keyhole, something turned over and fell back. Breathlessly, I twisted the ring and pulled. The door opened.

Inside it was gloomy, but I could make out a short flight of stairs and then, as I cautiously ascended them, what seemed to be a large room. No, not large, cavernous. It extended back a hundred feet or more and was about a third of that in width. It was lit by tall, narrow windows with leaded and stained glass depicting heroic scenes. All along the walls were bookcases and desks and boxes and piles of papers. I approached the nearest table and looked at the manuscripts arranged neatly on its top.

There was a pile of books of poems by a single author by the name of Brontelm, all of which seemed to be missing pages as the plays downstairs had. Beside the book, however, was a stack of paper. My heart jumped as I guessed that these were the excised pages. They would show me what the city authorities deemed so offensive that the library had to be decimated. I sat down and began to read eagerly, instantly realizing that the entire collection consisted of love poems. Censored love poems! This ought to be good.

My enthusiasm was unmerited. I got through the first ten sheets and stopped. I had read a dozen different poems about haughty mistresses, dark ladies whose crystal eyes shot death to their lovers' hearts, cherry lips which breathed jasmine flowers, and variations on the usual courtly love twaddle, and found nothing to offend, nothing racy or provocative. I had read Thrusian guides to grammar and pronunciation with more erotic content.

My gaze strayed to a box beside the table. In this were heaped other tomes, pamphlets, and books of various sizes and types, all still, all irreverently discarded, covers torn off, pages splayed and disheveled, crumpled and ripped. Given the care with which the books were preserved elsewhere, this seemed strange, so I plucked one out of the crate to see if I could figure out what it was that made it little more than refuse. It was written in some unintelligible language full of curls and dots and trailing lines like feathered tails, graceful but strong and forthright so that I found myself wishing I could read it. I carefully replaced the book in the box, but when I looked at the other boxes arranged around the room, a troubling pattern emerged. Every book bore the same graceful and unreadable script, and they were, it was clear, the sad remnants of a great many volumes. The boxes were grouped around a central hearth with a broad chimney which was blackened and choked with ash but quite cold, allowing me to paw through the cinders in the grate. I found the corners of pages and bindings, badly burned, but all showing the same beautiful, unintelligible script.

Libraries are not places you tend to associate with book burning. I supposed it was possible that the piles of mutilated manuscripts could have been infected with some parasite and had to be destroyed to preserve the rest of the collection, but it was bloody odd that every text in the other language had been set aside to be torched. I had seen none of these books in the halls downstairs, and only those in Thrusian seemed to have been painstakingly edited. It seemed clear that everything in this other tongue was being systematically rooted out and destroyed, but why? Maybe those who could read them were all dead, but could knowledge of a language die so completely that its literature was of absolutely no use to anyone? In this extensive library was there no grammar or lexicon to those feathery traces, nothing to make it worth keeping them?

Among the dead embers I found some pages printed with the cursive script that were less badly damaged than the others, and I took them, folding them into the pocket of my jerkin. I left the room quietly, and, in a few minutes, was able to click the lock on the heavy oak door into place. They would never know I had been there, whoever "they" were.

Well, they wouldn't unless they saw me standing around like the lingering ghost of someone who, well . . . did a lot of standing around. Sorry, but my mind was too preoccupied with the sound of footsteps on the stairs to waste time thinking up suitable similes. I came to myself and moved quickly, running on tiptoes around the gallery. On the far side of the dome was an archway and a corridor, but until I got there I was completely exposed. The banister around the gallery was made up of slim stone posts with a top rail and it afforded me no cover whatsoever. As I looked hastily around, two blond men reached the head of the stairs. I froze where I was.

They were each carrying a stack of books, leaning back slightly with their chins holding the tops of the piles to their chests. I caught a few muttered words from the sides of their mouths, but they were too preoccupied with managing their burdens to turn around and notice me. I started, very carefully, to move again, and stepped behind the cover of the great marble arch. From there I peered back while the men opened the door to the great room I had just left and disappeared inside. But any hopes I had of nipping out and down the steps were dashed as another pair appeared on the stairs, weighed down with books like the others. I ducked back into the arch and began to pace quietly down the corridor, trying to get away from all this officious activity. As I left the dome behind, the light lessened, but it was still bright enough to make out the doors set into the walls on either side and the larger, bronze-faced doors at the end.

These were set with intricately cast panels polished to a high golden luster, each seeming to show the construction stages of a great building which emerged from behind scaffolding in the topmost frames. Amidst the scenes of its great halls was a panorama of the structure from outside, and in the center of its roof was a broad dome, crawling with laborers. It was the library I now stood in. I put one hand on the handle to try it, and pulled it away hurriedly. It was warm.

I tentatively put the flat of my palm against another bronze panel. That, too, was almost hot to the touch, and throbbed faintly as if blood coursed through the metal and timber door. I was now conscious of a faint hum emanating from within, as if a swarm of bees had settled on the other side. But it wasn't just a sound. I felt suddenly dizzy, disoriented, and when I stepped back, my head swimming, I had to reach out to the walls to steady myself. I found myself leaning on one of the corridor's side doors. As I released my weight onto it, it opened suddenly.

I fell forward and collapsed on the floor. For a second I lay there, confused, then I rolled onto my back and found myself looking up at the long, graceful legs of Aliana.

She squatted down close to me, her face expressionless.

"What are you doing, Mr. Hawthorne?"

"There's a fire, I think, in the room at the end of the hallway. I felt it through the door."

She looked at me for a second and then got hurriedly to her feet. "The brass-paneled doors over there?" she said, stepping past me into the corridor and pointing.

"Yes," I answered getting to my feet. "I'm not sure, but I touched the doors and I felt something. . . ."

She had approached the doors and put her face close to them. Suddenly she turned back toward me and she was moving quickly.

"You're right," she said hastily. "I can smell the smoke, too. That is one of our largest storage areas. We must raise the alarm or we could lose the whole building."

And then she was marching away. I followed her out of the corridor into the dome gallery where she started shouting for assistance. The book carriers appeared, looking apprehensive and startled.

"There's a fire in the main storeroom," Aliana called. "You two, get everyone out of the building. Mr. Hawthorne, that includes you. The rest of you, help me get some water up here and we'll see how much we can save."

So much for my sneaking about. So much also for my claims to heroism. Here I was being turfed out like someone's elderly mother-in-law while others more capable looked to the valiant defense of the library.

"I can help, too," I began.

"No," said Aliana firmly. She gave me a quick look and added in a gentler, but still urgent, tone, "You are a guest of the king and I will not have you come into unnecessary danger. Please. Let us handle this."

"All right," I shrugged. "But be careful."

She gave me a long, strange look as if caught completely off guard, then moved rapidly back to where the blaze was raging, without another word or a glance back.

I was ushered down and out. Once in the streets, I ran around the building looking for signs of the conflagration. There was a pall of smoke over the building, but it was hard to see how much of it came from the various chimneys that peeped discreetly from around the dome. I caught a passing guard and told him of the fire and he ran to contact the appropriate authorities. I sat around to watch.

A few minutes later a horse-drawn cart with a great tank on the back drew up and a group of uniformed men with axes and pails alighted and entered the building. After that, nothing.

Time passed and the firefighters emerged, apparently none the worse for their labors. I watched them leave and then returned to the door through which they had come.

Aliana was there. "I thought you'd still be here," she said.

"I'm glad to see you unharmed," I replied.

"It was a minor affair," she said, still not inviting me in, "but it could have been much worse had you not reported the blaze as quickly as you did, though you should not have been here at all." She looked at me from beneath lowered brows, but the reprimand was almost playful.

"Sorry," I said. "But at least I was of use."

"Indeed," she replied. "Much of what was damaged was old binding material scheduled for disposal anyway, but it could have spread disastrously. We have had a narrow escape."

"Narrow enough to justify my asking you to join me for dinner?"

"What?" she asked, caught off guard again.

"Dinner with me. As a kind of reward. For me, I mean. There are a few things I'd like to talk to you about."

"Like what?"

"The battle for one," I said. "And the library. So what do you say?"

"Well, I don't know," she said. She seemed confused, as if this had never happened to her before. "I will have to think about it," she concluded.

"Fair enough," I said.

She smiled and began to close the door. "Farewell, Mr. Hawthorne. Till next time."

"Till next time."

So I hadn't lost all my charm, I thought to myself wistfully. Progress, of a sort, had been made. It was only a matter of time before she succumbed, and if that didn't get Renthrette's goat I was a pickled fish. Which I'm not. This return to erotic possibilities, however distant, suddenly reminded me of how I had heard of the library in the first place.

I fished in my pocket and drew out the letter which Renthrette had brought and read to me. Since I had never actually finished reading the thing, I unfolded it and looked it over. Being unused to love letters, especially *courtly* love letters, I was unsure of what to make of it, which was probably why I had all but forgotten about it. Of course, part of me was excited that there was someone here, someone pretty sophisticated and elegant, if her diction and perfume were anything to go by, who was apparently interested in me. This very elegance and sophistication constituted, however, a pretty major stumbling block for someone as out of his depth in the king's palace as I was. I could fake it a bit, from time to time, and I had as quick a brain as most or all of them, but I didn't have, and didn't want, the training in insincerity. This courtly verse and delicate verbal sparring bored the pants off me (and if that isn't the most inappropriate figure of speech ever invented, I don't know what is), and I wasn't about to work at getting it right for weeks so that some gorgeous tart in silk and rubies could reward me by presenting me with a scarf for me to wear in my hat, or whatever the hell they did round here in place of sex.

But I could not pass up female attention, however odiously it was versified, so I read the rest of the note. After that stuff about the play and the rather promising references to kisses and heaving breasts, it got down to the serious business of courtly metaphor. My eyes ran over two pages of rare stones, phoenixes, swans (and other—so far as I could tell—unchocolated fowl), sighs like clouds (hers), glances like javelins (mine), and a host of other tedious stock allusions. It was as if my self-proclaimed admirer had been locked in a small room for five years with nothing to eat but the most aristocratic of love poems, something far from unlikely around here. The second to the last paragraph, however, promised more than Renthrette had spotted or chosen to reveal, though I had long since quit trying to read something hopeful into her foiling of my amorous adventures. It ran as follows:

Be but at the gatehouse beyond the bridge as twilight falls and my coach will sweep us into such sweet bliss that angels will pause in their celestial music and sigh that only mortals could partake of such earthly rapture. For as the bluebird spies out her mate as night comes on and twines with him in flight, so will my hand seek yours and joy will bear us into heaven where lovers sing by the light of . . .

And so on, and so on. You get the picture. But, you must admit, it wasn't a bad picture, once you got past all that literary throat-clearing. All that intertwining birds business (what exactly is the fascination with birds in this town, anyway?) may promise no more than hand-holding, but either there was a spark of fire there that could light a real inferno, or I'm no judge of writing. I only wished my eloquent seductress had spent less time on similes and more on concrete arrangements. I mean, twilight is not very specific as a time for a rendezvous goes, and no particular day had been mentioned. Would she patrol the gates in her coach, sighing little love clouds out the window for the rest of the week, or what? Well, there was only one way to find out. As the proverbs say: Nothing ventured, nothing gained, and he who hesitates is likely to wind up spending the night by himself. Call me a hedonist, call me an irresponsible seeker of pleasure, a libertine, and a degenerate. While you do so, I'll be at the gatehouse waiting for a coach to take me to heaven by the fastest route I know.

A fast route, no doubt, but not one I had traveled in some time. Or that much at all, to be honest. This was a consequence of spending most of my first eighteen years in a dress (on stage, you understand) and the next with a bunch of high-minded adventurers who lived to denigrate my moral character. I needed to get into the right mood, and—if I didn't want to stifle my would-be lover—a clean shirt.

One problem with my scheduled assignation, of course, was that it meant wandering around the city after dark. The last time I had done that I had almost fallen victim to every assassin in the region. I wasn't going to put myself in that predicament again. The solution had already occurred to me, though: I would leave early, while it was still light—well in time for my assignation—and come back in the morning. This would mean being so irresistibly charming that my romantic correspondent would keep me closeted with her until daybreak, but surely I could manage that? Given my recent track record, it was a plan almost certainly doomed to failure, but I might be able to use the threat of my certain death if I returned to the city after dark as a way of keeping me enveloped in my beauteous lady's piteous bosom.

It never really occurred to me that she might not be beauteous. The fancy writing oozed sophistication and style, and all the courtiers I had seen thus far had been real lookers; in fact, I think they pretty much had to be real lookers in order to be courtiers, if you know what I mean. Everyone in the palace was so preoccupied with their appearance that you just couldn't imagine them daring to pass the time of day with any vile or misshapen old crone, assuming that the city of the fair folk even had the odd misshapen crone. I suppose I should have been outraged by this, but Garnet and Renthrette, who were usually pretty easy to outrage, would slit the throat of anyone who breathed a critical word about the court. If they thought it was all good and moral and wonderfully principled, how bad could it be? However much they played it down, of course, Garnet and Renthrette were attractive people themselves, in a chill and dangerous kind of way, and maybe this unspoken awareness made the exclusion of ugliness from the palace more acceptable to them. Maybe being part of the in-crowd of the court (and I had no doubt that they were part of that crowd now that Garnet was charging around heroically slaying goblins and Renthrette was drifting about in silk and jewels courtesy of the noble Sorrail) had dulled the edge of their righteous indignation. I don't know. However superficial all this devotion to beauty and the socially decorous might prove to be, I could see the upside: It would not be a vile and misshapen crone picking me up in her coach.

Then Garnet arrived and spoiled things. The only thing scarier than a hostile Garnet is a happy Garnet, because the things that cheer him up would make any sane person run screaming for cover. He strode into my room positively beaming and, more to the point, armed to the teeth. He was cradling his polished helm with its frightful steel mask and great horns in the crook of one arm, and his other hand was rested on the head of the immense axe pushed into his belt.

"Quick, Will!" he shouted unnecessarily. "We leave in ten minutes."

"We?" I asked, guardedly. "What do you mean, 'we'? And where are you going dressed like a grave statue anyway?"

"To battle!" he roared, his mouth wide and his eyes flashing. "And I have procured a horse for you."

"We're going to rescue Orgos and Mithos?" I asked.

"What?" he said, and there was that vagueness in his eyes again, but only for a moment. "No," he said. "Not now. That is already in hand."

"What does that mean?" I said.

"It's taken care of," he said. "We have another mission."

"Which is?"

He sat down hurriedly and spoke in an earnest, hushed tone. "The enemy who attacked the city have fled into the forest, but several of their foul companies have been spotted in the hills north of the city. Our scouts have reported that a large infantry unit has settled there and is probably awaiting orders to assault Phasdreille again. Their cavalry and the beasts they use are stationed elsewhere. If we wait for them to attack they will have a vast force composed of every type of soldier available to them. Right now, they are at a disadvantage. Several, in fact. They have not fully regrouped since their last assault and are missing anything resembling cavalry. They also aren't aware that we know their location, and their camp is poorly defended. We can strike fast and with minimal risk. Last time my service was scant. Today my sword will spill whatever goblins have in place of blood.

"You are here as my friend, Will. Now you must prove yourself true and valorous. Show the noblemen that your heart is stout and your weapon keen as your wit. Gird your loins, polish your sword, and leave your crossbow behind, for you will not need it. This is war, not a paltry trading of shots. We will go with sword and shield and helm and worthy steeds that will make the air sing with their strides. We will rain down upon these goblin filth like a storm god, and we will drive them from our land in a tide of their own blood."

See what I mean? To Garnet, loin-girding (what does that even mean?) and blood tide is picnic-in-the-meadow stuff, fun for all the family and a good time had by all. The more sharp bits of metal are flying around, the better he likes it, and these goblins had given him his absolute favorite thing in the whole world. moral clarity. And, in truth, it was kind of infectious. The idea of charging around with a bunch of honorable and well-equipped troops mowing down goblin scumbags armed with sticks suddenly sounded quite appealing, particularly once I'd reminded myself that if the opposition looked tougher than Garnet seemed to expect, I could always ride back, honor tarnished but hide intact.

And so, in a matter of minutes, there I was, sitting astride my worthy steed, my loins girded (I think), the reins gripped tightly in my shield hand while my leather-gauntleted right hand strayed uneasily to my sword hilt. I felt stupid, but I also felt the excitement and surety of victory of those around me, so I looked up proudly and tried not to feel like a fraud.

There was a company of fifty of us, horsemen all, mustered in the vast, pale courtyard before the palace. Sorrail rode at the head, clad in silver mail and brandishing a lance. Around him clustered Gaspar and several of the other prominent courtiers, all decked out for battle, their silken dalliance now barely conceivable as they spurred their horses and eyed their blades critically. Ladies and servants watched approvingly from the steps where Sorrail had greeted us on our arrival into the city. A woman in ultramarine taffeta strode forward and passed a veil or handkerchief to one of the riders. He kissed it ostentatiously and bound it to his wrist. Garnet, still beaming, cantered toward me as the horsemen fell into ranks of four and began to move off. My horse lurched as we began moving, but I stayed on.

Garnet, who lived for this kind of thing, raised his axe in the air and bellowed. I winced with embarrassment, but such displays were apparently considered acceptable to this crowd. Soon the courtyard rang with courtiers shrieking their valor and masculinity. I tried to smile away my fear and attempted a halfhearted cheer, but if anyone else was convinced, I certainly wasn't.

We passed through the city, whose streets were lined with admiring and encouraging faces, out of the inner gates, over the bridge, and through the main gatehouse. Our column veered north, moving swiftly through mown wheat fields and meadows of long, brownish grass, and Garnet talked about how he was going to win glory by killing thousands of goblins singlehandedly. I was amazed he didn't send the other forty-nine of us home so he could do the job by himself. Yet the company was part of it. He loved to be surrounded by like-minded men, all ready to show their skill and strength for a good cause. At one point he turned to me and said, "With these things you can smell the evil. You can see it in their eyes, in the shape of their limbs, in the malice scribed at birth into their faces. They are creatures of darkness, creatures of hatred and resentment. With each one you kill you can feel the world weeping with gratitude."

The words were strange, of course, especially from the usually taciturn Garnet, but I knew what he meant. I had seen them boiling around the city walls and I had tasted the righteous indignation he felt. I wondered if this was what people felt when they fought what they call a "holy war." By the time the camp was in sight, I had drawn my sword and set my teeth, almost as eager as my companions to encounter the enemy.

The fight, when it came, was short and glorious. We plowed through their camp before they really knew we were there. Those we did not kill instantly scattered in a rout before us, fleeing into the hills like geese with clipped wings. There were almost a hundred of them to our fifty, but they were thin, disheveled creatures with poor weapons and poorer spirits, and the sight of us bearing down upon them filled them with a shrieking terror so that they fled confusedly. We broke into two lines and funneled the stragglers into the center where they could not flee. For a few minutes, they fought desperately. Most of them could barely reach us, towering as we were on our saddles, so some took to hacking and stabbing at the horses until several fell.

I killed two goblins. One, a spindly fellow in gray rags brandishing a stick with a rock tied to the end, rushed into my sword point in a desperate charge. The other, a heavier creature with olive skin and deep-set, malignant eyes, stood his ground when he realized he could not flee. I charged my horse at him and plowed him underfoot before he could time his spear thrust. One of our men fell to a javelin thrust, but that was our sole casualty.

When we left the field, it was littered with the corpses of fifty-five goblins. The rest of their unit had completely dispersed. I felt utterly invigorated. Once the battle had begun, my fear left me and I never felt threatened or in serious danger. We were—as Garnet had said—like storm gods, unassailable, righteous, and potent beyond imagining. It was a good feeling.

We returned to the city as heroes. Women cheered and blew kisses and men applauded, promising to be with us next time. Garnet slapped me on the back and told me I had done well. His arm had been gashed by a goblin cleaver, but it was, he said, a minor injury. And the goblins had lived, but briefly, to regret doing him harm. Then he laughed and cheered with the rest. We were taken into the palace for a banquet, apparently the customary end to such raids. All damaged weapons, including my sword, which had been notched near the tip when I killed that first goblin, were collected and sent to the smith for reforging.

Here I made my excuses. Garnet was surprised that I did not want to indulge in this part of the proceedings, but he was also clearly impressed by the fact that I would fight and then not wait around to be wined, dined, and praised. His admiration, however problematic, came in my direction rarely, so I said nothing of my proposed rendezvous with the mysterious court lady.

Instead I bathed, dressed, and picked over the colorful, dainty, and tasteless morsels set aside for my private supper and went out, leaving the world of the palace behind. It was still light outside and the sky was pale and blue. The wind was fresh, and the city's towers, columns, and graceful, curving walls looked—it has to be said—astonishingly lovely, like something out of an old tale.

Well, so much for that. I had more immediate adventures on my mind. I crossed the scattered bridge where the goblins had led their feint and found workmen studying the small spots of damage where catapulted stones had chipped and cracked the masonry. Unlike the burly and rude types who labored on the streets in Cresdon when someone finally decided it was worth doing repairs, these men were as tall, slender, and clean as the guards, shopkeepers or, for that matter, the

courtiers. They were strong, no doubt, in that understated but powerful way that the men of their race seemed to have, but they looked
more like bakers than builders. They wore long tunics of a pale, sandy
color and stood around looking grave and doing, to my mind, very
little. At the far end I came upon some spots that had already been
repaired and noted the pretty shoddy job the workers had apparently
done. The stone blocks that had been shattered by the impact of the
monster had just been packed back into the crater in the wall, and one of
the laborers was in the process of painstakingly plastering over the damage. The finished job looked just about perfect, but the wall was structurally no stronger than before the "repair." Were they so short of
materials that they could not do a better job? Were they expecting another assault imminently and merely wanted to cheat the goblins into
thinking that the walls were as solid as they had been?

I approached the wall and looked closer, still riding a wave of confidence after my excursion with the cavalry. Almost immediately one
of the masons came over to see what I was doing.

"Just looking at the repairs," I said, lamely. "Rushed job, was it?"

He gave me an odd look and shook his head.

"It just looks," I said, "a little, well, flimsy. No. I don't mean
flimsy, exactly. I mean, well, I'm not sure. Not as strong as the rest."

"We have used a slightly different technique," the mason said, unoffended, "but the wall is as strong as when my great-grandfather first
hewed and shaped the stone which was laid as the foundation of this
structure. You see those columns by the gate? He carved those himself
with nothing but a chisel and mallet. He worked until his hands bled, refusing to rest until the job was done to the best of his ability. The intricacy of their carving is unmatched and, a hundred years later, they are
still as straight and flawless as the day they were finished. Since then the
goblin armies have broken upon this fortress like waves against cliffs and
it stands still. He taught the trade to my grandfather who taught it to my
father and my father taught it to me. This hammer," he said, hefting the
steel tool thoughtfully, "has been passed down through our family since
the days of my great-grandfather, who used it to shape these stones and
cut those pillars. We set a diamond into its handle to remember him
by, see? You need not worry about the strength of the walls."

I thanked him for his insight and moved on hurriedly, wondering
at how quick people here were to give you personal history lessons.
Beyond the barbican was a broad, paved road which skirted the edge

of the city in what looked like a circle. Presumably it led somewhere other than simply round the badly patched walls of Phasdreille, but I had heard so little about the immediate environs that I could not begin to speculate where it might go. When I met my secret assignation, would I be led into the city? And, if not, what else was there round here other than the forest, which was the domain of goblins and dead friends?

A coach drew up as I was mulling this over. My heart leaped and I tried to look conspicuous. It was drawn by a pair of white mares with red ribbons plaited into their manes and tails. A slender white hand parted the curtained window and stretched out, dangling a flounce of red-tasseled silk: a handkerchief, perhaps. Was this a sign for me? I faltered uncertainly. The coach and its offered invitation remained where they were. I took a hesitant step and then, quite out of the blue, a gentleman appeared from the bushes at the bridgehead. He wore a small mask spangled with glittering stones and a pale coat with forked tails and hemmed with gold. He strode up to the coach, took the handkerchief and stepped back as the door swung open in admittance. He climbed up and disappeared inside. The door clicked shut and the coach rattled away.

As it trundled out of sight I looked back to where the stranger had come from. Around the barbican grew dense laurel bushes and a scattering of sculpted bay trees. If I was not mistaken, these bushes were alive with casually hidden courtiers. Indeed, now that I looked, they weren't really hidden at all. Any attempt at concealment was purely token and, while they all wore elaborate masks, there was a similarly minimal effort to actually hide their identity. Clothes are expensive, and even a wealthy courtier can only run to a few suits of the kind of luxuriance that these blokes sported, so I could recognize several of them at a glance. One of them had been one of the principal players in the love debate we had witnessed while waiting to meet the king, and another had ridden with us earlier in the afternoon.

After another few minutes a different carriage rolled up and stopped. A lady's satin glove was dropped non-chalantly by the cloaked driver, and a masked dandy emerged from the shrubbery, returned it to the invisible lady inside, and was admitted. The whole thing took no more than thirty seconds. Then they were off to whatever prearranged pleasures they had in store—though whether this would consist of more than courtly wordplay, I could not guess.

For about a half hour this bizarre pantomime went on. Coaches would draw up, display their appointed signs, and collect their respective gallants. Passersby seemed used to the huddle of half-hidden lovers awaiting their trysts and would occasionally stop to chat with one or more of them. More often, however, they would simply watch from an admiring distance. On several occasions the masked courtier would make a courteous bow to the audience before climbing into the carriage. This invariably produced a little smattering of applause from those around, including those halfheartedly ensconced in the shrubbery.

Apart from bewildering me utterly, this strange sequence of events also raised a serious question in my mind. Since this seemed to be the official marketplace of love, how was I to recognize my designated lady? If there had been any mention of some significant token that would identify her, I couldn't remember it, and even if she stuck her head out of the window, I wouldn't recognize her. Perhaps she would hang a board with my name in big letters from the window, or the driver would lean over and bellow, "Hawthorne, you're on next." I feared I would get little applause from the crowd for that and, since I had neither mask nor sumptuous attire, it seemed I was going to get precious little in the way of panache points.

At that point two courtiers accidentally came out for the same carriage but, after careful inspection of the workmanship of the proffered signet ring, one of them politely retired with much bowing and scraping, for which he got a round of consolation applause. I was close to abandoning the whole farcical escapade when a canopied two-wheel buggy, stylish but probably quite fast, drew to a halt at the edge of the road. The curtain above the half-door stirred slightly and a white hand emerged. It was holding an envelope.

I looked about me, but no one else seemed to be claiming this one. I took a deep breath and strode purposefully up to the vehicle with its single horse and driver. The eyes of the crowd followed me and I sensed their amusement. I felt awkward, like I'd stepped onto the stage knowing only half my lines or couldn't remember how the scene ended. As is always the case in such moments, the audience smelled my uncertainty and fed on it. A titter rippled through the crowd. I flinched but kept walking, hoping against hope that I wouldn't have the further humiliation of being turned away. My steps were halting, uncertain, quite different from the confident and balanced strides of the courtiers who had preceded me. I turned to find some masked fop emerging from the trees in a clumsy, limping gait, which was clearly offered as a parody of mine. The crowd lapped it up, chortling delicately and pointing from behind fans and hats.

If I get out of this, I thought, I'll show that poncing git what I thought of his joke. He was dressed in deep, glowing blue velvet trimmed with lace and wore a rapier in a jeweled sheath. I'll remember you, I thought, you clever swine. I'll remember you, and we'll see if you can use that sword as well as mince about with it. Knowing that he was probably quite the expert with the blade only made me angrier.

"Mr. Hawthorne?" came a low, female voice from inside.

"What?" I said. "Er, yes, that's me. I'm in then, am I?"

Not the most romantic speech I could have delivered, I know, but it seemed to do the trick.

"Climb up," she answered.

And suddenly I forgot the smirking, disdainful crowd. The voice was breathy, passionate, and sent my heart pounding. I did not need to be asked twice. I climbed in and didn't even think to flick some rude gesture at the crowd as we rattled away.

SCENE XV

❧

A Long-Awaited Meeting

For a second I sat quite silently in the gloom of the hooded carriage. The girl was sitting opposite me and, like the gallants I had been lining up with, she was masked. It was an odd mask, glittery and shaped like the beak of a bird. Though golden and studded with green stones, it was eerie looking and, in other colors, would have been quite sinister. She was pale and blond, but since that went for the entire non-goblin population of this land, it was hardly informative. She wore her hair in golden ringlets which broke around her shoulders and the lacy enticement of her neckline. Her dress was of a rose-colored silk adorned with frills and some small amethysts. Her necklace looked like silver and tiger's eye or some similar semiprecious stones. And, strangely enough—for in other circumstances I would have thought her way too good for the likes of me—I was a little bit disappointed.

In my old Cresdon haunt, the Eagle, a woman like this would have turned heads like hands on a clock. Had she walked up to the bar where I sat, cheating some poor idiot out of his meager wages, I would have gaped, stared and, quite possibly, drooled. But I was getting used to beauty, elegance, finery, and riches; I was not quite so easy to impress these days. Before, I would have turned on my best performance for the chance of an hour alone with any woman distinguished by a lack of contagious skin afflictions and a fair limb count, but now I expected radiant perfection. The girl, under her mask and silk, might well be it, but her jewelry clearly wasn't, and this, strangely, bothered me. She would not have passed muster in the king's palace thus attired, and there would have been snickerings and knowing glances at her amethysts and tiger's eye. Perhaps there were the makings of a courtier in me yet.

"You are very quiet, Mr. Hawthorne," she said. Her voice, as I had noticed when she first spoke, had that rich and breathy character that spoke of both naïveté and knowledge, of coyness and sensuality. I caught my breath, began to answer, and had to pause, swallow, and try again.

"I am not sure where to begin," I said, beginning. "You know my name, but I do not know yours, nor do I think I have seen you at court."

She smiled. That much I could see, since the mask left the lower part of her face uncovered. She had good, even, white teeth, but I was struck not by them but by how few times I had seen courtiers produce anything so genuine. Their smiles were controlled wrinkles of their lips, as if someone had threaded a fishing line through the corners of their mouths and then tugged it gently upward. Such smiles were amused or sardonic, but always restrained, and no one showed their teeth.

"My name is not important," she said, "and I am surprised you ask it."

"Is it not normal to introduce oneself before"—I faltered, realizing I had dug myself a hole—"er . . . before, driving somewhere together?"

She giggled at my clumsiness. It was, again, both endearing and uncourtly, perhaps endearing *because* it was uncourtly. I smiled despite myself, but my doubts grew.

"So do you read many plays?" I said.

This stopped her smile like I had smacked it with a large fish. "What do you mean?" she asked, her voice losing a little of the refined politeness it had managed thus far.

"You made reference to a play in your letter," I clarified. "Have you read many?"

"The odd one," she said, with no real effort to conceal the lie. She beamed again.

The odd one? This was not the same mind that had conjured all those phoenixes and clouds onto the pages of the letter. As she seemed to relax and grow more playful, I found myself growing uneasy.

"You're not from round here, are you?" she said, and a little more of that aristocratic hauteur fell away from her accent.

"Not exactly, no," I answered warily.

"You're so tense!" she exclaimed. "I won't bite, you know. What do you go by, Will or Bill?"

"Either," I said, cautiously. "Usually Will."

"Right then, Will," she announced. "Turn round and let me rub your shoulders."

She moved suddenly, leaning across the carriage and pulling my upper body toward her. Usually this would be a promising step, but now I flinched like I'd taken an arrow in the gut.

"You're very highly strung, aren't you Will?" she said, as I recoiled slightly from her touch. "Your muscles are all knotted up like bits o' rope."

I pulled myself back abruptly and caught her wrist. "So that's the fashionable courtly speech, is it?" I demanded. "*Bits o' rope?* You didn't write that letter."

"Yes, I did," she said, lying playfully again.

"No chance. You don't sound like a courtier, you don't dress like one, and I'll bet my last farthing that you can't write like one."

"What does it matter who wrote the letter?" she answered.

"So you didn't?" I pressed.

"No," she replied, a trifle sulkily.

I released her hands, waiting for more information. She folded her arms and sat in silence for a minute or so. Then, in what I took to be her own voice—it was devoid of courtly affectation and touched with some regional accent that was round and earthy—she said, "And you don't think I look like a courtier?"

Her tone was hurt, and this seemed so completely genuine that my suspicion momentarily evaporated and I had nothing but a kind of pity for her.

"Well, I haven't really seen you yet," I said, as kindly as I could in the circumstances.

"There!" she said, snatching the mask from her face. "Now you can see me."

She was quite beautiful. Her face was fuller than was the fashion at court and she held a slight rosiness in her cheeks which would have seemed too countrified for the city, but she looked real as few of the women in the palace had looked. I was caught by surprise.

"Well?" she demanded, pouting slightly. Even in the dull light I could see that her eyes were hazel, deep and darker than any I had seen in the city.

"You look wonderful," I said, honestly.

"But not like a court lady."

"Better than a court lady."

She looked at me quizzically, a childlike skepticism passing over her face. Then she smiled broadly again. "Good," she concluded. "Look, we are nearly there."

She moved the curtain and the light fell on her face. We had been traveling for some time and were now far from the city. Trees grew out of darkening fields and, in the distance, isolated stone cottages showed lights at the windows.

"Where are we?" I asked.

"Nearly there."

"Yes, but . . ."

She reached across and laid her finger on my lips. I fell silent and then decided that this would be a good time to kiss her. I had no idea who she was or what she had in mind for me when the coach stopped, but I could not believe she meant me harm. Well, I preferred not to. It was conceivable that she would slip a stiletto in my ribs or hand me over to someone else who would, but she was no goblin, even if she wasn't a courtier either. I contrived to get closer to her on the pretext of looking out of the window and then made the move. As my cheek brushed against hers she backed away: a small but decisive gesture.

"Wait till later," she said.

But there was something in her glance, or the way she averted it and stared fixedly out of the window, that told me beyond any doubt that there would be no "later." It was my turn to sulk. I suppose I should have been more concerned for my safety, but I was too busy being disappointed in that petty, self-involved fashion that I've cultivated so expertly over the years.

⁂

It was quite dark when the carriage drew to a creaking halt. I had long since lost track of which direction we were heading in. I was thus rather alarmed when I looked out and found the dark, irregular silhouettes of trees hanging over the road. We were on the edge of that vile forest.

"Where the hell are we going? I demanded, petulance muffling my growing fear.

"We are at an inn," said my companion. "Climb down and go

inside. I have to pay the driver. When you go in, go straight up the stairs at the back of the bar and wait for me in room four. It will be unlocked."

"Why don't I wait for you here?" I asked, suspiciously.

"Because we should not be seen going in together," said she, with that provocative little smile, which seemed to promise so much more than I was going to get. "That just isn't done."

She wagged her finger at me. As she fumbled for her purse and replaced her mask, she added, "Go on in and I'll join you presently."

I wanted to believe her, but as I got down and walked across the cobbled yard to where the small hubbub of the tavern emanated, I knew she wouldn't be coming up. I considered having a few beers—if they were any good—and then getting the first ride I could back to the city, but I was too frustrated to be so passive. I sensed no malice from her and I wasn't about to threaten the girl, partly because I doubted that she knew entirely what it was that was about to happen. The assassins had got to me in Phasdreille. There was no reason for them to arrange so elaborate a ruse to get me out here in the middle of nowhere. No; this was something different, and I felt a rising sense of caution touched with anticipation. I wanted to see who had gone to so much trouble to get me out here and why.

So I started to go in. But first I took one last look at the masked beauty in the carriage, who was making a show of sorting through some coins. I didn't expect I'd see her again and had almost decided to go back to say something romantic and significant when the carriage suddenly launched forward and, with a clatter of hooves, vanished into the darkness. Well, that was my ride gone.

So much for romance.

For a minute or two I just stood there, not surprised, but feeling sort of confused and pathetic anyway. Then someone came out of the pub pushing a dolly with a barrel on it and the decision was made. He gave me a curious look. Suddenly conscious of how strange it must seem to be standing around in the courtyard in the dark, I took a few purposeful strides, gave him a "good evening" kind of nod, and stepped into the inn.

The barroom was curious. It had more of the Cresdon bustle than the other inns I had seen since we were transported to wherever we now were. It was smoky and loud—not like the Eagle, you understand, but it certainly had more character than the Refuge or anything in Phas-dreille. The atmosphere cheered me. Maybe the beer would even be decent.

I made my way to the bar and ordered. At first I didn't notice, but the patrons were a surprisingly mixed bag. In place of the tall, pale, and blond aristocratic types I had grown used to, these were tall, short, fat, thin, pale, dark, brunette, redheaded—in short, just what you'd expect in the taverns of Thrusia. My heart skipped at the idea and a thought struck me: Perhaps I had crossed back, taken another mystical carriage ride back across the edge of reality, back to Stavis. Then I tasted the beer: the same straw-colored ditchwater as before. I was still here.

As if to emphasize the point, I turned and found myself gazing across the room to the foot of a narrow staircase made of plain wooden boards. I took a sip of my "beer," left the rest of it on the bar, and walked to and up the stairs quite calmly, almost as if I knew what I was doing. Room four was the second from the head of the stairs on the right. I knocked, and, when no one answered, pushed the door open.

A candle was burning inside. There was a rough-looking bed with an uneven mattress stuffed with straw, a deal table and chair, and a large water pitcher and bowl. On the table was a bottle of beer and two earthenware goblets. Nothing else. I walked in, closed the door behind me, and sat on the bed. Drawing a knife from my boot, I stared at the door to a large closet and spoke aloud. "All right, let's get on with it. I'm in no mood for games."

The door swung open. "Nor am I, Will."

It was Lisha.

She stood there, small and still, smiling slightly. I stared at her, my mouth open. Then, without thinking, I threw my arms around her and squeezed her hard. This was the last thing I had expected and suddenly it seemed that I had never been happier to see anyone.

"What the hell are you doing here?" I exclaimed.

"Waiting for you, obviously."

"You sent the letter?"

"Of course."

"Why?"

"First," she said, "tell me how you got to Phasdreille and which of the party you have seen."

I still had my hands fixed to her shoulders, and now—perhaps at the mention of the others—it was like I remembered who she was, and I felt awkward and overfamiliar. I let her go and took a step back, gesturing vaguely and looking shamefaced.

"It's good to see you," she said.

I nodded and looked at the floor.

She poured me a glass of the beer (better than that in the city, but not by much) and I told my tale—all of it: Sorrail, the fight in the cave, the loss of Orgos and Mithos, our failed rescue attempt, meeting Garnet in the city, and everything that had happened since. After I had finished, she sat in silence for a long time, her narrow eyes almost closed with thought. She was, as ever, small and girlish. Her skin was dark, brown as leather, and her hair was black and glossy as the feathers of a raven. Sitting there so small in the candlelight of this unfamiliar room I was reminded of when I had first met the much-touted party leader and how bewildered and disappointed I had been. That seemed like a very long time ago.

"But you have had no news of Mithos and Orgos since your encounter in the forest?"

I shook my head.

"You think they are? . . ."

"I don't know," I answered, quickly.

"And there has been no other attempt to rescue them since you reached Phasdreille?"

"Not that I know of," I answered, "though I wouldn't be surprised to learn they weren't telling me everything. I'm not the most popular person in the city."

There was another long silence between us, then she sipped her beer and I shifted in my seat.

"So you also met the ambassador," she said. "Strange. I came here in similar circumstances and around the same time, but I arrived alone. I made my way toward the White City, though I did not get that far. Passing through a village near the forest on the east bank of the river, I found that I was being followed. Soon there was a growing crowd behind me, whispering and pointing. I made for an inn but they overtook me as I went in and let me know that I was not welcome."

"What?" I exclaimed. "Why not?"

"It seems they thought I was some kind of goblin half-breed."

Jaws often drop on the stage, but rarely have I been so gob-smacked in reality. This was one of those rare occasions. I just sat there and Lisha said nothing. It didn't take long for the pieces to fall into place. I looked at her, so small and dark, with her black hair and her narrow, eastern eyes, and I was suddenly embarrassed.

"How could they think that you were like that filth just because you don't, you know, look the same as them?"

She shrugged fractionally and smiled her tiny, knowing smile.

"You haven't come across the goblins, though, Lisha," I said, try-ing to sound conciliatory. "I mean, I'm not saying that it's under-standable that they took you for one, but the people round here have pretty good reason to hate them."

"Perhaps," she said, regarding me thoughtfully.

"I mean it's terrible that they misjudged you, but if you knew these things, you'd see why they are so paranoid. It's more misreading than malice, you know?"

She sat quite still and said nothing for a long time. Then she sighed and said, "I don't know, Will. This place just doesn't feel right to me. I've had to skulk around the countryside wrapped up like a leper so that no one would challenge me on the assumption that I'm some kind of demon. Out here, where the people are a little more mixed, I can just about get by, but even here I have to stay in my room and pay double the usual rate to keep the innkeeper happy. I can't get anywhere near the city. That's why I had to bring you to me, without making myself visible.

"I heard of your presence in the city but I did not want to risk drawing attention to myself," she said. "Apart from the danger such exposure might put me in, it could also jeopardize the kind of recep-tion you have been getting. I chose a way that would reach you but wouldn't attract attention if the letter should . . . go astray. You were the obvious target because I doubted Garnet and Renthrette would roll with something so underhanded. I assume they've adjusted to the court rather better than you have?"

"Yes," I said. "Odd, really. I've always prided myself on being flex-ible, on being able to play any role I was given, while they've always seemed rigid, unbending, and intolerant of whatever seemed suspi-cious. I guess the palace doesn't seem suspicious to them."

"And you? Are you suspicious?"

"No," I said, quickly and without much thought. "I don't think so. There are strange things about the whole city, but I suppose you'd find that everywhere."

"I suppose," agreed Lisha, noncommittally.

"What are you thinking?" I pressed. "You think something is wrong?"

"Probably nothing. I'm just not sure of a few things. I told you that I have word from the city via some of the few people who will talk to me."

"Does that include the girl who picked me up?"

"Rose? Yes. She doesn't know anything about me, but she likes to talk, and I have learned much from her. She . . . has contact with some of the courtiers from time to time."

"You mean . . ."

"Outside the city, people are not so wealthy as in it. Much of what is made or grown out here goes into Phasdreille, and many of the laborers struggle to make ends meet. Rose, like many others, has found a way to bring in some more money. That way she can keep her family, and her children, respectably."

"Ironic."

"Irony is a luxury many cannot afford," she answered. I dropped my eyes a little, but she smiled. "Come now, Will. Before you came here, your hide was a good deal tougher. I suggest you thicken it again, if you can. It may yet prove invaluable. But that wasn't my point. Rose and others like her told me of the arrival of people they called Outsiders. When you first reached the city, you created something of a stir. It seems that these Outsiders have been expected for some time. And though their interest in you has strangely dwindled lately, your first appearance prompted a good deal of excitement and some anxiety. Your names were on everyone's lips for a day or so, and then, quite suddenly, you were forgotten. Garnet is now a horseman of the fair folk. Renthrette is a court lady often seen in the company of the much esteemed Sorrail. Will Hawthorne has vanished from sight and, it seems, from memory. Rose spoke of you several times when you first came to Phasdreille, but when I sent her to get you, she appeared to have no recollection of you. It is, as you say, odd."

"I guess I'm kind of forgettable." I shrugged.

"But that's the thing," she said. "You're not. You should stand out, because you're not like them. You don't look like them and you certainly don't think like them, so why have people stopped talking about you?"

"Maybe I'm just the wrong kind of different," I said.

She looked at me sharply, and then nodded, as if I had said something shrewd or profound. "There's also this attempt on your life," she continued. "I don't know, Will. It's all very strange. It sounds like two separate entities—one goblin, the other human—want you dead. The cloaked figure only intervened when it seemed that the goblins might spare you. Why do two groups who hate each other *both* want you dead? And then there's the Orgos apparition in the forest. Do you have any ideas?"

"Not really," I confessed. "The goblin said, '*I have no faith in prophecy, Mr. Hawthorne.*' Could our arrival have been foretold somehow? It might explain why there was such interest in us at first. Then when it turned out that we either weren't what was prophesied or that the prophecy was bollocks, or whatever—then they lost interest in us? I don't ordinarily believe in such things, of course. . . ."

"Of course." Lisha smiled dryly.

"But this place is crawling with things I didn't believe in, so I'm sort of at sea in a leaky kettle. Maybe there *was* some kind of prophecy that seemed to refer to us."

"And then it became apparent that you weren't the prophesied Outsiders after all," Lisha suggested.

"That's possible," I mused. "But maybe a few fringe groups still think we're worth killing just in case. The Assassins' Convention, which I seem to have walked in on, took place some time *after* we fell from grace in the eyes of the king."

"We need to find out more about this prophecy, if it exists," said Lisha, rising and starting to pace the room. "I wish we could get Garnet and Renthrette out of there. I worry that . . ."

"What?" I asked, since her voice had trailed off into nothing.

"I don't know," she said, unsure of herself. "It's just a feeling, an uneasiness. I don't like the idea of them getting too . . . *involved* with the court in Phasdreille."

"If you say the word," I answered with a dry and knowing grin, "they'll jump back into line like their tails are on fire and you have the only bucket of water in the world."

"I don't know, Will," she said, "but I hope so."

She sat down again and stared at the tabletop as if her mind was miles away.

"I wish Mithos and Orgos were here," I said suddenly. It was the first time I had said it, and I was rather surprised by it. It was as if my private anxiety had been skulking through the jungle of my head for days, always a few feet from the path I was on, and had chosen this moment to ambush me.

"I think they are still alive," she said, looking at me in that compassionate but penetrating fashion of hers which always made me feel like she'd walked in on me as I was getting out of the bath.

"Based on what?" I demanded. I hadn't intended to sound hostile, but I did not want to be patronized by groundless hopes.

"I just feel it," she said. "Or rather, I do not feel they have died."

"Why would you?"

"I don't know. Perhaps I wouldn't," she said. "But we have been together a long time and I think their passing might register in me somehow."

Her eyes held mine throughout this curious speech. I hesitated only a second.

"That is the stuff of stories, Lisha," I said. "Brothers, friends, twins, parents, and daughters all die daily, and their loved ones are none the wiser till some grim-faced messenger arrives at the door. I'd love to think we were all connected by some sort of spiritual bond, some connection, but I have seen no evidence for it, and plenty to the contrary. I don't believe it."

"You are right not to," she said. "I don't believe it either. I merely hope that it might be true. Wishful thinking, perhaps, but I feel it nonetheless."

I shrugged, unconvinced, and began feeling depressed as a result. She smiled a little, as if this endeared me to her or reminded her of something she liked in me. Though she was the one talking fancifully and I was the cynical realist, she managed to make me feel, as usual, like a child. I smiled again and she clasped my hand impulsively.

"I am glad you got here," she said. "I needed to hear a voice of skepticism in this curious place. But now you must go back. I cannot come with you, and I feel that some of our answers still lie in the city. I will move in what limited way I can and gather information from the few safe sources available to me, but I have no wish to be hounded to earth and executed as a goblin spy."

"Where should I begin?"

"With the prophecy, I suppose, though how you will go about that without putting yourself in danger, I do not know. Beware of trying to sour the city for Garnet and Renthrette too quickly. They may turn against you."

"Again."

"Quite. In fact," she added, "now that I think of it, it might be better if you don't tell them I'm here."

"You want me to lie to them?" I said, pleased by the idea.

"No," she insisted. "I just want you to keep what you know of my presence to yourself. For now."

I grinned. One day I would get some real mileage out of this, her trusting me over them. Still, it was unlike her to mislead her friends.

"I just think it might be for the best," she added. "For them, I mean. We'll tell them soon."

"We don't need to," I said.

She ignored that.

"Be careful, and bring me word through Rose," she said. "I will send her to the bridgehead gate two days from now and every day thereafter. If I can, I will come in the coach; otherwise, you should give her any letters for me that you have. I think she can be trusted, and I do not think she can read. Leave no writings in your quarters as long as you are in the palace. I hear the general practice of being a courtier involves a good deal of spying just to see who is on the way up and who on the way down and out. I have no doubt that servants are paid to bring stray letters to their masters. Don't get caught up in the factions of court life, Will. There are too many daggers in such places, and you can't protect yourself from all angles."

"It's a good thing we know who the enemy is," I remarked.

"Indeed," she said.

I spent the night on the floor of Lisha's room and left as close to first light as I could manage. I journeyed back to Phaadreille by means of the same carriage in which I had left, but Rose, alas, did not make the return trip with me. I arrived at about nine o'clock, passing the barbican sentries with a nod which they returned with the smiles of men who thought they knew what I'd been up to all night, and made straight for the palace and my room.

My sword had come back from the smith, but instead of the notched blade having been reforged, they had just cut the end off and then ground down what remained. It was now less a short sword than long knife. I was irritated enough to have a word with the nearest guard, who pointed me to the armory next door. I marched in like I owned the place, slammed the sword down on the counter, and asked what the hell *that* was supposed to be.

"It's a fine sword," said the duty officer.

"It *was* a fine sword," I said, "before you idiots chopped three inches off the end. Now it's a bread knife. Can't you make it like it was?"

"Longer, you mean?" said the officer, blankly. "How?"

"I don't know; I'm not the smith. Melt it down, add more steel, and beat it out again," I suggested. "Isn't that how these things work?"

The officer looked confused, but he went back into the forge. When he didn't come back after a couple of minutes, I went in after him. I noticed two things right away. The first was that, though the smithy was large, with several furnaces and anvils set up, there was only one person working, and all the other hearths were cold. In fact, they looked like they hadn't been used for ages. The second thing I noticed was the way that the smith in his leather apron studied the sword with the same blank look the duty officer had given me. These people were clueless.

"I could weld a setting for some diamonds to the hilt," said the smith, sauntering over, "or I can give you a new one."

"Oh," I said, taken aback and rather pleased. "Fine. Yes. I'll take a new one."

Since I seemed to be the only person in the city who didn't go about with a wheelbarrow full of diamonds, it seemed the smart choice.

He turned to a door and opened it. Briefly I saw beyond him and noticed rack upon rack of swords and other weapons. He drew one out, seemingly at random, and brought it to me.

It was, if anything, finer than the one I had broken, with a filigree patterning in the steel where it had been folded and reforged many times. I swashed it about in a professional sort of way, which seemed to satisfy the smith.

"I'll take it," I said.

So I was feeling pretty good about myself as I made for the library.

Things had gone without a hitch thus far. I was beginning to feel as smooth as a greased otter when I got to the side door of the library and found it closed and guarded. I paused in the long morning shadows of the colonnade that ran along the sides of the square and considered my next move, while trying to look like I was out on a morning stroll. Not that anyone round here ever went on strolls. It was all lolling about spouting poetry or charging into battle. A good stroll would probably do them good.

None of which helped me. I needed to get into the library because I felt sure that it was there that I could learn the most about the prophecy. But that wasn't all. My curiosity had been piqued about the fire which had evacuated the building on my last visit but left no noticeable damage anywhere. I had paced around the entire building, focusing particularly on the great dome itself, but there were no signs of cracking, no scorching of brick, no shattering of window glass, no blackening of stone. If there *had* been a fire, it had been a bloody small one. Perhaps I had just felt the heat from another incinerator, in which case Aliana either had no idea what was going on in the library or she was trying to keep their little book-burning project under wraps. If I got inside again, the first thing I would do was look over that room with the great brass doors.

But getting in, like many things in life, was easier said than done. The only way in that I knew was guarded, and the alternative was to knock politely on the door and ask them what the big secret was. I hadn't forgotten the spectral "Orgos" or the rival assassins in the alley. They, whoever "they" were, probably had suspicions about me already, but there was no point in confirming those suspicions unless I was going to achieve something in the process.

You will have noticed that my brand of adventuring is subtly different from that of Garnet or Renthrette. Perhaps "subtly" isn't the right word. In this instance, neither of the noble siblings would think anything of shinning up the walls like secretive steeplejacks, clambering ape-like down chimneys, or knocking holes in the dome with their heads. That was not my style, partly because such feats were beyond me. If I started hoisting my awkward frame up ropes and squeezing through windows I'd probably rupture something crucial or hang myself in the process. The general populace would wake to find me sheepishly dangling from a turret, flapping about like some absurd flightless bird. No, I was not Garnet (thank God) and I must stick with whatever talents I had.

Unfortunately, these were few. I could talk myself into a rich man's good graces and his theater-loving daughter's bedchamber (well, nearly). I could act the part of a crippled beggar or a sleeping drunk whenever there were coins to be donated or pilfered. I could get onto a stage and make a crowd believe I was a warrior, lover, tyrant, or clown. But I wasn't going to get into that library, and the reason was perfectly simple. Out in the slightly seedy tavern where Lisha was staying, I had blended in with the other lowlifes and disreputables. Here, I was a man alone.

The average height of the men in Phasdreille was a good two or three inches above mine. They were lithe and slender, I am—as Renthrette was fond of pointing out—thicker about the waist than I should be, and my limbs tended to the scrawny. They had long, flaxen hair, bright as sunlight through hay, and pale, icy blue eyes. I have hair so brown that it gives a new dimension to the term "nondescript." My eyes, likewise. And while, in my former life, these features had helped me lie low, they now stood out like a beacon, a sign that singled me out, identified me by name, and reminded all and sundry what a gutter-crawling degenerate I was. While I could live with such barely concealed distaste and skepticism—it had never really bothered me before—it meant that there was no way I could dress as a guard or a librarian (complete with book-burning stove) and sidle in as if everything was normal. I either had to go in as myself, or I had to go in one hell of a disguise.

I tried the former.

It took me a moment to convince the guard on duty that I knew Aliana. He sent word inside to confirm my story. She met me at the main door fairly promptly.

"I'm back," I announced, redundantly. She met my genial smile with a tiny replica of her own touched with a certain reserve.

"Yes," she said.

"How was the fire?" I asked, jauntily, as if it had been some kind of holiday excursion.

"It's out," she said.

"Much damage?"

"Not much."

"I was worried about you."

"There was no need."

"And the fire's out?"

"Yes."

"And there was no real damage, to speak of, as it were?"

"No."

This was not going all that well. She was holding the door open just wide enough to poke her head round, and showed no sign of inviting me in.

"So," I tried, trying to sound casual, "can I come in and do some, you know, reading?"

"I'm afraid not," she said, not bothering to soften the blow much. "The library is closed, as you know, and, since the fire, we have been obliged to tighten our security and speed up our work."

"What work?" I demanded, a trifle testily.

"Cataloging," she said. Her smile had evaporated like a ground mist under a morning sun. The door, if anything, had closed an inch or two. "Now I really must get back to work," she said.

"Right, right," I beamed, falsely. "While I remember," I added before I walked away, "I was wondering if you might mention to Sorrail what I did during the goblin siege."

"The goblin siege?" she said, suddenly hesitant.

"Yes. You know, when we were up on the walls and the goblins were attacking. You had your crossbow. I was on the other side of that big breach in the walls over there as the goblins were coming through. Well, no one seems to remember me doing anything and, when I mention it, people don't seem to believe me. I wasn't expecting them to put a life-size bronze of me in the town square, but a little less contempt would be nice, you know? After all, I did earn it. Pretty heroic, I thought: gigantic monster poised to ravish the city and . . . Well, I'm not especially popular right now, so I thought you might mention it to Sorrail or the king or something. I mean, fair's fair."

She gave me a long, blank stare, as if I was speaking a foreign language. She showed no animation at the memory of the battle, no astonishment that I hadn't got some kind of official award, and, in fact, no sign that she could recall the event at all. When I finished she merely nodded distantly, as if her mind was on something else, and said, "Yes. Now I really have to go."

I made understanding noises and the door shut heavily in my face. A key turned and then a series of heavy bolts thudded home. I wouldn't be going in that way.

❧

"The lover returns," said Renthrette. "Been breaking hearts, Will?"

"Jealous, Renthrette?"

"Desperately," she said with a look that would have curdled milk.

"How did you know where I've been, anyway?"

"Gossip, Will, gossip. I thought you would have figured that out. What do you think courtiers do all day? It's not all banqueting with the king, you know. A lot of talking goes on here. I expect you'd like it. That's your strength, isn't it, talking?" She smiled, wide as a grave and twice as nasty.

"We can't all be semiliterate baboons like you and your brother," I responded.

"I can read, so can Garnet."

"I said semiliterate, not illiterate. Yes, you can read in that 'see the dog run' fashion you think is adequate, but it unsettles your stomach, doesn't it, all that brain juice flowing? And killing things is so much more fun."

"It's not about fun—" she began.

"I know," I interjected, "it's about principle. It's about honor and chivalry and sunshine and the forces of light. I heard the litany, Renthrette, so spare me."

"I'm just verbalizing," she said. "I thought that was what you liked: words."

"Thank you," I muttered bitterly. "You're a chipper little thing when you've got an evening with Sorrail to look forward to, aren't you?"

"Not just Sorrail," she said. "The whole court. It will be tremendous. So tremendous that even your presence won't spoil it for me."

"Mine?"

"You're going, too."

She reached out, brandishing a cream-colored envelope sealed with red wax and edged with gold. My name was etched in a curly script marked by so many flourishes that the letters were almost unreadable.

"Your invitation," she said, staring at me significantly. She didn't actually say *don't screw this up for us*, but it was there in her face.

I reached for the envelope and she pulled it fractionally away until I met her eyes and gave a shrug of acknowledgment. Then she gave it to me.

And so were my evening's plans made. It might even be fun. And, besides, I was still floating slightly on the knowledge that Lisha had trusted me while Garnet and Renthrette didn't even know she was around. When Renthrette taunted me, it was all I could do not to whistle *I know something you don't know*. But I said nothing. It was more fun that way.

⁂

In truth, I was faintly relieved. Being at the banquet meant I would be safe and could put off any attempts to break into the library until some less rational hour. Tonight, I thought, I would do my best to enjoy the pleasures of the court by blending in, something that would have been close to impossible were it not for assistance that came from a rather surprising quarter. An hour or so before we were due to go, Garnet appeared at my door with one of those earnest looks in his emerald eyes.

"I've brought you something," he said, kind of sheepishly.

"Come in," I said, trying to see what he was holding behind him. "What is it?"

Garnet lowered his eyes, hesitated, and, with a sharply intaken breath that suggested both embarrassment and resolve, he whisked a suit of black silk and brocade out from the bag he was clutching. It was adorned with a white lace collar and cuffs—not too flouncy, but enough for elegance—and buttoned with silver. I gave a long, tuneless whistle. "Where did you get this?"

Garnet muttered something and walked over to the window with a nonchalance that was totally unconvincing.

"What?" I said.

"I found it in the town," said Garnet, fidgeting and looking pointedly out of the window.

"You what?" I said.

"I found it," said Garnet, looking at me suddenly with something like defiance, "you know, in the town."

"What, lying around?" I demanded.

"Of course not lying around," he snapped, irritation clouding his brow.

"You bought it?" I exclaimed.

There was silence for a moment.

"Kind of," said Garnet, dropping his eyes again and gesturing vaguely so that he knocked a small flower vase off the window ledge. It broke and he instantly stooped to pick up the pieces.

"Kind of?" I repeated. "What does that mean? Did you buy it or not?"

"Yes," he hissed, not looking up.

"You bought this for me?" I persisted. "Garnet, I didn't know you cared!"

He looked up, and his usually chalky face was flushed with pink. "Don't make a big deal of this, Will," he spluttered. "I got it because you'll need it for tonight. That's all. I don't want you embarrassing yourself. Or us."

"That's really very sweet of you."

He rose quickly and his fingers flexed as if he were looking for the axe he normally wore in his belt. "Listen, Will, don't start. . . ."

"I'm grateful, Garnet. I really am," I said, honestly. "I'm just surprised that you would think to do this for me. Was it expensive?"

"I got a good deal on it," he said, a little sulkily.

That I didn't doubt. He and Renthrette would argue for hours to save the kind of change you find under bar stools. The suit was unlike anything I'd ever worn before, excepting some of the cast-off fashions with which the nobility had supplied the Cresdon theaters. I felt the fabric. It was flawlessly smooth, and the brocade felt like the pelt of a meticulously groomed mink. I grinned at Garnet and he shuffled.

"Thanks, Garnet."

"Don't mention it," he said, and meant it in all possible ways.

I changed quickly. The suit was a perfect fit. Garnet had completed the outfit with suitable hose, boots, jewelry, and a tastefully discreet codpiece. I felt like an impostor at first, but I walked up and down a few times and practiced holding one arm crooked while the other hand rested on the pommel of my sword, and the role started to feel more natural. I began to walk slower and straighter, with my head back and my lips curled in a self-satisfied sneer. Soon I was bowing fractionally, practicing delicate little smiles and applauding with two fingers of my right hand against the palm of my left. Garnet rolled his eyes.

"It's just a suit," he said. "You're not supposed to change your entire identity."

"Rubbish," I said, admiring myself in a pocket mirror. "I am what I look like. Enter Viscount William, courtier, poet, sophisticate, and lover. This is going to be fun."

And indeed it was. For a while.

A Fly in the Ointment

It was, as you might imagine, a glittering affair. The entire court, serving maids, footmen, and nobles, counselors, and the king himself, were all turned out as if panache, elegance, and looking like they had been rolled in something very sticky and then pelted with jewelry would save them from the goblin hordes. As they filed formally into the banquet hall, each one seemed more dazzling than the last, each vying to outsparkle the polished crystal of the great chandeliers with their gold and diamonds. Each wore a paper-thin veil of humility over self-satisfaction verging on smugness, and each dropped their witty words like a king on a balcony casting rubies into the outstretched hands of the peasants below. In seconds the hall was buzzing like some insane beehive, all poetry and studied laughter, clever songs and felt-lined applause. And in the middle of it all, dressed to kill and brandishing his rapier wit and disarming charm, was Sir William Hawthorne.

Well, let's face it, if there's one thing I can do, it's fake pretty much anything. More to the point, what passed for wit and wisdom here was pretty obviously the usual recycled courtly twaddle about beauty, truth, taste, etcetera, and if I couldn't fake that by now I wasn't the duplicitous cad I prided myself on being. I had heard it all before and I was sure I could match the best of them. Pretty sure, anyway.

Now, there may be a handful of people out there who live for bad love poetry and dressing up as lovelorn and unfeasibly wealthy shepherdesses, but I'm banking that they're few and far between, so I'm not going to go into a lot of detail about the wonderful costumes and the wonderful speeches and the wonderful songs and the wonderful smiles that were smiled so wonderfully at the wonderful poems. To those few of you who thrive on this kind of saccharine and overpolished pigs' offal, my apologies. Here, then, are the salient facts, unadorned by satin and pearls.

First: Will Hawthorne, looking like someone's terribly debonair great aunt, makes his entrance into the king's banquet hall to a general raising of the collective eyebrow. "How handsome!" they remark. "How stylish!" "Could this be," they wonder among themselves, "the same degenerate hog's turd of an Outsider who sullied our court only days ago?"

Second: Will sparkles. Not satisfied with merely looking impressive, he opens his store of golden words and charms his hearers dumb. Rarely have such wit and poise, such timing and ease, been so impeccably combined. This man could break wind loudly and his audience would swear they had never heard anything more wryly apposite all season. Such a man cannot fail to win the hearts and admiration of the entire court.

Third: Will spectacularly fails to win the hearts and minds of the entire court, and is forcibly ejected as if he is some slimy form of pond life which was accidentally tracked in on the sole of someone's boot.

In retrospect, it started out far too well. With my history, I should have anticipated calamity looming overhead like a thirty-pound hammer, but foresight, hindsight, and any other kind of sight which doesn't originate in the very second in which I exist is something of a mystery to me. The thirty-pound hammer (augmented by murderous-looking spikes) hovered just long enough for me to start feeling comfortable, and then pounded me through the floor.

But enough of these ominous metaphors. I woke at about five o'clock the following morning. The banquet and its subsequent revelries had been over for about three hours, though I had been absent from them rather longer. I had been curled up in the drafty corner of one of the palace's anterooms, sleeping fitfully, when the toe of Garnet's boot prodded me imperiously. As I gazed wretchedly up at him and his iron-faced sister, the whole miserable affair gradually came swimming back to me.

"Get up," said Garnet, more exhausted than angry. "We've been looking for you for ages. Get up and we'll get you to bed."

I stirred vaguely, but my legs were not interested. I paused to consider the drool and vomit that had stained the front of my new suit while they looked at each other and sighed. At first, Renthrette refused to help, but eventually Garnet persuaded her to brace me up, and between them they dragged me half-senseless to my room. There they maneuvered me onto my bed, where I lay on my side, wheezing and hacking the thin, foul-smelling remnants of whatever had been in my stomach into a tin basin. Once, I tried to sit up, but the room tossed and spun as if I was bound to the sail-less mast of some storm-wracked ship. I retched something that looked liked orange oatmeal onto the pillow and my gut contracted as if my entire midriff had been clamped into a vice. My eyes watered with pain and my open mouth strained, voiding nothing but air in a long, agonizing gasp. Pleasant, eh? When the nausea subsided I collapsed back onto the bed, my eyes shut against the lamplight and the humiliation. And in this blissful condition, I passed the rest of the night.

Now, this was not the first time I had been a little the worse for wear after an evening's carousal, but it was, I think, the first time that I had passed into this miserable state without the slightest idea how it had happened. One minute I had been the life and soul of the party, sipping some flavorless fruit drink while bantering to the admiration of all; the next I had been launching the partially digested remains of my dinner over someone in lemon velvet. My lyrical depiction of the pangs of love went into a hideously rapid decline, and before I knew what was happening, I was trying to organize some kind of impromptu orgy using language that would have made the most experienced harlot blanch. But how this all came about, I could not say.

Garnet and Renthrette, naturally, just assumed that I had let the side down by drinking beyond my limit. Now, I know for a fact that I could drink either of those two under several tables and go on to perform every role in several full-length plays without dropping a line. Moreover, everyone had been drinking the same yellowish muck as I had, and I would go before the highest authority on earth and swear that I had had no more than two glasses of the treacherous filth. In fact, I knew that many of those about me, including the stoically sober Renthrette, had had a good deal more than me, so engrossed was I with my courtly patter. I suspected foul play and said so, but Garnet would have none of it.

"Someone doctored your drink?" he exclaimed, his anger now showing through his disbelief. "Why would anyone do that? These are not the kind of degenerates you used to spend your time with."

"I'm not a degenerate," I muttered unconvincingly.

"Really?" barked Garnet with nasty hilarity. "So you're just a normal, civilized person, are you? And normal, civilized people always end the evening by announcing that Lord Gaspar, the chief justice of the land, couldn't fill his own codpiece."

"I didn't do that," I said, hopefully.

"Yes, you did," Garnet exploded. "You said that you bet there was nothing in there but old stockings, and that if his wife went home with you instead she'd get to see, and I quote, 'the one that got away.'"

"I did not say that," I said bleakly, my voice muffled by the rancid pillow.

"Yes, you did," said Renthrette, leaping into the fray. "In fact, you went on for a full five minutes about your bait and tackle, about eels and fishing poles, about how once she 'nets this one' she'll never mess with minnows again, and every other stupid, degraded fishing image you could come up with, all the while rubbing yourself against her and leering until everyone in the room . . ."

"Everyone!" agreed Garnet.

". . . was staring at you in horrified silence," she concluded. "You only stopped when Lord Gaspar and Viscount Vallacin physically moved you away. And then you started drunkenly swinging at them and calling them a 'pack of poncey-assed nancy boys who dressed like girls.' It was only their honor and decency that stopped them from skewering you on the tips of their rapiers like the pig you are."

"It can't have been that bad," I replied, lamely.

"No," said Garnet, "it was worse. You sneezed all over Baroness Drocine's dinner plate and then told her that you could bet safely that your snot was more palatable than anything that had been served all night."

"Well, you know, the food here . . ." I inserted, semi-apologetically.

"And then you climbed onto the table and offered to urinate into any glasses that needed filling. Thank God Sorrail was on hand to get you down before you had a chance to lower your breeches."

"I thought the worthy Sorrail would have been a witness to all this," I said, the surge of resentment I always felt at his name rising as quick as the bile in my throat.

"Sorrail saved your neck," Renthrette spat. "You could have been executed on the spot after what you said about the king being a bloated and flatulent old fornicator."

"I never said that," I tried again.

"You said he had a private room full of small animals with which he practiced immoral acts," said Renthrette, her face prissily straight.

"I'll bet I didn't put it like that," I said, managing a smile for the first time since this nightmare had begun.

"No," she said flatly, "but I wouldn't sully my lips with one-tenth of the things you said last night. You also called the king's private secretary a 'whoreson swamp-sucking varlet' and the captain of the palace guard an 'unctuous, civet-reeking, pus-dripping clodpole,' whatever that is."

"I can get rather colorful when the mood takes me," I admitted.

"Most of the time no one had any idea what you were talking about," Garnet said. "But they got the message, all right. How much did you have to drink?"

"Nothing!" I exclaimed. "Maybe two glasses, but no more! Somebody put something in my drink! You think I can't hold my beer? I could outdrink everyone in that entire court combined."

"How impressive," said Renthrette.

"It's not meant to be impressive," I returned. "It's just a statement of fact. I lived on beer—*real* beer—for over a decade in Cresdon. I worked in a theater that was also a tavern, remember? Someone spiked my drink, and I don't mean they put a shot of grain whiskey in my tankard. I mean they added something serious, some drug that would . . ."

"No one in the court would do such a thing," Garnet said. "It's completely implausible."

"And I'm telling you that it's the only possibility," I shouted back. "Someone in that court set out to discredit me, and they did so by . . ."

"Spare me your lies, you snake," Renthrette snarled, cutting me off. "The insults you threw at the top of your lungs; the indecent suggestions you made to virtually every lady in the room, regardless of whether her husband or betrothed or admirers stood listening to every disgusting word; the people you offended . . ."

She paused, unable to finish. Then she looked me in the eye. Complete resolve came over her, and, when she spoke again, it was like watching a raging torrent freeze suddenly. "Last night, Will, you crossed the line. You have always walked a dangerous path, but last night you shamed us all, and that, as far as I am concerned, is it. Henceforth, do not speak to me. Do not associate with me. Do not even look at me. If you so much as mention my name I will find you and I will run my sword up to the hilt through your stomach. I will cut out your heart if you ever claim any kind of connection to me again. I have waited with you all night to tell you this, and now I am going. As soon as you are fit to walk (if you were ever fit for anything), leave this place. Forget my name and that of my brother and those who traveled with us. If I ever see Orgos, Mithos, and Lisha again, I will say you are dead—and that, I think, is a kindness more than you deserve. From this moment on, you are alone, as you always wanted to be."

Before half of this had sunk in, she was gone. Garnet faltered for a second. His eyes met mine and there was uncertainty in them, but he looked to his sister as she stepped through the door, and a hardness came into his face. "Good-bye, Will," he said, stiffly. And with that, he followed her out the door.

❧

This was a bit of a setback. I had toyed with the idea of abandoning the party from the first day I had met them, but it was usually an empty threat. I needed them in this strange land and, though they could all get on my last nerve, I had grown to like them. Laughable though this now seemed, I had once thought that Renthrette might turn into something more than a friend. Garnet was a tougher nut, perhaps, but I had never really considered the possibility that they might just dump me on the side of the road. I had always assumed that I was just valuable enough to them to make them put up with my idiosyncrasies as I put up with theirs. Apparently this was not so.

Yet, however much Renthrette fancied herself party leader, she did not speak for Lisha and the others. I had briefly flirted with the idea of brandishing my secret knowledge about Lisha as a way of derailing their righteousness, a way of showing that the person they respected most thought me useful, may think me somehow more trustworthy than them in ways I couldn't quite explain. But I didn't. I had promised Lisha, and that meant something. So did the sense that there was something more important than whether or not Renthrette liked me.

Lisha had left me with a task, and whatever else it might achieve I figured that my one chance of staying with the party was by completing my assignment. I slept for one more hour and then dragged myself out of bed, washed, dressed in my new suit (the collar and vest front sponged as best I could), and stumbled out into the frosty morning.

Oh, and I stole Renthrette's dress. The one she had worn the previous night. She wouldn't be happy about it, but I couldn't slip any further in her esteem, so I just concentrated on not getting caught. I rolled the thing up as best I could and shoved it under my arm as I went outside. I did it because I needed it, though I'd be lying if I said that the fact that it would seriously piss her off didn't add to the appeal.

The cold air skewered my lungs like one of the elegant rapiers which had surely been aimed in my direction last night, and my head swam. For a moment I thought I would faint, which led me to sit with hurried clumsiness in the street. After a few minutes I struggled gingerly to my feet and walked to a small piazza where I found a pump, splashed the icy water on my face, and took a tentative drink. A gaggle of courtiers who were exchanging amused recollections about the evening's frivolities caught sight of me and stared in hostile silence. I returned to my drinking, ignoring them as they turned pointedly from me and walked away. I drank a little more while they got out of the way, then set off again, miserable but determined.

My stomach sloshed about as I walked, but my light-headedness passed and I felt no urge to vomit what I had just drunk. I begged a stale crust from a bakers' shop, and, though I felt no desire to eat any more, I managed to keep it down. I sat for a while in the square by the library, feeling better apart from a pulsing ache in my temples. Now all I had to do was get into the library one last time. Then I could run, my tail firmly between my legs, from the city to Lisha, the one person on the planet who might still be pleased to see me. Of course, if I couldn't get into the library—particularly if Lisha had gotten word of my evening's activities—even her patience with me might reach its limit.

I found my way to the exclusive little gallery of shops adjacent to the marketplace where I had sampled the chocolate bird. A quick glance at the wares in the overstuffed windows and my mission was clear. I took a long breath and tried to screen out the pain in my head. Then, selecting the most ludicrously sumptuous of a number of establishments dealing in cosmetics, I barged in as if I had sprinted across town.

"Is it ready?" I demanded in a loud, impatient tone. "Is it ready? Come on, I don't have all day."

"Is what ready?" said a venerable old lady behind the counter. She was absurdly made up with cheeks of a uniform flamingo-pink and a blue-green shadow in the sockets above her eyeballs. She was sixty-five if she was a day.

"The package my mistress ordered!" I screamed back. "She wants it immediately."

"I don't know what you mean," said the shopkeeper, with a glance at one of the serving girls who was ministering to another customer. "A package?"

"Yes, a package!" I spluttered. "Two complete wigs, face powder, lip tint, and colored spectacles."

"And this was ordered when?"

"Last week. Maybe earlier. You must have it. She needs it now and she said she'd never employ you again if it wasn't . . ."

"Now, let's not be hasty," the old woman cut in. "Your mistress's name is . . . ?"

I glanced pointedly around the store. Several ladies paused in their perusal of false eyelashes and hairpieces and regarded this little scene with interest.

"My dear lady," I began, as if offended, "surely you do not expect me to utter the name of so venerable a court lady as my mistress before common ears." I leaned close to her. "She is a little . . . sensitive . . . about what time is doing to her beauteous features. Surely you would not have me . . ."

"Certainly not!" exclaimed the shopkeeper. "But it would help if I knew. . . . You say she has employed our services before?"

"On a regular basis."

"As a personal dresser as well as supplier?"

"Indeed," I confirmed.

"And she is more advanced in years than say, myself?"

This seemed tough to imagine, but I nodded knowingly.

"Would I be correct in saying that her name began with—" Here she leaned close to my ear. As I struggled not to keel over at the stench of her perfume, she breathed the letter "W."

"The very same," I smiled, remarking to myself how easy this had turned out to be.

"Then I am scheduled to meet with her this afternoon."

"Err . . . yes," I said, "or, rather, you were. She wants you to send this package to her today, though it seems my fellow the valet did not relay this information to you."

"I think not."

"It would not be the first time," I said, sighing at the fallibility of servants. "But that is no matter. If you can compose the package now, then she will meet with you tomorrow instead of today and will pay you then."

"At the usual time?" asked the shopkeeper.

"Half an hour earlier, please," I said, for no particular reason.

⚜

I left the store with a parcel of brown paper, which I opened as soon as I got to a side street. Despite having to time my actions around the motions of passersby, it took me no more than five minutes to slip on Renthrette's dress, powder my face after the courtly fashion, rub a little of the red grease on my lips, and don the ringlet wig. This last item was perhaps the most risky, but it was also the most essential. It was an odd sensation, returning to my days playing ladies on the stage, doubly so because I wasn't actually on stage at all, was actually in an alley where being discovered could get me into real trouble, and it took me a few minutes to steel myself for my return to the main street. As soon as I slipped the tortoiseshell spectacles with their bluish lenses (such as I had been assured were "absolutely the first choice of all the *right* courtiers this season") onto my nose, Will Hawthorne effectively vanished. My disguise wouldn't stand careful scrutiny, particularly from someone who knew me, but I had spent the bulk of my theatrical apprenticeship playing women and had often been told that I did it well; better, in fact, than some actual women. I was never sure what that meant, but I took it as a compliment. And now, moving back through the elegant streets of Phasdreille, I clung to the idea like it was the banister of a steep and narrow staircase.

I reached the library and made straight for one of the guards monitoring the side entrance. He was a little taller than most of the "fair folk" and his limbs were heavier, more aggressively powerful-looking than the sinewy strength of the other troops. He caught sight of my rapid approach, but his gaze was blank. I touched the fringe of my wig self-consciously and proceeded.

Fishing into my stocking-padded cleavage, I produced a sheaf of official-looking papers marked with sealing wax. I was taking a chance, of course, but I hadn't seen much devotion to learning outside the privileged circle of the court, despite the magnificence of the library. That a lowly sentry would be able to read seemed unlikely, and I might thus get away with the fact that what I was brandishing was actually the formal invitation to the king's banquet, the same banquet at which I had so endeared myself to the Phasdreille elite.

The guard's eyes stooped to my face expressionlessly.

"Lady Fossington," I announced, modulating my voice and conscious that I was perspiring slightly. "I'm here on behalf of the Committee on Textual Rescription."

I paused and gave him an expectant look as if this made my business clear. His brow wrinkled slightly and his mouth opened, but he said nothing while his eyes strayed to the document I was holding. I could tell at a glance that he was taking in the parchment and the official-looking seal rather than the words, so I held it up for him to get a better, but no more helpful, look.

As he did so, I kept talking in a rapid and slightly nasal manner. "At the second semiannual general meeting, the committee reviewed the minutes from the previous meeting and found certain items of business unresolved. The most major of these was the updating of the list of titles to be permanently erased from all but the Former Titles list. But my business today is more directly concerned with item four on the original meeting minutes—that is, what is now item 2b on the recent meeting agenda: Maintenance Subsistence Levels for Book Redirection and Clarification of Furnaces. The earlier think tank report on this matter suggested that said furnaces were not adequately monitored for the accumulation of post-incineration written matter detritus, which was directly impacting the efficiency of said furnaces in subsequent acts of textual modification by means of incandescence. According to the report, said accumulation was inversely proportional to said furnaces' available volume and may have further repercussions correlating to issues of temperatural generative capacity. My task is to make detailed observations on the post-incineration condition of said furnaces in order to ascertain the necessity of further detritus removal operations."

The blank look in the soldier's eyes tried to hide, but it wasn't going anywhere. He hesitated, trying to look engaged, then nodded. I pressed the advantage. "So if you would conduct me on a tour of the furnaces so that I can complete my examination, I'm sure that the library staff and the king's palace will be appreciative."

"Oh," he said. "Right. Yes, um'mm."

And I was in.

The next trick was to lose my guide. That might prove more difficult. The soldier chaperoned me everywhere I went and insisted on guiding me straight to the room I had already been in. He watched me as I poked around in the embers of the fireplaces, sifting through ash, and taking little scrapings of burned matter from the chimney lips with the point of my knife. Periodically I would pause to sniff significantly. Once I even tasted the gray-white powder, all the while scribbling meaningless words and figures on my sheet of paper. This clearly fascinated the trooper, and he showed no signs of leaving me alone for a second. We moved from room to room, seeing nothing I hadn't already seen. I was in continual dread of bumping into Aliana or someone else who would be less accepting of my story.

"This is the last one," said the guard as we entered a small circular chamber with a dead hearth in its center.

"What about the brass doors at the end of the corridor there?" I asked.

"There's no furnace there," he said. "This is the last one." The look on his face was completely guileless. He was unaware that anything significant had been said. As far as he was concerned, he was telling the truth.

No furnace. So Aliana's story about the source of the heat behind those doors had been a lie.

So what was through those doors, I wondered? I had to see, and I was fast running out of time. I had not been spotted, hadn't run into Aliana, and, though I hadn't knocked my absurd wig off, I also hadn't learned anything, and the soldier was still gazing rapt at the way I was pawing through the cinders of all those Redirected and Clarified Texts. It made me nervous, having him watch so closely while I did nothing. I tried to distract him.

"Nice room," I said, glancing around at the heavy timber beams and imposing stonework.

"Yes," he said.

"Must have taken years to build," I added, aimlessly making conversation until I could think of a way to get rid of him.

"Yes," he said. "I'll be a mason when I retire from the army."

"Really," I said, "how very interesting."

This was said sarcastically, nastily even. I thought vaguely that offending or belittling him might make him leave, but he apparently misread my remark altogether. That's the trouble with idiots: You can't even offend them without working overtime.

"Yes," he said. "It's a family trade."

"Well, you mustn't try anything too intellectually challenging," I tried.

His face showed nothing. In fact, he seemed, if anything, strangely distant as he began to reply. "My great-grandfather first helped to hew and shape the stone which was laid as the foundation of this structure. You see those buttresses? He carved those himself, with nothing but a chisel and mallet. He worked until his hands bled, refusing to rest until the job was done to the best of his ability. The intricacy of their carving is unmatched, and, a hundred years later, they are still as even and flawless as the day they were finished. Since then the goblin armies have broken upon this fortress like waves against cliffs and it stands still. He taught the trade to my grandfather, who taught it to my father, and my father taught it to me. My hammer has been passed down through our family since the days of that great-grandfather in whose memory we set a small diamond into its handle. Soon I will continue his work."

An odd chill had started to come over me halfway through this speech as it began to resonate through my mind. It was like smelling something that invokes some ancient memory which you can't quite place. The experience left me confused and, stranger still, a little afraid. He finished his speech and gazed back at me, as if just realizing that I was there.

"A hammer passed through generations," I said. "That must give a fine sense of continuity and history. I didn't think people did that with tools. More with weapons. You don't have an heirloom weapon passed through the family as well, do you?" I ventured.

"An axe," he said. "My great-grandfather bore it when Phasdreille was besieged by a vast goblin horde which crossed the river to sack the White City. He rode with a cavalry force raised in the borderlands, and they met the goblin ranks as they lay outside the great city. The horsemen caught the goblins unawares and routed them, though many tall and fair soldiers fell in the battle. My great-grandfather survived, but he was killed shortly afterward. That was the last time he wielded his mighty axe. With it he struck down many dozens of goblins, cleaving a path through their ranks until he came upon their chieftain: a huge brute dressed in red and black, great ugly spikes on his helm and a weapon like a vast cleaver in his massive claws. My ancestor faced the beast and, after many blows were struck on both sides, felled him, cleaving his skull in twain. But the goblin was wearing an iron collar and the axe was notched, though it is still functional, and we set a diamond taken from the goblin chief and set it into the haft. I don't carry it because it is not regulation-issue for sentry duty, but I long for the day when I can wield it as he did in the open field of battle."

"Shouldn't you be guarding the door?" I suggested hurriedly, anxious to get rid of him and the strangeness he suddenly seemed to exude.

"I was finishing my shift when you arrived," he answered. "There'll be another guard down there by now." His manner rapidly shifted back to how it had been when I first spoke to him. All trace of the distance I had felt from him as he recited those oddly familiar words was gone.

"Then perhaps you can help me," I said, unsure exactly where my words were leading me, but desperate to have him leave.

His face lit up. "Certainly," he said. "What can I do?"

"You see this bluish dust in the ash?"

He stooped over and nodded thoughtfully. "What is it?" he asked.

"Well that's what I need to find out," I said, straightening up and trying to sound professional. "It may just be a little calcined sulfur such as is commonly discharged when the err . . . celedine fibers are exposed to intense heat in the presence of anthracite, belomnites and, you know, cellulites. It could also, however, indicate the build-up of vitrilic carbon mandible particles."

"Is that bad?" said the soldier, reading my expression.

"Let's just say that if I'm right—and I hope to God that I'm not—the next spark kindled in this room could create an explosion which would leave nothing of this building but a dirty great crater in the ground."

His jaw dropped. I went on. "I need you to go outside and find me a cup full of bird droppings. Preferably from er . . . a kind of hawk. Female. It has to be female. Put male droppings in there and the alcolyde mercurials will spontaneously combust, and then we'll be in real trouble. But you must walk very carefully. If you create a spark with your armor against the stone walls, we've had it."

"I'll get right on it," he breathed, and began to tiptoe out.

"And don't tell anyone!" I added hastily. "I mean, we don't want a, you know, *panic* on our hands."

He left me, creeping with arms spread for balance and uneasy glances back at the mound of ash which I was poking thoughtfully. *Imagine*, I mused as he left, *how much easier life would be if all the people I met could be relied upon to be as dim as the worthy trooper who has just left me. Alas, such special gullibility is all too rare, and the world is a correspondingly tougher place for the rest of us.*

I was so wrapped up in these considerations that I almost forgot to capitalize on the opportunity that that special gullibility had won me. I sprang up, dusted off my hands, and tried the door. It opened onto the gallery that skirted the great dome, and there was no sign of life that I could see or hear. I trotted hurriedly down the corridor to the great doors with their brass panels, lifting my skirts as I ran. When I got to them I found myself again aware of the dull hum which seemed to come from inside. As I stood there listening, my gaze fell upon the metal relief work which covered the doors. Before, I had noticed the images of the library with its great dome, but I hadn't considered the details. I leaned closer to consider the figures depicted in the panels, noting that the builders were small and squat. I was just thinking about how odd this was and leaning on the door in a pensive kind of way when I recoiled suddenly. It was as warm as before, and pulsed with energy.

This was no fire. I guess I had always known that, but it struck me like a crossbow bolt through the forehead that I had been lied to on all sides. It also meant that there was something behind this door which I was not supposed to see, something which perhaps explained the strange secrecy which hung over this building. Without thinking further, I took the great brass ring in my right hand and twisted it sharply. The door clicked and yielded. The door opened. Nothing could have prepared me for what I saw next.

The room inside was vast, and both walls and floor were stone. It could have been magnificent, and probably was, once. Now it was a scene of devastation and chaos. Much of the stonework was shattered and all the huge, carved images which stood like columns supporting the roof were disfigured so extensively that it was impossible to discern if they had been men or beasts. The intricately worked wooden paneling, which seemed to have borne remarkable pictures in marquetry, had been hacked to splinters. Only fragments of the beautiful wooden inlay could still be made out where the vandalism (for such it seemed) was limited to severe scoring and the crude strokes of a paintbrush dipped in scarlet. The same savage desecration was everywhere. The immense paintings which hung from the ceiling buttresses were slashed to stained tatters, the bookcases had been emptied and their contents violently shredded, and the statues which stood on either side of the great throne at the far end of the hall had been beheaded and daubed with crimson paint. There was, and had been, no fire. There was no smoke staining, no ash, no charred timber. The ruin before me was man-made and it had been effected with what I can only describe as hatred: a hatred so profound that it had unleashed a fury beyond words, beyond reason. Furthermore, it had not happened recently.

On everything, from the brutalized statues to the torn pages of the books which littered the floor like a confetti carpet, was a gray furring: dust. It looked as if the room had not been disturbed for years, decades even.

But it was not uninhabited. In a stone chair at the far end of the chamber, overlooking this ruined wasteland and flanked by crippled statuary, sat a man. He was robed and hooded in purest white and his hands were lost in the sleeves. He was motionless, though he was turned toward me, and, though I could not see his face under his pale and heavy cowl, I felt his eyes upon me.

He did not move. I, seemingly paralyzed, was unable even to speak. The pulsing throb which I had felt through the door seemed to be all around me, not pushing me out of the room, but swirling at me from all sides. It was as if I was at the center of an eyeball whose iris had contracted tightly about me. And then, as if the room had suddenly dwindled, the walls rushing in until the entire chamber was only a few feet square, I stood at the man's feet and he was gazing down at me from his throne. My mind emptied. Then he spoke—or, rather, I heard a word in my head. The voice was cold and unfamiliar. It said one thing only, and it was not a question, comment, or exclamation. Rather it was the tone of someone acknowledging my presence—someone who had expected, even *sent for*, me.

"Outsider."

My eyes were fixed on the dark hollow within the hood, the space where the man's face should have been, and I could not tear them away. But however hard I stared I could not guess what that face would be like if I had the strength to reach up and tug the cowl back. Pale and old beyond reckoning, I knew, though where this idea came from, I could not say.

I felt cold, pinned like a bug under a lens, and then I had the strangest and most uncomfortable sensation of being read like a book, the pages of my life torn open and riffled as if he could see into me, into my past, into my mind and heart. I felt exposed, naked. I fought to close myself to him, but couldn't. He had me in some sort of inverse vice that forced me apart, separated my very thoughts and feelings.

It was horrible.

I knew I couldn't stop it, but somehow I lighted on another possibility, something that might distract or unsettle him. He had called me Outsider. Through the confusion and fear I managed to shape a defiance that was also a kind of question.

"As prophesied," I thought.

Then, as my eyes burned futilely into his, I became aware that the charge in the air, the energy that rushed about me like liquid, had acquired a color. It was now visible as a grayish smoke tinged with violet. As it surged and darted I saw, from the corner of my eye, that it was lit by flickers of blue-white lightning ripping through sullen clouds. I tried to look away from the seated figure, but my eyes would not leave his hooded visage. The air grew heavier and darker until the flashes of light burned themselves into my vision for seconds after they had passed. As the light faded, I felt the hatred which had ravaged the room and the coldness of the mind which had gripped mine and I was overcome with fear. In desperation, I tried to shut my eyes, but they stood open as if their lids were pinned back. They burned. The black hollow of the man's head filled my vision, but around me the room was growing still darker. There was another flash of light, more brilliant than the rest, and it forked right through my head. I cried out with a defiance born of fear and again tried to shut my eyes. It was like closing vast, iron-bound doors, and required all my strength. For a moment, my eyelids were immobile and staring, dry, smoldering so badly that I thought they would clot over with blood; then they were moving. I drew them down as if I was winching some great weight over a pulley. When they were no more than cracks through which I could see the seated figure, he shifted.

And in that second I heard a voice. It was not the voice of the hooded figure who had gripped my mind, but a voice from long ago echoing down a tunnel of memory, a voice which seemed vaguely familiar but unplaceable. The voice faded in and out, each word almost just out of the reach of hearing, resonating like a bell struck years before but somehow still ringing.

"Outsiders will come to Phasdreille," said the voice in my head. "A small group of men and women from beyond your maps. They will alter the course of the war and of your world. They will bring change."

If there was more, the being in the library shut it out, as if slamming a door. I felt his uncertainty and anger at the memory of the words. Then there was darkness, a subsiding of the fear and panic and a stilling of the air. I waited, and when I opened my eyes again, I was where I had been when I walked in. The room was huge again, and the figure robed in white was a good hundred yards away from me. I knew instinctively that my window for escape would be narrow, so I turned hurriedly, yanking at the handle of the great brass door. His eyes burned into me and I felt the air thickening again as he strove to hold me, but I was already out and running as fast as my dress would let me.

I had good cause to run. Not only could I still feel him watching me, I felt sure that some strange alarm had been triggered and the guards would be after me. I glanced wildly around at the library's passages and doors, unsure of whether to bolt from the building or find somewhere to hide.

The decision was made for me. In the hall which lay directly at the foot of the stairs that led up to the dome gallery, doors boomed and a dozen soldiers in white and armed with shortswords and silver helmets burst in. They moved with the resolve of men pursuing a bear that has eaten their wives. An officer shouted and pointed, and a pair of the library's own guards joined them, their voices raised and sharp.

"The Outsider is disguised as a court lady," said one. "He's upstairs."

The company divided, drew their swords, and moved toward the double staircases, their faces strangely grim. They apparently thought me dangerous, and that would make them lethal. I moved quickly out of the gallery and toward the door from which I had once seen Aliana emerge. I had reason to doubt that she could be trusted, but given the choice between doubt and the certainty that those soldiers would kill me on the spot, I'll take doubt any day. Call me an optimist. I tried the handle without knocking and burst in, tearing the wig and spectacles off as I did so.

She was standing inside, clad as before in a long, pale smock, open at the throat.

"They're after me!" I spluttered.

"Will?" she said, peering at me.

"Yes. They're after me."

"Who?" she asked, stepping toward me, her brow clouding with concern.

"Soldiers," I said. "I don't know why. But I think they plan to kill me."

"Stay here," she said. I just stood there. A wave of fear had hit me as I remembered the looks on their faces. I was damp with sweat.

She grasped my shoulders and looked into my face.

"Will?" she asked, her face earnest, almost pleading. "Are you listening?"

"Yes," I managed.

"I said, stay here. I can get you out, Will. Just give me a moment."

"Right," I answered, and began to pace beside her desk below the window.

She left the room, closing the door behind her. I sat and listened to the sound of my fractured breathing and my thumping heart. Outside, it was quiet. That unnerved me. Before, there had been booted military feet drumming on the steps and the polished stone floors. Now there was nothing.

What is she doing?

I got up and stepped closer to the door and heard, or thought I heard, stealthy movement behind it. I backed toward the window and I thought about what she had said. She had called me Will. Not Mr. Hawthorne, not William, *Will*.

Suddenly we were friends?

Opening the window, I peered out down forty feet of sheer stone to a flagged courtyard below. No chance.

Though small, the chamber was thoroughly furnished and the walls were lined with books: destined for the fire, no doubt. There was a miniature furnace with a narrow pipe chimney. Beside it at floor level was a hatch, about three feet square, with a heavy winch mechanism and a braking lever set in the wall above it. I pulled at the hatch door and it moved upward, sliding in a pair of grooves. The floor inside was a square wooden panel suspended by chain at its corners. Dropping to a crouch, I climbed awkwardly inside, feeling the base shift and swing alarmingly. Then I reached one arm back into the room, groped for the winch handle, and pulled the lever downward.

Several things happened simultaneously. The panel beneath me dropped as my weight sent it tearing down a dark shaft, almost severing my hand in the hatchway as it fell. At the same moment, I heard the chamber door crash open as the soldiers entered. As I plummeted downward, the thought of hitting the bottom suddenly seemed at least as bad as whatever the troopers up there had intended to do with their swords. The chain rattled through its pulleys and all light but the receding square opening into Aliana's room dwindled to nothing as I hurtled noisily down.

Then there were faces peering down from that square, leaning down into the shaft. I saw the shadows of gloved hands grabbing at the chains, trying to stop my descent. Their efforts were in vain, though they slowed my fall slightly. This, ironically, made my impact with the ground less jarring. I crumpled and rolled, too delighted to be on solid ground to be too concerned with the inevitable bruising that the fall would leave me with.

I was getting to my feet in what seemed like another storage room piled high with books destined for censorship or destruction when Aliana's voice, distant and echoing like the ghosts in old plays, pinned me to the spot. She was leaning into the shaft and her voice was cool, gloating, so that I almost didn't recognize it. "You didn't really think I'd help you, did you, Outsider?" she whispered. I paused, astonished and touched with dread. It was as if a veil had been plucked from her face and I was seeing her as she really was for the first time.

"I should have known," I shouted back. "Never trust a book burner."

"You are as stupid as the goblins," she added. "You can't possibly get out of here, you know. A gross and degenerate creature like you, evade us?"

There was a hint of bitter amusement there; I could hear it. She started to say something else about how I was going to get the death I deserved, her voice never losing that calm, insinuating tone with which she had begun, but I wasn't listening. I stuck my head back into the shaft and turned to shout something up at her, and found that the crossbow, though awkward in the confined space, was already aimed. I saw the light on her face and in her hair, but I never saw her eyes until I sensed the crossbow bolt speeding at my face.

I cried out, I think, and pulled back just in time to feel a rush of air and see three inches of steel-tipped quarrel slam into the splintering wooden platform. She began to talk again, but I knew she was just stalling till the soldiers got down to me. I didn't stick around to listen.

I was in a stone room piled with boxes of books. There was a single wooden door, and through this was a corridor which joined up with the passage I had used to enter the building from the side. I ran out into the cold sunshine, unlacing my bodice and stepping out of the dress as I did so, knowing that they were mere yards behind me. I let the dress lie where it fell.

❧

My course of action was clear: I had to put Phasdreille behind me. Nevertheless, I had returned to the palace, intending to stay just long enough to get my belongings and think for a moment. It wasn't a great idea, I suppose, but I didn't know where else to go, and I suspected the city gates were already held against me. I was in the palace for no more than two minutes, but it was long enough for Garnet to find me. Perhaps that was what I'd gone back for.

"What did you do?" he demanded, storming in without knocking.

"Last night?" I asked, alarmed by the look on his face.

"No," he said. "Since then. Something worse."

"Nothing!" I said.

"Don't lie to me, Will," he shouted suddenly. "You did something. The entire garrison is looking for you. I do not think . . ."

He paused as if uncertain what to say, but then I realized he was uncertain what to *think*.

"You don't think what?" I pressed him.

"I don't think you will talk your way out of this."

There was none of his usual righteous glee in the statement. There was, if anything, a glimmer of anxiety, even fear. Garnet knew I was capable of all kinds of appalling actions in word and deed, and he would happily watch me flogged with something spiky if it taught me the error of my ways and, more importantly, proved the rightness of his. But this was different. His face was paler than ever and his eyes were downcast. There was a studied blankness to his features and a rigidity to his posture that suggested a tremendous effort of will. He was being strong, and while this usually came naturally to him, the effort was nearly killing him. And as I thought this, it came to me. "They're coming to kill me, aren't they?" I mouthed.

He look at the floor and said nothing.

"Aren't they?" I demanded.

He looked up very slowly and there was doubt in his eyes. "They are coming to apprehend you for trial," he began, but his voice failed him and he paused. His eyes met mine and the doubt was gone as he answered me without knowing how he could be so sure: "I think so," he said. "Yes."

"Tell Renthrette I'm sorry about her dress," I said.

I was already grabbing my things and running for the door. He stood where he was, asking quietly, desperately, as if this would make everything clear, "What did you do?"

SCENE XVII

The Dead Forest

You may have noticed that running away is not a frequent feature in the lives led by the heroes of literature. You may also have noted that running is something I do rather a lot of. The fact of the matter is that dying, which is rather more popular in heroic tales, has never especially appealed to me, particularly when it involves pain and humiliation. I wasn't sure which method of slow torture the so-called "fair folk" preferred, but I was pretty sure that I would rather be otherwise engaged. I'm not particularly stoic when it comes to pain and, since I'm far from sure what may or may not lurk in the hereafter, I have learned to spot danger before it spots me and move away from it very, very quickly. Not particularly honorable or even dignified, I admit, but I can live with that. At least I'll live with something.

So I ran from Phasdreille, from its handsome book-burning soldiers, from that poisonous Aliana bitch and the valiantly murderous Sorrail, like a rabbit from a greyhound. The bridge sentries were still searching the palace, so I clambered into the back of a wagon of empty soap boxes packed in straw, and tried to still the hammering of my heart as we moved out over the bridge, through the barbican and out of the city at last. Garnet's warning had, it occurred to me, saved my life. I suddenly wished I had told him that his beloved Lisha was alive and only a few miles away.

Well, too late for that now.

I waited a few minutes and then slipped down from the wagon, rolling into the ditch by the road and lying still till I could hear no sign of life. I moved quickly into the woods to rest. I was not in the best shape, and my exertions, augmented by a stifling panic, had left me breathless and just about incapable of action. I was lying on my stomach and staring back toward the city while I tried to figure out what to do next when a company of horsemen came charging over the bridge and out of the barbican. There they clattered to a halt, divided into two, and set off in opposite directions on the road. This was not encouraging. I didn't actually hear them distributing my portrait, but their mission seemed clear: Find Hawthorne and put one of those carefully polished lances through his gizzard.

I wasn't sure what my gizzard was, but I was fairly confident that I had other plans for it, so I lay in the bracken and did my best to stop breathing for about ten minutes. Then another group of soldiers, this time on foot, came out of the city and my blood ran colder than Renthrette's eyes on a frosty day. At the head of the company, yelping and lunging forward with disturbing eagerness, was a pack of hounds.

It seemed about that time again. So I ran, straight into where the forest seemed deepest, diving through bracken and bounding over fallen trees like . . . well, like someone with a company of soldiers and a pack of dogs at his heels. I figured it would take the dogs a moment to pick up my scent, but once they had it, my days, and—for that matter—my seconds, were numbered. I knew that I should be thinking up some brilliant ruse, but my legs had taken over and my brain was trying to keep up. I knew that even if I climbed a tree (presuming I could do that without killing myself) or hid in some conveniently positioned hollow, the hounds would track me down and I would gain nothing more than another minute or two to reflect upon those teeth and lance tips. So I kept moving with nothing more in my mind than getting as much distance between me and my pursuers as possible. Far behind me, the barking swelled and became unified: They were coming. And suddenly, as I blundered through a screen of hemlock, the stench hit me.

It had probably been growing with each footstep, but I had been too preoccupied with my footing to reflect upon the sweet and fragrant aromas of the forest. These aromas had now become a good deal less sweet and fragrant as a sour note overpowered the resin scent of the pines and brought me to a nose-wrinkling halt. The dogs answered, right on cue, with a bloodthirsty baying, so I silenced my offended nostrils (if you know what I mean), and pressed on. A huge spruce barred my path and I had to press blindly through its pale extremities. I shielded my eyes from the needles as I did so, and then, as I broke free, found myself gaping at my feet. One of my boots had sunk into the earth up to the cuff at the knee. I plucked it out with a long, sucking draw and the smell broke upon me like a cloud. Looking

up, I found that the trees here had fallen away. Across a few yards of
dark and stinking mud was the river, black, oily, and still as death.

I remembered the winding river instantly, of course, how it divided the fair woods and Phasdreille from the foul realm of darkness
on the south bank, and as I stared across, it was all perfectly self-
evident. The trees which sprouted from the stagnant water or stuck up
at wild angles from its surface were blackened poles stripped of
leaves, with branches like ragged claws, and on the far side of the river
the woods were reduced to a thicket of the same dead pikes stabbing
at the sky from dank and swampy beds. The air was chill and heavily
silent for a second, and I could smell the evil through the decay. But
then the silence was broken by the voices of the hounds and their han-
dlers, and my dilemma hit me between the eyes like a pickaxe. Should I
stay on the bank and wait for the soldiers to drag my bleeding remains
from their dogs for formal torture and execution in Phasdreille, or
should I brave the horrors of the water and whatever lay beyond it?
Put like that, I seemed to have only one option. The stinking waters
might even throw the dogs off my scent.

I took three more gurgling strides through the struggling reeds
and mud and then felt the chill of icy water rushing over the tops of
my boots. It was an inconceivably unpleasant sensation. Another step,
and the bottom, which was treacherously slick with what I took to be
rotting leaves and branches, shelved sharply. The water rose up to my
chest, driving the breath from my body as the surprising cold overcame me. I stood there gasping the noxious air and gazing, stricken, at
the far bank, which looked about a mile away. I had just remembered
that I couldn't swim.

There was a rustle in the vegetation behind me. It could have been
a deer or a rabbit, but I assumed the worst and took another hurried
couple of steps. The water rose and its frigid and viscous surface
closed about my neck, so thick and dark that I could barely see my own
body beneath it. I tipped my head back and closed my mouth, almost
retching at the thought of this stinking fluid getting on my face, in my
nose, in my mouth. The surface was mottled with a foul-smelling scum,
unnaturally white and clotted with bubbles like oversized frog spawn.
My every movement roused a thick cloud under the water, black and
heavy as blood.

Luckily, it got no deeper. I could hear the soldiers and their pack
through the birdless trees, but their calls were of confusion. I might

make it yet. Indeed, perhaps I didn't need to venture into the haunted forest, or whatever it was, on the other side at all. Perhaps I could just stay where I was, freezing quietly, until they left. But how long would that be, and how could I hope to reemerge from the woods onto the road without being seen and apprehended? So I continued to wade across, slowly, being careful not to slosh the heavy water which congealed about me, my joints beginning to seize as the cold shrank my sinews and froze my muscles. But then, quite unexpectedly, the river bottom seemed to swell and the water receded from my throat. The shelving was almost as steep here as it had been on the other bank, and it took both hands digging into the mud and clasping hold of stray logs before I could clamber, filthy and stinking, out of the water.

I say I got out, but in fact the water never really went away. It just turned into shallow stagnant pools and broad, still basins from which the dead trees emerged like some ruined palisade. I knelt shivering on the edge of one such pool and gazed back the way I had come, but I could see nothing. A heavy silence had fallen like a blanket of snow over the entire forest. For the moment, I was safe, but this was hardly prime picnicking territory. A brooding gloom suffused the place, filling me with slow dread. Out of the frying pan, as they say, and into the demon-infested swamp. . . .

For what seemed like a long time I did nothing but wonder what to do. If I was trying to get to Lisha, I should follow the riverbank west; but if I was headed for the mountains where we had entered this hellhole, I should go east. Both routes would take me on a several-mile stroll through the sinister expanse of death that lay stinking all around me, and I did not doubt that there were goblins and things still fouler lurking throughout the forest on this side of the river. But if I crossed the river, the "fair folk" would take one of their fair axes and remove useful parts of me. The world, apparently, wasn't my oyster.

I had almost decided to head west for the village tavern where Lisha was staying when I caught sight of smoke from the direction of the mountains, which would have been upstream if there had been any movement in the water whatsoever. It seemed close by, though I couldn't tell which side of the river it came from. Without thinking further, I began walking toward it, following a winding track around water-filled pits and shifting earth.

I came upon the source quite unexpectedly. Rounding a bend in the river I found myself no more than fifty yards from where it spanned the river: a great building, half-dam, half-mill, and constructed of what looked like new but stained and blackened brick. Chimneys spouted along the length of its roof and each belched thick and sulfurous smoke into the sky. As I stood there, the wind caught the smoke and it drifted, sagging toward me like some overweight and drunken cow. The smell was appalling. It was like both the air of the dead forest and the stagnant water of the river and pools; but it was, if anything, stronger, and touched with a rancid edge like butter left in the sun for days. I clutched my stinking hand over my nose and mouth to shut it out and fought to keep my gorge down. Then, driven by the curiosity which kills more than cats, I approached, skulking through the gray reeds.

It was a graceless structure, windowless and devoid of ornament. Along its side, about two yards above the level of the stopped-up river, was a series of five pipes, each a foot or more in diameter, and each trickling some yellowish filth into the water below. It congealed, this effluent, into greasy pools, sometimes collecting on the surface, sometimes sinking and drifting for a while until it settled elsewhere. One look at or sniff of that putrid glaze as it slopped out of the pipes and I no longer wondered why the river and forest were dead and stinking.

Right beside the bank where I crouched, a chute crudely constructed of heavy lumber emerged from the building and emptied into the marshy shoreline. As I edged closer to peer into this, a hatchway somewhere inside opened and I heard for a moment the sounds of boiling, churning fluid and clanking pans. Then there was a clatter and a heap of objects came tumbling down the chute and into the river. Some sank without a trace; others missed their mark and fell around me like the rain that falls in nightmares. There were bits of armor, pieces of fabric, the broken hafts of weapons and fragments of metal, but mostly, there were bones: ribs, thighs, fingers, skulls, some almost human, but most ridged and heavy set. These were, there could be no doubt, goblin remains.

What the hell? . . .

I looked toward the mountains. Since the river ran fairly straight for about a mile, I could make out two similar structures straddling the river. There were sounds from inside the brick building, but it never occurred to me to see if the people within might protect me. Whoever—or whatever—they were, I did not want them to see me. I glanced across the river as I moved away, and there I glimpsed the

wagon in which I had sneaked a ride from the city, incongruously
bright and clean, painted elegantly in cream and trimmed with purple
and gold. A man, tall and dressed in a buff leather jerkin, was loading
crates onto the straw-packed back of the wagon. I knew what went
into those boxes and recalled Garnet's words on how proud of their
cleanliness were the citizens of Phasdreille. Through the stink of the
smoke and the stuff which was pumping out into the river, I thought I
caught a distant whiff of rose petals.

So, this is how they make their soap.

I wasn't sure if it was this realization or the sickly sweet aroma
which finally pushed me over the edge, but I vomited quietly into the
reeds where a cluster of pale bubbles puffed fat like fungus.

Being sick got rid of whatever lingered from the previous night's
drinking binge, and though I was now thirsty and hungry, I felt better,
clearheaded and ready to think. Of course, it didn't take much detailed
analysis of my predicament to see that I was like a man who, coming
home after a night on the town, finds that what he took to be his bed-
room has become a cage full of tigers. The only thing more bewildering than how I had got into this insane situation was how I was going
to get out of it.

Staying where I was would clearly be as dangerous as it was offensive to my nostrils, so I moved inland, if that is a fair term for the
quagmire which stretched back into the blasted forest. I was still wet,
and a cold wind had picked up and was coursing through the dead
trees like a thousand sighing phantoms. I kept moving, for warmth
more than to get anywhere specific, though after a close encounter
with some quicksand—or its black and slimy equivalent—I picked up
a stick and probed the earth before each step. Thus, with slow and uneven strides, I inched my way back from the river and into the dead
forest.

I had been walking no more than ten minutes when my finely
tuned adventurer's ears picked up movement behind me. In fact, my
three-quarters-deaf aunt could have heard the clomping around in
the reeds behind me, and she's been dead several years. I stopped and
considered my options. Either whoever or whatever was behind me
wanted me to hear them, which was not necessarily a good thing, or
whatever it was was so immense and hulking that this pounding
through the underbrush was what passed for stealth among its kind.
Since neither option was particularly optimal, I decided to get my

weapon ready and turn slowly. I hadn't had time to arrange my pack as I would have liked, but my sword, now muddy and probably rusting, hung by my hand. I dragged it quietly from its sheath and wheeled rapidly as if I was ready for anything.

I wasn't, of course, but things could have been worse: a good deal worse, in fact. Behind me was a small woman, olive-skinned and with narrow black eyes and small features. Her long, raven-black hair was held back by a silver pin. She leaned on a silver-shod staff of ebony.

"Lisha?" I gasped.

"You're deaf as a post, Will," she remarked. "I've been following you for ten minutes, trying to make sure it was you and that no one else was tracking you on this side of the river. I thought I was making enough noise to wake the dead."

"I heard you," I replied, guardedly. This was not the first friend I had met wandering in these woods and the last one had turned out to have been dead some time. "How did you find me?"

"I heard from Rose that the city was up in arms looking for you."

"There's no way she could have gotten word to you that quickly," I replied, keeping my sword raised and level. "I've only been running from them for an hour or so. It would take her three times that just to get back to the inn and give you the news."

"She didn't have to," said Lisha, unoffended by my skepticism. "I came with her in the carriage, hidden, of course. I was concerned that we hadn't heard from you, and then one of Rose's other clients mentioned your behavior at the banquet. . . ."

"I was set up!" I exclaimed. "I could drink all those tarted-up clowns into the middle of next week, especially with that gutless rubbish they call beer around here. . . ."

"I know, Will," said Lisha, smiling her small and cryptic smile. "That's one of the reasons I thought you might be in trouble. Someone was obviously trying to discredit you, or worse."

"Exactly," I agreed, huffily.

"So I hid in the trunk under the carriage seats and came down with Rose to the city gates. We arrived just after the soldiers had come this way looking for you. Everyone was talking about it. I guessed that your only possible escape would be on this side of the river, though I'm still not clear why they wouldn't cross over and continue to search on this side."

"Why aren't you wet? How did you cross the river?"

"I used the dam where that building is—"

"Yes, all right," I interrupted, reluctant to talk about that ominous and disquieting structure for fear of articulating what went on inside it. She fell silent and watched me and as I looked at her closely, I realized that I no more expected her to start falling into dead bones and powdered flesh than I expected her to sprout another head and sing a duet. Relief and pleasure crept over me. "God, it's good to see you," I exclaimed.

"You, too," she answered, smiling. "Now we must move. You can tell me your news while we walk."

"Which way?"

"It doesn't matter, so long as we get away from the riverbank and those search parties. They may yet cross the water. The way you were heading seems as good an idea as any."

"But this takes us deeper into the haunted forest," I said, trying not to whine.

"*Haunted*?" she said. "Will, are you all right?"

"I know, I know. But I've seen things here that, well, don't make sense. I don't know what's real. My gut says that you are Lisha, and I'm trusting to that because I want you to be Lisha. I'm making some kind of leap of faith. Or maybe it's a leap of desperation. Can you make a leap of desperation? I believe you are you because if I allow myself to think that you are really some tentacled demon in a cunning disguise, I'll probably go mad, and I'd prefer not to do that just yet, thank you."

She extended her hand. "Here, Will," she said. "Take my tentacle."

I started and gave her a look of alarm.

"A joke," she said with only the smallest crinkling of her lips. "Come on."

I took her hand and it felt real enough, small and warm. She led me through the paths of the swamp like a child leading an indulgent adult. Still, it occurred to me again, I had rarely been gladder to see anyone in my life.

❧

"And this hooded figure in the library was not the assassin who chased you in the alley," asked Lisha.

"No," I said. We had paused to eat some bread which she had brought with her, seated on the trunk of a tree that had torn up its entire root system as it fell. I continued, thoughtfully. "This was someone I had never come across before. *Something*, perhaps. I don't know. He was more than just some old coot in a cloak. He was more than old, for a start. He was phenomenally old. And he knew things, and not just about the prophecy. I don't think he even wanted me to hear that—I'd swear it wasn't his voice. It was almost like I was hearing his memory, a memory he wanted to keep hidden. That's the impression I had more than anything else: he remembers. It's like he's an embodiment of the people or the city. . . . Something. And he knew about me. About us. About the city. I'm not sure how I know, but he could see . . . maybe not everywhere at once, but he could see a lot more than was in that room. It was weird."

Lisha munched silently while I finished this lame and embarrassed account. I tried to grin, expecting her to dismiss the whole thing as the product of an overactive imagination, but even though I'd spent a lot of time with the likes of Renthrette, I should have known better. Lisha nodded thoughtfully, uncritically, and shaped a smile that was compassionate, as if offering sympathy for what she could tell had been a harrowing experience.

I pressed on. "Aliana knew, too. The girl who ran the library, I mean. There was more to her than met the eye. She knew there was no fire behind those doors, but she pretended there was to get rid of me. Somehow, finding my way in there and seeing him—it; whatever—was what shot me to the top of the most-wanted list. I don't know why, partly because if I'm supposed to have learned something crucial from what I saw, I didn't, and partly because I just walked in. It wasn't guarded. It wasn't even locked."

"They must think you are dangerous," said Lisha. "It must be the prophecy, though I am at a loss as to what it means or where it came from. Garnet is a greater warrior than you and they have accepted him, so it must be something you know or something you might guess."

"I've eaten rabbits that knew more than me," I mused. "No, if that old bloke in the library is some state secret worth killing for, I have no idea why. Yes, he was creepy and scared me to death, but that seems the rule rather than the exception round here. The line between the exotic and the downright terrifying has gotten very thin of late."

I took a woolen blanket from my pack and wrapped it around myself. I was still damp, and the air was, if anything, getting colder.

"What about these recurring accounts of old battles and

buildings?" she asked. "Could this mysterious old man have any connection to those?"

"I hadn't thought about it, but now that you bring it up, I'm
tempted to say yes. Each time I heard one of those strange, formulaic
accounts, I felt like the words were coming from somewhere else."

"From him?"

"It's possible. I know it sounds absurd, but I think it could be true."

"Why, though? What do the stories have in common?"

"I only heard a couple of variations and they were quite different," I said. "One was about a particular family heirloom, a weapon.
The other was about the building of the city, as I said."

"And both were about continued family involvement," she answered, reflectively. "Heritage. History. I don't know, maybe—"

I cut her off, blinded by a realization. "History," I thought aloud.
"That's got to be it. There were no history books in the library,
and all the other books were being changed. Many were destroyed
altogether. Some were in an unreadable language, but some were in
Thrusian almost the same as ours or the 'fair folk's.' I have some
here."

I fished in my pockets and pulled out a handful of burned scraps
which I had taken from the furnaces. Lisha peered at them and I
looked over her shoulder.

"A lot of it's just old love poetry," I remarked. "That was the batch
they were burning, I guess. It doesn't make sense. None of what I read
was offensive in any way. Look," I said, choosing the largest fragment
of verse and beginning to read.

> *"My soul and I have traveled through the world*
> *And yet in forest dark or ebon sky*
> *I never have beheld a hue more black*
> *Than that which pools and gleams in your fair eye."*

"Pretty predictable stuff," I added. " 'Pools' is nice, I suppose.
Hardly worth burning though, don't you think?"

"Hardly," said Lisha, reading the other pieces silently to herself.

I watched her for a moment, and she noticed, glancing up at me
suddenly. "What?" she said.

"Nothing," I shrugged, flushing slightly. "I was just thinking about that line, you know, about blackness pooling in your eyes. Your eyes have that kind of look." She looked confused, and I stammered hurriedly, "I don't mean anything by that. I mean, I'm not, you know, trying to . . ."

"It's all right, Will," she said, smiling suddenly. "I'll take it as a compliment. Thank you."

"It was a compliment," I admitted stuffily. "But the words struck me because you don't often see poetry that addresses people who, you know, look like you. Usually it's all written for golden-haired ice queens with sky blue eyes and ruby lips . . ."

It finally hit me.

I froze, then leaped to my feet. "That's it!" I yelled. "That's it! There is no history because the history is all wrong. The 'fair folk' didn't write the books in that library. How many women with black eyes have you seen around Phasdreille? If there were any, they wouldn't be the subject of poetry, I'll tell you that, not unless things used to be very different."

My mind was racing. Things were slotting into place, and I talked quickly to let them all out. "The brass panels on the doors that feel warm? They show the library being built. But the builders are squat and heavy-looking, not like the 'fair folk' at all. God, Lisha! Goblins built that city! Is that possible? It would explain why the new stonework looks so inferior. The masons had nothing to learn from. There were no hammers passed on from father to son, no heirloom weapons notched on goblin collars. It's all been a lie. The history is being rewritten. Every part of that culture is being remade as the work of the 'fair folk.'"

"But that would mean . . ."

"That Sorrail's ancestors are the newcomers," I said. "They took the city from the goblins and the goblins want it back. No wonder the goblins don't know their way around the Falcon's Nest. They may have carved it out of the rock generations ago, but they haven't used it in just as long. The so-called fair folk know about its secret entrances because *they* moved into it. It was *their* fortress, their base when they first invaded. That's what they do. They commandeer and appropriate, and when it's theirs, they ornament. But they don't build, not really. They don't construct. They don't have the skills. They capture or they con their way in and then they make everything theirs. You see? It makes sense. That's why the statues have been defaced. That's why the library has been closed down while the books are edited for any reference to the goblin past."

"But why?" demanded Lisha. "Why spend so much time and effort trying to convince the people of something they must know isn't true?"

"They might not know," I said. "I think the library, and that one room and whoever lives in it, is somehow affecting or altering the people's memories of the past."

"But you said these stories started cropping up long before you got near the city," said Lisha. "Can his power have that kind of range?"

"What if the hammers and swords somehow do it, or focus his sorcery?" I said, thinking aloud. "They are all set with diamonds. We've seen stones that had power before. Maybe they serve as a kind of matrix for storing those bogus personal histories. But how he's doing it is less important than what it all means. There were no great goblin invasions and no 'fair folk' builders, but the war and the city have to be explained, so history is being rewritten, even in the minds of those who live there. It's the ultimate way to prop up their own sense of righteousness: Rather than feeling like the aggressor, the people of Phasdreille get to think of themselves as the victims, the righteous ones on the receiving end of evil and malice. I can't think of a better way to make people fight than in defense of something they believe to be their ancestral home. Maybe this is what they expected me to realize earlier, though who the 'they' is, I couldn't say. The king? Sorrail? Aliana? The hooded figure in the library? Him, at least."

There was a long silence between us.

"And this would be enough to want you dead, I think," said Lisha.

"Yes," I agreed. "I see now. I seem to have become dangerous. Though what I could do with this knowledge, I really don't know. Still, we can't go back there now. I suspect that being caught by Sorrail and his fair-haired and perfectly attired men-at-arms would not be much better than being taken by goblins in these swamps."

And before Lisha had time to agree, perfectly on cue, as if I had set the whole speech up just for dramatic effect, the swamp was swarming with them: goblins, gray and olive and yellowish and black, all snarling, all staring at us, all approaching cautiously with weapons at the ready.

Lisha leaped to her feet and swung her metal-shod staff up before

her. I drew my sword hurriedly and stood at her back. Together we ro-
tated slowly in some absurd dance as goblins crept closer, sputtering
their foul words at each other. I don't think that holding a sword had
ever felt so pointless. There were dozens of them emerging, as if from
the vile pools themselves, and through a thicket of tangled vines a
goblin the color of sandstone riding a great bear led a dozen wolves,
heads low and menacing, toward us.

The goblins came on, creeping watchfully, as if making sure we
had no escort, until they formed a rough circle around us and stood
no more than twenty feet away. There was a good deal of shouting
from outside the circle and some rapid movement, but I was watching those goblins that were closest to me, those near enough for me
to see their ragged armor and gnarled hands; their twisted, skinny
frames; their eyes. They were glancing from us back to each other,
and they were talking. Something strange was happening, and my
sense that they were about to rush us en masse and tear us to pieces
faded. The confusion which replaced it was shattered when the circle
broke and a great black goblin came bounding toward us, brandishing
a long and lethal-looking sword.

"Lisha!" I cried and stepped around to block the brute's assault.
It came toward me, taking huge strides and shouting. Then my sword
arm was seized and held, my weapon twisted from my grasp. I
wrenched my head around and saw Lisha taking my weapon and tossing it on the floor as a scrawny goblin came from behind me and
pulled my arms behind my back.

"You *are* one of them!" I screamed at her. "You are. I'll kill you.
I'll kill you all!"

Lisha, or whatever it was that seemed to have taken her shape,
stepped up to me so that her face was only inches from mine. She
caught my face in her hands. I spat at her. "I'll kill you, you foul bitch.
What have you done with Lisha?"

"Will," she said, and her voice was soft. "Will, look."

She pointed me toward the huge black goblin who had almost
reached us before stopping dead in his tracks. I looked.

It was Orgos. His armor was grimy and his tunic torn, but it was
Orgos. I don't know how I could have failed to recognize him.

"It's all right, Will," said Lisha. "You see? It's all right."

She broke from me and wiped her face.

My eyes fell on Orgos. He had dropped his sword, the one with the yellow stone in the pommel. I think he had been running to embrace us, but now his eyes were full of doubt.

"I'm sorry," I said. "I thought . . . I saw the other goblins and I thought . . . Sorry."

The goblin who had pinned my arms released me and Orgos stepped up to me.

"Hello, Will," he said. And it was him: No goblin. No undead apparition. It was Orgos, my friend. Slowly, a smile as broad as only he could manage spread across his face.

"I missed you," I said as he flung his great arms about me. Over his shoulder I saw Lisha embrace another large man: Mithos, still bandaged, but walking and well.

"And now you have to tell us how you come to be here," Orgos said, still grinning, "and we'll introduce you to our new friends."

"Friends?" I spluttered.

"Friends," said Mithos firmly.

The impact of the word put the finishing touch on all my former thoughts about Phasdreille, the rewritten history of the "fair folk," and all the other suspicions which had been mounting in my head. I watched Orgos casually say something to one of the "goblins" in their own tongue and watched the listener smile with understanding. The goblin features shifted as easily as any human face and I found myself looking not at the spawn of hell, but at a person. The unavoidable conclusion came charging through with the rest of the wild horses that were my thoughts, and I grew instantly cold and struck with horror.

"My God," I breathed aloud. "What have I done? Lisha . . ."

She turned to me and her eyes were full of a sad understanding. She wanted to make me feel better and knew it was futile.

As the full weight of my realization hit me, I felt my eyes well with tears, and, staring at her, I managed to say it.

"Lisha, I've been fighting on the wrong side."

⚜

Goblins

I was still cold, and evening was coming on. One of the goblins, a thin, gray creature with deep-set eyes and high, angular cheek-bones, was adjusting a blanket strapped to a small backpack, using his long, bony fingers. The blanket was worn in places, but it looked clean and dry, unlike mine. A matter of hours ago I might have killed him for it, or tried to, but now I didn't know what to do. I shifted uneasily, hardly daring to meet the creature's eyes and fearful of what would follow if I did. I coughed. When his gaze fell blankly on me, I looked jealously at the blanket.

"You want this?" he said in perfect Thrusian. "Here. Dry yourself off. The swamp may freeze tonight."

I gaped at him. It was as if I had sat down to milk a cow and the beast had turned to me at the first squeeze of its udders and said, "Gentler, if you don't mind."

There's something about hearing words come out of someone's mouth that changes the way you look at them. I guess it's the casual ease with which the lips and tongue shape sounds so intimate and meaningful to you, putting the two of you on the same level, establishing an equilibrium of sorts. A talking cow, then, would not merely be a curiosity; it would violate your understanding of the universe and your place in it. It would force you, I suspect, to rethink every action you had ever performed. It would change more than your attitude to steak, I'll tell you that.

This was where I found myself now. The goblin unfastened the buckled straps and tossed me the rolled blanket without another word. I stood there doing my world-famous impersonation of a fence post, waking only when the parcel hit me in the chest and fell into my hastily raised arms. It—or perhaps I should say *he*—grinned broadly and walked away. I watched him go.

His grin had been genuine and yet somehow alarming. It reminded me that he was a goblin, for his jaw was heavy and his teeth were over-large, but it also seemed so ordinary, so human. Before I could take my eyes off him, Lisha appeared silently beside me.

"Will?" she said. "Are you all right?"

"I'm not sure," I said, my eyes still on the back of the receding goblin. "I . . . I'm really not sure."

"We should talk," she said.

"Yes, we should," I echoed distantly.

"Will! Look at me!"

I turned slowly and met her eyes. They pooled at me in the twilight.

"We made a mistake," she said. "That's all. We were given false information and, without any reason to doubt it, we believed it."

We. The extent of her mistake was getting mistaken for one of them. I, however, had . . .

Don't think about it.

I nodded and managed a smile, but it was a thin ruse. She knew as much, knew also that, for once, I didn't feel like talking after all, and she respected that. She touched my cheek and walked over to where Mithos and Orgos were studying a map.

I sat on a log, dazed with shock. How could I have been so stupid? I had trusted my eyes and ears and, as a result, fallen for the oldest theatrical ploy there is. I was taken in by the desire to believe something preposterously convenient was real. I had forgotten to read between the lines. I had known something was wrong but I just went on standing there like the idiot in the pit who thinks everything on the stage is real because a few paid con men tell him it is. It had all been a show, just storytelling and spectacle, and I had fallen for it hook, line, and sinker. I had risked my life for the "fair folk" and—and here was the scorpion in my underpants—I had killed for them.

Now morals aren't my strong suit, and I still had a hard time thinking of the goblins as *people* exactly, but my glorious ride with the cavalry, my brave defense of the city, and my valiant raid on the Falcon's Nest fortress were beginning to look a little tarnished, as if my heirloom silver tankard had turned out to be made of oven-baked cow dung. The "fair folk" had said that all the light-against-dark, good-against-evil rubbish that I'd been laughing at my entire life was actually true, and I had believed them. They had told me that every old tale, every fairy story about ogres and goblins, every half-baked morality play aimed at children and the mentally deficient was right, and the world as I had always known it was wrong. Beauty (of the right kind) really *is* virtue, they had said, and ugliness (someone else's) *is* evil. And I had believed them. Cynical Bill, Will the realist, had polished up his sword and gone out goblin slaying, glad to be doing his bit for goodness and light and fluffy bunny rabbits. I should have known Garnet couldn't be right.

I *had* known, too. Kind of. A bunch of things had not seemed right. I should have just listened to my hunches and not to those dandified idiots in Phasdreille. Well, from here on it would all be Will Straight-from-the-Gut Hawthorne.

"Feeling better?" said Orgos.

"Yes," I lied. "The blanket helps. How long did it take you to realize what was going on?"

"Not long," said Orgos. "But that was because they told us and we believed them. Maybe we would have believed Sorrail if our positions had been reversed."

"You don't really think that," I said.

Orgos shrugged. "Well, we also had the evidence of how they treated us," he went on. "They were suspicious because we had been caught in the company of one of their greatest enemies, but we had our looks on our sides, which, frankly, helped."

"They believed you because you're black?" I asked, eyebrow raised.

"It made it a lot less likely that we were working with the so-called fair folk, said Orgos.

"But they kept you locked up," I said, not sure who I was trying to convince or what I was trying to justify.

"Like I said, they were suspicious of us, and most of that fort hadn't been lived in for decades. Their rooms weren't much better than ours."

I frowned and said nothing.

"Come on," he concluded. "The sooner we get there, the sooner we can eat. I have a feeling you're going to like these people."

I gave him a quick look, but the remark seemed to have been genuine enough, so I said nothing and followed him.

We wended our way through the swamp trails and the light faded fast. In half an hour it was almost too dark to see. Since no one produced a torch or lantern, I edged closer to the pack and studied the ground ahead. Orgos said that "they" had good night vision. I grunted and kept walking without even bothering to ask where we were going.

We came upon a thicket of healthy young pine trees, all slender and stretching skyward like wading birds, and as I paused to study the trees, the column of goblins dwindled to nothing. I stopped, glancing wildly about and wondering if I had been led out here as part of some elaborate and ghostly hoax. Even Orgos had gone.

"What the? . . ." I began. Then what I had taken to be a dark pool showed movement and Orgos was there.

"Come on, Will," he whispered. "You're the last."

I approached cautiously.

"I can't see you properly," I said. "It's a tunnel?"

"Kind of," he said. "Here, take my hand. I'll show you the way. You'll like this place. It was hollowed out of the rock perhaps a century ago, maybe longer, and has been carefully maintained so that the swamp water is sealed out. Lately the damp has become a greater problem as the forest above it has fallen into decay. How much longer it will be livable, I don't know. But, for the moment, it is more than just a hiding place on the enemy's doorstep."

"Assuming the 'fair folk' are the enemy," I muttered.

"That, you will have to figure out for yourself," he said, with the carelessness that suggested the matter was self-evident.

"As you have done?" I pressed.

"Yes, Will. As I have done. You still aren't sure?" He asked this with a note of surprise in his voice and turned toward me so that I could just about make out the light of his eyes in the gloom.

"Not yet," I replied a little frostily.

He was unaffected by my tone and, in truth, I didn't know why I had taken it. He just shrugged and turned back to the descending passage, pulling me slightly toward him as he stepped down. There was a hole, no more than a yard across and almost invisible in the long grass, and in it was a tightly spiraling stairway. I fumbled for a rail, grabbed an outcrop of bare and polished rock, and lowered myself in. Feeling for the edge of each step with my foot, I descended slowly into the darkness, until I could smell smoke and candle wax. Then, quite suddenly, a yellowish light played over my feet. I took two more steps and then bent down to peer into the chamber below.

A broad cave spread out around me and firelight flickered on the walls. Voices raised in song and laughter rose from below and, if my ears did not deceive me, I thought I caught the familiar clink of pewter mugs. Things were looking up.

Briefly. The moment I made my appearance on the stairs, a strange hush fell on the chamber. Faces turned toward me and the last patterings of speech trickled into nothing but the roar of the fire. Their gazes fell on me and held me, their eyes burning quietly and their mouths closed. Somewhere one of their immense bears growled.

I faltered, and then, seeing Mithos turn back toward me, continued my descent, slowly, watchfully.

"Come on, Will," said Mithos, with a deliberation which refused to acknowledge the change in the assembly's demeanor. "Let's get you a drink."

I looked at him expressionlessly and stepped down, half expecting the two of us to be overwhelmed in a rush of hostile goblins overturning tables and chairs, shrieking and raising heavy, cruel weapons.

Instead, the swell of conversation grew again, gradually at first, returning to normal in a matter of seconds. The goblins turned back to their food and to each other and soon after that there was singing and the sound of a small harp.

I gave Mithos a hard stare as soon as the last face was turned from us. "What the hell was that? Are you so sure these are the good guys? They look like the only reason they haven't slit my throat yet is because they're saving me for dessert."

"Cut it out, Will," said Mithos, stern now.

"They aren't exactly rolling out the red carpet . . ." I began.

"Do you know how many of them you killed when you came with Renthrette to the Falcon's Nest?" said Mithos, his eyes glittering hard and black.

"We came to rescue you!"

"And did it never occur to you that we might not need rescuing?"

"No!" I said loudly. "No, it bloody didn't. And you know why? Because these half-animal degenerates attacked us in the mountains and did their best to kill us all. You have a pretty damn funny way of picking friends. Is it part of your bloody adventurer's code? Do I have to hack one of your legs off before you'll consider me a buddy, too? With friends like this, who needs . . ."

He stepped up close enough that I could feel his breath on my face when he whispered, "Do you remember how that fight started, Will?"

I said nothing.

"It started," he said in the same scarily hushed tone, "when you assumed that the beasts that had come into the cave had come to attack us, and you threw a stone."

"A pack of wolves and some grizzlies marched into the place we were bedding down! What did you expect me to do? Offer them tea?"

"I'm just saying that you started it, and it might have gone differently. If we hadn't given Sorrail an excuse to 'rescue' us, we might have all gotten a clearer perspective on this thing. . . ."

"Oh, of course!" I shouted suddenly. "It's my fault! How *very* surprising. When in doubt, blame Hawthorne. Thanks for the encouragement, Mithos. I'll tell you what; I'll just go and drown myself in the swamp, save everyone the trouble."

"Fine."

"What?"

"Fine. Go and drown yourself. You know where the stairs are."

"What," I stuttered, "*now*?"

"Don't say things you don't mean, Will," said Mithos, walking away.

I had a good mind to go right back up, but it was damn cold outside and wandering around the swamp at night—or, more likely, sitting sulking just out of sight of the stairway—wasn't what you might call a grand night out. If I didn't manage to drown myself as threatened, I'd probably get eaten by something long and slippery. At least the goblins had a fire. I'd stay right where I was. That would show them.

It turned out they had a good deal more than just a fire. They had a banquet including roast pork, two kinds of wine, and three kinds of beer. Initially, of course, it was all dust and ashes in my mouth, torn as I was between doubt and misery, guilt and anger, but that passed fairly quickly for reasons that will become rapidly apparent. The pig was stuffed with rosemary and sage and was served with a thick fruit-based sauce. There were half a dozen different cheeses, all excellent, ranging from a firm-fleshed but delicate yellow smoked to a full-bodied blue that you could cut with your finger. There was some kind of venison *pâté* served with crusty bread, and mushrooms stuffed and sautéed with buckets of garlic. There was a pot of highly spiced beans that warmed me more than the fire.

And then there was the beer. After the gnat's piss they drank in Phasdreille, this was like liquid divinity. One was a lager, golden and

sharp with a hoppy aftertaste that woke you up and suggested another mug. There was also an ale: nut-brown and rich with a hint of
spice, like afternoon light on a leather chair. Lastly, there was a stout,
full bodied and velvet-smooth, black and opaque with a head like
fresh cream. I had one of each, and by the time I had gone back for
seconds, I was slipping my arm around the shoulders of the meanest-
looking goblins and suggesting we play some cards. I took another
mouthful of the herbed pork, swilled it down with a gulp of ale, and
the idea that these good fellows around me could possibly be the enemy faded like a memory from childhood. And in my inebriated state,
oscillating between sublime insight and rank stupidity, the quality of
the goblins' beer seemed like a perfectly good reason to switch sides in
a war.

The following morning, I still wasn't sure if that last thought had
been genius or insanity. Last night I had felt at one with the goblins
and with the cosmos generally, which is something good beer often
does to me. Today, waking bleary-eyed with a dull ache in my temples,
cold in my bones, and with a company of goblins about me, some of
whom still shot me looks that would have skewered a horse, I wasn't
so sure. In my lowest moments, I reflected that climbing into a leaky
stone pit under a marsh with a goblin army, complete with its bear
mounts and wolf scouts, was rather like smearing myself with honey
and then sitting on a wasps' nest, though these wasps had stingers several feet long. This wouldn't have bothered me so much if the goblin
community as a whole had been busily extending the hand of friendship, but no one wished me good morning and suggested hangover
remedies. Nobody brought me breakfast, showed me the way to a fresh-
water spring outside in the swamp-forest, or told me where I could best
relieve myself without nettling my bum. Conversations would peter out
as I walked by, and small, slanted eyes would follow my path with, if
not actual hostility, then at least suspicion. Once one of them muttered
to his companion and felt the edge of his knife thoughtfully. I found myself walking aimlessly around and staying out of the way, afraid that
falling asleep or bumping into someone would give them the opportunity or motive to slit me some new orifices. In the circumstances, how I
felt about them hardly seemed relevant.

Orgos thought otherwise, but rather than lecture me himself, he called over a gaunt-looking goblin with brownish skin and lively green eyes. "This is Toth," said Orgos. "He is a worthy soldier and a respected bear-rider. Mr. Hawthorne," he said, turning to the goblin, "wants to know why your people do not regard him favorably."

The goblin turned to me and shrugged expressively. "They see the way you look at them," he said, in a gruff voice that sounded like it should come from a larger frame, "and they remember your attack on the Falcon's Nest. Some of them may have respect for what you were trying to do, but it is grudging at best. You fought for their enemy, an enemy that has stolen everything from them and set out to wipe them out utterly. You can see why they are a little leery of you. Let me see your sword."

I drew it, grateful for something that didn't require me to speak. He peered at the blade.

"Yes," he said. "One of ours, very old. The gilding on the hilt is new but the blade is excellent and will stand many reforgings should it take damage."

"They don't reforge," I said. "They either grind them down or throw them away and get new ones."

"Yes," he said, and he looked sad somehow. "I know. Except, of course, that new really means old. Our ancestors forged these blades and few now have the skill to remake them—none, I think, in Phasdreille. Some of our men still have the skill, but since we left Phasdreille we have had neither the raw materials nor the equipment to make more than a few good blades a day. It is not enough. Meanwhile the enemy use the swords we stockpiled over decades and throw them away when they need repair."

"Is that true of the stonemasons, too?" I asked. "I got the impression that most of the repairs to the city were sort of shoddy."

The goblin called Toth nodded solemnly. "My people were once great builders," he said. "Before the Arak Drül came—those you call the 'fair folk'—we relied upon our hands and our wits, and we made fair and mighty things."

"So how did they take over?" I demanded, feeling defensive.

"Guile," he said. "Deception. And there is no doubting their military prowess. Their energies go into ornamentation and into war. They may not build castles or forge swords, but they have learned to use both as well or better than those who made them."

I nodded. Ornamentation and war. The former for the bland,

vapid entertainment which was designed to stir neither mind nor heart, and the latter to ensure that no one entered their world uninvited, and to make all other parts of the world look like theirs.

Toth wasn't done. "They also had access to some power we did not recognize until it was too late," he said. "We still don't fully understand it, though I suspect it will come into play in the struggle which approaches. We welcomed them into our city because they seemed to have much to share with us, but by the time we realized how little substance there was to what they offered, strange things had already begun to happen."

"What kind of strange things?"

"Most of the people around were like us, but many were different, their blood mixed with other races in generations past. It was not a problem, until the Arak Drül came, and then—almost overnight—it *was* a problem. Many who had stood with us turned against us, and a new hierarchy was established, one which centered on the pale, blond newcomers. Their king came to Phasdreille and there were enough people of his complexion that he soon took over. One night, the Pale Claw sect—a guild of Arak Drül assassins and politicians—led a series of raids. My people's leaders were arrested, many were executed, and others were banished. From then on, the city became a dangerous place for us. Within a month, our property was being confiscated in accordance with the new laws, so we left the city: some fleeing, some driven out. We left with only the clothes on our backs, and the Arak Drül chased us to the mountains, butchering all they could. They took the city—our city, generations in the making—and all it contained, without fighting a single real battle."

He smiled bleakly and made his little half-shrug again, so that his head bobbed and his eyebrows raised a little. It was an alarmingly human gesture.

"This Pale Claw sect," I said. "They attacked me in the city. As did some of . . . your people."

"There is something about your presence here that I don't fully understand," said the goblin. "For years now it has been rumored that Outsiders, neither my people nor what you call the fair folk, would play a decisive role in the war. Many here see you as those Outsiders, and while this gives some of us hope, it scares others. Factions on both sides of the war feel it is best to destroy you, while others seek to draw you into their respective camps to help them to victory. Garnet and

Renthrette have been wooed by the Arak Drül as Orgos and Mithos have been wooed by us. Lisha was hidden until very recently. That left you, and your position was—perhaps still is—unclear to both sides, making you a target to both."

"If the 'fair folk,' or whatever you called them, the . . ."

"Arak Drül."

"Whatever. If they wanted me dead, why didn't the king just execute me?" I asked.

"Some in Phasdreille's ruling council expected to be able to use you as a weapon. But the Pale Claw sect, who are bent on the destruction of all who are not pure-blooded members of their race, were sufficiently doubtful of your natural inclinations that they tried to kill you before your allegiance had become clear. I suspect that they were also responsible for trying to discredit you in the eyes of the court during the palace festivities two nights ago. Yes, we have heard much of your experiences through your friends and they have spoken for you. If they had not . . ." his voice trailed off and he shrugged again. "Well," he concluded, "they did. We trust them. So."

It wasn't a ringing vote of confidence but it was as good as I was going to get.

"Now you are here," Orgos cut in, "and Mithos and I have spoken on your behalf, but you can't expect them to instantly treat you as one of them. But don't worry, Will. You will have time to prove yourself to them soon enough."

Splendid, I thought. It was almost funny how keen my friends were for me to prove myself by risking life and limb. Whenever Orgos talked of "proving myself," part of my intestine seemed to wrap itself around my kidneys and squeeze. To less flamboyantly noble people, "proving oneself" might hinge on an enthusiastically worded testimonial from Someone High Up. To Orgos, it meant facing sizable armies while armed with a modestly sized baguette. When Orgos says that you're going to show them what you're made of, you can usually take it literally.

"You want me to storm Phasdreille by myself?" I suggested.

"That wouldn't be practical at the moment," Orgos answered seriously.

"Fine," I replied bitterly. "Later this afternoon, perhaps. In the meantime, I could clean up the forest; you know, drain the swamp, make everything grow, and build a row of gazebos along the riverbank.

Do goblins like gazebos? I mean, I'd *hate* them to be disappointed in me."

"Don't call them goblins," Orgos answered, with a look at Toth.

"What?"

"Don't call them . . ."

"I heard what you said. It was a rhetorical 'what?' As in: You must be joking."

"I'm not joking."

"Then what should I call them?" I demanded petulantly.

"This land is called Stehnmarch," said Toth. "It was called that long before those you call the fair folk came to it. We, its inhabitants, are therefore the Stehnish, or Stehnites. That's all. 'Goblin' is a foul word and no one here uses it. You might bear that in mind."

Sure. A name is a name. If it kept their steel out of my spinal cord, I'd call their enemy the Arak Drül and I'd call them the Stehnish, but they sure as hell looked like goblins to me. But you know what they say: If it looks like a duck and quacks like a duck, it's probably something altogether nobler, like maybe a unicorn.

I was considering this, absently watching Orgos shave with his leaf-bladed dagger and wondering why he bothered going through this little ritual every day, when one of the worthy Stehnites graced us with his company. "Captain Orgos," he said. "You are required in the meeting hall immediately."

Orgos nodded promptly and put his knife away. I watched the honorable Stehnishman leave with Toth, then turned on the sword-master with astonishment. "*Captain*? You've allied yourself with this rabble?"

"Why not? Their cause is just."

"You think."

"I know."

"That's not the point!" I spluttered. "Look at them! Not at whether they're goblins or not," I added hastily, seeing him ready to interject. "I mean, look at their army, if you can call it that. They're disorganized, untrained, poorly armed . . ."

"The last I'll grant you," said Orgos, wiping his face and heading back to the stairs. "But they are not disorganized, and they *are* passionate soldiers."

"But untrained."

"Well, yes, largely, but—"

"And you've joined up with these goblin idiots—sorry, Stehnite idiots—to fight against the likes of Sorrail and his archers and his horsemen?"

"They need me," Orgos answered.

"So you have to fight for them?"

"Yes."

"Do you have to stand up with every weak and crippled force that you think has a genuine grievance regardless of whether they're going to get flattened like a ladybug charging a rhino?"

"Yes," he said. And that, I suppose, was the end of that. And him, probably.

"I'd better get my sword sharpened," I said, miserably.

"So, you will fight?"

"No. I was planning on slashing my wrists now," I answered. "You know, nip all that pointless hope in the bud."

"They need you, Will," said Orgos, giving me one of his level, sincere looks.

"No one needs me," I replied quickly. "And no, I'm not looking for sympathy. I'm just telling the truth. I'm virtually useless in a battle. I can shoot a crossbow, but I've seen farm animals that could be trained to do that. I can barely draw a sword without slicing something crucial off myself. My best hope is that the enemy will laugh themselves to death."

"But if your heart is true—" Orgos began.

"Rubbish," I cut in. "And anyway, my heart isn't true. In fact, if we're being honest, lies are my strong suit. You need someone to swear on everything holy that black is white, I'm your man. But give me something pointed and ask me to lay down my life for truth, virtue, and some very dodgy-looking Stehnites and you're on a loser."

"I get the point," said Orgos.

"Sorry."

"Well, you'll probably change your mind."

"I doubt it."

"Let me rephrase that," said Orgos thoughtfully. "You'll have to change your mind."

My internal alarm bells began clanging heavily. "What does that mean?" I demanded.

"Well . . ." Orgos began with a look as close to sheepish as he was ever likely to manage. "How long have we been friends, Will?"

"Nowhere near long enough to justify whatever you're about to say."

"How many times have I saved your life?"

"What have you done?"

There was a weighty pause and he took a long breath. "We had a meeting last night after you had gone to bed."

"Who's we?" I demanded, now surly and apprehensive.

"Mithos, Lisha, and several of the Stehnite leaders."

"Why do I wish I had been there?" I mused aloud.

"I knew you wanted to, well, prove yourself to the Stehnites, so . . ."

"That was you!" I exclaimed. "I never wanted to prove myself to anyone. You wanted that. I wanted to prove how little I cared about anything, and did so by drinking about eight pints."

"Well, I made it sound like you'd volunteered," Orgos continued, undaunted and smiling, as if I would thank him for all this one day.

"To do what?"

"It's best if the Stehnite Council tells you."

"No, it's not. It's best if you spill your guts before I have to spill mine less figuratively."

I had been so engrossed in this ominous exchange that I hadn't noticed Mithos's soundless approach. Suddenly he was beside me. He gave us a brief look and said, in a tone whose seriousness was almost sinister, "It's time."

❧

The Stehnite Council was eighteen men strong—or rather, as Ren-thrette would have annoyingly pointed out, was eighteen *persons* strong: Eight of them were women. All of them were dressed in darkly grand fashion, many sporting armor made of ancient metal and leather laced together at the edges and shaped outlandishly into horns, veined wings, and other animal parts, many hung with colored horsehair or feathers. Some wore armored masks, others clasped heir-loom weapons finer than any I had seen in Phasdreille, and all of them seemed lost in memories of ancient times. Among them was Toth, so quiet and dignified that I did not initially recognize him. He was seated with a naked blade across his knees and, like the rest of them, his face was somber and thoughtful.

They sat in a circle in a swept corner of the cavern, a brace of large, swarthy Stehnites a good ten yards away from curious by-standers, though still within earshot. This last was of no consequence that I could see since the assembly was completely silent. Ominously silent, you might say. They sat like statues, eyes downcast like attendants at the funeral of someone they didn't know very well. I can't say I liked the feel of this, particularly as Mithos shepherded me into the center of the circle, his fingers curled round my upper arm with a grasp that could not be argued with. Then the grip was relaxed and I was left by myself in the middle. The council's eyes rose from the floor to meet me and I decided I liked this still less. The funereal atmosphere was now augmented by something stern and sacrificial. If I was watching a funeral, it was likely to be my own.

For a moment, no one spoke. But then a sigh, as of resolve, seemed to escape several, maybe all, of them simultaneously, and, without any visible cue, they began to speak in unison.

"William Hawthorne,"—their voices were slow and somber, even sad—"reviewing your assault on the Stehnite settlement known as the Falcon's Nest, this council finds you guilty of four separate counts of murder. Do you have anything to say?"

My jaw dropped and the room spun as if I had been slapped in the head by a roofing beam. Murder? How could an adventurer be tried for murder? I had killed a few goblins while trying to rescue my companions. That's what adventurers did. I was the hero here. Heroes don't murder, they . . . well, they kill the evil and degenerate. But that wasn't going to work as a defense. Maybe I could blame Renthrette. . . .

No. I began to speak. "Worthy council members, that I slew . . . er . . . people I believed to be enemies, I cannot and do not deny. That I slew them maliciously or knowing their worth, I do deny. I did what I believed was right because I had been . . . misinformed. I do not mean that someone misinformed me on that particular day, that I hold the Arak Drül solely responsible. No. I was misinformed from the day of my birth. I was raised in a society where all people are judged according to their appearance. We shun the deformed and the sick; we despise those who are different from us. We even deride those who do not dress according to our customs and fashions. What we think of as abnormal we consider degenerate. What is different from our standards, we consider to have failed to meet them.

"As a child," I said, warming to my subject, "my grandmother told me tales of hideous goblins whose appearance matched their evil, just as her mother had told her. When I came to this land, I found what I thought was confirmation of those tales in the words of Sorrail and the Arak Drül, and the strange (to my eyes) creatures that lived in the mountains. The Arak Drül culture lined up beside that which I had been raised in, so I believed them all too easily. I was wrong, but at that time I could not have assessed how wrong I was. I now know differently. I see you are an intelligent, subtle, and sophisticated race. I have read your literature and paced the sculpted streets of your city and I know your quality. This is why I do not despair. I know your virtues and, humbly, I throw myself upon them. You value truth, so I have given it to you. And as you are just, so, I beg you, be merciful."

That went quite well, I thought. I concluded with a searching and soulful look, turning to look upon each of them in turn, then I bowed respectfully and waited. Nothing happened. Then one of them, a female swathed in a robe of blue so dark it looked like the night sky, made a minute gesture with one hand and one of the larger guards escorted me from the circle. I was turned loose and began to stroll away when a low murmur of discussion rose from the seated council. I wandered to a corner, where I sat on a low bench and poured myself a small beer from a leather flagon. Orgos followed me.

He stopped a few feet away from me, watching. I offered him a cup, but he shook his head and stayed where he was, looking at me keenly, his eyes narrow and thoughtful.

"What?" I asked. "Was it not enough?"

"I'm sure it was plenty," he said slowly. "It was a good argument, and they will take it seriously."

"Good," I said, drinking.

"Did *you*?" he asked, his eyes still level on me.

"Did I what?"

"Did you take it seriously?"

I thought for a second, then hedged: "What do you mean?"

"You know what I mean, Will," Orgos replied, coming no nearer, and standing stiffer than ever. "Did you mean it? Any of it? Or was it just another bit of theater, a speech designed to manipulate?"

"Of course it wasn't," I said, but my voice had been hesitant.

"Of course it wasn't," he echoed, blankly. Then he turned on his heel and walked away.

Had I meant it? The damnedest thing was, I really didn't know.

A good performer has to believe what he's saying as he says it or the audience smells deception. It had made sense to me, and I knew it would make sense to them, but how much I thought all this cultural upbringing stuff was a sufficient excuse or explanation for what I had done, something that would rightly stop them from stringing me up and testing their spears on me, I couldn't say.

But it did work. Kind of.

They didn't string me up. Instead, they gave me a mission, which sounded like good news until I heard the details of what they wanted me to do.

Stringing me up would have been a lot quicker.

SCENE XIX

The Halls of the Dead

The bridge guards bear out your story," said Sorrail grimly, "but you can't expect anyone here to believe that you have returned to Phasdreille of your own accord. Look at me when I speak to you!"

He took hold of my chin and yanked it up, slapping me hard as he did so. The guards around me hoisted me roughly into an upright, kneeling position, one of them dragging me by a fistful of hair. My cheek was so swollen with bruising that my left eye was a sightless slit. I looked at Sorrail with my right and gasped an attempt to speak. Blood spattered from my mouth in a fine spray, and a droplet fell on Sorrail's white linen tunic. He scowled at it and then, almost casually, kicked me hard in the ribs. I collapsed onto the stone floor coughing and spitting blood.

I had no idea how long this had been going on: An hour? Two? I had been picked up by the bridge guard and brought directly to Sorrail who, assisted by his more enthusiastic troops, had beaten me periodically ever since. As I got my breath back and cleared my throat, I wheezed out my story again. "I told you already. I ran from the city and into the forest. I walked into a huge goblin army. Some of them saw me and came after me. I ran. I knew the city guards would take me in as a criminal and, with half a dozen bear-riding goblins on my tail, that seemed the best plan. I also thought that by bringing word of the enemy force, I might make up, at least in part, for my past crimes in the city. That's all there is to tell."

I sank to the floor again, coughing, exhausted by my narrative and feeling, more than ever, the ache in my jaw where I had been punched.

"These goblins," Sorrail demanded, and as he came close to me I could smell his scrubbed body, still fragrant with the soap they made by boiling down goblin fat. "What standard did they bear?"

I thought for a moment. "A white half-moon—a crescent—on a red background."

Sorrail looked at me, and though his gaze was hard and hateful as before, it held a hint of uncertainty.

"He could have seen that in the last attack on the city," suggested a burly sergeant, scornfully.

"No," said Sorrail, distantly. "That device is borne only by the mountain tribes to the north. They have not been seen here for many months, and certainly did not participate in any of our recent engagements. If they were here . . ."

His voice trailed off and he stood for a moment in silence. Then he squatted suddenly and spoke directly to my face. "These goblins, the ones riding the brown bears, were they—"

I cut him off, spotting the test. "The bears weren't brown, they were black. Kind of charcoal but . . ."

"Kind of?"

"They looked black but they had, like, a sheen that was bluish and silvery, like steel."

The guards looked at me, then at each other, then at Sorrail. His eyes burned into mine and he knew that I was speaking the truth. I could not have come up with that kind of detail unless I had seen them.

"And these were the only beasts they had with them?" he prompted.

"Yes. No. There were wolves, too, like the ones that attacked us when you found us in the mountains."

He hesitated, caught slightly off-guard by this remark and the memories it evoked, perhaps because I had been unable to conceal the bitter amusement in my voice. Then I had taken him as a savior, someone who might keep the hand of evil from my throat. It was a nasty irony, but I think I was able to swallow that back before it showed in my face. As it was, he merely smiled darkly and said, almost comfortingly, "No one here need fear their wolves. They know me by the foul pelts I have flayed from their loathsome fellows, and have learned to avoid me in the mountains, no matter how many of them there are. They will learn to flee me on the battlefield also. But their goblin masters: You did not attempt to speak to them, or? . . ."

I gave him a wide-eyed stare. "They're goblins!" I sighed. "I may not be one of you, but I am also not one of them. Do you think a race that lives by murder and destruction, creatures that despise all things including their own filthy kind, would suffer me to live? I saw them, and I ran. They came after me and they did not want to talk."

And suddenly, it was over. Sorrail rose, turned, and stalked out of the chamber with his officers at his heels, muttering, "Clean him up," to the guards left with me.

❧

Cleaning me up was easier said than done. My lip was split, I had a long jagged cut over my right eye, and my left was no more than a thin, dark line across a plum-colored distention. I was fairly sure I had a cracked rib or two (they had kicked me repeatedly and struck me across the back and shoulders with thin but heavy clubs apparently designed for the purpose) and my entire body felt like one great bruise. Every touch of the guards' sponge set me moaning and squirming like a dying eel, slow and agonized but too resigned to the pain to really fight it. Only when I caught the distinctive rose-petal scent and my mind flooded with images of the factories in the forest and what they did to make their soap and cosmetics did I recoil and insist on them leaving me alone. They went sheepishly, like bullies who had tried to make it up to their victim, failed, and now fear he will report all to his mother.

I crawled toward a couch, dragged myself painfully onto it, and lay there, throbbing. The door opened behind me. Turning toward it proved too painful, so I lay there and waited till my visitor came to me. For a split second I considered the possibility that it was an assassin or that Sorrail had changed his mind and sent some lackey to finish me off, but I did not move. Oddly, and perhaps for the first time in my life, I genuinely did not care. I waited, my good eye closed until I sensed a presence near me. Then I looked.

It was Renthrette. She stood there looking down on me, her face expressionless. By this I don't mean impassive: She was clearly thinking, even feeling, a great deal as she looked at me, but exactly what was going on in her head was impossible to discern. I wondered if my assassin had indeed come—it would be ironic if all those poems about a distant beauty who kills her suitor with disdain turned out to be literally true. The idea made me smile, slightly, and the muscles of my face cried out with pain. "Hello, Renthrette," I whispered, my eyes closed.

"What are you doing here, Will?" she replied. The last time I saw her, this would have been a rhetorical question which meant "get out of here before I use your intestines to string a lute," but now her tone was not so much hostile as cautiously inquiring.

I opened my eyes. "I ran into the goblins in the forest and ran back here. . . ."

"I heard that version," she said, quickly. "What is really going on?"

"Nothing," I said. "Just what I said."

"I don't believe you."

"No one is asking you to," I answered, closing my eyes again.

She paused, turned, and, by the sound of her heels on the stone, I judged that she was leaving. The door closed firmly. Then she came back and knelt beside me.

"I don't believe it," she repeated. "This has all the marks of a Hawthorne scam and I will not be taken in by it. Why are you here? What is going on? What do you know?"

I was going to ignore her questions, but the last one sounded odd. I looked at her and saw something similarly odd in her face. There was an anxiety there which had been in her voice when she first came in: an anxiety which had replaced the hatred with which she had been brimming when last we met. I hauled myself onto my elbows painfully and looked at her. "What do I know?" I repeated. "What do you mean?"

She hesitated, shot a hasty look at the door, and lowered her face toward mine as if she was going to kiss me. When she spoke, her voice was almost inaudible, and halting, as if she was finding each word, each thought, as she spoke. "I feel that something is not right here. And you feel it, too—no, you *know* it. Since you left, Garnet and I have been, well, ignored, it seems. Everyone—I mean *everyone*—seems to have forgotten us. Garnet is happy. He rides against the goblins every day. I am a court lady and I do what they do, though not as well as they do it. Sorrail . . . I have barely seen Sorrail since you left, and when we meet at court he treats me exactly as everyone else. But it's more than that. I think . . . there is something more, something much bigger.

"The people here don't seem *real*. Different people have told me the same stories, *exactly* the same, word for word, and no one reacts. I have heard two different people in a group recite the same pieces of poetry and no one comments. It isn't just politeness; it's as if they *don't remember*. They are like empty shells, going through the same actions day after day. The only thing they show any real passion for is their war against the goblins. I know the goblins are terrible, but their passion . . . it doesn't make sense to me. And when you ask about it, you get the same stories repeated verbatim. Like what they have done to you now: I don't understand it. For a while, before you left, I thought I did. But that was when I was more like them—when I was *becoming* one of them."

She paused, glanced over her shoulder again, and then breathed, "I also feel *watched*. Kind of like when we were in Harvest. I do not know by who, but there is someone or something here in the city trying to reach me: a mind stretching out to mine. I feel very sure that I do not want it to find me. I . . . I fear it may have already found Garnet."

Not just a pretty face, Renthrette. Still, I wasn't sure, but then she paused and spoke again.

"Back in the mountains," she said, "the night this all began, you told a story about a girl whose family was attacked by Empire soldiers. Remember?"

I winced at the recollection and nodded fractionally.

"I think you owe me another story," she said.

❧

I told her everything. It might not have been wise, and I had been advised against it, but I trusted her—or, at least, I trusted my gut feeling that she wasn't that good an actress. Anyhow, I found it hard to believe that she had been selected to wheedle the truth out of me, given the terms on which we had parted. No, the very fact that there had been no love lost between us made me take her revelations seriously. There was also a part of me which suspected that an agent of the "fair folk" would not be able to articulate the oddities of their city quite so baldly; they certainly didn't seem too self-aware when cheerfully recounting by heart the history of some notched goblin-crushing weapon. And if they could identify the inconsistencies in their own tales, I doubted they'd announce them to Renthrette, even as part of some larger ruse.

I have to say that most of these carefully thought out justifications of my actions came to me *after* I had already confessed all to Renthrette, but I like to think that I had already recognized them intuitively. In fact, it probably had more to do with Renthrette's earnest face, bent so close to mine that I could feel the breath from her lips on my skin, but why split hairs? In any event, I told her: quickly, in a whisper, and with one eye on the door, but I told her everything.

If it had not done so already, her allegiance switched in a heartbeat. "And they are all alive!" she gasped, joy breaking out all over her. "Lisha and Orgos and Mithos?"

"Yes. But be quiet! Part of the story I told Sorrail is true. There is a large Stehnite force mustering in the forest, but they know they can't assault the city. They built Phasdreille, after all, and they know that storming the main gate will get them nowhere. The breach in the walls is largely blocked, but it is still their best chance of getting in. Sorrail and the rest of them know this, of course, and will have it heavily defended. The only chance for the Stehnites is to significantly reduce or distract that guard. That, I'm afraid, is the task dumped on me, and because I didn't want it in the first place, I expect you to help. I know that makes no sense, but people in pain are permitted to abandon logic. If I'm in, you're in."

"We can't do it alone."

"We won't have to, supposedly," I said ruefully. Part of me had hoped she would denounce the plan as foolhardy, in which case I could have abandoned it and still say I'd tried. I should have known better.

"So what's the plan?" she asked, a flicker of animation coming into her eyes.

I looked at her, sighing pointedly. She misread the gesture as being a symptom of my discomfort, and began pushing pillows under my painfully bruised back. I began talking, hoping to stop her ministrations before she did real damage. "Orgos and a company of Stehnites— the people you call goblins—are making their way to a secret entrance into the city. It is narrow and can only be opened from the inside, but it seems that the 'fair folk,' or whatever we're supposed to call them now— the Arak Drül, I suppose—are unaware of it. We have to let them in. If the king and his 'fair' friends *do* know of the entrance, we will find out very quickly, I would think, but Orgos assures me that all will be well. So that's that settled."

"Where is this entrance?"

"There is an abandoned Stehnite necropolis beneath the city—"

"A what?"

"A goblin cemetery. Sounds like fun, doesn't it? A real holiday jaunt. Apparently we are supposed to go there—limp, in my case—and find some tomb which is actually the entrance to a tunnel under and out of the city. Having avoided being seen by the inevitable legions of guards with the aid of some device they seem to have forgotten to pass on to me, we then open the tomb, greet our companions warmly, and destroy the forces of darkness. Or, in this case, light. 'And be home in time for supper,' I think the original orders read," I added dryly. I had already gone through a pretty bleak time with Sorrail and his men, and the plan that the Stehnite chieftains had produced, with Mithos and the others nodding gravely in the wings, now seemed an even bigger death trap than it had at the time.

"Can you stand?" asked Renthrette.

"I suspect so," I replied miserably, "but I choose not to."

"Come on. We have work to do."

She slid the door bolt back and had her hand on the handle when the door exploded inward, throwing her heavily against the wall. I rolled panic-stricken from my couch as a man stepped into the room. He was hooded, but his posture somehow conveyed both strength and agility. It also seemed familiar. When he spoke, all doubt in my mind vanished. The assassin from the alley had caught up with me as he had promised. "Well, Mr. Hawthorne. So nice to see you again. And in the company of the Lady Renthrette, I see. Sorrail *will* be shocked."

Renthrette had fallen facedown, but she was turning over quickly and her hand was fumbling for her dagger. He kicked at her wrist, a single, explosive snap that sent the knife skipping across the floor. I made a movement toward him, but he turned easily, ready for me, idly remarking to the prone Renthrette, "How quickly you people change allegiances."

"And what side would you have us on?" I demanded, stalling.

"No side," he remarked simply. "I want you dead."

A bit of a conversation killer, a remark like that, and maybe not just conversation. He passed his right hand across his chest and his fingers flexed oddly, like a magician performing a sleight-of-hand trick. Then he doffed his hood with his left hand, revealing the thin, balding features of Lord Gaspar, and drew his right arm back close to his head.

Part of me wasn't surprised, not because I had suspected Gaspar of being a highly proficient murderer, but because I hadn't liked him much. Not much of an insight, I know, but enough to make my next action a tiny bit more efficient. I lunged at him headfirst before the

missile could leave his poised hand, crunching into his midriff just below his ribs. He gasped and fell back, but he was surprised more than
winded, and his recovery was virtually instantaneous. The guards had,
of course, taken my weapons—not that I could fight an assassin on
anything like even terms in this condition if I'd had an entire armory to
select from. He stepped back from me and I barely stopped myself
from falling facedown. Renthrette was gathering herself into a crouch
by my side, but he watched her from his place by the door and seemed
smugly unconcerned. In his right hand he now brandished a length of
fine chain which ended in a cluster of thin spines and razor blades. He
was whirling it round faster and faster like a lasso, so that it whined
thinly in the air.

"Just a scratch, Mr. Hawthorne," he smiled, "that's all it will take.
One skill we have perfected since the time of the first goblin wars is the
art of poison. This is a distillate from Briesh root. Very fast, very
painful."

He smiled again. His skin seemed to stretch transparent over his
skull and his deepset eyes twinkled like polished stones. The pitch of
the sound rose as he spun his weapon faster and advanced upon us.

Renthrette and I shrank back. He had raised the chain so that the
weapon hummed like a swarm of bees over his head, and now he
backed us into the cold stone wall. I spared a glance at Renthrette;
she was standing now, straining back to stay out of the range of the
poisoned blades that cut the air in front of our faces, but her jaw was
set and resolute. For a moment my heart leaped, thinking she had a
plan and was on the edge of action, but then I saw the truth: She was
steeling herself for death. The realization brought a thin yelp of terror to my lips and she turned quickly to look at me, perhaps hoping
to see an idea in my face, a promise that Reliable Will, Hawthorne the
Resourceful, had one more trick up his sleeve. I checked my sleeves.
Nothing. Gaspar took another step toward us and his mouth buckled
into a small and satisfied smile. This time the Pale Claw would have
their way.

Suddenly the door behind Gaspar opened inward and a sentry
armed with towels and sponges stepped in. It took a second for him to
react, but his hand went instinctively to his sword. Gaspar swung the
chain wildly at the astonished guard, who raised one thoughtless arm
to protect himself. A cut opened up along the edge of his wrist and he
fell back clutching it. Gaspar turned hurriedly to us again but he was

already off balance and Renthrette had moved sideways. Gaspar let out a few more inches of chain and spun the weapon faster. Renthrette sucked her breath in and slid down the wall toward the door. Gaspar paid out more chain and the deadly circle expanded. I wondered if I could time a lunge at him between the passes of the poisoned razors, but I felt the wind of it on my chest, heard it like some lethal mosquito in my ear, and my courage failed me. Renthrette, though, moved again, edging toward the still-open door. Gaspar grimly let out a few more inches of chain. Almost immediately there was a sharp thud and, in the silence that followed, a quavering tone, like the fading end of a bell's peal. The needles and blades of Gaspar's weapon had bitten hard into the wood of the open door.

Renthrette dived, rolled, and came up with her dagger. In about the same instant, Gaspar seized a long knife from his tunic and slashed at the air to keep her at bay. I, not realizing that Gaspar's lethal spinning toy was out of commission, had dropped to the floor with a gasp of panic, which was quickly succeeded by a squawk of pain as I landed awkwardly on my elbow. Gaspar, perceiving this as an indication of attack, wheeled to faced me. As he did so, Renthrette lunged meticulously with her dagger, low and hard, held it for a moment, and then drew it out, bloody. Gaspar stood paralyzed and his eyes showed first shock, then pain, then nothing. He fell heavily forward.

The sentry was already dead. Whatever Gaspar's other virtues, he hadn't lied about the speed of his venom.

"Shouldn't we be moving?" said Renthrette, wiping her knife clean. She was breathing heavier than normal, but otherwise she might have been suggesting that we leave a rather dull party.

"What?" I gasped, hardly able to speak.

"Don't we have a job to do?" she demanded, her blue eyes transferring from the now-spotless dagger to my face with a hint of impatience.

"Can I have a moment to recover?" I sputtered, irritably. It had been intended as a rhetorical question, but Renthrette had never quite learned to spot them.

"Why?" she demanded. "We aren't hurt."

"I am!" I riposted. "Still. And someone just tried to kill us!"

"Tried," she said, "and failed. So let's go."

"Where to?"

"You tell me," she answered, "it's your show."

My show. I considered that, uncertain which was worse: the fact that I was indeed responsible for getting the Stehnites into the city, or the fact that Renthrette considered such an operation, a mission not so much audacious in its daring as suicidal, to be a "show." Tough call.

"We'd better move quickly," said Renthrette. "If Gaspar was one of the Pale Claw assassins you mentioned, then who knows who will be after us now."

"They'll all be after us once they find his body," I said, "Pale Claw or not. What was Gaspar?"

"Chief Justice," said Renthrette, bleakly.

"I thought it was something like that. Whether Sorrail and the king shared his politics seems rather immaterial, don't you think? I wasn't especially appreciated to begin with, and with the murder of one of their chief ministers under my belt I think we can rest assured that my popularity has entered a decline. Well, I don't intend to wait around for them to find us."

"Good," said Renthrette. "I was beginning to wonder."

"Do you have that oil lamp with you?"

"Always," she said, as if I'd asked her if the sun was strictly a daytime thing.

We considered hiding Gaspar's body to buy us some time, but we couldn't conceal both Gaspar and the sentry under the small half-bed, and that was the only piece of furniture in the room. We considered locking them together as if they had killed each other, but they were too heavy, and I doubted it would help. Finally, we did what we did best: we ran.

There had been no point in my bringing either weapon or disguise into the city since the guards would confiscate them, so I was in the intriguing position of being totally recognizable and unable to defend myself. Renthrette may, for the moment, go where she pleased, but my unwelcome and beaten face would certainly excite inquiry. I didn't know what would be best: to walk brazenly down the palace's long echoing corridors, to skulk in the shadows, or just to sprint until my lungs exploded.

Renthrette led with a brisk walking pace that looked like she was going somewhere, and I scuttered behind in a kind of jog that looked like nothing of the kind. We passed a sentry getting a dressing down from his corporal for a dirty tunic. As we got clear, Renthrette muttered out of the side of her mouth, "Where are we going?"

"To the wine cellars."

She almost broke stride and shot me a look that challenged me to say anything about feeling like a drink. Instead, she said, "The fair folk don't drink wine."

"I know," I said, "but the Stehnites did."

"Stehnites?"

"Goblins."

"Right. So what do we call the 'fair folk'?"

"I told you," I said. "The Arak Drül. That's what the er . . . Stehnites call them. Deadly Dull, might be a good translation."

"And where are these cellars?"

"Under the kitchen that serves the main banqueting hall."

"That's right by the main garrison," Renthrette exclaimed.

"Yes. Keep walking."

"It's where the palace guardhouse is and where the king's elite troops live."

"Yes."

"We have as much chance of getting out of there alive as we do of walking on water."

"About that: yes," I agreed. "And it looks like we're about to get our feet wet."

A company of six soldiers and an officer had just rounded the corner and clearly intended to speak to us. "Lady Renthrette," began the officer, "where are you taking Mr. Hawthorne?"

Renthrette looked at me blankly and opened her mouth like a large carp.

"I was hungry," I inserted. "After a hard day of getting lumps kicked out of me by your worthy men, one gets a little peckish."

"So I was taking him to the kitchens," said Renthrette, throwing the carp back.

"I'm sure something could have been ordered for Mr. Hawthorne in his room," said the officer.

"I'd just as soon stretch my legs," I said weakly.

"I mean," said the officer with a labored earnestness, "that though you are presently our . . . guest, you should probably stay in your room until we get express word from Sorrail or one of the other duty officers."

"Fair enough," I said. "The moment I've eaten, I'll go right back to my room and stay there."

"No, sir," began the officer, "I'm afraid . . ."

"Now you listen to me," I snapped, raising my voice, "I've had just about as much of this as I can stand. I came here as a witness to aid your army and was set upon by your thugs. Now all I ask is something to offset my hunger and rebuild the strength your troops knocked out of me."

"Even so," said the officer, a little sheepishly, "I really must insist that . . ."

"Mr. Hawthorne has a rare blood disorder," said Renthrette, to everyone's surprise. "He must eat on the hour, or he is likely to collapse."

I nearly did. My mouth fell open and I began to burble something, but she kept going:

"His feeding time is long overdue, and the only way to keep him awake is to keep him moving. Come on, William, stir yourself up and down a little."

I gave her a wide-eyed look. She stared at me and said, "You must keep your blood flowing, William. Keep those legs moving."

She slapped at my thighs and, in slow disbelief, I began to hop lightly from one foot to the other as she seemed to be suggesting.

"That's right," she commended. "A little higher. Now," she said to the soldiers, "I promise I'll take him back as soon as he is fed, all right?"

The officer hesitated and glanced awkwardly at his men. I continued to dance about, executing some bizarre form of jig, while trying to look as if this was perfectly normal. I flicked my heels up behind me, now humming to give myself something to cavort to. The soldier watched me for another moment and then nodded silently. We set off immediately down the passage, Renthrette marching swiftly, I reeling off some lunatic country dance.

As soon as we were round the corner I began walking normally. I growled at Renthrette, "And what the hell was that supposed to be?"

"I thought that was rather good," she remarked, without looking at me. "You know, *inventive*." She shot me a sly smile and I frowned at her.

" 'His feeding time'?" I muttered. "What am I, some kind of sideshow ape?"

"William Hawthorne in a sideshow?" she remarked archly. "No, you're strictly a main stage attraction."

"But still an ape," I added.

"A pretty smart one," she said, grudgingly.

"Thanks. Where are these bloody kitchens?" I muttered.

We rounded a corner, chose a door, moved quickly down a narrower passage that ran around a small, cloistered herb garden where the air was cold and fragrant, and passed through an arch into a broad room floored with ceramic tile and dry with the heat of ovens. In one vast hearth a woman was stewing cabbage, and the scent, sour and slightly metallic, hit us like a large animal. Several others went on with their chopping and skinning and whatever else they did in this hellish place to ruin whatever food came near them. No one paid any attention to us at all.

It didn't take us long to find the cellars. There was a narrow flight of steps down into a bricked arch with a heavy door whose paint was black and flaking. There was no keyhole and the bolt was clumsy and ill-fitting. We opened it and descended.

I had been shown a plan of the palace cellarage, but it was several generations out of date and no one knew exactly what it would look like today. The Stehnites were pretty sure their enemy didn't know about the secret means of egress from the city, but *pretty* sure wasn't *absolutely* sure, so we would have to be alert for guards, though we hadn't seen any in the kitchens or the lower chambers so far.

The area below the kitchen had once held an extensive wine store, but the wine had long since been used or thrown away. The Arak Drül did not replenish, I had been assured; they merely consumed. There were a few shelves of salted pork, some bags of white flour, and several barrels of the thin, flavorless yellow beer they made, but otherwise the place seemed empty. There were alcoves and cupboards with shelves, stone cold chests, and a meat locker with hooks, but little of it looked used. You could imagine the place fragrant with cheeses, hanging with sausages, and piled high with bottles of rich and flavorful wines and barrels of hearty ale, but the palace's new inhabitants apparently ate merely to stay alive. With me, I thought dryly, it was rather the other way round.

Renthrette watched me as I paced around the dank and freezing cellar. "Well?" she said.

"Well what?"

"Where is this passage?"

"I'm looking for it, aren't I?"

"It looks to me like you're thinking about food."

I gave her a shocked look. "You misjudge me," I lied. "Give me a hand with this. My ape strength seems to be failing me."

Between us we shifted a large—but empty and partly rotten—cabinet. One of its doors flapped open as we lifted it, twisting its corroded hinges till it was barely hanging on. Setting the piece of furniture down we found a large hatchway where it had stood. This was latched but not locked, and it opened upward with a long, high-pitched creak. Renthrette lit her lamp and the cellar flared with leaping orange tongues before settling down to an amber glow.

"It's just a stone cistern for cold storage," Renthrette whispered, beginning to lose patience. It had, after all, been minutes since she'd killed anything.

I climbed in and looked around, stretching to take the lamp from her. By its light, a rusted iron grill shone dully in the corner of the floor. The shaft beneath it looked like a drain of some sort, but it was quite dry.

"I think this is it," I said.

"You think?" said Renthrette, dropping easily in through the hatch and peering at the grate.

"See any other possibilities?"

"Not here."

"Then this must be it."

The grill was held in place by heavy nails driven into a timber frame. We hadn't brought tools, so I squatted down beside it, wondering how we were going to move it and smelling the cold, damp air that drifted out of the shaft. Renthrette nudged me aside and planted her boot squarely in the center of the grate. She pushed and it bent noticeably, scattering red flakes of iron into the hole beneath. Leaning on my shoulder she stomped at it twice more, until I hushed her, sure that someone would be attracted to the noise. We waited, holding our breath and looking at each other. Then, without warning, she did it again, and this time her foot went straight through.

Two bars of the thin metal had snapped clean out, and several more had buckled enough that they could be bent out of the way. Renthrette went first and I lowered myself awkwardly into the shaft after her, her hands closing about my waist, drawing me down toward her in ways far less erotic than they sound.

"Drop," she said. "It's only a couple of feet."

I did so and she braced me against the impact embarrassingly.

"I'm fine," I spluttered. "You don't have to heave me around like a child, you know."

"I was just trying to help," she said, affronted.

"Don't. Now where the hell are we?"

We were in a passage. The shaft we had just dropped through had been alarmingly narrow and I had had visions of crawling, as we had done through the cistern drain at the Falcon's Nest. But this was quite different. Once in the tunnel proper, we were able to walk upright and side by side. The lamp showed the same carved buttresses and gargoyle ornaments that we had seen elsewhere in the city, but here you could see the goblin heads that had been smashed elsewhere. The ancient kings or tribe leaders of Stehnmarch stood proud, though strange to our eyes, and noble. Renthrette lifted the lamp and gazed at them.

"So it's true," she said, her voice hushed. "They were here first. The 'fair folk,' Sorrail . . . It's all been a lie."

"I hate to say I told you so but . . ."

"No, you don't," said Renthrette. "You love it. And to be precise you never *told me so* at all."

"I implied it," I said. "I was skeptical."

"You always are."

"Thank you," I said, smiling and bowing slightly as if she had paid me the highest compliment. Renthrette was moving off down the passage, however, staring at everything except me, and didn't notice.

The passage was straight and there were no doors or corridors leading off it, so we made rapid progress in what felt like a slow turning and descending spiral. The flint underfoot seemed newly cut and showed little sign of wear, but patches of dark moss clung to all the surfaces and water dropped from the arched ceiling in places and coursed in rivulets down the walls. It seemed to be getting colder as we progressed, and in minutes I was catching sight of tiny icicles gleaming in the lamplight like quartz.

Then came a staircase, broad and steep, and at its foot, a round chamber, with relief carvings on its walls showing the Stehnites laying out their dead. There was a single door leading out of this chamber and I stopped Renthrette before she opened it.

She gave me an impatiently inquiring look.

"Did you look at the carvings?" I said.

"No. This is hardly the time for artistic appreciation."

"They're funeral engravings," I said.

"So?"

"This is a burial chamber."

"I thought you said this was an escape route from the city," she said.

"That was its secondary function, yes, but it was also where they brought the bodies of their rulers and dignitaries."

"So?" she parroted.

"So we are about to enter an underground graveyard, a mausoleum. I thought you should know."

"You said," she said, unmoved, and in truth I wasn't sure what I was trying to say. I suppose I thought we should somehow feel a sense of respect for those who had died, but since we had recently been doing our best to kill their successors, that didn't make a lot of sense. Maybe I wanted her to feel guilty like me.

She pressed the handle until it clicked dully, then she pulled the heavy door, its timbers dragging, wide open. Inside, though the tunnel was about the same size as the one we'd just come through, it seemed tighter, more restricted. The air had a dusty staleness that you could smell through the damp, and where the walls had formerly been plain, they were now lined with doors, each no more than a few feet square and set at waist height. They were made of some hard, reddish lumber designed to resist decay, though few had after all these centuries. There were dozens, maybe hundreds of them, and where the portal timbers had crumbled or been eaten away by worms, you could see the black, arched hollows where the corpses lay.

The place smelled of death. Not death like in a butcher's shop, all caked blood and internal organs, or the stench of decay like a rat left out in the sun, but ancient and forgotten like the world the people buried here had inhabited. It smelled of age and all the time that had gone by since their passing. Some of the bodies had monuments carved into their sepulchers and the corridor around them swelled into a kind of vault, others were marked only by a line of indecipherable script. We inched along the passage, Renthrette, for all her earlier casualness, slowing as if awed by a sense of dread or sadness. And around us, stacked and arrayed in their decayed finery, lay the dead.

The tunnel ended abruptly in a tight spiral staircase that wound upward.

"We must have missed it," I said, suddenly afraid for reasons I couldn't say. I began to bustle about in the low and shifting lamplight, scanning the various tombs with growing alarm. "It must be here," I muttered into the stillness. "We must have passed it."

"What are we looking for?" said Renthrette, calm and quiet.

"A mausoleum with a figure of a warrior carved into a pillar: life-size. Tough to miss, you'd think."

"We've seen a lot of tombs."

"But have we seen *that* tomb?" I hissed, my patience beginning to strain. The place—the silent and forgotten passage with its corpses arranged rank upon rank—was beginning to get to me.

"How would I know?" she returned.

"Brilliant," I remarked. "So we're stuck here."

"If worse comes to worst we'll go back the way we came," Renthrette answered with a reasonableness that sounded labored. It was getting to her, too, however much she pretended otherwise.

"What if we can't?" I barked. It suddenly seemed more likely that we would be locked in, that we would be entombed here forever. The idea chilled me to the bone.

"We have to get out," said Renthrette, urgent.

"We can't," I replied, suddenly quite sure. "We're going to be walled up with the dead. We'll never get out. . . ."

"Stop it, Will," said Renthrette, slapping her hands over her ears. "Don't say that. There's something trying to stop us, distracting us. The dead are confusing us."

For a moment I thought she was right, but then it hit me.

"No," I said, suddenly clear and moving away from her. "It's not the dead. But something *is* trying to stop us. We must keep looking."

"Why must you?" said a voice.

I turned hurriedly and found myself looking at Garnet. He was coming down the corridor toward us, armed for battle. Renthrette ran to meet him.

"Garnet! Thank God," she cried. "We have to let Lisha and the others in. I'll explain it all later."

"I already know," he said, smiling. "I have spoken to them and they sent me to you. Come back this way."

He started to move back the way we had come, and Renthrette took a step toward him.

"No!" I shouted. "Renthrette, wait. That's not your brother."

She shot him a quick look and then called back to me, half laughing as she did so. "Of course it is. Who else could it be?"

"Look at him closely," I answered, walking quickly toward them. "Make sure."

She glanced at him, but only for a second. "Of course it's him," she said.

"Come," he said, extending his hand to her.

"No!" I bellowed, breaking into a run.

She took his offered hand and he began to draw her back and up. She moved with him, easily, and as she turned from me, I had the distinct impression that she had forgotten my presence utterly. I called after them, but they did not turn or answer. I ran and, rounding a corner, saw where a black hollow had appeared in the rock wall: a tomb door, gaping open. Only yards from it, Garnet and Renthrette paced arm in arm. The oil lamp lay shattered and sputtering on the ground and Renthrette's posture seemed limp, as if she were drunk.

The tomb they now stood before was little more than a vertical coffin carved into the rock. To my horror, Garnet slid his back against the wall and into the recess, drawing Renthrette after him. I shouted and flung myself at them. Garnet's free hand caught my wrist, but now I saw it for what it was: a fleshless, bony claw.

It began to pull me in.

I tried to tear it away but some greater strength was guiding it, giving power to its dusty, fleshless bones, and in moments we were all three pulled in a horrible embrace into the tomb. The corpse which had taken on Garnet's form released Renthrette, whose eyes were cloudy and sightless, and used that free hand to reach for the stone slab which was the sarcophagus lid. I kicked and flailed as best I could but the skeleton hand now had me firmly by the shoulder and its grip was like a vise. Renthrette was muttering to herself like one on the edge of sleep, and the door, the great stone slab that would entomb us, was shutting out the light. I stopped fighting, knowing that since Renthrette's illusion was giving the thing power, only she could stop it.

I called her name. "Look at him, Renthrette!" I cried. "Look at your brother."

Her eyelids flickered and opened for a second. They rested on the skull beside her face and she smiled.

"Yes," she whispered. "Garnet. Now rest."

"No," I shouted, as the tomb door inched further across the opening, "it isn't him. He's different."

"No," she murmured, her eyes still shut. "No."

"How did he find us?" I tried, desperate now. "How did he know we were here? He says he spoke to Lisha: Where? When? How could he have found them and why would he have gone looking? He didn't know they were here. Lisha is outside the city and couldn't have come to him. He must be lying. Renthrette, *it's not your brother.* Look."

Her eyelids rippled again and confusion crossed her forehead as the last of the lamplight was closed out of the tomb. In the last second before the darkness took us, her eyes opened all the way; she saw the hollow eye sockets, yellow and gnawed by rats; and she screamed.

In that instant the grip which seized me broke, the finger bones shattered, and the tomb door quavered and fell slowly into the passageway, crashing full length and breaking upon the flint floor with a deafening roar that seemed to resound through the earth. I staggered out after it, gasping the air, and Renthrette followed, shrieking and brushing at the torn limb which had encircled her. The rest of the corpse seemed to stand for a second and then tumbled in pieces, many of the bones turning to powder before they hit the ground.

Renthrette sank back against the opposite wall, the back of her hand pressed to her mouth and her eyes fixed on the empty tomb. She was wheezing, rather than sobbing.

"It's all right," I said. "It wasn't him."

For a while she said nothing, so I sat down beside her and slipped my arm around her shoulders. I had, after all, seen this little trick before. She didn't rebuff me, or react at all, for that matter. She just sat there, breathing heavily and biting into the back of her wrist till the print of her teeth showed bone white.

"What was it doing?" she asked.

There were lots of possible answers to this, some of which I preferred not to consider, so I kept it simple. "Trying to stop us."

"Why?"

"We're about to fulfill a prophecy," I said. "But we'd better be quick. If he, whatever that thing in the library is, has sensed us here, he'll be sending troops. We have to find that passage."

I helped her up. She could have rested a while longer, but I dared not risk it. We moved back down the passage to where the largest tombs were. The lamp oil was still burning in a pool on the floor, but we couldn't carry it with us and visibility at the far end was almost nil.

"This is impossible," I said. "How could we have missed it?"

"What's that?" said Renthrette.

I followed her gaze steeply upward and my heart stopped. High above the other tombs was a figure, armored and crouching, ready to pounce. I took a step back, but the warrior didn't move and, now that I got a second look at it, it seemed unlikely that it would.

"That's it!" I said. "That's the statue. Let me give you a lift."

I locked my hands and she stepped into them wordlessly, using them as a stirrup to hoist herself up. Then she grasped the masonry and hauled herself the rest of the way.

"Are you up?" I said. "All right. Now, take hold of his spear, above his hand. Got it? Now, pull it toward you."

For a moment nothing happened, then the spear seemed to break off and snap forward. But it didn't fall, and as it moved, something heavy behind the wall disengaged. Renthrette jumped back hastily as the entire section of wall lurched back a few inches and then dropped vertically into the earth with a great rush of dust and a thunderous rumble. Behind where it had stood there was first darkness, then a lean, gray Stehnite face under a steel helm. It was Toth.

"You have proved many people wrong today, Mr. Hawthorne," he said, as soon as he had leaped down. "I am glad, and grateful."

Renthrette stared at him. I thought I saw her hand stray toward her sword.

"Renthrette," I said, "this is Toth, a Stehnite chieftain."

"Enchanted," he said.

Renthrette returned his half bow with a kind of stunned nod, but there was no time to dwell on courtesies. Others were appearing at the hole in the wall and dropping cautiously into the passage. Among them were Orgos and Lisha. Renthrette came to herself instantly, embracing them heartily and with real joy.

"Quick!" I said. "They know we're here. They'll try to shut us in."

"They will try," said Toth, darkly, "but now that I have set foot in the city of our fathers, I will not leave it."

At this utterance, many of those gathered in the passage made sounds of assent, but a glance up at where the statue had been told me that there were not many of them. About three dozen Stehnites and a pair of sleek gray wolves had come in through the passage. The rest would lay siege to the walls with Mithos and the other chiefs. I doubted it could possibly be enough.

Orgos, taller than almost everyone else there by a hand, conferred with Toth, and the unit began to move quickly back the way we had come, their weapons drawn. For a second I found myself face to face with one of the wolves and I saw thought, or perhaps even recollection, in its yellow eyes. It was a huge, pale beast, its fur gleaming like brushed steel and with a white blaze on its throat. As I looked at it I knew I had seen it before, long ago in that mountain cave where we had met Sorrail, and that it also remembered. The wolf held me in its gaze, and I, overcome by a rush of guilty regret for a lot of things, swallowed hard and held my breath. It watched, considering, then moved off, following the others. I blinked the memory away as best I could.

We hurried through the monuments and sepulchers, past the open tomb which had so nearly been my last resting place, and into the circular chamber near the steep staircase. There we stuttered to a halt. Orgos, at the front of the line, had raised his palm in a call for silence. No one moved.

Over the sound of my heart I heard a sloshing sound, like barrels of ale being drawn up from the cellar, followed by a harsh splitting thud, like an axe biting lumber. An acrid scent drifted down the stairs. With it, trickling black down the steps and collecting in pools at our feet, came the oil.

A dozen of the Stehnites realized the same thing in the instant that I did and began shouting in their own language and jostling backward. We moved as a unit, panicked and erratic as the flames started rushing down the steps toward us, bluish for a second, then red.

A young Stehnite who had strayed to the front of the column found himself suddenly engulfed in the blaze. He came running toward us, screaming, but I suppose the shock was too intense, for he fell suddenly, and was lost in the fire. The heat followed a moment later. It filled the passage like a wall, and our attack broke against it like water on stone.

SCENE XX

The Soul of the Arak Drül

I s there another way out?" demanded Orgos.

Toth shook his head. "Not that I know of, but it's been generations since we were last here. There may be an exit that we don't remember."

"We can't go this way," said Orgos, "and if we wait for the flames to die down, the battle will be over and we will be at the mercy of our enemy."

"There is another way," I said.

"What?" said Orgos, wheeling.

"There are stairs at the other end," I explained. "I don't know if they go anywhere, but I saw them when Renthrette and I first came down here. They may also be burning, but if the enemy reacts to our actions as we think of them, we may have a moment's advantage."

"What do you mean?" Toth asked.

"I think that whatever it is that lives in the library senses our actions rather than truly reading our thoughts, and only when we are either physically close to him or unusually focused. It can feel the impulse behind an action, but nothing more complex. It didn't know I was lying to Sorrail when I came back. I'm guessing, and it would be too much to hope that it doesn't know we're here now, but I think it can only act through other people, so we may still have time. Follow me!"

And with this dangerously heroic cry I bounded off, a pack of Stehnites at my heels. The perceptive reader will need no reminding that running toward the stairs I had seen beyond the tombs was also running away from certain death in a blazing stairwell, so you can hold back the "hero" judgment for a bit. We retraced our steps for, it seemed, the dozenth time, passed the gaping hole through which our companions had entered, and found the tight spiral staircase I had glimpsed earlier in the shadows beyond the rubble.

I didn't even have to point it out before Orgos and Toth had barreled past me like a pair of startled bison and bounded up the steps with their weapons drawn. I hesitated for a second, wary of getting caught in another cascade of fire, but we seemed to have a moment's advantage, so I joined the pack behind Lisha which was, I thought, as good a place to be as any.

The stairs went up for some distance and the whole unit began to slow perceptibly as we got higher. I slipped closer to the back of the column with each step, my breath coming in great sucking gulps as if I was a tadpole in a drying mud puddle. But unless I missed it somewhere, your average tadpole never has to climb stairs for the privilege of doing hand-to-hand battle with a vastly superior force, a prospect which rarely quickens my step.

And suddenly the company stuttered to a halt. I crawled up to them and lay wheezing on my back while the Stehnites above me relayed the message: The way ahead was blocked. A heavy slab of stone (at the very least, since no one knew what was on top of it) lay over the stairwell. We were stuck. I sat on the steps, breathing heavily. I was wondering whether it said something about my heroism that I had started at the front of the unit and was now at the very back, when something sounded below.

I had not minded being the last of the group on the stairs since the fire had cut off any possible pursuit, but now something was moving a bit below us. It was an unhurried, shuffling sound, but it was getting louder. Uneasily, I took a cautious step down, but the spiral was too tight to see anything more than a few feet away. I took another step, then another, and was considering going lower when a figure half-dragged, half-lurched around the bend in the stairs.

It was large and it bore an ancient sword, and though the light was too low to see detail, I needed no time to consider the nature of what was facing me. I had seen its hand, the pale bones wound tight round the sword hilt. As I fled upward, I looked over the rail of the stairs down to where the ancient Stehnite tombs were emptying one by one, their bodies moving with single and uncanny purpose.

For a moment my voice forsook me, and I ran headlong into the Stehnites on the stairs before they had even seen me coming. "Move!" I managed, unhelpfully. "They're coming. The dead are coming after us."

I didn't need to say more, because the first was already upon us.

I pushed past one of the Stehnites and then turned, astonished at his lack of response to what he saw. But then, I don't know what he saw. He looked on the foul and ragged skeleton and he did nothing. None of them did. Only when it leaned forward and precisely thrust its rusted sword through his lungs did any of them react.

In the screaming that followed I took the scimitar which fell from the dying Stehnite and hewed the arm from the ancient corpse. It came on and its bony fingers reached for my face. With an instinctive and horrified surge of emotion, I cut wildly at its neck and the head tore free in a spackling of dust and tiny bone shards. The body fell under the feet of those that followed it and we, pawing desperately to get away from them, climbed over each other in the madness of fear.

Then Renthrette passed me going down and her sword sang on their dead crowns. After they had got over the initial shock, some of the Stehnite turned to aid her. I, on the other hand, kept moving until I was in sight of Toth and Orgos, their shoulders set against the slab of marble above them and sweat glazing their features. Others pushed along with them, and one of them counted, trying to time their surges of energy.

"Dead goblins!" I sputtered. "Coming from behind."

"We heard," said Orgos. "But we're kind of busy. . . ."

"Try harder," I said, glancing behind to see if the corpses of the ancient Stehnites were cutting through our ranks yet. "It can't be *that* heavy."

"You'd be surprised," said Orgos, with commendable patience.

"Too bad you didn't bring one of those immense beasts that you had with you the last time you attacked the city," I said.

"Alas," gasped Toth, "she was the last of her kind. Her aid now would indeed be . . ."

"She?" I repeated, aghast.

He glanced at me and a question rose in his face, but whatever he was going to say was forgotten as they heaved at the slab once more. With a great shout they all strained at the rock and something seemed to shift. More joined in, pushing upward, levering with the hafts of their weapons until a crack of light appeared around the stone rim and spread like the sun breaking from clouds. With one great surging roar, the slab was pushed up and clear and gray light fell into the shaft.

Toth was the first out, swinging himself up and into a crouch like a hunter. Orgos followed, with a brace of Stehnites on his tail. Then me, and I needed only a second to see where we were. Ranged about us were shelves of books, and two vast staircases led up to a gallery that skirted the great translucent dome which arched above us.

We were in the library, and there were soldiers everywhere.

They seemed to be coming from all sides, running fast like hounds converging on a wounded sheep. Arrows whistled through the air and skipped off the marble floor. One of the Stehnites fell clutching his leg and rolling, as the others spewed out of the hole like water from a geyser. I ducked and scuttled toward a pillar, thinking vaguely that this is where I would normally be taking leisurely shots with my cross-bow. But the crossbow was lost and I was left diving for cover, clutch-ing a rusted scimitar and wondering what the hell kind of use I could possibly be, even if I could stay alive for another five minutes.

The Stehnites were a valiant group and they ran at the enemy with the kind of self-restraint I was used to in Orgos, meaning none. Orgos himself was in the thick of things, of course, his sword sweeping in great lethal arcs. I think only Toth, who had hacked his way past at least a couple of the tall, pale soldiers, showed a similarly furious dig-nity. But there were dozens of the immaculately dressed and trained Arak Drül, and they burned with a deep, smoldering hatred for the goblins. High on the gallery stairs, an officer arranged his mail-clad archers and they showered us with arrows in audible sheets. Beside him was one of those who I had seen on the city walls during the bat-tle. He was dressed in flowing pale vestments, his eyes shut but his fin-gers moving rapidly, as if he were drawing out invisible thread.

"Get down!" I shouted.

The arrows came again, but this time we were blinded by the flash of brilliant emerald flame that came with them. A cry of despair rose up from those around me, and the Stehnites that had survived the first wave of the flaming missiles scattered and ran for cover.

Except Toth. He sprang up the stairs four at a time, his great cleaver before him. The archers turned their sights on him, but by luck and speed they could not find their mark, and the volley was weak and erratic. Then he was almost upon them and their line quivered in panic as several fumbled for their swords. One of the wolves, the paler of the two, bound up after him and burst upon the line of soldiers, which buckled, then broke. Some fled, others just dropped in horror as their ancient enemy tore into them. The priestly figure's eyes snapped open and he staggered back, his spells forgotten in the face of those ravenous lupine jaws.

Then Orgos leaped from the balustrade into the fray, and Lisha, seeing how the scattered Stehnites had taken heart, attacked the stairs, her dark spear flashing its electric blue fire before her. The Stehnites followed her lead with a shout of defiant unity, forcing the Arak Drül soldiers back up into the domed gallery. Renthrette, who had held off the skeleton soldiers almost singlehandedly, now emerged from the hole in the floor, looked briskly about her, and leaped after the rest. I broke cover and joined the pack. At the top of the stairs, the Arak Drül sentries were fighting a losing battle, many having fallen to the Stehnite onslaught. Those that remained were white-faced and wild-eyed. Several cast down their weapons in desperate submission, and it seemed it might be over.

But as I climbed the stairs to join the victors I heard the library's great external doors clang wide and heard the unmistakable sound of horses—many horses. I turned, suddenly cold. Below me, polished and grim, came the pride of the Arak Drül cavalry, pouring in through the huge doors, riding two abreast. There were too many to count, and, at their head, still and resolute, rode Sorrail.

He wore silver armor made of rings and riveted plate, but he bore no helm and his hair was brushed back like spun gold. A cape of fur varying from gray to black was draped about his shoulders, and at its hem the pelts ended in half a dozen wolf heads, snouts hanging down around the flanks of his mount, eyes sightless in defeat. His face was hard and cold but his mouth held a hint of disdain, even amusement, that such rabble should dare to challenge him. He led his horse toward us, and his cavalry followed, a study in confidence and unnatural composure.

Their horses hesitated at the foot of the stairs, but only for a moment. Then—implausibly—they were coming, lances lowered like a gray thicket of death, and there was nowhere for us to go. I had never seen horses move like that. It was like they weren't actually horses at all, or had been taken over by some controlling mind. The Stehnites shrank back and even Toth and Orgos lowered their weapons and stood watching as the horses clattered up the steps toward us.

"Any ideas?" Orgos asked me, a lightness in his voice that did not register in his face. "Any pearls of wisdom you picked up in their company that will give us an edge?"

"They're afraid of cheese," I suggested.

Through one of the high ecclesiastical windows I could see the city walls, where tall, pale soldiers fired volley after volley of arrows onto the army that boiled around the city. Mithos was out there with the Stehnites, but their only hope of victory was if we could open the breach to them. The walls—ironically, the walls they themselves had made—were too strong. I looked desperately around, but we were badly outnumbered, and fighting was useless. It was only a matter of time now before the Stehnite attack outside the city failed, our little incursion having been utterly contained before we could even threaten the walls from the inside. Now we would be captured or slaughtered, Sorrail would return to the siege, and the ancient mind that lived in the library would vanquish the Stehnites once more.

The mind in the library. The force that was guiding those horses and making the army behave as if it had one conciousness. The heart of the Arak Drül, their purpose, their guardian angel, their guiding, blinding light . . .

And suddenly our path was clear to me, though the thought was dreadful and I immediately wished I could put it back and forget it, *unsee* it in my head somehow. Through the throng of anxious Stehnites huddled together on the great dome-lit landing, I could see the corridor that led down to the brass-paneled doors where I had met and wrestled with the guardian of Phasdreille. I pointed through the crowd and shouted, "That way! Run! Open those doors. Quickly!"

Toth was the first to move and he was down the passage before I had taken a step. But as he stretched out his arm to the door handle, a throbbing pulse of light coursed up and down the brass and, in a brilliant flash, he was thrown heavily backward. One Stehnite ran to him, and another tried the door, with the same effect.

"Degenerate fools," said a voice.

I turned and found Sorrail, still mounted, only feet from me, and watching us with a scornful leer distorting the features that had once seemed so perfect.

"Do you think we would leave our holiest shrine open to their defiling hands?" he snarled.

No one spoke. The Stehnites shrank back from him and his men, sensing that they were heavily outnumbered. Sorrail continued, still smiling nastily. "No one can enter there unless the soul of our people permits it."

"I wonder," I said, aloud.

"I thought I might find you here," he said, "blending in with the sub-humans. And I see your lies have dragged the fair Lady Renthrette with you. That is unfortunate, but I suppose it was inevitable: Corruption cannot be washed away. Now, throw down your weapons."

There was a moment of silence, then an irregular clatter as some complied. I knew beyond any doubt that he was lying about the door, but I didn't want to prove it. I didn't want to go back in there with whatever it was that looked like a hooded man but wasn't. I couldn't bear to let him inside my head again, let him tear out my thoughts like some creature scooping out my brains and entrails.

So stay right here, I thought. Surrender. You're not a goblin. They may still spare you. It's not your war. You don't even belong here. You're an Outsider.

And then I realized that those weren't my thoughts at all. They appeared in my head, but they came from inside the chamber.

That rather changed things. I launched myself against the brass doors and threw them open easily. Before I even looked inside, I turned back to the astonished faces, Stehnite and Arak Drül alike, and I shouted, "You lie, Sorrail. Your whole world is a lie. The doors are guarded only against those who belong in your war. I, however, am an Outsider."

He spurred his horse at me, and a dozen of his cavalry came with him, charging me down. I stood in the doorway of the huge ruined chamber with its wrecked furnishings and devastated manuscripts, and in the same instant Orgos leaped out between me and the horsemen, engaging them with a great swinging flourish of his sword. I permitted myself only the briefest glance at the clash which followed as Sorrail stormed into the fray before turning and stepping through the doors and into the great, ravaged room.

He was there, waiting for me, the ancient hooded figure whose mind I had felt moments before.

His thoughts caught me like a dozen hands and pinned me where I stood. Toth tried to come after me, but the moment he entered the chamber he was caught up, as if seized by a great wind, and flung heavily back against the wall. His weapon splintered at the handle, and he cried out in rage and pain. The cloaked figure in front of me had barely moved, and his eyes were still on me. Dimly I knew that only the Outsiders were a threat to him for the same reasons that only we could pass the great brass doors. We didn't belong here in their world, their war. But what we could possibly do to him, I didn't know. How do you harm someone you suspect is really a spirit or, worse still, an abstraction, an idea which holds a culture together? Even if I hadn't already been paralyzed, my own indecision would have prevented further action.

Then the grip on my mind and body fluttered for a second, and I became aware of another figure entering the room. Actually, there were several. Half a dozen or more of the Arak Drül cavalry burst in, their horses oddly placid, as if sleepwalking, and with them came a disordered rabble of Stehnites. These were lifted and scattered by invisible hands, but one kept coming, cutting at the horsemen as he did so: Orgos. I felt the mind that held me struggling, but it was momentary. Whatever threat my sword-master friend posed to the hooded figure evaporated almost immediately. Immobile though I was, I heard the distinctive snap and rush of a crossbow. Orgos fell to the ground, clutching his midriff. In the second of semi-freedom which followed, my eyes flashed up to where the sound had come from. There, poised on a stone balcony over the central throne, was Aliana, methodically fitting another bolt into her weapon.

Any awareness of what was happening around me was promptly shattered by a voice in my head, ancient but clear and hard as glass, which broke in upon my thoughts like a brilliant light. The words bit like steel into my brain: "Outsider, I am the Soul of my people, a people as strong as they are beauteous, a people immune to the corruptions your kind bring with you. But you and your dogs have dared to challenge your betters, and you must therefore be educated in courtesy. You will not like the lesson."

I think he was laughing, though the scornful amusement was overshadowed by his terrifying hatred. But then the impression of his voice flickered and I could see and hear the horsemen methodically lining up in front of him. Around the room I glimpsed crumpled figures: Orgos, Toth, other Stehnite warriors. Whether they were paralyzed or dead, I could not say. Among the horsemen was Sorrail, stern and implacable as before, his dark cape of wolf hides making him grotesque, nightmarish. But I was temporarily free, and, turning, I could see why: Lisha and Renthrette were walking purposefully into the library. Whatever had held me had bigger fish to fry.

I moved quickly. There was a narrow flight of steps up the dark stone, and I headed for it, blinking away the lingering slowness which still gripped my legs, focusing on the stairs and running up them. I broke out from the top as Aliana was leaning over the low, carved rail to shoot.

She spun to face me, her eyes cold and narrow as they brought the heavy crossbow in line with my chest, her full mouth pursed into a crack of concentration. I shouted desperately, but it was a cry of rage as much as of panic, and as I did so I threw myself at her, arms outstretched. At the same instant her finger tightened on the crossbow trigger. I felt the bolt tear through my jerkin under one arm, grazing my side with a rush of heat, and I thought I was dead. For that briefest of moments, I didn't care.

I suppose she had been entirely focused on her shot, and not on planting her feet properly. I don't know. In any case, I caught her off balance somehow, and before I knew it, she was falling. She didn't even cry out as she toppled over the balcony and dropped the twenty or so feet to the stone floor below. I drew myself up in shocked horror and looked down.

Lisha and Renthrette stood paralyzed a matter of yards from the figure that had called itself the Soul of the Arak Drül. Lisha's eyes were closed and her mouth set tight as if her mind was trying to wrestle free, but Renthrette's eyes were open and in them was pain, fear, and burning anger. Sorrail and the cavalry had dismounted, and the soldiers were slowly approaching the two women, their weapons drawn. I stood watching, powerless. Aliana's crossbow had fallen with her, and there was nothing I could do to prevent the slaughter which would inevitably follow. I focused my thoughts on the cloaked entity below, whose back was to me, struggling to grapple with him and set the others free to defend themselves, but his mind was like a wall of ice and though I could sense it, I could not penetrate its defenses.

Sorrail took a step toward Renthrette. His spear burned white at the tip so that its light reflected in her wide, upturned eyes. Then he turned to the soldier by his side, and I noticed for the first time the sharp emerald green of the Arak Drul officer's eyes beneath his silver helm: It was Garnet.

"Wait," Sorrail commanded the soldiers. "We two will strike together. I will deal with the traitor, Captain Garnet with the she-goblin."

A hush fell upon the chamber as the soldiers stepped clear, leaving room for the two officers to complete their task.

"Garnet," I screamed. "It's Lisha and your sister, for God's sake!"

He turned sharply and looked up at me. "Take that traitor," Sorrail said, and a pair of soldiers broke from the rest and began to climb the narrow steps to the balcony.

"It's all lies, Garnet," I called down. "They have lied to you. They are not what you think they are."

"How dare you, of all people, accuse them of such a thing?" he replied, scornfully.

"It's true," gasped a voice.

I looked back to where Orgos, still stuck against the wall, struggled to speak. "Will's right," he managed, before the soldiers moved to silence him.

"Is this your idea of honor, Garnet?" I shouted desperately. "To stab them while they stand paralyzed by a sideshow magician?"

"The creatures of darkness are beyond honor," said Sorrail.

"The creature of darkness you are about to hack to death is Lisha," I yelled at Garnet. "Look at her! Look . . ."

And then the soldiers were on me. One of them punched me hard in the stomach. I doubled up, but my eyes stayed fixed on what was happening below us as if my life depended upon it. Garnet was looking at Lisha, axe in hand, but his back was to me and I could not see his face.

"Strike," said Sorrail, raising his weapon over his shoulder like a javelin, his deathly cape of fur rippling with the movement, "Strike as I do."

Lisha stirred, twisting free of the mind grip for the briefest moment, and her eyes opened and fell on Garnet. Her mouth moved and I thought she said his name, but her voice was a mere breath and I could not be sure.

Kill the goblins, commanded the voice in my head. *Kill them all.*

Sorrail pulled back his spear to strike and Garnet took two sudden steps backward, spun around, and brought his axe down heavily on the hooded man. You could hear the steel bite into flesh and bone, but then the robes folded in on themselves and the body vanished. The mind, or soul, or whatever it was, became an absence that stood out like a sudden silence after the unnoticed drumming of rain on the roof. Renthrette's sword arm came to life. She struck at Sorrail's spear as he lunged, deflecting the glowing tip from her breast. Then there was a blur from the chamber door and the great pale wolf, flashing like silver, streaked toward them and leaped, jaws wide, at Sorrail's chest. He staggered under the weight of the great beast, but did not fall. It snapped at him, and its guttural growl slid into a menacing hard-edged bark. Sorrail jabbed with his spear and the wolf scuttered back, biding its time. Then the man froze. For a long moment he seemed to just stop as if lost in thought, then he turned his head fractionally so he could see Renthrette pulling her sword from his bleeding side. He stared at her as if amazed before slumping to his knees. Then the wolf was at his throat. I averted my eyes.

The other soldiers turned toward Renthrette, but Lisha's spear spun in her hands and she warded them off as if with a charm, and in truth it was no longer clear that they meant to attack. A slow confusion was settling on the enemy and the library felt as if a great cloud bank which had obscured the sun had unexpectedly stirred and melted away. The soldiers' grips on my arms relaxed, and they peered at me as if unsure of who I was or what they were supposed to do with me. Around the room, fallen Stehnites were cautiously picking themselves up. Toth, bruised but otherwise unharmed, moved quickly to where Orgos lay and began to tend his wounds, then—bizarrely—one of the blond men who had been conjuring fire for the Arak Drül archers joined him and held his hands over Orgos's belly as if warming his hands at a flame. Orgos's eyes flickered under their lids, then opened, and he smiled weakly at Toth.

All around us things were changing, and not just the people. Horses were waking up and moving like animals again, shifting and breaking ranks in casual disinterest. The Arak Drül troops looked at each other, their faces bewildered, and many of them laid down their weapons as if they were unsure of what they were or where they had gotten them.

Garnet embraced his sister, then Lisha, but his face was serious. I wondered what he was thinking and, more importantly, what had changed his mind so completely. That Garnet could act decisively when he was clear on what he thought was right had never been in question; the problem was that I had not seen enough to account for a change. Had it all been a ploy, a cleverly staged ruse in which he lulled them into vulnerability and then struck? I doubted it. He had come in as one of them, and then he had changed and cut them down. I couldn't explain it beyond proffering the woolly and inadequately obvious: that the sight of his sister and his friends about to be slain by his new comrades had forced an instant and dramatic reappraisal of his values and allegiances. Or perhaps Sorrail's attempt to make him see Lisha as a goblin had backfired, forcing an altogether different conclusion. But I remembered how Orgos had once come running to greet me and I had seen him as a goblin bent on murdering me where I stood. I just didn't know what to think.

I turned and found the huge wolf, its face streaked with Sorrail's blood, looking thoughtfully at me. I swallowed hard and reached out uneasily to pat its head. But as I did so, a low rumble came from its throat, and I snatched back my hand as if bitten. I opened my mouth to say something, but could not think of suitable words, so I closed it. At that moment, something came across the wolf's face and it took a step toward me, briefly brushing its thick fur against my thigh. I gasped, but stayed quite still. The animal, if that's the right word, looked up into my face once, its deep yellow eyes fixing me as before, and then slipped away into the crowd.

I was mulling this over in the heavy and confused silence which followed the flurry of activity when, from outside the city, a great rolling shout broke out. Everyone raised their heads, listening. The sound continued and, one by one, we remembered the battle outside, which would define the fate of this land.

I ran from the library and through the unnaturally silent streets down to the gatehouse, and found the same bewildered inactivity: soldiers of all ranks standing there unsure of themselves, bows and spears held idly as if they had just awoken and couldn't recall what they were doing.

"Open the doors," I shouted, running up the stairs to the wall that connected the gatehouse at the head of the bridge to the barbican at the far end, which was surrounded by the Stehnite host.

I didn't know how long I had before some form of normalcy would return. Maybe it never would, but I had to do this while I had the opportunity. Behind me, spilling out of the library, were Garnet and Lisha and Renthrette, with half a dozen uncertain-looking Arak Drül and some equally uncertain-looking Stehnites following behind.

"Open the gate," I repeated, shouting at the first officer I saw. "Who's in charge here?"

He looked around, unsure, then pointed to a turret where a man in brilliant armor stood beside a white and gold banner: King Halmir, son of Velmir, lord of Phasdreille. I had almost forgotten him, and now I found myself wondering how he would adapt to what had just happened in the library. Would he fight to the death for all that the city and court had been, or would he wake up like the others had done as from a strange and consuming dream. He turned to peer at me, since I was the only thing moving and making noise on the otherwise silent battlements, and his armor flashed in the sun. He was about fifty yards away, but his visor was up and I could see his face. It was blank, perhaps confused.

"Open the gate," I shouted. "Give the order."

He watched me for a second, then seemed to glance sideways, as if waiting for some counselor to offer advice. Not finding one, he looked back to me and—without great conviction, but clearly, unmistakably— nodded his assent. Almost immediately, the grinding mechanism of the gates began to creak into action, and I ran back down to where the others were assembling.

The guards on the walls continued to watch, impassive and not making a sound. Some had set down their weapons and leaned out over the ramparts to get a better view, but no one was speaking or moving.

It was utterly surreal. The massive doors groaned their way open, and I found myself gazing out across the bridge to where a great Stehnite army stood as silent and still as the defenders of Phasdreille. Then, at last, there was movement: The army began to shift to let a figure pass with slow and silent purpose through the ranks of Stehnite warriors in their outlandish armor and masked helms, onto the bridge, and into the city. It was a man, sitting astride a great black bear, and behind him came the chieftains of the Stehnite Council, but it wasn't until he was at the gates themselves that I realized that the bear-rider was Mithos.

SCENE XXI

Aftermath

And that, Rose, is how I won the war," I concluded.

Orgos gave a single howl of laughter.

"What?" I protested, injured. "It's true."

"Kind of," laughed Orgos. "In a Hawthorne-esque fashion."

"Hawthorne-esque?" I exclaimed. "What the hell is that supposed to mean?"

"I think you know what it means," said Orgos.

"I'm pretty sure *I* know what it means," said Toth, smiling, "so I know you do."

"Come on, Rose," I said to Lisha's former informant, now stripped of her courtly makeup, "let's go somewhere where we are appreciated."

Orgos roared again and poured himself another beer.

It was good beer, rich and dark and sweet, and we were drinking it in the palace in Phasdreille, something I wouldn't have believed possible a few weeks before. But things had changed in the White City. The beer, the books, and many other things but, most importantly, the faces. The Stehnites had reentered their ancient city and the pale invaders had left or surrendered. Memory slowly came back to them, and some refused to believe what those memories brought, but most quickly abandoned any claim to the lands they had so recently conquered. Lisha and Mithos negotiated a settlement between King Halmir and the Stehnite chieftains in which areas of the city were preserved for the Arak Drül community, though the nature of their housing and employment was still under consideration. Resentments lingered on both sides, and twice in the last week there had been incidents of fighting between the rival factions, but a bipartisan force had been established to police such incidents, and casualties had been minimal. Things would improve in time, we hoped. How much time, it was impossible to say. In my darker moments I was sure that a real settlement would take generations and squabbling might erupt into open war again before then, but things seemed to be progressing as well as could be expected.

Garnet was not so sure. He had, I suppose, surrendered to the hatred more than any of us, but he had also been the one to reverse his position most drastically. It took me a while to realize that what resentment lingered in his mind was directed not at those he had considered goblins, but at the fair soldiers and courtiers who had ridden with him and who had taken him in, in more ways than one.

"They are liars," he said simply, on the one occasion I persuaded him to talk about it. "Just like you said."

"*Were* liars," I corrected him. "That was in the past, when they were under some kind of controlling influence. Now they're different. Most of them."

"Maybe," he said.

"And that's why you attacked that . . . whatever it was, their soul?"

He shrugged, as if unsure, or unwilling to talk about it.

"It never occurred to me that any of us could attack him physically like that," I said. "I was racking my brains to think of some brilliant way to undermine the heart of a culture, and while I'm standing there anxiously philosophizing, you just drew your axe and smacked him one."

"Maybe I'm just a shallower person than you, Will," he said. "Less complex."

"I didn't mean it as a criticism," I stammered, blushing.

"I didn't take it as one," he said. "I never particularly valued complexity. Sometimes it seems paralyzing."

Ironic, really. The simplemindedness that had made him believe everything that the Arak Drül had stood for had also made him the only one capable of destroying them. I considered this for a while, but couldn't turn it into a useful lesson to take away. Perhaps it served to remind me merely of the extent to which all of us—Lisha, Renthrette, Garnet, Mithos, Orgos, and myself—depended on each other. Perhaps it meant nothing, and any attempt on my part to read significance from it was no better than Sorrail reading the signs of evil in the perceived deformity of a Stehnite. Perhaps it was just a warning, a reminder that when things look too good to be true, you can bet there's something nasty and dangerous underneath, just

waiting for a moment to leap out and expose your stupidity by tearing your limbs off. I don't know.

Whatever control the "soul" in the library had exerted, not everyone had needed it. The Pale Claw cabal melted away, but within hours
of the surrender it became clear that they had not simply thrown
down their weapons with the rest. They had left, quiet and close to
powerless, but with an unsettling deliberation. Where they were now,
no one knew for sure, but there had been reports of attacks on
Stehnite hunting parties in the mountains, and the newly formed city
council had started compiling a list of the Arak Drül's key courtiers,
generals, and politicians who could not be accounted for. The Pale
Claw had needed no hooded sorcerer to make them hate goblins, and
I suspected that Phasdreille had not heard the last of them. Whether
some of those still in the city were only masking their true feelings
about the present détente, and how close to the throne the Pale Claw's
influence had spread, no one knew. As tidy as the end to the war had
been, there were loose ends, though how far they would trail into the
future, I could not begin to speculate.

I returned to the attentive Rose and my excellent beer, but our little chat was disturbed almost immediately by a knock at the door. It
was Renthrette.

"We need you in the banquet hall, Will," she said, her eyes falling
on Rose. "Now."

I scowled at her and tried to look imploring. "Right now?"

"Right now," she answered, still looking Rose up and down un-
abashedly.

I sighed and muttered a promise to Rose that I would be back
soon.

"I'm not sure you'll keep that promise," said Renthrette as we
closed the door behind us.

"Why?"

"You'll see."

We walked along the cold corridors of the palace, through empty
antechambers that had once been packed with courtiers entertaining
themselves and pressing for a glimpse of the king. Inside the banquet
hall, the party was gathered in a whispering huddle. At the far end of
the room stood a man in black, the same man who had offered us a
ride in his coach from Stavis.

"Will," said Renthrette, "you remember Ambassador Linassi?"

I stopped in my tracks. How could I forget?

I had planned for this meeting, rehearsed my anger and outrage, mentally staged the way I would fly at him and beat him. But now that the moment had come, I forgot my lines and could not think what to do. I was corpsed. My mouth opened and nothing came out.

He looked at me, smiled his undertaker smile, and it was almost like being back with the hooded soul of the Arak Drül. But I felt his thoughts and they were at once benevolent and mildly amused. I said nothing. He looked at each of us in turn, then said, "Ready to go home?"

No praise, no thanks, no apology; just that. I found my voice again. "Oh, no," I began. "Not that easy, mate. You're going to do a lot of talking before I get in that magic hearse of yours. You can't just whisk us across the world—presuming we're still in the world—and drop us into a war from which we emerge by the skin of our teeth, having been chewed by talking bears and generally inconvenienced by an elaborate collection of things that shouldn't exist in any rational . . ."

"Shouldn't exist?" he smiled.

I hesitated. I was suddenly overcome by the sense that I had a significant moment in my grasp, and could easily get us all into a lot more trouble by saying the wrong thing. The rest of the party seemed to be holding their breath. "Shouldn't exist," I said, "but apparently do. Here. Wherever that is."

Lisha moved. I caught her eye and she nodded fractionally, as if with approval.

"But, look," I began. "I still don't understand a lot of this. That's a state of mind that I've gotten quite used to. But the fact is that I think we need some explanations. I mean, we were *prophesied* to be here, or something. Now what's all that about, for a start?"

"I don't think there was ever a real prophecy," said Orgos. "Not in the sense you mean."

"But they knew we were coming," I said. "They said we would have a hand in their war and they were right."

"There's nothing in the library," said Lisha. "I've been looking. I think the prophecy was just a rumor that came from paranoia and xenophobia. The world of the Arak Drül was defined against the Stehnites. It makes sense that the one thing they might fear above anything else was people who would not fit in either camp, outsiders who would not see good and evil in the ways they wanted. Such people might erode the Arak Drül's sense of order just by being here."

"So they learned to watch for strangers," agreed Orgos, "for anyone who wasn't 'goblin' but didn't see the world as the Arak Drül did."

"That's it?" I said. "No prophecy? No cosmic hand writing us into the future? No promise that we were destined to shape the world?"

"No," said the ambassador, simply.

I thought for a moment and then nodded.

"Good," I said. "I don't believe in destiny."

Everyone looked to the ambassador to see how he would respond to this, and when, after a tense moment, he smiled, you could feel everyone breathing out with something like relief. I caught Lisha's eye and she nodded again, but this time the approval held a note of warning. I was being told that what I had said thus far was plenty, and now I should shut up. I thought about it, and shut up as requested.

"Then we are ready to move on," said the ambassador.

I wasn't entirely sure what that meant, and was suddenly struck by a reluctance to leave at all. Rose was waiting for me in my room, I thought. I was a hero, an honored guest.

But "guest" was right. I didn't belong in this land of sorcery and chocolate-covered birds. I didn't know where I did belong, but it wasn't here.

"All right," I said. "Let's go."

There was a tiny ripple among the group, a kind of resolution that did not come easily, but came definitively.

"My coach is outside," Linassi said. "As is your stallion."

"Tarsha!" exclaimed Renthrette, and everything else, the pain of parting from Toth and his people, the strangeness of all we had seen, and the various extreme feelings that accompanied all we had done since we had got here was forgotten. As soon as Renthrette imagined meeting her beloved warhorse, her memories of Sorrail and what, if anything, she had felt for him evaporated as only the memories of old love can. I defy any man to compete for her affections with that bloody horse.

We didn't even get to say good-bye, though that was probably a blessing. I had been popular briefly enough that I wasn't sure I knew how to leave those who valued me, if only as someone who had done Significant Things. I wouldn't even be leaving any friends, not exactly. I was on the verge of getting to know Rose, and I no longer jumped a foot in the air when Toth showed up at my door, but I had spent too much of my time here alone to have made lasting acquaintances.

I left Rose a book of poems that I had been carrying about with me. They were addressed to people with dark eyes, but I didn't think she'd mind. It was odd to think that a few weeks before she might have been revolted by them.

Toth was there to see us off, but no one else knew we were leaving. He bowed to each of us in turn, including me, and embraced Orgos and Mithos. Then the coach was moving off, silent and dark as before, with Renthrette mounted on Tarsha at our rear and Garnet sitting beside the coachman. Orgos's eyes met mine and he smiled. "Worried, Will?"

"Always," I answered, honestly.

Mithos grinned, a real smile that split his face so you could almost see his teeth. It was like glimpsing a very rare bird, and within moments I had convinced myself that it had been a trick of the light. I peered out of the window as Phasdreille, white and glorious, receded slowly behind us and we got onto the road proper. It was a clear, cold day, and the early afternoon light was turning the city to gold as it had been when I first saw it. Back down the road, a familiar silver wolf with a flash of white on its throat was loping easily after us. The ambassador touched my arm and I leaped in my seat.

"I wish you wouldn't do that," I muttered. "It's like rolling over and finding you're in bed with the grim reaper. No offense."

"None taken," he replied. "I was merely going to suggest that you pull your head inside the carriage. I think I hear a storm coming."

I glanced hastily out of the window and saw that the land around me was darkening fast. Overhead, I heard the distinct rumble of thunder. Then the heavens opened and a great torrent of rain came crashing down upon us, lashing the carriage and the horses. As the lightning flashed hard and white, I remember thinking that so much water might just wash the world away.

"Brace yourself, Will," said Orgos. "We're going home."

"That," said the ambassador, "remains to be seen."

I was about to ask him what the hell he meant by that, when there was another brilliant flash which seemed to linger impossibly, and then I was thrown face-first onto the carriage floor. When I opened my eyes and got up to my knees, everything had changed. There was no storm, and the light from outside had dropped to almost nothing.

I fought with the latch on the carriage door to get out of that oppressive darkness and bundled myself out into the dim courtyard of the Fisherman's Arms, the tavern where we had first met the ambassador.

"Stavis," I muttered to myself. "We're back in Stavis."

"Like we never left," said Mithos, cautious, as he stepped down from the carriage behind me.

"But we did," I said. "Right? You're not going to give me that 'and-I-woke-up-and-it-was-all-a-dream' bollocks, are you? Because that is the single worst ending to a story ever."

"No," said Orgos, wonderingly. "It was real. I can still feel the ache of my wounds."

I felt my face, but the bruising Sorrail had given me had healed long before the ambassador had showed up in Phasdreille. I glanced wildly around, expecting to have lost some of the group, but they were all there, Garnet still sitting beside the driver with a dazed look, Renthrette sliding out of Tarsha's saddle, Lisha stock still, her spear somehow ready.

"The same place," said Orgos, still in an awed whisper, "and the same time."

"What?" I said. "What do you mean?"

I was trying to sound defiant, dismissive, but a part of me knew what was coming and guessed he was right. He was staring at the corner of the sky where a quarter moon was beginning to rise.

"This is how it was when we left," he said.

"Oh my God," I said. "There will be Empire troops all over looking for us. We're right back where we were!"

"Almost," said the ambassador, stepping down from the carriage.

I had assumed he was gone, and his voice made me jump, but I recovered quickly.

"What do you mean, 'almost'?" I said.

"Times change," he answered. "See for yourself."

As he was speaking, the door into the tavern had been thrown open and a bored-looking stable boy trudged out with a bag of oats. Orgos, ever stealthy, ducked behind the carriage, reaching for his sword. Mithos and Lisha followed. The boy, who was about fourteen, frowned at us.

"Oh," he said to me. "I didn't know anyone was here. I'll get my master."

"Wait," I insisted. I had no idea how to proceed. "So," I said. "How's business? Busy night?"

He frowned again, then shrugged.

"Same as usual," he said.

"Any excitement in town?"

"Excitement?"

"Commotion," I said, speaking through a fixed and wholly unconvincing smile. "Tumult. Uproar. Hullabaloo. People running around and shouting . . ."

"Sir?"

"Are the streets quiet?" said Renthrette, like she was wading in to save a man drowning in two feet of water. "Or is there a lot of Empire activity?"

Subtle, I thought, and waited for the boy's face to cloud with suspicion. Instead, his bafflement seemed to increase.

"Empire?" he said.

"Empire," repeated Renthrette. "The Diamond Empire. Are there more than the usual patrols, or? . . ."

But the kid was shaking his head, brow still furrowed.

"What Empire?" he said. "What do you mean?"

"The people who run Stavis," Garnet called, jumping down from the carriage.

"*Run* Stavis?" the boy repeated. "Not sure who runs Stavis. Depends who you ask, I suppose. The Merchants Guild control half the city council, my master says, but it's supposed to be freely elected . . ."

"But who controls the city?" I inserted. "Who polices it? Who makes the laws and suppresses rebellion? Who is the power here? Who are you scared of?"

The boy hesitated and something uneasy shot through his eyes.

"There's the Fraternity," he offered. "They are the police. They keep the bad people out."

"And this Fraternity is an army? White cloaks with a diamond motif . . ."

"There are twelve of them," said the boy. "There is no army."

"Wait," I said. "Are you saying that the Diamond Empire has no presence in this city?"

"I'm sorry, sir," said the boy. "I don't know what the Diamond Empire is. Is it a trade league? There's a Goldsmiths' Guild. Maybe it's part of that."

"No," I insisted. "I mean an army. A massive military and political presence which came south from Aeloria. They took Cresdon and

Bowescroft, then Cherrathwaite, remember? Then they came here. They built a road across the Hrof and they took Stavis, which is now their easternmost frontier. There was a big troop buildup here a few months ago when there was fighting over in Shale and Graycoast. Right? The Empire. The Diamond Empire. Ring any bells?"

"I'm sorry, sir," said the boy. "I have no idea what you're talking about. Cresdon was conquered by an army from the north? No chance! We might be a bit far afield, but we would have heard. When did that happen?"

"Almost twenty years ago!" I exclaimed.

"Oh," said the boy, as if he was finally understanding a joke we had been making at his expense. "All right. I get it. Stavis is a long way from anywhere and we don't know what's going on in the world. A big army could take over the whole area and we wouldn't notice because we're too busy counting our money. Very funny. You know, if you're going to be here long, I'd get that kind of humor out of your system quickly. People won't like it. So, you need your horses stabled or what?"

"Yes," said the ambassador, stepping forward. "Perhaps you could fetch the innkeeper. We may need rooms for the night."

The boy, looking surly, returned to the inn and I got a brief glimpse inside: a few patrons at tables eating and drinking. No crowds. No soldiers. No Empire presence of any kind.

"What the Hell is this?" I said.

Orgos, Mithos, and Lisha emerged from the shadows behind the carriage.

"The boy is deluded," said Garnet. "Or dim."

He said it loudly, throwing out his chest as if defying the world to contradict him, but there was something in his eyes, a flicker of uncertainty. Even he knew there was more to it than that.

"Open the street door," said Lisha.

"Lisha," Renthrette cautioned, "if there are Empire troops on the road outside . . ."

"Will," Lisha said. "Open the door. Carefully."

I wanted to ask why it had to be me, but I also wanted to know. I walked across the inn yard, lifted the bar across the door and cracked it open. It was dark out, but I could see all the way down the road. There were shops and houses, and taverns, mainly closed for the day, and a few people wending their way home to bed. There were no soldiers. I opened the door wider and realized that something was missing.

"There's no tower," I whispered into the night.

"What?" said Garnet, striding up behind me.

"There was a stone watchtower just down there," I said, pointing. "It was a small fortress for the Stavis garrison. The Empire must have built it when they took the city. It's not there anymore."

"Maybe they pulled it down," said Garnet.

"No," I said. The beginnings of the truth had started to register. "They never built it. Did they?"

That last was aimed at the ambassador, who was watching us, smiling in his cryptic and unnerving way.

"That's right," he said simply.

"That's not possible," said Garnet. "It was there. I saw it. How can they have never built it?"

"Because the Empire isn't here," I said. "The Empire doesn't exist."

"What?" sputtered Garnet. "What are you talking about?"

"Where did we just come from?" I asked the ambassador.

"From the city which was once called Phasdreille," said the ambassador.

"And *when* did we come from?" I asked.

Garnet started to protest but Lisha silenced him with a gesture.

The ambassador stood there saying nothing for a long moment and his eyes moved over us as if he was deliberating how much to say. When he finally spoke, it was in a low, even voice like someone delivering the epilogue to a play.

"You came from four hundred years in the past. You came from Phasdreille in the mountains of Aeloria, from a place where, once upon a time, a mighty Empire was born. The Arak Drül were conquerors who assimilated other cultures into their own through a combination of military might and sorcery. They drove out other peoples before them, though in time they became simply a war machine, funded by the natural resources they had taken from others, funded, in particular, by their control of the mining and trade of diamonds."

"Diamonds," I said, thinking of the courtiers and the fashionable jewelers' shops I had seen in Phasdreille. "Of course."

"We went into the past," said Orgos. It wasn't a question. It was an answer that made sense to him.

"Yes," said the ambassador.

"Oh my God," said Renthrette. "The fair folk became the Empire?"

"In one version of reality, yes," said the ambassador. "But here, where we are now, history tells a different story. Instead of building from Phasdreille, pushing south from the mountains and conquering all of Thrusia, including both Cresdon and Stavis, the fledgling Empire was never able to stretch its wings. Its control of Phasdreille was lost in a great battle with a race who had once lived there, a battle in which a small group of Outsiders were instrumental, and with that, the Empire's military ambitions collapsed."

There was a long and loaded silence.

"Wait," I said. "We defeated the Empire—the whole Empire—without even knowing we were fighting them?"

The ambassador's lips twitched in that smile of his and he said, "In a manner of speaking."

"I don't understand," said Garnet. "We were in the past . . . and what we did there changed the present?"

"Made a different present, yes," said the ambassador.

"So we're not wanted men," I said. "And women. I mean, we're not outlaws! We won, and we're not on anyone's hit list! This is fantastic! It means . . . I don't know. Lots of things. It probably means . . . Wait: Are there theaters here now?"

"There are theaters here, yes," said the ambassador.

"So I could go back to being an actor and playwright!" I said, laughing with joy at the idea.

"You could," said the ambassador. "If you wish."

"Oh believe me," I said. "I wish."

I turned to the others. Orgos had settled into a kind of crouch, as if his head was swimming. He was smiling softly, but he still looked dazed and unsure of himself, and he was breathing hard. Mithos and Lisha were looking at each other, their eyes wide but their faces blank. Garnet was still demanding explanations and Renthrette was trying to soothe him, but none of them were exactly celebrating the downfall of their old enemy.

"What is the matter with you people?" I demanded. "The Empire is gone! We defeated them! It's a new world. It's . . . I don't know, better! Definitely better."

"I just can't imagine it," said Orgos softly. "No Empire? What am I without the Empire? What do I do?"

"You get joyously, raging drunk and then help me prepare for an audition," I suggested, but he wasn't listening, just sat there, gazing at his hands.

"Other things will define you," said the ambassador. "There will be other battles to fight, other principles to champion."

Before he had a chance to respond, the inn door opened again, and the boy returned with a burly man in an apron. He had a pink face and arms like tree trunks.

"Ned here says you'll be wanting rooms," he said, as he strode over. "I'm the innkeeper, Wigrun Bartels. He said he only saw four of you, though it looks like you'll be needing . . ."

His voice trailed off. He had been looking at me because I was closest, but his welcome was a general one, and it was as he looked over the rest of the group that his words stalled. He was staring at Lisha. Then at Orgos.

For a moment I thought we had made a terrible mistake. The Empire could not simply vanish. All this talk of moving through time and changing the future was the kind of nonsense you wouldn't even put on stage. There were soldiers everywhere and they were looking for us. The innkeeper had been told to watch for a group with a black man and a small woman from the Far East. . . .

But that wasn't it. The innkeeper just stared with his mouth open, and then took a nervous step backward. He was afraid. Then he turned to the boy.

"Run," he said. "To the Fraternity. Tell them."

The boy, whose eyes were as wide as his master's, sprinted through the door like all the devils of Hell were after him.

"Wait," I said. "There has been some misunderstanding."

"Stay back," said the innkeeper, pulling a carving knife from his belt.

"Look," I went on, "I don't know what the problem is but I'm sure we can sort it out. We're not from round here. . . ."

The innkeeper laughed once, a caustic bark that fought through his fear. I ignored it.

"I'm sure we can explain things," I said. "This Fraternity: These are your leaders, your law enforcers?"

"They keep the bad people out," said the innkeeper. The echo of the boy's line unsettled me. "Bad people," he went on, nodding at Orgos and Lisha. "People like them. You can explain things? How will you explain to the Fraternity that you have brought goblins to our city? You think they will understand? You think the ancient Fraternity of the Pale Claw will welcome them to Stavis? They know them of old."

Well, put *that* way . . .

"Right," I said. "Fair enough. Well, thanks again, ambassador. Other battles to fight and principles to champion. Yes. Thanks. Always a pleasure. Now, to the rest of you," I said, turning to Orgos, Lisha, Renthrette, Garnet, and Mithos, "I'm going to suggest running. Fast. Who's with me?"

And we ran.

❧

THE END